MIDNIGHT AND MAGNOLIAS

REBECCA PAISLEY

An Avon Romantic Treasure

AVON BOOKS ◆ NEW YORK

MIDNIGHT AND MAGNOLIAS is an original publication of Avon Books. This work has never before appeared in book form. This work is a novel. Any similarity to actual persons or events is purely coincidental.

AVON BOOKS
A division of
The Hearst Corporation
1350 Avenue of the Americas
New York, New York 10019

Copyright © 1992 by Rebecca Boado Rosas
Inside cover author photograph by Kent McCarty
Published by arrangement with the author
Library of Congress Catalog Card Number: 92–90332
ISBN: 0–380–76566–7

First Avon Books Printing: December 1992

AVON TRADEMARK REG. U.S. PAT. OFF. AND IN OTHER COUNTRIES, MARCA REGISTRADA, HECHO EN U.S.A.

Printed in the U.S.A.

RA 10 9 8 7 6 5 4 3 2 1

For Paisley and Emo

How does an author-mommy dedicate her book to her children?

Thanks for eating 7,849,325 sandwiches and twice that many cans of soup since I started writing full-time.

Thanks for making your friends understand that there is a tad of difference between a crazy person and a writer, and that I'm the latter.

Thanks for wearing the same pair of socks for six days in a row when I don't have time to do the laundry.

Thanks for licking five trillion envelopes and stamps when promotion time rolls around.

Thanks for kissing my tears away when I believe I'm the worst writer in the world. And thanks for rejoicing with me when I've had a good writing day.

Thanks for gathering around the computer to clap when I type "The End" after months of writing.

Thanks for remembering where Federal Express is when "deadline panic" erases my memory.

Thanks for explaining to Papa that I'm not *really* in love with the heroes in my books.

Y'all are the best kids God ever made.

Thanks for being mine.

"WE'RE MARRIED NOW, AND WE WILL SLEEP IN THE SAME CHAMBERS. INDEED, IN THE SAME *BED*."

She squealed when she saw him coming toward her. There was a purposeful intent in his stride, and something powerful in his eyes.

"Peachy," he said huskily. His voice had a tinge of irritation, a touch of arrogance, a lot of impatience. And something else, too, something she could find no name for.

"Quit it," she said. "I done tole you I cain't fight what yore blue-as-mornin'-glories eyes do to me. It's like you got a spoon inside me, a-stirrin' up all my feelin's."

"Peachy, you're afraid. I understand that. But I will not be denied."

"I ain't a-stayin' in here tonight! I tole you it's too soon fer any o' that kinda stuff, and iffen you think . . ."

His mouth smothered the rest of her words . . .

If You've Enjoyed This Book,
Be Sure to Read These Other
AVON ROMANTIC TREASURES

AWAKEN MY FIRE *by Jennifer Horsman*
FIRE AT MIDNIGHT *by Barbara Dawson Smith*
MY WILD ROSE *by Deborah Camp*
ONLY BY YOUR TOUCH *by Stella Cameron*
ONLY WITH YOUR LOVE *by Lisa Kleypas*
RAINBOWS AND RAPTURE *by Rebecca Paisley*

Coming Soon

THE MASTER'S BRIDE *by Suzannah Davis*

Prologue

Possum Hollow, North Carolina

"What do y'mean, I'm gonna *die?*" Peachy McGee exclaimed. Staring at the doctor who'd just examined her, she sat upright in the feather bed, her thick red-gold curls falling in wild disarray around her slim shoulders. "I ain't but twenty years old!"

Solemnly, Dr. Greely folded his stethoscope and dropped it into his medical bag, and looked into her pale green eyes. "There's no doubt in my mind, Miss McGee. It's tipinosis."

"Tipinny-what? I ain't never heared o'—"

"Not many people have. It's an extremely rare disease. In fact, there are medical men who have never come into contact with it."

Swallowing hard, Peachy pushed her fingers through her hair and tried to untangle her many thoughts. "But— but I was s'posed to git wedded up with a real rich black-haired man whose first name starts with 'S'!"

"Married?"

She took hold of his hands and squeezed them so hard that her arms shook. "I ain't gonna die, hear? I swallered a gnat a week ago."

Dr. Greely scowled. "You ate a gnat?"

"The gawdang thing flied straight down my throat. It's a omen. Means I'm gonna git married real soon. After I et the bug, I picked up the first rock I laid eyes on to see what color it was unnerneath. It was black. So that's the

1

color hair my man's gonna have. That night I dreamed I catched a fish the bigness of a gawdang horse. Ever'body knows that means my man's gonna have more money'n God. Sunup the next day, I put a snail on the porch railin'. It slimed out the letter 'S'. So that's—"

"The first letter of your future husband's name," Dr. Greely finished for her. "Miss McGee, you don't really believe—"

"Omens don't lie!" she shouted, releasing his hands. "They ain't never wrong. Doctors . . . they can be wrong. Maybe *yore* wrong. Could be I ain't sick a'tall."

Dr. Greely pulled a chair next to the bed and sat down. Massaging the back of his neck, he glanced around the one-room log cabin and was surprised to see a tiny gray squirrel eating something out of a battered pot on the stove.

Cheeks bulging, the squirrel sprang to the floor and scampered to the bed. Dr. Greely watched it jump onto Peachy's lap, where it commenced chewing.

"Y'hear what I said, Dr. Greely?" Peachy queried, her gaze still aimed into his.

Watching Peachy scratch the squirrel's ear, Dr. Greely realized the animal was her pet. He dismissed the rodent from his mind and concentrated on his patient. "I wish I were wrong, Miss McGee, but I'm afraid I'm not."

"But—"

"Are your parents still alive? Tipinosis . . . it's hereditary," he hinted.

His implication struck her instantly. "No. They're both gone." Her bottom lip trembled; she cast a glance out of the window, watching the breeze drift through the magnolias her father had planted years ago. "We funeralized Maw nigh on ten years ago. Her name was Tilly. She tuk her last breath a-birthin' my baby sister, Lulu. Lulu tuk her last breath right along with Maw. And Paw . . . Laid outen Paw jest three months back."

Memories of her father came to her. She curled her fingers around the bedcovers, a feeling of doom passing through her. "Paw," she whispered, "he—he commenced a-feelin' draggly fer a spell afore he passed on. I give him a tonic o' sulfur and yaller root and merlasses ever'day, but he— I ain't never unnerstanded what finally stiffened him up."

Dr. Greely patted her hand. "It was tipinosis, my dear. I'm sure of it. Tell me, did he experience strong tingling on the bottom of his feet? Did he begin forgetting things?"

"I—"

"Did he ever say anything about trembling muscles? Twitching eyes? Sudden mood changes? Did his neck ever hurt? Did he mention being unable to sleep well, or perhaps he slept too much?"

"No! He didn't never carry on about none o' them things."

Dr. Greely rubbed his short white beard. "Then your father was a very brave man, indeed. No doubt he kept his suffering to himself so he wouldn't worry you."

Peachy lapsed into thought, wondering if she should trust the physician. He was much like all the other traveling doctors who offered their services throughout the small towns near the Appalachian foothills. She'd been examined by such doctors many times before, but none had ever found anything wrong with her.

"Iffen yore right about me not a-bein' pert ..." She turned toward the window again. "I jest cain't unnerstan it. I ain't never spit on no cat. I don't never lace one shoe afore I got the other one on, and I ain't never in my whole dang-blasted life kilt no cricket. There's rimptions more death-like omens, too, but I swear to God Almighty that I ain't never did a one of 'em."

Still staring out the small window, she spotted a large bird circling in the sky. For a moment its significance didn't register in her mind, and she merely watched as it sailed gracefully above her cabin.

But in the next instant she realized the bird was none other than a turkey buzzard. Her throat constricted. She closed her eyes and felt her stomach twist into a hard knot.

A turkey buzzard.

She needed no other proof now. The buzzard was a warning of impending death. Indeed, it was one of the most powerful omens of all.

She yanked off the sheets and jumped out of bed. Clad in a thin shift, she wandered aimlessly around the room, trying desperately not to cry. Like some kind of terrible predator stalking its prey, the word *death* kept creeping into her mind, and no matter how hard she tried to dismiss it, it continued to haunt her.

This couldn't be happening, she told herself. It wasn't real. Die? How was it possible? She was so young! And what about the fact that she was to be married soon? The marriage omens had been so clear.

Her heart hurt; she wondered if the pain was but the beginning of the dreaded symptoms. Tears glimmering in her eyes, she turned to Dr. Greely. "You—you didn't never say how long afore I . . . Afore I'll be a-ringin' the knell."

He collected his bag and stood. "It's hard to predict with any accuracy," he answered softly. "Watch for the symptoms. It's possible you won't notice any for a while, but as the disease progresses you'll experience them more often and to a greater degree."

He crossed the room. As he neared the door, he spied a hand-carved crucifix hanging near the threshold. The sight helped him to think of a good farewell to give to Peachy. "May God grant you peace during the rest of your lifetime, my dear."

"It ain't death I mind . . . really," Peachy whispered, unaware that the doctor had spoken to her. "Ever'body's gotta die sometime. It's jest that— Well, I—I didn't git to do nothin' special whilst I was here in this world. Ain't hardly never even set foot outen Possum Holler."

Dr. Greely opened the door. "Try to rest, Miss McGee."

I'll be a-restin' fer all eternity purty soon, Peachy replied silently. She heard the door close; one tear slid down her cheek. Rubbing her hands over her upper arms, she sat down on a small stool by the fireplace and moaned softly. "Always wanted to eat me a mess o' them fish eggs called caviar, and warsh 'em down with that French likker called champagne," she said on a quivering breath.

"I—I had me some big plans to live one o' them lifes o' leisure so's I could grow outen my nails and see what they look like all long and purty. And sleep in a bed with one o' them silky canopy things a-hangin' down all around me. And git tea brung to me whilst I'm a-layin' in that bed. And . . . and wear a lavish o' jewels jest like a princess."

She felt more tears fill her eyes and spill down her cheeks. A myriad of emotions swept through her. Sorrow such as she'd never before experienced. Dizzying fear, sheer black defeat.

She was going to die, and she hadn't even had a life yet. Her fragile control finally snapped; she sobbed so hard her entire body shook.

She didn't realize how long she'd cried until she noticed that the small room was washed with the muted colors of the setting sun. Her head hanging low, sadness still rippling through her, she shuffled to the door, making the sign of the cross as she passed the crucifix.

On the porch outside, she picked up the newspaper that lay folded on the porch swing, then sat down. Her squirrel jumped up beside her and buried a hazelnut in a fold in her shift. While she stroked his velvet-soft fur, all her wishes and hopes for the future came flooding back to her. "Wanted to live in a big, big house," she whispered. "Ride a purty horse and drive a purty carriage. 'Pears to me, Thurlow Wadsworth McGee," she said to her squirrel, "that only a gawdang *king* could pay fer the kind o' dreams I got." Her sorrow deepening, she placed her hands over her face and gave in to a second bout of tears.

Night had fallen before they stopped, before she had no more to shed. Her hand shaking, she lit a small lamp that hung from the porch railing and tried to decide what to do. She needed to eat supper. She needed to bring in firewood, fetch fresh water, wash the breakfast dishes, and sweep the porch.

But she didn't feel like doing any of those things. "What a great big world this is, Thurlow Wadsworth McGee," she murmured, her gaze pinned to the star-splattered horizon that loomed above the shadowed mountaintops. "And I ain't got the time to see or enjoy none of it."

She glanced down at the squirrel, seeing the newspaper he was lying beside. Absently, she skimmed the articles about that great big world she'd just pondered. "Sardinia," she choked, reading the story titles aloud, "is a-declarin'

war on Austria. Swiss railroad a-doin' good in Zurich and
Baden. King Zane of Aventine commands son, Prince Seneca, to choose a bride. Revolt in Rome."

She sighed. The world would go on without her, she
mused sadly. Everything would . . .

Her thoughts trailed away. Her brow furrowed. Quickly,
she looked back down at the newspaper, her gaze sweeping to the story concerning the wealthy island kingdom of
Aventine. "King," she whispered. "Prince. Bride."

She scanned the article, slowing only when she reached
the brief description of Seneca, Crown Prince of Aventine.
"One o' the richest bachelors in all o' Europe," she read.
"Thirty-two years old. Blue eyes. Black hair. Tall and . . ."

Her eyes widened; her heart pounded. "Seneca," she
whispered. "Richest . . . black hair." The significance of
what she'd read hit her full force. For a moment, she was
too stunned to think clearly. But in the next instant, she
impatiently gathered her chaotic thoughts and recalled the
words she'd just spoken.

'Pears to me . . . that only a gawdang king *could pay
fer the kind o' dreams I got.*

"A king," she murmured, barely able to take her next
breath. "Or— Or a p-prince."

She fairly burst with newborn hope. The newspaper
fluttered to the ground. "A prince who has black hair.
Whose name starts with 'S.' A rich prince . . . who's gotta
git him a princess. And me a-findin' this here story right
when I needed it the mostest. Omens. *Omens!* Sweet Lord
o' mercy, there ain't nary a doubt about it!"

Shakily, she stood, grabbing the porch post for support.
"It's true what the Bible says, Thurlow Wadsworth
McGee," she whispered. "When God shuts one door, He
always opens another one. He's a-fixin' to shut my door
ferever, but not afore a-lettin' me git a peek inside another
one. Don't this jest beat all, boy? He's a-openin' up the
biggest door of all. The door to a palace."

She stared out at the twinkling horizon again. "The castle of Aventine."

Chapter 1

The cold North Sea breeze stinging her cheeks and whipping through her hair, Peachy climbed out of the small dinghy and bid good-bye to the Scottish sailors who'd rowed her ashore. Foamy waves lapping at her boots, she turned, took a few steps, then dropped her bag of belongings to the starry white sand. She shivered, not with cold but with deep excitement, and covering her mouth with her chapped hands, she squealed so loudly the vibration of her voice traveled up her arms.

Here it was. Right before her eyes, beneath her feet, all around her, here it was.

Aventine.

Though it was nighttime, bright moonlight frosted her surroundings, enabling her to see a tree-lined path that led inland. Her squirrel scampering along beside her, she began to follow it. Her legs shook. Accustomed to the rock and sway of the ship, she wobbled, and before she could find her balance, she fell into a soft mound of sand.

It glittered. "Sweet Lord o' mercy, Thurlow Wadsworth McGee," she whispered, "this here Aventine sand's got diamond dust in it."

The woodsy path soon gave way to wide-open meadows. The brilliant moonlight made them seem like green velvet seeded with gleaming pearls. Large flocks of sheep milled about in the beautiful fields. Peachy burst into loud, joyful laughter and raced among them, slowing only when the moon slid behind a patch of clouds.

Proceeding more cautiously in the midnight shadows,

7

she walked for a long while before the clouds drifted away from the moon. As the pale light poured over the landscape, revealing what lay ahead, Peachy stopped abruptly.

Nestled snugly among a cluster of emerald hills, a dazzling river flowing in front of it, was the palace. In all its glory. In all its grandeur. Spasms of pure astonishment rippled through Peachy's entire frame, stealing her voice, her breath, and all rational thought.

Once again, the moonlight performed its magic, painting the magnificent gray stone edifice with hues of shining silver. "God Almighty," Peachy murmured. "Diamonds in the sand, pearls in the velvet grass, and a palace builded o' pure silver. I ain't never seed the beat of it!"

Her mind a tangled mixture of excitement, hope, and happiness, she set forth toward the castle.

Her prince, she thought blissfully, was waiting for her there.

"I will speak to her father tomorrow." King Zane turned from the tall velvet-draped windows toward his son. "I cannot think of a reason why he would object to the betrothal. You are, after all, heir to the throne."

Seneca showed no sign of his fury. After years of practice, he was a master at hiding his emotions. Tapping his fingers upon the arm of his blue satin chair, he cast a relaxed glance around the immaculate room, then motioned to a stone-faced footman. Immediately, the elegantly attired man poured him a snifter of brandy.

"Callista Inger is a beautiful woman," King Zane commented as he, too, accepted a brandy from the servant.

"True." Seneca finished his brandy in one swallow.

"She's young. Healthy. She is capable of giving you many children, one of which I hope will be a male heir."

"Then let's toast her, shall we?" Seneca suggested, waiting for the servant to fill his glass again. "To Callista Inger." *Royal brood mare*, he added silently.

The king gave his son a long, thoughtful look. "It is my will that you wed her, Seneca. Therefore I shall let it be known that you are much pleased with the match."

Seneca gripped his glass tightly; the brandy sloshed up the sides. It was all he could do to continue sitting there with a nonchalant look on his face. Mute with anger, he watched his father limp across the spacious sitting room.

His sire was showing serious signs of his seventy-eight years. With age, his gout had worsened, especially in his knees. Though a cane would help, his vanity wouldn't allow him to accept one, and the pain he stubbornly suffered made him bitter and furious.

Age, pain, bitterness, and vanity had turned his father into an unreasonable tyrant, Seneca mused, a ruthless dictator over not only his people but his own son as well. It was obvious to all that the king was becoming less and less fit to wear the crown.

"My marriage with your mother was an arranged one, Seneca."

Seneca saw that his father had stopped in front of the elaborate portrait of Queen Arria. "I am aware of that, Father."

The king bent to rub his aching knees. "In fact, Callista reminds me of your mother. Surely you can see the resemblance. I never found anything about your mother to fault, and Callista is also a paragon."

Every memory Seneca had of his flawless mother came back to him. The recollections left him feeling nothing, nothing except a gnawing emptiness.

"A man cannot ask for more than sheer perfection, Seneca," the king continued. "You would do well to thank me for arranging your betrothal to such a woman. Had I left it up to you, you would have undoubtedly taken another ten years to find your bride."

Carefully, Seneca kept his features void of all emotion. He stood no chance of swaying his father's decision. As a child, he'd learned that the man never cared a whit for any opinion other than his own. "I see no reason to continue with this discussion, Father. It is apparent that you have made up your mind."

"Indeed I have."

"Very well." Seneca placed his glass on the marble table beside his chair and stood. "By your leave?"

"You may go."

Seneca walked toward the mirrored doors, anxious to escape but keeping his pace dignified.

The palace clocks struck midnight. "Seneca?"

Seneca stiffened, angry that he hadn't made good his escape. He turned, noticing his father's smug smile and wondering what it meant.

The king took his time swallowing a sip of brandy. "You do not want to wed Callista, am I correct?"

Seneca felt a shred of hope. Did he dare believe that his father would change his mind?

The king's smile broadened. "Never let it be said that I did not give you every possible chance to find your own wife, Seneca. If it's more time you want, I will grant it to you. I speak with Callista's father tomorrow at nine. And so, my son, you have exactly nine hours in which to find a wife of your own choosing. Should you succeed in coming upon your princess before morning, I will honor your choice of brides."

Seneca didn't miss the taunting gleam in his sire's eyes. With all the regal bearing he possessed, he inclined his head. "Ah, then never let it be said that King Zane of Aventine is not a generous man. Thank you, Father." His body rigid with contained fury, he arrived at the doors.

There, the king's personal attendant, Rupert Tiblock, bowed stiffly. "Please allow me to be the first to congratulate you on your betrothal, Your Royal Highness."

Seneca saw malicious amusement on the man's bony features. He'd detested the haughty servant ever since Tiblock had joined the castle staff twenty-one years ago. Because Tiblock possessed the king's special favor, he had the run of the palace and authority over all its inhabitants, and he didn't hesitate to take advantage of that authority.

Seneca longed for the day when he would have the power to discharge the man. But that day would come only when he claimed the throne, a day that at times seemed centuries away.

He didn't deign to give Tiblock a reply, just left the room and proceeded down the long, lamplit corridor that led to the grand staircase.

"Nine hours," he muttered to the royal portraits lining the hall. He stormed up the spiral staircase and glared at the star-filled glass dome above. "Nine hours," he flared at the gleaming suit of armor that stood guard at the upper landing of the staircase.

Mumbling all the way, he stalked down another long hallway that led to his apartments. Upon entering his rooms, he dismissed his valet, Latimer, and disrobed beside the huge, ornate fireplace, leaving on only his white pants. Jerking his fingers through his thick, ebony hair, he kicked a piece of kindling into the fire and watched as the blaze quickly consumed it.

"Callista." He growled the name. It was true, he mused angrily. She *was* a paragon. Like an exquisitely carved ice statue. Perfectly beautiful to the eye, perfectly cold to the touch.

Worst of all, she was his father's choice. *That* rankled Seneca more than anything else. The man had ruled Seneca's every action—indeed, his every *thought*—for over thirty years.

Viciously, he kicked another piece of kindling into the fire. "Callista," he seethed again.

Unless some other woman materialized out of nowhere within nine hours, he would be bound to Callista forever.

Nimbly, Peachy released the bowed oak branch and landed neatly on the stone balcony that surrounded the second floor of the castle, her squirrel following suit. Huffing both with exertion and aggravation, she looked over the ledge and spied the contingent of guards who had unceremoniously removed her from the palace grounds some time earlier. Dammit, because of them she'd had to swim across the river twice and was wetter than a widow's handkerchief!

"Yoo-hoo," she called quietly to them, knowing her voice wouldn't reach them. "Here I am, you gawdang sword-totin', agger-pervokin' varmints, you."

She stuck her tongue out at them, then smiled. The soldiers undoubtedly thought they'd effectively gotten rid of her. But what they hadn't taken into account was the huge oak tree that grew beside the palace. She'd skinned her knee while climbing it, but what was a little scrape compared to spending the last of her life in this fairy-tale castle wrapped in the arms of her fairy-tale prince?

She slipped her hat back on, retrieved her satchel from where she'd thrown it, and advanced toward a big wooden door. "Please God," she whispered, "don't let it be locked."

It wasn't, and creaked loudly when she pushed it. It opened into closed damask draperies. Peachy moved them aside and peered into dim chambers. As her eyes adjusted to the softly moonlit room, she gasped in awe and struggled to take in air.

Decorated in shades that ranged from vivid purple to lavender, it was the most gorgeous room she'd ever imagined could exist. Everything she saw glittered with the evidence of boundless wealth. There was only one thing wrong with it.

Prince Seneca wasn't in it.

Her squirrel in her arms, she crossed to gilded double doors and proceeded down a brightly lit hallway. From either side of her, painted people, forever locked inside their golden frames, stared down at her. Unnerved by the feeling of being watched by so many eyes, she quickened her pace.

She soon came to a huge spiral staircase with a crimson runner snaking down its marble steps. Looking up, she saw a glass dome directly overhead, and watched mesmerized as hundreds of stars sparkled down at her. "Wouldja look at that, Thurlow Wadsworth McGee? They got 'em a little piece o' night right here inside the castle."

Before she realized it, she was climbing the winding staircase. It was a long, long way to the top. When she reached the upper landing, she saw she'd come to another endless corridor.

She saw a man there. A big one. From head to toe, he was covered with steel. In one gloved hand he held a gleaming spear; in the other he brandished an ax.

For a moment, Peachy couldn't move. But as fear gushed through her, it lent strength and momentum to her body. Holding back a scream, she raced past the man of iron.

But her skirt caught on the metal soldier's leg. He tottered violently and with a nerve-shattering crash spilled to the floor. Peachy's fear turned to terror when she saw that his fallen ax had nicked the toe of her boot. And when she watched his head roll down the hall and the rest of him clatter down the staircase, full-fledged hysteria exploded inside her. "Oh, God, he— He's slashed plumb to pieces! I done *kilt* him!"

Completely panicked, she turned and began to run, sure that every guard in the palace would soon be looking for the assailant who'd murdered their fellow soldier. Not knowing what else to do, she stopped at the first door she came to. Twisting the knob, she rammed her shoulder against the wood paneling.

The door opened more easily than she'd expected and banged into the wall behind it. She fell to the polished marble floor and slid several feet along the slick tiles. She might have gone farther had she not crashed into a solid oak chest.

"Dang it to hell!" she cursed, rubbing her throbbing head. With no time to waste, she scrambled up, raced back to the door, and slammed it closed. Her heartbeat hammering in her ears, she bolted the door and laid her forehead against it. Her breath came in ragged heaves.

"Who are you, and what are you doing here?" a deep voice demanded.

Another scream filled her throat, but she was too startled to release it. Terrified to turn and see the man behind her, she stood as still as she was able. Hot tears flowed down her cheeks so quickly she felt her cold, wet blouse grow warm with them.

"Who are you?" the voice demanded again.

Peachy realized the voice came from a very big man. He was probably dressed in steel, like the one she'd killed. She swallowed—so hard her throat ached. She was going to have to face the man; if she tried to escape, he'd catch her.

"I didn't mean to," she squeaked, her face still turned to the door. "He must've cut his own head offen. He— He landed on his ax. His head . . . It rolled down the hall! And the rest of him clanked down them stairs! Sweet Lord o' mercy, it weren't my f-fault!"

Seneca frowned, confused by her tears, her story, her

very presence in his chambers. "What are you talking about?"

"The soldier a-wearin' steel clothes," she tried to explain. "He falled down and hacked hissef to bits!"

From his spot by the fireplace, Seneca could barely see her, but he heard her clearly. Her unusual accent, one he'd never come across before, told him that not only didn't she belong in the palace, she didn't belong in Aventine. "Step out of those shadows."

His voice filled the room like a blast of cold wind. Preparing herself for the sight of his metal suit and sharp, wicked ax, she turned slowly, her eyes tightly closed. When her back was to the door, she clenched her fists, praying as she'd never prayed before, and opened her eyes.

She gasped.

The man wasn't wearing iron clothes. He was barely dressed at all! Only a pair of snug white pants covered his tanned, lean form. The pants were the whitest things she'd ever seen, whiter even than the Appalachian snow. Gold braid was sewn down the sides of each pant leg, its shimmer drawing her eyes to the thick muscles in his thighs. Peachy felt her knees wobble.

He stood beside a huge and elaborately molded fireplace. The mellow light of the fire flickered through his thick, wavy hair. His hair . . . was black. Black like charcoal. Like raven feathers. Like midnight.

A thrilling thought clicked into her mind. Could this be Prince Seneca? "You— Is yore name . . ."

Her voice fading, she cocked her head and examined him more intently. No, she decided, this wasn't Seneca. This man wasn't wearing a gold crown with jewels all over it. Everyone knew royal folks always wore their crowns. They even wore them to bed. And they certainly didn't walk around with their chests naked like this man was doing. Royal people covered up with red velvet robes. "Who are you, mister?"

Seneca couldn't believe her nerve! "Who am *I?* The question, young lady, is who are *you?*"

"I'm—I'm a killer," she remembered, sniffling and blinking back more tears.

"The soldier at the top of the staircase is a decoration," Seneca explained impatiently. "An empty suit of armor."

It took Peachy a moment to understand. "Y'mean I didn't kill nobody? That man weren't—"

"You didn't, and he wasn't. Now come out of those shadows so I can see you."

She wasn't altogether sure she could trust him. "No."

"No?" he thundered. "What do you mean *no?*"

Peachy let out a small shriek. "God Almighty! Y'ain't gotta scream at me! I ain't done nothin' a'tall to you! Jest who the hell do y'think you are?"

Seneca inhaled sharply. "Do you curse at me?" he asked incredulously.

The unmitigated astonishment in his voice made her smile. "No, I'm a-whisperin' sweet nothin's."

Seneca's first reaction to her sarcasm was disbelief. In the next moment, he felt his lips twitch. His near smile amazed, baffled, and angered him all at once. What did he think was so amusing? The girl was actually taunting him! *Insulting* him!

His expression stern, he started for her but stopped suddenly when a tiny gray animal darted in front of his path. It sprang to a satinwood table near the fireplace, selected a shiny red apple from a fruit bowl, and commenced to eat.

Peachy clapped twice, her action bringing the squirrel to her immediately. He leaped into her arms. "Yore a sorry rascal, Thurlow Wadsworth McGee. A-hepin' yoresef to a apple when you ain't been offered as much as one o' them there grapes."

She looked back at the man, who now stood in the middle of the spacious and luxurious room. "Can I stay in here till them guards stop a-huntin' fer me? Y'know, I'm mighty glad I didn't kill nobody. I was a-wonderin' how many years in Purgatory I'd git fer it. I'm Catholic, y'see. 'Course, I ain't been to mass in a right long spell on account o' Father Sullivan up and went back to Ireland. Now the nearest priest's a whole lot further away than jest a look and a holler. Anyway, us Catholics? Well, we believe in Purgatory. I don't know if folks who ain't Catholic believe in it or not, but I can tell you right here and now in this day and time that it's real."

Seneca frowned again. "Purgatory?" God, he thought. Who was this strange girl, and why was she telling him such odd stories? More importantly, *what* was she doing here?

"Purgatory's where y'go afore y'git to heaven," Peachy explained, casting another appreciative glance around the opulent room. "I ain't rightly shore where it is, but I think it's betwixt earth and heaven. There's holy fire in Purgatory. You have to stand in them flames till all yore sins is burned offen yore soul. When you've done roasted half to death, you git to go to heaven. I— Ha! Did y'hear what I said about a-roastin' half to death? Ain't that funny? Yore already dead once yore in Purgatory! Wonder why I said sech a dumb thing?"

Seneca didn't know how to respond to such ludicrous conversation. It was the first time in his life that he'd felt so bewildered by a situation.

"Well, looky there," Peachy said, pointing to the wall behind a dark blue and burgundy striped sofa. "You got swords a-tacked over yore sofer. Ain't you never afeared them swords'll fall offen and cut yore head open? You know how to use them swords, feller?"

Irritated over being called "fellow," Seneca glanced at the ancient set of broadswords attached to the satin-covered wall. Though he never used those particular weapons, his skill with swords was well-known throughout Europe. Indeed, he was a master fencer.

"Anyhow," Peachy went on, giving him no time at all to answer, "I been a-wonderin' how many years I'll have to spend in Purgatory. I'm a sinner, y'know. Ever'body is, even you. Fer ever' sin y'commit, y'git time added to yore stay in them Purgatorial flames. I didn't used to be too worried about Purgatory till I larned I was so long in the neck, but I'm powerful worried now." Nodding at her own words, she set her squirrel down on the floor.

"I ain't a-doin' too good at not sinnin', though," she admitted sheepishly. "Cain't seem to quit a-cussin' to save my life, and when I come into this here room? Well, I was tickled clear down to the inside o' my innards by the sight o' yore nekkid chest. You and me ain't married, so me a-lookin' at you the way I done was a sin prob'ly worth at least seven thousand years in Purgatory. Tomorrer I'll do some penance so's I can git a few hunnerd years tuk offen my stay there. I'd do penance tonight, but I'm too gawdang tired to put up with any sufferin' right now. Yeah, plumb pizzlesprung's what I am."

Seneca was totally perplexed. Long in the neck? Pizzlesprung? The girl certainly used some odd expressions. He couldn't help wondering what they meant.

"Look, mister, I can see by that survigorous look on yore face that yore—"

"You will cease speaking to me in such an incomprehensible fashion! If I do indeed have a . . . a *survigorous* look on my face, it would please me enormously if you would tell me exactly what kind of look that is!"

"Survigorous? Well, it means vicious. Riled clear down to yore gizzard. You look jest about as sour as dog breath." Satchel slung over her shoulder, arms folded across her chest, she stepped out of the shadows by the door, but remained a good distance away from the man, who appeared to be even more angry now than he had been before.

"I know yore plumb agger-pervoked and that I ain't yore favorite person in the world right now. Yore near about as nekkid as a parched peanut, so you was prob'ly a-fixin' to go to bed when I come a-bustin' in here. That, or you was a-waitin' on some girl so's you could squeeze in a little sweetheartin' afore mornin'."

She saw him glower, but continued quickly. "I swear I'll git outen here, but can I stay jest till all them guards quit a-huntin' fer me? I'm in a real hurryment to find my beloved, but I know them hound dog soldiers is a-sniffin' around the castle on account o' that man o' iron? Well, when he commenced a-fallin', he maked more noise'n two skeletons a-makin' love on a tin roof. So can I stay here with you fer jest a little while?"

Seneca gasped softly. He'd never heard a girl use such language! "No, you may not—"

"That a onyx on yore hand?" Peachy asked, staring at the black stone set in a heavy gold ring. "Ain't nobody never tole you that onyx means inner troubles and deep down sorrer? You a sad man with problems inside you?"

Unmitigated astonishment fell over him. God, could the strange girl see inside his very soul?

"You orter wear emeralds, mister. They mean happiness, unnerstandin', and love. Sapphires is good too. They hep y'be peaceful inside. Rubies is the worst y'can wear. They mean anger and cruelty and all sorts o' cold feelin's."

Instantly, Seneca pictured his father's ring, a huge blood-red ruby that covered half his hand. *Anger and cruelty and all sorts of cold feelings.*

" 'Course I ain't never weared nary a jewel in my life," Peachy informed him, "but there's rimptions o' omens about 'em. All true, too. True as true could ever be truthfully true."

She was the most talkative person he'd ever met. Accustomed as he was to long periods without speaking at all, it was difficult to adjust to someone like her, a person who barely took a breath between sentences. "If you don't tell me what you're doing here, I'm going to call the very soldiers you fear and have you hauled away."

Peachy took a few more steps toward him. "To the dungeon? I heared all about them cold, wet, dark, smelly, rat-infested dungeons y'all got in castles. The thing is though, iffen you have me tuk to the dungeon, ole Seneca'll jest come and git me outen."

Her last statement captured Seneca's full attention. "Oh really? And why is that?"

She gave him a smug smile. "On account o' the gnat I swallered, the black rock, and the 'S'-slimin' snail. Oh, and the lilac leaves, too. My maw's name was Tilly. I always loved that name. Maw's gone now, and so's Lulu, my baby sister. Anyhow, Maw was always a-sayin' that iffen a girl eats five lilac leaves, she'll marry whoever she wants to. Jest to be on the safe side, I et ten. Doubles my chances, y'see. Omens is powerful strong."

Her explanation was so bizarre, Seneca comprehended none of it. But for reasons he couldn't fathom, the very outrageousness of her personality intrigued him. He didn't, of course, condone her wild character, but it didn't repulse him, either. His emotions fell somewhere in between, and he thought that very odd indeed.

He still couldn't see her face well, but he could see her attire. She wore some sort of fur cap on her head, its striped tail lying over her thick red curls. At first glance, Seneca thought the raccoon it was made from might still be alive. Beneath her long buckskin coat she wore a multi-patched skirt that looked to be homespun. Old, scuffed boots peeked out from beneath the skirt, and a long and lethal dagger gleamed at her waist.

He looked back at her shadowed face. "You have five seconds to explain your presence here. Go a second over that time and—"

"I know, you'll have me throwed in the dungeon." Noticing again his lack of a red robe and jeweled crown, Peachy smiled. The man definitely wasn't royal, but his bossy attitude sure made him seem like one. She decided to stall for more time. "Five seconds, huh? Well, that ain't enough time to tell you nothin'."

"You will, however, tell me."

"Yeah? Make me."

At her insolence, Seneca's eyes widened.

It looked to Peachy that they were about to fly out of his head. "Oh, all right, I'll tell you. 'Pears to me that iffen I don't, you'll work yoresef nigh into a frenzified frazzle. Prince Seneca's why I'm here."

Seneca's curiosity was too strong to squelch. "Why?"

"On account o' only a prince could make all my last earthly wishes come true. I got this 'Must Do Afore I Die' list, y'see, and most o' the things on it have to do with a-livin' one o' them lifes o' leisure. I been a-workin' ever' single day since I was old enough to be able to do it, and now all's I want to do is nothin' but fun things. And I always wanted to know what it's like to wear a crown, too. Who else 'sides a prince could do that sorter stuff fer me? 'Course, I ain't had no death-like symptoms yet, not nary a one, so I prob'ly got a while longer yet. But I 'spect them symptoms'll be a-showin' up afore too much longer."

"Symptoms?"

"Of tipinosis. That's what's gonna rid the ground o' my shadder. S'what kilt my paw, too."

Tipinosis, Seneca repeated silently. He'd never heard of it. The girl certainly didn't act sick. Indeed, she looked to be the epitome of health. Why, she didn't even show signs of being upset! "You say you're gravely ill," he began, watching her closely, "yet you don't seem distressed at the prospect of dying."

"Yeah, well you shoulda seed me when I first heared about it. I was all broke up. Cried and carried on fer nigh on all afternoon and some o' the night, too. Even after I larnt about Prince Seneca, my feelin's was still fair whipped down. But afore I leaved the hills? Well, you prob'ly won't believe this, but a ruby-throated hummin'-bird flied into my cabin."

He got the distinct idea that he was supposed to be impressed by her announcement. "A hummingbird. I see."

"Well, *ever'body* knows that's one o' the most rarest omens there is! It means that the purest and lastin'est kind o' happiness is gonna fill yore days. So when I git to feelin' dolesome-like over all my woes, I jest commence mem'ryin' that sweet little ruby-throated hummin'bird. That omen ain't never, ever been knowed to fail, so I'm shore and sartin that fer whatever time I got left, I'm gonna be happy."

God, Seneca thought. The girl had the wildest imagination he'd ever encountered. "What—"

A sharp rap at the door cut him off.

"Oh, Lord, I knowed it!" Peachy whispered hysterically. "They're a-lookin' fer me!" She understood she hadn't killed anyone, but the fact remained she *had* broken into the palace and destroyed the empty steel man. Terrified that she'd be put in chains before having had the chance to find Seneca, she raced into the bedchambers.

Seneca followed her. For a moment, he didn't see her, but in the next instant he heard her behind him. He turned just as she threw herself into his arms. Caught off guard by her quick action, he careened backwards, the girl clinging to his neck, her legs dangling between his.

"Don't turn me in!" Peachy whispered into his ear. "Please don't—"

"Let go of my—"

"I'll do anything you say iffen you don't—"

"Release my—" He had no time to finish his command. His feet met with the bottom step of the dais that supported his bed and, in an effort to keep from falling to the floor, he stumbled up the steps and toppled to the mattress instead. The girl fell with him, landing directly on his chest. Her raccoon hat slipped off her head, its tail tickling his nose.

"They'll prob'ly chop my head offen!" Peachy moaned, her face pressed against his neck. "Or have horses pull my body to pieces! Or press me into a bed o' iron stakes! Oh, God, don't let 'em git me!"

Her voice muffled in his shoulder, Seneca understood nothing of what she said. Hands curled around her waist, he started to lift her from his person.

But a sudden movement by the side of his face stilled his actions. He saw her squirrel staring at him. The creature began sniffing his temple. Seneca wondered if the small, sharp-toothed beast was going to eat his ear.

This was truly the oddest experience of his entire life. With one smooth action, he successfully removed the girl. When she rolled to the mattress, he got to his feet and headed back into the sitting room. He knew full well that it was the castle guards who were knocking. They'd found the fallen suit of armor and had come to see to his safety. He intended to allow them to perform that service, for he'd had quite enough of the outlandish girl and her squirrel.

"Please, mister! I'm on my knees a-beggin' you to keep me safe! I'll kiss yore ring! Yore feet! Hell, I'll kiss yore *ass* iffen you'll jest hide me!"

At her shocking language, he rolled his eyes, halted beneath the archway of his bedroom, and cast a glance at her over his shoulder. He was unable to move, to breathe, to blink. An extraordinary feeling passed through him.

He hadn't seen her clearly before. He did now.

She knelt before the flame-filled hearth, her hands folded, her arms outstretched in a pleading gesture. Soft firelight glowed all around her, making it seem as though she were bathing in a pool of liquid gold.

She was lovely.

Radiant.

Like an angel.

He heard the guards pound on the door again. "Leave me!" he shouted to them, his gaze still pinned to the girl's. The profound feeling inside him intensified. As it deepened, a memory came to him. A barely-there kind of memory that floated on the edge of his consciousness, too far away to remember completely. The harder he tried to recall the whole of it, the faster it disappeared altogether.

There was something about the girl . . .

The gentle shine in her eyes beckoned to him. Slowly, he walked toward her, stopping when he was directly before her. He was struck anew. Her long red-gold hair seemed so familiar to him. He felt as though he'd admired its brilliant softness many times . . . that he'd always loved the way it curled sweetly about her heart-shaped face. Her skin . . . was like magnolia blossoms. He'd never seen such creamy, flawless skin. Or had he? He certainly felt as though he had.

And her eyes . . . Two glistening chips of pale jade. He seemed to remember having been comforted by them a thousand times. He even felt as though he'd made wishes and whispered secrets into them. But where? When?

She was the most incredibly beautiful woman he'd ever seen. "I— Have I ever met you before?"

She shook her head.

"Tell me who you are," he murmured, extending his hand.

Peachy placed her fingers lightly in his palm.

Immediately, Seneca was aware of her warmth. He helped her to rise and brought her closer to him, so near that he could see his own reflection in her eyes, her compelling eyes.

"Who are you?" he whispered. Without realizing what he was doing, he drew her closer still. Desire slammed into him when he felt her lush breasts touch his chest. Astonishment melded with his passion. He'd never felt such deep and instant attraction for any woman. "Tell me your name," he entreated.

Spellbound by the tender glow in his eyes, the even softer caress of his whisper, Peachy could not immediately answer. "Peachy," she finally said. "Peachy McGee."

He knew instantly that no other name in the world would suit her. "Peachy."

She felt his heartbeat between her breasts. He was staring into her eyes, peering so deeply into them that she wondered if he was reading her thoughts.

Something inside her awakened. Something she'd never realized lay dormant. It sprang to life, igniting within her a feeling of intense yearning. For him. For this man she didn't even know.

Confused, she tried to step away. He wouldn't let her, and held her as though she belonged to him. She thought to protest, but her body wouldn't obey her mind's commands. Stunned, she watched her own hand cup his cheek. Her fingers slid through the unruly black curls at the nape of his neck; her eyes never left his.

A long moment passed before she realized what she was doing. "This . . . It ain't right." Quickly and forcefully, she wiggled out of his embrace. "You ain't the man I'm gonna marry, and there I was a-rubbin' up to you so close that it's a gawdang miracle I didn't raise a blister! God Almighty, that prob'ly got me another ten thousand years in Purgatory!"

Flustered by her strong response to him, she turned and faced the fire. "I gotta go now."

He took note that she made no move to leave. "You're going to marry?"

"Look," Peachy snapped, still staring into the blaze and trying to get hold of her wild emotions, "I been through hell a-tryin' to git here, and I ain't gonna mess ever'thing up jest on account o' yore knee-weakin' looks, hear? I been a-travelin' fer s'long I done lost count o' how many days it's been since I leaved Possom Holler."

"Where?"

"Possum Holler. It's a little place near the Blue Ridge in North Caroliner. Ain't but about twenty folks who live there. From Possom Holler, I rided in a wagon to the port o' Wilmin'ton. From Wilmin'ton I sailed in a big ship-boat that was a-headed fer Scotland. The captain-sailor was nice enough to drop me offen here. I paid fer passage with the little bag o' gold dust Paw hanged onto fer s'many years. That little sack o' dust was all the money me and Paw ever had, and now I done used up that, too."

She sensed he was still watching her in that intense way. Her tension increased. "Paw got the gold dust from our stream, but that ole crick don't got nary a grain o' gold in it no more," she rambled nervously. "Ain't got much water in it, neither. I can still git my drinkin' water from it, but I do all my warshin' in the Mackintoshes' stream. They're my neighbor-people.

"Anyhow, I jest got here tonight. It's a right fur piece up here from the seashore, y'know, but I walked it. Got here, then I had to fend offen all them varmint guards. They come at me like piss ants a-pourin' outen a log. I swum that gawdang river twice, clum up a oak tree, and skint my knee. Then I near about busted my head wide open when I crashed into that blasted table in the other room. All's I want to do now is git up with my dearest beloved.

"He's the onliest person in the whole world who matters to me now, y'see," she said, trying to make him understand. "'Course I got a distant aunt and cousin in Elroy's Corner, North Caroliner, but I ain't never laid eyes on 'em afore. Orabelle and Bubba. Aunt Orabelle used to write to Paw, but all's she ever wanted to know was how much gold we was a-gittin' outen the crick. I writ to Aunt Orabelle and Cousin Bubba when Paw died, but they didn't show up fer the funeralizin'.''

She frowned, suddenly realizing how far off the subject she'd rambled. "Anyhow, yore a real handsome feller, and it shore don't hurt my feelin's none to look at you, but you ain't the one I come to be with, hear? You ain't the one who's gonna make all my wishes come true, who's gonna hep me live the rest o' my short life to the fullest o' full. Now, iffen you'll jest tell me where I can find Prince Seneca, I'll be on my way."

When he offered no immediate answer to her query, she wondered if he understood why she was so desperate to find the prince. Slowly, she turned from the fire and faced him. "The king's a-makin' him marry," she explained. "Seneca needs a princess, and I need a prince. I cain't make it no clearer'n that."

Seneca felt as if he'd been struck by a bolt of lightning. With blinding intensity a myriad of thoughts exploded into his mind . . .

Seneca needs a princess, and I need a prince.

His father's smug smile . . . His father's taunting promise . . .

Should you succeed in coming upon your princess before morning, I will honor your choice of brides.

Nine hours . . . Nine hours.

He raised an ebony brow and deliberated with calculating intensity. Two questions echoed through him:

Would he submit to his father's decree and marry the cold and impeccable gentlewoman, Callista Inger, whom he'd known for years?

Or would he defy his father for the first time in his life and take to wife the outlandish but warm and hauntingly beautiful mountain girl, Peachy McGee, whom he'd known for all of twenty minutes?

He almost smiled. "Peachy," he whispered. He took her hand and lifted it to his mouth, brushing his lips across her slender fingers. "I am Seneca."

Chapter 2

His words floated to her as if borne on a summer breeze. They sang with sincerity. But doubts nagged at her.

"You? The prince? But— What about yore crown?"

"My crown?"

She didn't miss the confusion in his startling blue eyes. A real prince, she knew, wouldn't look like that when asked about his crown. Indeed, a real prince, if he wasn't wearing his crown, would go to the closet and take it out to show her. She took her hand from his and backed away a few steps. "You ain't got no crown, do you?"

"I have three of them."

"Ha!"

"I do."

She nodded. "Yeah, shore, and iffen you want more, all's y'gotta do is go pick 'em offen the crown tree a-growin' in the castle backyard. I s'pose y'got three o' them sceptor-sticks, too. And a few o' them gold balls that look like worlds that royal folks hold in their hands?"

"Orbs," he corrected her. "No, I'm afraid I do not own any orbs or sceptors."

"No?" She narrowed her eyes. "What's a-matter? The Aventine orb and sceptor-stick trees ain't a-doin' so good this year?"

"Only the sovereign may possess the royal orbs and sceptors. They will not pass to me until I am crowned King of Aventine."

Peachy smiled, then burst into loud laughter. "Sweet

26

Lord o' mercy, feller, you got one hell of a nerve, a-tellin' me them lies! I'm a-fixin' to become Princess Peachy! Cain't you unnerstand that afore long I'll have the power to have you throwed in the alligator moat? Seneca'll be on my side, y'know."

He didn't know whether to feel insulted or amused. "I *am* Seneca."

Giggling, Peachy turned toward the mantel, rubbed her finger across it, but found not a speck of dust. "I readed this story once? Well, it was about this princess who come to a strange castle a-wantin' to git outen the rain, see. Nobody believed she was a princess, so the castle folk, they maked her sleep on a hunnerd feather beds. They'd put one little dried-up pea under them beds on account o' only a *real* princess would be able to feel the pea unner s'many mattresses. When the princess waked up? Well, she was black and blue all over from a-sleepin' on top o' the dried-up pea. I mean to tell you, she was some *kind* o' swolt up."

Seneca tried to remember if he'd heard the story, but the only tales he could recall hearing his literature tutor read to him were those of Greek and Roman mythology.

For a brief second, he found himself wondering how the princess-and-the-pea story had ended. But no sooner had he caught the question in his mind than he dismissed it as nonsensical. "Are you suggesting I sleep on a pea to prove who I am?" he flared, angry with her for not believing him and irritated with himself for wasting time wondering about that stupid story she'd told him.

Peachy took one of her auburn curls and glided it across her lips. "No, jest feeled like a-tellin' you the story, is all. Y'ain't gotta take a snit over it, y'know. 'Sides that, I think that pea thing only works fer princesses. Fer a prince it prob'ly has to be some other kind o' vegetable. Maybe a pinto bean."

"I will not sleep on a bean." As the words left his mouth, he couldn't believe he'd said them. He'd never heard himself speak so ludicrously. Sleep on a bean indeed!

"Why not?" Peachy dared. "Afeared y'won't wake up all black and blue?" Tapping a finger to her chin, she decided to make him a more realistic offer. "Tell y'what, feller. Call yore servants and git 'em to fetch them crowns o' yores up here."

It went completely against his grain to obey what was obviously a command, but Seneca didn't know how else to make her believe him. He strode to his massive bed and pulled a gold satin sash that hung suspended from the molded ceiling. In moments, a soft knock sounded at the door in the sitting room. "Stay here," he ordered Peachy.

When he left the bedchamber, she peeked around the archway and saw him open the door in the other room. Standing in the corridor was a finely dressed man.

"Latimer," Seneca said to him, "bring me my crowns. And make haste."

"At once, Your Royal Highness."

His back to Peachy, who he knew was spying from his bedchambers, Seneca remained at the door until Latimer returned bearing a solid gold tray. Upon it rested the three precious headpieces. Seneca took the tray, dismissed the servant, and carried the priceless burden into his bedroom to the bed. Then he returned to the fireplace and waited for Peachy's reaction.

Her gaze was pinned to the glittering array of crowns. She couldn't suppress a long sigh. In a daze, she made her way to the canopied bed, walked up the dais, and reached out to touch one of the crowns.

Her finger slid across a diamond that was as big as any of the plump walnuts that grew in the Blue Ridge. She took off her raccoon cap and reverently lifted the crown from the bed, mesmerized as hundreds of gemstones twinkled at her. Hands trembling, she placed the crown on her head. It slipped down to the bridge of her nose. With one finger, she pushed it back up.

"Look at me, Thurlow Wadsworth McGee," she murmured to her squirrel, who sat in the midst of the cluster of midnight-blue pillows at the head of the bed. "I'm a-wearin' a crown. It's plumb full o' gold and jewels and sparkles, and I've really and truly got— Got it . . . on."

Shock waves tingled through her. The man, she thought. Upon his command, the crowns had been brought to the room by a servant. *At once, Your Royal Highness,* the attendant had said to him.

"Highness," she whispered. Slowly, almost fearfully, she turned and looked at him.

At His Royal Highness, Prince Seneca of Aventine.

Seneca met her wide-eyed gaze directly. "You believe me now."

Unable to speak, she nodded.

"It is unbefitting for a princess to doubt her husband. You will never do so again."

Hands shaking, she took off the crown. As she began to lay it back on the tray, the full implication of his statement struck her. The crown fell from her grasp and rolled across the rich burgundy coverlet. "Princess— You—" Moistening her lips, she looked at him again. "Yore . . . gonna marry me?"

He took a moment to ponder the changes his wedding her would bring about in his life. He could think of only two: he wouldn't sleep alone anymore, and his father would be forced to cease badgering him about attaining a wife. Otherwise, marriage with Peachy wouldn't alter his days in the least. Indeed, he'd see little of her.

He would, however, demand that she conduct herself in a proper manner. "You will consent to become the lady fit to wear the title of Princess of Aventine?"

"I . . . I promise to wear my crown ever'day."

He glanced at the floor, struggling to keep from smiling over her inadequate oath and trying to think of a way to rephrase the question. "And do you also promise to learn the *ways* of a lady? Do you give me your word that you will endeavor to acquire proper etiquette?"

"Etiquette?"

"Manners."

"I never put my elbows on the table, and I use a napkin instead o' the back o' my hand," she rushed to reassure him. "I don't never sneeze or cough afore a-coverin' my mouth. I don't pop my knuckles or spit, neither."

He was glad to know she didn't spit, for that was one particular that it never would have occurred to him to caution her against. "That's all well and good, but I'm afraid

I must insist that you promise to learn other aspects of good behavior, too."

"I— I promise to be the mostest mannerized princess this island's ever had."

He looked into her eyes. They glowed with what he hoped was sincerity. "Very well. Then, yes, I am going to marry you."

She stared at him, taking in every inch of his tall, sinewy form. His dark skin gleamed in the firelight. He moved slightly; she saw the muscles in his smooth chest ripple. His thick sable hair curled rakishly around his face.

His features appeared refined and rugged at once, as though a master sculptor had chisled them from the finest, rarest wood.

There was nothing subtle about his looks. He was boldly handsome.

And he belonged to her.

Instantly, exquisite excitement whipped through her. She fairly flew off the dais, sped across the room, and leaped into his arms. "Oh, my most dearest beloved! I knowed you'd say yes! I jest knowed it! Them omens, they don't never lie!"

Grinning, she slipped out of his hold, reached for his hand, and held it to her heart. She'd wondered if he would object to marrying a girl who wouldn't be alive for long, but he didn't seem to mind, for he hadn't said much about it. His calm acceptance relieved her enormously. *She* wasn't going to cry and carry on over her dying, and she didn't want him to, either. Life was too short and precious to spend in sorrow.

"Sweetest, darlin'est man o' mine," she said, "fer as long as I'm alive? Well, I swear to God Almighty I'll try my dangest to give you a lavish o' wedded bliss."

He failed to think of a proper response. He could only feel. She held his hand between her breasts. Indeed, they formed two lush cushions around his wrist. If he moved his hand only slightly, he could touch her. Intimately.

Desire returned. God, she was beautiful. Sleeping next to her night after night wasn't going to be the least bit difficult.

"I'm gonna love you like you ain't never been loved

afore, Seneca," Peachy promised softly, watching his sapphire eyes darken to a deep, stormy blue. "I cain't love you right away on account o' I don't know you good. But once I know you? Well, I'm gonna adore the plum puddin' outen you. And ... And maybe you'll love me back. That's one o' the things on my wish list, y'know. Fer you to love me. Fer the last days o' my life to be full o' love. Love from me and love from you."

Her request for his love caused him to start. He took a step away from her.

"Seneca?"

"Yes?" he answered absently.

She puckered her lips. "It's time now."

He frowned, her statement bringing him out of his daze. "Time? For what?"

"To swap spit."

His scowl deepened. "I beg your pardon?"

"Swap spit. *Kiss.* We cain't do nothin' more'n that on account o' it'd be a sin. It'll be a spell afore we can commence a-doin' the real good stuff. 'Course I ain't never done it, but my neighbor-woman, Miz Mackintosh? Well, she let on that it's good stuff. She called it a-gittin' gravel fer her goose. She has thirteen young'uns, so I don't reckon she was a-lyin.' Anybody with thirteen young'uns must really like a-gittin' gravel fer her goose."

Seneca was at a complete loss. Her unseemly way of describing a kiss ... Her even more shocking way of defining lovemaking ... One part of him urged him to severely upbraid her for talking in such an indecent way. But another side of him ... some part with which he wasn't at all familiar, struggled with the temptation to laugh out loud.

It dawned on him that this wasn't the first time she'd brought him such contrary emotions. Ever since she'd fallen into his room, he'd battled with anger, confusion, shock, and amusement all at once.

" 'Course now that I think on it good," Peachy amended suddenly, "it might even be too soon fer a kiss. I don't know you good yet, y'see, and it's prob'ly a real horrible sin to kiss a man afore y'know him good. And I ain't a-takin' no chances with them sin-burnin' flames. Sorry,

Seneca, but y'cain't kiss me tonight. I don't know when y'can, but it ain't tonight."

He fought the desire to laugh again. "You think to deny me?"

"Jest till I know you good."

He felt the overwhelming temptation to take her into his arms and kiss her breathless. It would be a pleasure for him, and it would show her that he would not allow her to refuse to give what he wanted from her.

But as her big green eyes peered up at him, the innocence and trust in them made him take another step away from her. "You will retire now."

"Retire? From what?"

"From what? From being awake, I suppose."

"Oh, y'mean you want me to go to sleep?"

"Yes."

"Then why didn't you say so?"

"I did. You'll sleep here."

She gasped. "The hell I will! We ain't married yet! I ain't *that* kind o' girl, Seneca."

Her announcement was further proof of what he already suspected. Virginity was required of all women marrying into the royal family of Aventine. She would, of course, have to submit to an intimate examination by the court physicians. "In the future, please refrain from using obscenities. Now, you will sleep in my bed, and I will sleep on that sofa."

She glanced at the huge velvet sofa across the room, then at the bed. Its shimmering burgundy canopy was so long that its gold-tasseled ends lay spread all over the floor. Sleeping in a canopied bed was one of the things on her wish list. "All right, but don't go a-gittin' no ideas in the middle o' the night, hear? Yore one o' the gawdangedest handsomest men I ever seed in all my born days, and iffen you commence a-oozin' outen with that there charm o' yores, I won't be able to say no."

Her confession pleased him, but her uninhibited honesty took him a little aback. He experienced a fleeting curiosity about how it felt to speak with such openness.

He decided that perhaps her candidness was why he'd thought he'd recognized her earlier. She had a way about her . . . a certain something that made one feel as though one had known her forever.

It was almost a shame that he would have to teach her to keep her emotions carefully concealed.

He inclined his head. "I give you my word that you will be quite safe from my attentions tonight."

Satisfied with his promise, she retrieved her bag and proceeded toward the bed. But before she arrived, she noticed a third room beyond another ornamental archway. She was astonished to see it held a bathtub that was actually sunken into the marble floor. The tub gleamed with the richness of what could only be pure gold. Beside it lay piles of plush towels and stacks of immaculately white soaps. Every wall in the room was made of solid mirror. The gleaming reflection of gold danced everywhere Peachy looked.

"Sweet Lord o' mercy," she whispered. "I ain't never seed a tub like that afore. Back home we always used a wooden one in front o' the hearth. It rotted a while back, though, and Paw, he never did git around to a-makin' another one. After that, we warshed in the Mackintoshes' crick. Lord, that water was colder'n a witch's boobies in a cast-iron corset. Paw said fer me to go on and warsh in that icy water anyway. Said it'd grow hair on my chest. 'Course I didn't never grow none, a-seein' as how I'm a girl, and all."

She turned from the tub and faced Seneca again, her eyes making the delightful journey across the heavily muscled expanse of his chest. " 'Pears you ain't never in yore whole life tuk no baths in icy cricks, Seneca. Yore chest's jest as smooth as a moth's nose."

He looked down at himself, thinking about how smooth a moth's nose really was. Her comparison of his anatomy with that of an insect was . . . Well, it was a bit amusing, highly absurd, as well as rather insulting. Again, he felt confused over his conflicting response to her. "You will keep such unladylike comparisons to yourself, Peachy. Is that clear?"

She wasn't certain what he meant, but to please him, she nodded in agreement, then moved the tray of crowns to a table. Sitting on the bed, she removed the dagger from her belt and the worn boots and bright red socks from her feet. "I usually sleep buck nekkid," she explained while slipping between the dark blue satin sheets, "but— Well, you a-bein' in here and all, I reckon I cain't tonight. So I'll jest sleep in my clothes. They're all dry now."

"I will hire a brace of seamstresses as soon as possible. You will not wear homespun clothing or old boots. Nor will you wear a man's hunting knife." However, he added silently, it was perfectly all right with him if she wished to sleep naked. In fact, he liked the idea very much.

"How come y'don't keep yore crowns in yore room?" she asked. "What fer do y'keep 'em somewheres else in the castle?"

"They are far too valuable to leave lying around. They're kept locked in the crown room, along with all the other royal jewels. The room is well guarded."

"Well, that don't make a bit o' sense to me. Somethin' purty as them crowns ... Purty stuff should be enjoyed, not locked away where nobody cain't even see it. When I git my crown and princess jewelry, I'm a-wearin' it all the time. I won't never take it offen, 'cept to take a bath, and that's all. Yeah, I'm gonna dote on my purty stuff with ever' bit o' my heart."

In answer, he shrugged.

"Can we talk fer a while?" she wanted to know. "I need to tell you what all's on my 'Must Do Afore I Die' list, see. Like I done tole you, I ain't got a whole lot o' time left. I got all sorter stuff on the list. Some's plain stuff like a-sippin' tea in a bed jest like this one. But other stuff's real thrillin, like a-dancin' with gypsies. Ever since I seed a paintin' of a gypsy in a book I used to have, I *always* wanted to dance with real live ones. They beat on tambourines whilst they're a-dancin'. Y'know, Seneca? You look sorter like a gypsy with all that black hair and dark skin o' yores. You kin to gypsies?"

He wondered if her mouth ever got tired. "No."

"Prob'ly are and jest don't know it." Humming a merry tune, she withdrew a sheet of paper from her bag. "All right, gypsy prince, here's my weddin' gown," she informed him, pointing to the drawing on the paper. "I drawed a picture of it whilst I was on the ship-boat. It's my dream dress, Seneca, and I been a-hopin' fer it ever since I first knowed I was gonna marry you."

He couldn't understand why she'd been so sure he would wed her. Her trust in omens was, of course, ludicrous. As was her belief that she was dying. Indeed, she appeared healthier than any woman he'd ever seen.

"Seneca," she said, pointing to the drawing of her gown, "these little dots I drawed is diamonds. See how I want 'em sewed on? They start up here at the middle o' my waist and go clear down the front o' the skirt to the floor. They spell outen yore name, Seneca, see? S-E-N-E-C-A. My dearest beloved's name. Ain't that jest the most romantic thing? And o' course I want my princess crown, too, Seneca. It'll be what my veil goes on. Purty, huh?"

"You may place it on the table beside the bed. I will examine it tomorrow." To pacify her, he would glance at the drawing, but he already had specific ideas concerning the design of her wedding gown. As his bride, she would dress as befitted a princess, in satin, lace, and flowers.

And she would bow to his will on the matter. "Lie down," he instructed her.

Weary clear down to her bones, she settled happily and deeply into the soft mattress. A multitude of silky pillows spread all around her, she felt as though she were cushioned within a sun-heated cocoon. Thurlow Wadsworth McGee burrowed into the covers with her, providing her with yet more warm softness. Drowsiness drifted through her.

"Tomorrow," Seneca began, his hands clasped behind his back as he walked around the room, "you will meet my father. However, I will speak to him privately first, so you will remain in this room until I come for you. It will be quite early in the morning—around eight, I believe, which means, of course, that you must begin to stir at seven in order to have sufficient time to dress. I apologize for the ungodly hour."

Vaguely, Peachy heard him talking to her. But she was so warm, so comfortable, and so terribly sleepy that she couldn't quite concentrate on what he was saying. All she made out clearly was the word *tomorrow*. "Tomorrer," she murmured. "Yeah, tomorrer at daybust I'm gonna go outen to them green fields and play with all them purty sheep."

Seneca heard her muttering and supposed she was giving him her consent. "After you have met Father, you will spend the rest of the day—indeed, most of the next two weeks—with the court seamstresses. That, of course, will not give us much time to work on your manners, but I assure you that I will begin your lessons shortly after the wedding."

Her eyelids were becoming heavy. She yawned and snuggled even more deeply into the thick blankets. "I ain't never played with sheep afore," she whispered, closing her eyes. "I'm gonna git barefoot and run all over with 'em. Gonna go a-fishin', too. We'll have us a picnic, Seneca. And maybe yore paw can come, too. Tomorrer."

Her continued whispering assured him that she was still listening to him. Her close attention to what he was saying gratified him. "All right, Peachy, now that I have given you your schedule for tomorrow, go to sleep." He turned, noticed how very still she was, and strode over to the bed. Gazing down at her, he realized she was already fast asleep.

Her instant obedience to his order pleased him very much. Although her behavior left much to be desired, it was obvious there was a docile and acquiescent side to her as well, for she was making a strong effort to abide by his commands.

He would see to it that she spent her days quietly, staying out of his way unless he summoned her. He would grant her wishes for a life of leisure, and she would immerse herself in gentle and feminine pleasures. As for her dream of dancing with gypsies and whatever other outlandish items were on her wish list, they would, of course, be denied to her.

Highly satisfied with his plans for her, he retired to the sofa. As sleep came to him, he smiled at a comforting realization . . .

His union with Peachy McGee was going to solve all his problems.

* * *

She was going to drive him insane.

Her bedcovers crushed between his fists, Seneca glared down at the empty mattress. Only hours after having received his instructions concerning what she was to do this morning, the wayward wench had already disobeyed him.

She was gone. God only knew where she was or what she was doing.

He threw a glance at the enameled clock on the mantel, his fury swelling when he noticed the hour. His father was probably already on his way to the morning chambers, where he enjoyed having tea before breakfast.

Seneca flung the bedcovers aside, stalked down the dais, and strode angrily into his mirrored bath. His reflection told him that he was ill prepared to meet with his father. His neckcloth was tied improperly, there was lint on his coat, several wrinkles snaked down each of his pant legs, and his shoes were scuffed.

He'd dressed himself after having denied entry to his valet, thinking to keep Peachy's presence a secret for a while longer. He'd dressed quietly, making as little noise as possible just so she could sleep longer.

And his efforts had been for naught. He knew now that she'd left his apartments before he'd even opened his eyes!

Wiping as much lint off his coat as he was able, he stormed out of his chambers and headed down the hall. At the expression of thunderous rage on his face, servants scurried out of his way.

Downstairs, Seneca proceeded toward the morning chambers. Dismally aware of his appearance, he tried once more to clean his coat, and gritted his teeth when he accidentally tore a button off his cuff. He watched it roll across the floor and rest beside a pair of sturdy leather shoes. Raising his gaze, he saw two young housemaids, their dark brown frocks spotless, their pristine collars and caps freshly starched. God, he thought. The maids looked better than he did!

He held out his hand. "My button."

One of them retrieved it, curtsying as she handed it to him.

"Your names."

"I'm Ketty, Your Royal Highness," one said quietly. "And this is Nydia."

"Have either of you anything I can use to remove this lint from my coat? I also need the button sewn back on."

Blushing, they both smiled. It was a rare occasion when either of them ever got close to the handsome prince.

Quickly, they both bobbed curtsies. Nydia withdrew needle and thread from her pocket while Ketty took a clean handkerchief from hers. With all haste and the utmost pleasure, they set to work.

Nydia reattached the button, but Ketty was unable to remove all the fluff from the prince's coat. Seneca, however, was pleased with both girls' efforts. He started to join his father, but a sudden thought caused him to address the maids again. "Your duties take you all about the palace, do they not?"

"Yes, sir," Ketty replied, thrilled because the prince had deigned to continue speaking to them.

"I assume you rise early," Seneca continued. "Tell me, during the course of the morning have you seen anyone who doesn't belong here? A girl?"

"A girl, sir?" Nydia repeated.

"She has long red hair," Seneca elaborated. "She's wearing boots and a skirt and blouse of some sort of homespun fabric. A dagger is more than likely hanging from her belt. Oh, and she's probably accompanied by a gray squirrel."

Ketty and Nydia looked at each other, then back at the prince. "No, Your Royal Highness," Ketty said.

"We've seen no one like that, Your Highness," Nydia added. "But if it would please Your Highness, we could search for her in the servants' quarters."

Seneca sighed deeply. "She's not a servant," he muttered, turning back to the door. "She's going to be your princess." With that, he opened the door and stepped inside. "Good morning, Father."

The king faced the huge window. "Seneca, are you aware that there was an intruder in the palace last night? The men-at-arms failed to apprehend the ruffian. I ought to dismiss the lot of them. Tell me, what good does it do me to employ a contingent of guards if they cannot catch one man?"

Seneca shut the door and crossed to the tea table. A footman handed him a full cup of the dark, fragrant brew. Seneca accepted it, wishing it were hard whiskey. Being intoxicated sounded like the only way he could survive this morning. "Father, I would like to speak to you about—"

"I had a terrible night," King Zane announced. He limped away from the window and sat down in his favorite chair, a monstrous piece of furniture with gilded arms and red velvet upholstery. "My knees pained me to such an extent that I was unable to sleep. They are still aching."

"Perhaps if you would accept a cane, you—"

"I will *not* hobble around on a cane! Such devices are for the weak!"

Seneca strove for patience. "Very well. As you wish. Now, if I may talk to you—"

"And I was awakened at six o'clock by my advisors," the king grumbled, setting his cup of tea on the table beside his chair. "Six o'clock! It would seem that some of the peasants have refused to report to the fields today. Some excuse about their blasted sheep. The only thing they care about is their sheep! Idiots, all of them! I sent soldiers out to see to them. The workers will be back in the fields soon, you may be sure of that." With a great huff, he picked up his cup again.

Though Seneca was impatient to discuss Peachy, his father's announcement both worried and angered him. "What orders did you give the soldiers?" he demanded.

The king frowned. "Do you dare to question me?"

Boldly, Seneca met his father's accusing eyes. "I do."

"Though you wish it were so, you are not the sovereign yet, Seneca."

Seneca's temper rose. "Nevertheless, the peasants are my people, too. Have you no sympathy for them? They're shepherds, not farmers. Forcing them to abandon their flocks and work the fields is—"

"Until you are given the throne, Aventine is mine to rule. I advise you to remember that."

As if he could forget it, Seneca seethed silently. All he

had to do was look out any palace window and see the beleaguered peasants to remember that he had no way of helping them. His sire may as well have tied his hands behind his back. "Father—"

"I will hear no more on the subject, Seneca. However, you can calm yourself over the matter of the workers' defiance. The soldiers are not going to draw and quarter the peasants, but simply escort them back to the fields where they belong. Now, did you want to speak to me about something? Do be quick about it. Our meeting with Lord Inger is but an hour away, and we've yet to break our fast. What is wrong with the kitchen staff, I ask you? For that matter, what is wrong with your valet? Are you aware that you are disheveled, Seneca? I don't believe I have seen you in such a state since you were a small boy. Even then Lady Muckross immediately corrected your unseemly appearance."

Seneca stiffened. Lady Muckross had been both nanny and governess to him. The woman had never seemed to age, but had swept from one position to the other with an ease and efficiency that endeared her to Seneca's parents. Seneca understood now that the king and queen had taken such delight in her because she effectively kept him away from them.

The mere thought of her dredged up feelings of intense hatred in him. He managed to bury them again, but only with extreme effort. "Father—"

"I told Tiblock I wanted my morning meal precisely at eight, and already it is eight and a quarter! Oh, what a morning this has been, Seneca," he lamented and shook his head. "Indeed, I cannot think of another vexing occurrence that might arise. Well, Seneca, what do you want?"

Calmly, Seneca set down his teacup, his tranquil actions a direct contrast to the emotions he felt inside. Every nerve he possessed pulsed with apprehensive yet pleasurable tension. "Father, do you remember what you told me last night at midnight?"

The king scowled. "Good night?"

Seneca shook his head. "No." *You've never said good-night to me,* he added silently. "I refer to the vow you made."

"Vow? What vow?"

Seneca almost smiled. But he wasn't at all used to smiling, so he didn't. "You said that if I were to succeed in finding my princess before this morning, you would honor my choice of brides. You do remember making that oath, do you not, Father?"

The king drummed his fat fingers upon the gilded chair arms. "What is your point?" he snapped.

"I'll come to it straightaway if you will tell me whether or not you recall making the promise."

"Yes! I remember!"

Seneca inclined his head. "I have found her."

King Zane glowered hotly. "Found her? Found who?"

"My bride."

"Your bride?" the king shouted.

"I will marry her in a fortnight."

It was a moment before King Zane could think of his next words. "How— What— Who—"

"Let me go, you gawdang, bedevilin', confounded, worthlesser'n sour owl manure varmints, you!"

At the string of expletives that came from outside the doors, the king fairly sprang from his chair, the action causing considerable pain to his knees. Doubled over his large stomach and holding both kneecaps, he glared at the threshold.

Seneca rolled his eyes. Introducing Peachy in this manner hadn't been his plan, but there was naught he could do about it now. The palace guards must have found and arrested her, he realized. And judging by her colorful ranting and raving, she was not at all pleased.

Mastering his rising anger, he walked to the doors and opened them. At the sight that met his eyes, he curled his hands into tight fists.

There stood Peachy, struggling with the two soldiers who held her. Her skirt was soiled with grass stains and mud. One of her boots was missing, and there was a hole in the toe of her red sock. Her face was smudged with some sort of yellow paste, and her hair, tumbling about her shoulders in chaotic disarray, was filled with what Seneca recognized immediately as sheep fleece.

And she reeked of fish.

Peachy stilled instantly when she saw who'd opened the doors. "Seneca! Tell these here varmints that I—"

"Your Royal Highness?"

Seneca saw it was his father's personal attendant who addressed him. "Tiblock," he said, the name filling him with distaste. He stepped aside, giving unspoken permission for the fussy man to enter.

Hands clasped at his waist, Tiblock marched into the middle of the room and bowed before the king, the guards who held Peachy following suit. "Your Majesty, we found this slovenly person preparing to make a meal in the kitchens."

"Look, mister," Peachy said to him, "I don't know who the hell you are, but I'm—"

"I am Rupert Tiblock, personal attendant to the king. I oversee the running of the palace as well, and you have no right to speak to me in such a brazen manner."

Peachy eyed the thin, bald man with ire and disdain. He was the ugliest human being she'd ever seen. His eyes were two black dots pushed into his head, and his nose reminded her of a spring onion, skinny at the top and rounding out to a fat little bulb at the end.

"Well, Rupert-Dupert-Figgymoopert, you listen to me!" she blasted at him. "I catched five trout this mornin', and I was gonna make a fish-and-cornbread breakferst fer Seneca and the king!"

Seneca understood then that the yellow paste on her face was batter. And she smelled of fish because she'd been fishing. That also explained the mud and grass stains on her clothes. But how she'd been able to get sheep wool in her hair was beyond his comprehension. The only feasible answer he could come up with was that she'd been frolicking with the livestock. And who would want to do that?

He rolled his eyes again.

Tiblock snorted. "I called the royal men-at-arms immediately," he bragged to the king and the prince. "Several of them recognized her as the intruder who breached the palace walls last night."

"Intruder?" the king shouted, still holding his throbbing knees.

Tiblock nodded imperiously. "Yes, indeed, Your Majesty, and a positively *revolting* person she is, too. With Your Majesty's permission, I shall have her removed—"

"Who you a-callin' revoltin', you meaner'n gar broth varmint?" Peachy yelled, still struggling with the two guards. "You orter take a good look at yoresef! Yore skinny enough to lay unner a clothesline in the summertime and not git sunburnt. And about them itty bitty black eyes o' yores . . . Ever seed two rat droppin's in a snowbank? And what do y'brush that fine head o' hair o' yores with? A sponge? Sweet Lord o' mercy, yore so ugly, I reckon that when you was born yore maw didn't know which end to diaper! And iffen you think fer one dangblasted second that you can git shed o' me, you'd best wipe yore onion nose on account o' yore brains is a-leakin' outen it!"

Seneca inhaled sharply. Instantly and without warning, laughter exploded inside him. It distressed him deeply that he found her tirade so amusing, but he simply couldn't contain himself. To prevent his laughter from escaping, he coughed into his hand.

"Is Your Royal Highness all right?" Tiblock queried, thinking the prince was choking.

" 'Course he's all right!" Peachy flared. "Ain't you never seed nobody cough afore? What's a-matter, Seneca? You swaller yore spit down the wrong way?"

Her question sent more mirth bubbling through him. He barely managed to quell it. God, what had come over him that he was having such trouble governing his own emotions? Such a thing had never happened before.

Straightening, he looked at Peachy, the cause of his dismaying loss of control. However inappropriately amusing he found her outrageous behavior, and however deserving Tiblock was of her insults, he had to put an end to it. It was wrong, and he was equally wrong for allowing it to entertain him. His jovial reaction would only make her believe he condoned it, which he didn't, not in the least. "Peachy, that is quite enough."

Tiblock tossed her a smug smile. "Not only is the girl slovenly and repulsive, Your Majesty," he continued smoothly to the king, "but she is deranged as well. Why, she actually believes she is to marry—"

"You don't know nits from noodles!" Peachy hollered, so angry she could hardly think straight. "Roses is red, violets like rain, thimbles is empty, and so's yore brain!"

Tiblock gasped. He'd never been so insulted in all his life! And in front of the royal family, too! Rage sluicing through him, he raised his hand to strike her.

"Hold!" Seneca shouted.

The command came too late. Tiblock's palm smacked across Peachy's cheek.

Seneca saw fire. With long and furious strides, he strode to where Tiblock was standing. "You will never lay a hand on her again! Release her!" he commanded the guards.

As soon as she was free, Peachy went into action and yanked open her skirt pocket. "Git him, boy!" Quickly, she pointed to Tiblock.

Before Tiblock was even aware of what was happening, he saw a gray blur, then felt something pierce the top of his hand. Immediately, blood seeped through his pale skin. Though the wound was only a tiny one, he screamed and staggered backward, clutching his hand as if it were about to fall off.

"Atta boy!" Peachy yelled as her squirrel jumped back into her arms. Smiling, she looked at Tiblock. "Rupert-Dupert-Figgymoopert, meet Thurlow Wadsworth McGee. His teeth is so sharp you could use their shadders to shave with. But I reckon you jest finded that outen fer yoresef, huh? Yeah siree, ole Thurlow Wadsworth McGee's the best guard-squirrel who ever lived. Iffen I was you, I'd think twice afore a-tryin' to meller me again."

Tiblock opened his mouth to speak, but stopped abruptly when the prince raised a hand for silence.

"Leave us," Seneca demanded. "All of you. And I would remind each of you once more that you are never to touch this girl again. If it comes to my attention that you have done so, I assure you that you will regret your actions."

At the look of extreme displeasure on the prince's face, Tiblock and the soldiers left. Tiblock snorted and threw Peachy a withering glance before shutting the doors.

Seneca took Peachy's hand and turned toward his father. The expression on the king's face could have reduced a mountain into a pile of sand. And the man was obviously in shock; he was still doubled over and holding his knee-caps, which was the same position he'd been in five whole minutes ago. "Father—"

"Yore the king?" Peachy asked, staring at the silver-haired, overweight man across the room. "But you ain't got no crown on. Seneca, he don't—" She frowned, noticing that Seneca's head was bare as well. "You ain't got yores on neither. Why—"

"Seneca, explain this immediately!"

Seneca saw fat veins pop out on his sire's forehead. He felt that same inappropriate amusement rise again, but this time he was successful in squelching it immediately. "Father, allow me to introduce—"

"I'm Peachy McGee, Yore Royal Majestic Highness," Peachy told the king. She grabbed handfuls of her dress and executed a low curtsy.

The king had never seen such a low curtsy; the girl's nose actually touched the rug.

"Peachy," Seneca said quietly, helping her to rise, "the king is *His Majesty,* and there is no need for you to curtsy to the ground."

"Who is this girl?" the king demanded. "What is she—" Good God!" he shouted, backing away from the small gray animal that was scampering toward him. "Good God!"

"Y'orter not take the Lord's name in vain, His Majesty," Peachy advised him. " 'Course I do it, too, so I reckon I don't got nary a right to tell you not to. That little feller there who's a-twitchin' his nose at you? Well, like I done tole Rupert-Dupert-Figgymoopert, that's Thurlow Wadsworth McGee. He's a small and puny little thing, but he's got him a big heart. That's why he's got him sech a big name. I've had him fer nigh on a year now. He was a orphan, y'see, on account o' ole Burris Splatt kilt his maw.

"I mellered Burris good after I seed what he done," she continued, nodding her head. "I don't hit folks much, but I'm a-tellin' you the truth—Burris is s'mean he'd put a rattler in yore pocket and then ask you fer a match.

Thurlow Wadsworth McGee, say hey to the king." With a flick of her wrist, she motioned to the squirrel.

The little beast obeyed instantly and leaped onto King Zane's shoulder. There, he commenced ruffling through the king's hair with his tiny hands.

"He's a-lookin' fer fleas," Peachy explained. "He don't eat 'em, or nothin' like that, though. He jest likes a-pickin' 'em outen. 'Course I'm shore y'don't got none, His Majesty, but a-tellin' Thurlow Wadsworth McGee that is about as pointless as whitewashin' horse manure and a-settin' it up on end. He's gotta find outen fer hisself. Stubborn little feller s'what he is."

At the expression of horror on his father's face, Seneca didn't know whether to be concerned, to apologize, or to laugh. He maintained a straight face, however, and swore to speak to Peachy about her squirrel. It could not be allowed to jump on people, nor could it be allowed freedom within the palace. He would suggest Peachy keep the creature outside, where animals belonged.

For now, though, he couldn't help liking the little beast exactly where it was.

"Father, it is not yet nine o'clock," he announced, pretending not to notice the king's absurd predicament with the squirrel. "I believe it would be in good form to send a message to Lord Inger advising him that your meeting with him has been canceled. His estate is but a short ride away, and I'm sure the message will reach him before he sets out."

Taking Peachy's hand again, he led her to his sire. "You see, Father, there is no longer a reason to meet with Lord Inger. I present to you Peachy McGee. I found her shortly after midnight. And as your vow of last night gives me every right to do," he added, pausing for a moment to savor the look of intense apprehension on his father's face, "I will make her my princess."

Disbelief soared through the king. Rage boiled. A thousand questions exploded inside his brain. But he didn't dare move a muscle.

The squirrel was now perched directly on top of his head.

Chapter 3

Fiddling with the bit of lace at the cuff on one of her new gowns, Peachy stood at the window of the Pink Rooms, a suite that Seneca had selected for her. She looked down at the gleaming carriages which formed a long line down the road that twisted through the sheep-filled meadows.

Aventine's aristocrats were arriving for the wedding. For a moment, Peachy wished she'd been able to invite guests of her own. She'd have asked her neighbors the Mackintoshes and her only living relatives, Aunt Orabelle and Cousin Bubba Hoggard.

But she couldn't have invited them and wishing she could was a waste of time. Her thoughts turned back to the wedding.

It was a gorgeous day to be married! she mused, admiring the cloudless azure sky and the way the bright sun spilled its lemon and tangerine rays all over the verdant landscape. Even the sea, which was clearly visible from her rooms, seemed bluer than usual this afternoon.

Only one dark spot tainted her happiness. She wasn't going to let it ruin her day, but it wasn't easy to forget it, either: she hadn't slept well last night. And insomnia was one of the tipinosis symptoms Dr. Greely had warned her about.

She sighed and made herself think of the ruby-throated hummingbird omen. She was to be happy, she told herself. *Happy.* Her last days on earth were to be cherished and lived to the fullest.

She nodded at her own positive thoughts, determined not to forget them again. "I might not have too much longer on this here earth, Thurlow Wadsworth McGee," she told her pet as he jumped to the windowsill, "but sweet Lord o' mercy, the time I got left is shore gonna be nice. And look at my nails a-growin' boy. They ain't real, real long yet, but they're outen purty good, ain't they? Had me some tea brung up to me yesterday, too. Weren't sassafras, but I drinked it anyway on account o' a-drinkin' tea in a canopy bed is on my wish list. Yeah, things is really nice here, little feller.

" 'Course I ain't seed much o' Seneca lately," she remembered aloud. "What with all them long, pin-stickin' days he maked me spend with them sewin' girls, I ain't had barely a minute to speak at him."

She blushed suddenly, recalling the last time she'd spoken to him. It had been after that humiliating examination she'd endured at the hands of the palace physicians. She'd sworn on every saint she'd ever heard of that she was a virgin, but because of some dumb Aventine law, proof was necessary.

Well, Aventine had received its proof, and that proof would allow her to become a princess in a few short hours.

She wondered what kinds of things she was supposed to do as a princess. She thought princesses threw a lot of gold coins to peasants while riding in a carriage. As soon as she got her princess crown, that was what she was going to do.

How she'd dreamed of her crown! She'd made sure to draw it very clearly on the sketch she'd given to Seneca. The drawing had disappeared two weeks ago, so she knew he had it.

A knock at her door broke through her reverie. Realizing someone had finally arrived with her gown, she spun around, clasping her folded hands beneath her chin. "Come in! Come in!"

Two young maids entered. Between the two of them, they carried a heavy mass of immaculate white satin and lace.

"My name's Ketty, milady," one of them said, her apple cheeks dimpling.

"And I'm Nydia," the other chimed in as she tucked an errant chestnut curl back into her cap. "We've brought your gown, milady. We've just finished pressing it, and now we're to assist you into it. His Highness himself sent us. Is it true that you really have a squirrel? Oh, is that him?" she asked, pointing to the furry gray animal perched on the windowsill.

"Nydia, hush up," Ketty scolded her friend, then turned back to her new mistress. "The prince says we're to hurry, milady. The wedding is only three hours away, and he gave us instructions to prepare a bath for you. We're also to do something pretty with your hair and—"

"Hold it up!" Peachy begged loudly. "Sweet Lord o' mercy, let me see my dress!"

They obeyed instantly. The gown rustled luxuriously as they lifted it.

Dumbfounded, Peachy stared at it. She didn't blink, she didn't breathe.

Her gay mood shattered. She felt her heart do likewise.

The gown was not her dream dress. There were no diamonds on it. There was nothing sparkly on it at all. There were only pink flowers and lace. And there was no crown attached to the veil, either. Only a wreath of more pink flowers. Tears stung her eyes.

"Milady?" Nydia asked. "Is something wrong?"

"My diamondy dress," Peachy whispered. "And my crown veil. I give Seneca the drawin'. But— He . . . My dress . . ."

Ketty took a moment to look at the gown again. "You don't like it?"

"Don't—don't you think it's beautiful?" Nydia queried.

Slowly, as if each step she took caused her pain, Peachy walked to where the two girls stood. "It ain't beautiful," she choked, a lone tear sliding down her cheek. With a trembling hand, she reached out and touched a finger to one of the pink flowers. "It ain't my dream dress. I wanted diamonds on the skirt, a-spellin' outen Seneca's name. And a crown . . . I was s'posed to have a crown."

Nydia cast a worried glance at Ketty. "But the prince has had a set of seamstresses working on your gown around the clock, milady. They followed his instructions to the letter."

Peachy drew back her hand, as if the gown had stung her. *"What?"*

The maids didn't know what to say. They remained silent, uneasy.

"That high-handed varmint," Peachy murmured, fury sliding hotly through her veins. "That no-account, sneakier'n a sheep-killin' dog, contrary as a set-down jackass, *varmint!* God Almighty, when I git holt o' him, I'm gonna smack his fool head right offen his royal shoulders!"

"Milady!" Nydia gasped. "Someone might *hear* you!"

Ketty let go of the gown and rushed to the bedroom doors. She peered down both ends of the long corridor, then shut the doors. "There's no one about, thank the good Lord in heaven."

"I don't keer nary a jag iffen anybody hears me," Peachy informed them. Sniffling, she glared at the gown; then, without another word, she marched to the mammoth dresser across the room, her pale green skirts swishing. From the top drawer, she retrieved her hunting knife. "Hold up that dang gown again."

When they did as she asked, she returned to where they stood. "I ain't a-havin' these here flowers on my dress." She pinched one of the flowers between her fingers and heard it crackle. "Hell, they ain't even real! They're maked o' gawdang *paper!*"

"Oh, milady, no," Nydia corrected her. "The flowers are dried paschal blossoms. Our people tend the crops. But we are shepherds by tradition. It isn't fair that—"

"Nydia!" Ketty hissed, giving her friend a warning look. "Paschal grows only in Aventine," she explained to Peachy, casting one last admonishing glance at Nydia. "Nowhere else in the world. And see, milady? Even dried, the flowers retain their bright pink color. They're much in demand throughout Europe, and His Majesty has had huge crops of them planted for export."

"Yeah?" Peachy said, holding out her knife. "Well, I ain't a-havin' these here *paschal* flowers on my dress then!" Quickly, efficiently, and ignoring Nydia's and

Ketty's horrified gasps, she proceeded to cut every single paschal flower off the gown and veil, then kicked the pink blossoms away. "Iffen I had me a pile o' diamonds right now, I'd sew ever' dang one of 'em on this here— On this here . . ." Her voice trailed away; her head snapped up.

"Milady?" Ketty asked, wondering what the future princess was thinking now.

"Can you girls sew?" Peachy blurted loudly, encouraged when they both nodded. "Can you git me to that big ole room that has them two thrones in it? They're a settin' under a red velvet canopy that has gold tassels a-hangin' all over it."

"The throne room?" Nydia queried, throwing a look of total confusion at her companion.

Their bewilderment didn't last long. In mere moments, they found themselves escorting Peachy to the massive and highly ostentatious throne room. It was situated well away from the part of the palace where the wedding festivities were being held; not so much as an errand boy worked nearby.

"Yeah, this is it," Peachy said, her gaze sweeping the ceiling. "I wandered in here the other day whilst I was a-lookin' fer the dinin' room. I cain't never mem'ry where nothin' is here in this great big castle. I git so lost that not even my own bloodhound could find me in a week's worth o' good weather. 'Course I don't got no bloodhound, and ole Thurlow Wadsworth McGee couldn't keer less how lost I git. Now, y'see all them crystal chandeliers up there? This here room's got more of 'em than any other room I've seed s'far. I counted twenty-four."

The girls peered up at the glittering chandeliers.

Peachy stared at the sparkling ceiling one last time, then began walking around the room, finally stopping in front of a tiny marble table upon which was a gleaming brass candelabra. It wasn't big and tall like the other ones scattered around the room; its eight candle holders were slender points that rose from the round foundation.

She removed the candles it held and smiled. Caressing the candelabra, she looked up at all the twinkling chandeliers again.

Ketty watched how tenderly her new mistress held the

candle holder. She saw, too, how delighted her mistress was with all the many chandeliers hanging from the ceiling.

Comprehension shook Ketty all the way down to her toes. She inhaled so quickly she almost choked. "Milady! Surely you aren't thinking of—"

"Yeah, Ketty, I am. And my name ain't Melody. It's Peachy. Y'all call me that, hear? Now, Nydia, you go fetch glue, needles, and spools o' thread. Carry 'em up to my rooms. Ketty, you stay here and hep me. We gotta hurry. The weddin's less'n three hours away."

Huge arrangements of red and white roses occupied every available spot in the palace chapel. Gilded statues of angels gleamed in the late afternoon sunshine that poured in from the tremendous stained-glass windows. Soft organ music flowed throughout the beautiful sanctuary. Along the lengths of two walls stood the most prestigious members of Aventine's nobility, each of them dressed in his or her finest, each overcome with curiosity to see Prince Seneca's chosen bride. No one had seen her, and no one understood why the prince had kept her so tightly concealed within the confines of the castle.

For that matter, no one had seen the king recently either. Rumor had it that the sovereign had taken to his bed and only just gotten out of it this morning. His Majesty was seated in the royal balcony now, however, and though he appeared to be out of sorts, his presence did much to relieve his worried subjects.

A hush fell over the crowd when the prince stepped up to the altar and took his place beside the court minister. Reverend Charlecoate looked up at the king, received the royal nod to proceed, and then inclined his head at the two servants who stood at the end of the flower-strewn aisle.

Every eye in the room was trained on the two attendants, who were to open the chapel doors. But no one present stared as hard as Seneca. Excitement and pride burst inside him. Peachy was the most beautiful woman in the kingdom, and that fact would soon be known to all. Not only that, but her gown was exquisite. Simple, but very elegant, it would compliment her natural beauty. The seamstresses had outdone themselves.

Peachy would look every inch a princess.

Seneca felt as though several eternities had passed before the chapel doors were opened. The first person he saw in the threshold was Lord Fonthergill, one of the king's advisors, who had been chosen to give Peachy away. The man appeared flustered and agitated. In the next moment, Seneca understood why.

Peachy stumbled to Lord Fonthergill's side.

Seneca's mouth dropped open to a wide "O."

She was wearing a brass candelabra on her head! It was so heavily encrusted with shiny beads that she could barely hold her head up. Indeed, Lord Fonthergill was forced to support her waist as she wobbled up the aisle. But even with her escort's help, she had to stop frequently to push the unwieldy headpiece back on top of her head.

And her dress ... Seneca's eyes widened. Down the front of the satin gown were sewn what looked to be hundreds of shiny beads. As sunlight glinted off them, creating rainbows of colors within their crystal depths, Seneca saw that the beads spelled out S-E-N-E-C-A.

His first reaction was stunned shock, followed by disbelief. Finally, when he heard muffled murmurs rising from the crowd of guests, raw fury blinded him.

Blithely unaware of her beloved's murderous thoughts, Peachy took her fill of him. Her senses fluttered at the sight he presented.

Dressed according to Aventine custom, he wore a suit of solid white, its starkness relieved only by the gold epaulettes on his broad shoulders, the solid gold buttons down the front of his waistcoat, and the gold braid sewn down his pants legs. Across his chest shimmered a scarlet satin banner, it, too, embellished with gold decorations and medals, many of which contained a multitude of glittering gemstones. Lying along the muscled length of his left leg was a long and dazzling gold sword, its hilt thickly studded with more jewels.

And upon his head rested a crown.

Peachy missed a step when she saw it. Its base was of white fur. Above the fur gleamed a solid gold circlet peppered with rubies, and from the twinkling circlet rose eight gold arches that curved to meet at the top. The hollow space under the arches was filled with crimson velvet. A gold cross crested the royal headpiece, a stunning diamond set in its middle.

Sweet Lord o' mercy, she thought, Seneca looked every inch the powerful prince. But though her senses continued to pulse with awe and admiration, she silently damned him to hell and back. It was painfully obvious the royal varmint had spared no expense on his wedding clothes. From head to toe, he shone.

Her only comforting thought was that her own wedding outfit was now equally resplendent.

No thanks to him.

With superb effort, she managed to quell her anger. This was her wedding day, she was marrying the handsomest—albeit the sneakiest—man in the whole wide world, and after the ceremony her name would be Princess Peachy. Considering all those wonderful things, it was silly to stay mad.

When she reached the steps that led to the altar, she allowed Lord Fonthergill to place her hand in Seneca's. Her gaze spilling with happiness, she smiled brilliantly into her beloved's eyes, and was not a little taken aback when she saw that those eyes glittered coldly with what could only be fury. Her gaiety faded instantly.

Seneca glared at the candle holder on her head, realizing that the shiny stones surrounding it were chandelier crystals. And the glue she'd used to attach them was still wet. One of the crystals had slid off the brass circlet and was now stuck to a lock of her hair—hair that was supposed to have been put up in a smooth chignon.

He grasped her hand with more force than was necessary; his rage demanded it. "What," he whispered without moving his lips, "did you do to your gown?"

The suppressed anger in his voice brought her own fury back to life. "I fixed it into my dream dress," she replied through a false smile. "And afore you commence a-back jawin' me about it, you'd best be glad I didn't sew the word *varmint* on the front. The thought crossed my mind, y'know. Now hep me up these here steps. My clothes is s'dang heavy I cain't hardly keep a-standin'."

"What did you expect?" he asked, his words hissing between his clenched teeth. "You're wearing a chandelier on your skirt and a candelabra on your head."

"I wouldn't have had to wear a candelabra iffen you'd gave me my crown," she returned hotly.

He helped her up the last step, stopping her in front of a very puzzled Reverend Charlecoate. "We will discuss this later, Peachy," he ordered quietly.

"Let's not," she said sweetly, and gave the minister a grin. "Today ain't the day fer argufyin' with each other."

"We *will* discuss it," he insisted.

"All right," Peachy said, lifting her chin, "but mem'ry one thing, Seneca. You've done invited trouble. Don't complain when it arrives."

The royal banquet room, where the wedding feast would be served, was sumptuous. Its walls were covered with white and gold silk, but the predominating color was pastel yellow. Indeed, every satinwood chair lining the astonishingly long dining table was covered in yellow damask. Gracing the table were beautifully folded yellow linen napkins set in long-stemmed crystal glasses, huge gold candelabra, a multitude of finely cut bowls of bonbons, and an immense epergne of angels holding a dish of exotic fruits and emerald ferns. Masses of fragrant yellow roses, solid gold eating utensils, and fragile ivory china completed the gorgeous table setting.

After Tiblock seated the king, Seneca escorted Peachy to the opposite end of the table, helped her into her chair, and took his place beside her. Only then did the liveried footmen assist the guests.

Evening had fallen; two fires and a multitude of tall white tapers had been lit, their mellow light creating an atmosphere of luxurious warmth throughout the room. But though the room invited a sense of tranquility, the tension that filled it was thicker than the ocean fog that blanketed Aventine each morning. King Zane said nothing, nothing at all, only glowered at everyone and everything in his line of vision. The guests also remained quiet, many of them keeping their heads bowed low. Seneca managed to effect a calm demeanor, but it was only with the utmost effort, and a skill perfected by years of experience.

Peachy herself barely noticed the disquiet. Her attention was focused on the food. She'd never laid eyes on so much! It seemed to her that every edible thing in the whole world was being offered. The numerous sideboards fairly groaned with the weight.

And she was hungry. Earlier, in the picture gallery, she'd stood in a receiving line for well over an hour, met most of Aventine's aristocrats, and then had been forced to withstand the long and countless toasts made to her and Seneca. She *had* gotten her first taste of French liquor, though. Wondering if she'd get more, she looked up at Seneca. She sensed the cocky varmint was still mad at her, but she was too hungry to care right now. Later, after she'd eaten, she'd tell him to hang his arrogance on his ear and twist it twice.

"Are they gonna put jugs o' that bubblin' French likker on the table, Seneca?"

Though his and Peachy's place at the end of the table prevented any of the guests from overhearing their conversation, Seneca kept his voice to a low growl. "*Champagne* is not liquor, but a wine, It does not come in *jugs,* but in bottles, and, no, you will have no more." He smiled and nodded at a gentleman four seats down.

"What's this?" Peachy picked up a small gold frame that held a cream-colored card with writing on it.

"That is the menu," Seneca answered stiffly.

Peachy studied it carefully, recognizing not a single word on it. "I cain't read this. It's—"

"French."

"French? But I don't know no French. How the hell am I s'posed to know what to eat?"

Seneca seethed inwardly. "Never mind the menu. Now, take that ludicrous thing off your head. If you keep it on, you will not be able to eat without it falling into your plate."

Just to defy him, Peachy wished she could keep her homemade crown on, but she realized he was right. The headpiece was much too heavy. She took it off, laid it on the floor beside her chair, and prepared to indulge in all the wonderful food. She wanted to taste every single thing.

A small bowl of hot soup came first, followed by a cold one. She finished both soups quickly and looked forward to sampling the rest of the many delicacies. Much to her dismay, however, Seneca quietly forbade her to eat more than a tablespoon of each of the various dishes, ones he selected for her himself.

"When attending a formal dinner party," he murmured sternly down to her, "a lady is expected to simply pick at her meal."

He hadn't planned to begin her lessons in proper etiquette at the wedding feast, but he was still utterly enraged over what she'd done to her wedding clothes. The rebellious spitfire *would* learn to obey him. And there was no time like the present to begin showing her the supreme authority he had over her every action. He would show her discreetly, of course, but he *would* show her.

He saw her eyeing the platter of juicy roast beef a butler was serving to a nearby gentleman. Another attendant offered the man a slice of venison accompanied by tender pearl onions.

Seneca knew what she was thinking. "And under absolutely no circumstances, Peachy, is a lady allowed to eat anything strongly flavored during an elegant occasion such as this," he informed her. "Game and beef fall into that category. Even cheese is forbidden to you. There are many more foods that you may not consume as well. They are for gentlemen only."

Her stomach growling loudly, Peachy glanced down at her plate. Upon it sat a small bed of young lettuce, a few new potatoes, and a shred of turkey breast about as big as her finger.

She knew Seneca was furious at her, but did the man think to starve her to death? Her temper simmering, she proceeded to devour her meager meal.

Seneca watched as she lifted the last potato to her mouth. "Do not eat everything on your plate, either," he added. "That is unladylike."

She put the potato back on her plate, then noticed an elderly woman sitting several chairs down from her. The lady's plate was overloaded with food of all sorts. "That there woman—"

"Lady Yarwood is almost seventy years old," Seneca said. "When you have reached her age, you may become a glutton if you wish. For now, you will eat the way I tell you to."

His last statement unleashed her tethered anger. She'd tried valiantly to keep from talking back to him, but now he'd gone too far. "Eat the way you tell me to, most dearest beloved husband?" she repeated quietly. "What about the way I breathe? Do I have to do that the way you say, too? Shorely there's some sorter rule that says I can take only so many breaths in a minute. What is it, about ten per ever' sixty seconds? Or is it more ladylike to take only eight? I ain't allowed to eat enough food to fill a gawdang flea, so it 'pears to me that I prob'ly ain't s'posed to breathe too much air, neither."

"You may breathe however you please," he replied stiffly, "as long as you do not pant." He knew full well she'd come back at him with another saucy retort, and she didn't disappoint him.

She looked at him from the corner of her eye. "Oh, well then, you ain't got nothin' a'tall to worry about, darlin'. The onliest time I pant is when I'm a-doin' dog imitations."

He gritted his teeth, but still felt the intense urge to smile. "Your sarcasm displeases me." He put a bite of tender beef in his mouth, waiting again for her mocking reply.

Her mouth watered as she watched him chew. It seemed to her that he was exaggerating the chewing motions, probably to infuriate her.

He succeeded. But two could play at this game, she fumed. Since the royal varmint didn't like sarcasm, sarcasm was exactly what he'd get. She'd pay the price for her transgression in Purgatory, but not even the thought of those hot flames induced her to keep a civil tongue. "After this here party's over, y'want to play house with me, Seneca? It'll be real fun. You'll be the door, see, and I'll slam you."

The bite of meat almost got stuck in his throat. His immediate reaction was pulsing anger. But edging his wrath, indeed, *tempering* his extreme ire, was amusement. *You'll be the door, see, and I'll slam you.* He'd never in his life been so outrageously insulted, but even so he couldn't keep from seeing the humor in her insolence.

He laid his fork down, so confused with his own conflicting emotions that it was a long moment before he could form a reply. "Peachy, you will stop this offensive banter." His brow furrowed in irritation, his lips twitching with mirth, he turned away from her and raised his glass of wine to a distinguished woman who sat a few places down the table on his left. "Aunt Viridis," he greeted her. "You're looking well."

Viridis Elsdon's eyes snapped with disapproval. She merely lifted a silver eyebrow in response.

Seneca was not insulted. Affecting a stern demeanor was her way; indeed, he respected her utterly proper manners. He raised his wineglass higher.

Peachy followed his example. After all, she was mad at Seneca, not her guests. She, too, picked up her glass and toasted a nearby couple. The overweight and bearded man looked to be about sixty years old; the lady couldn't have been more than twenty and appeared unhappy. Peachy wondered if they were father and daughter. "Who are y'all again?" she asked them. "I done meeted s'many folks whilst me and Seneca was a-standin' in that what you call receivin' line that I declare, I jest cain't seem to keep all y'all straight."

"I am Veston Sherringham," the man replied gruffly. "And this is my wife, Agusta."

His *wife!* Peachy exclaimed silently. No wonder Agusta looked so sad, being married to that fat old man. And he had thin lips, too, a sure sign of meanness.

She studied Agusta carefully, deciding the woman was the thinnest, unhealthiest woman she'd ever seen. Her gaunt face was whiter than Seneca's clothes, and her bony hands shook terribly. Peachy felt instant compassion for her. "Agusta?"

"Yes, Your Highness?" Agusta answered timidly.

Peachy gave the shy woman a brilliant smile. "Yore so skinny that iffen I was to feed you a little bit o' cranberry juice, I could use you fer a thermometer. Git yoresef some more food, hear?"

"Peachy!" Seneca whispered loudly. "What—"

"The woman needs to eat, Seneca, and I aim to give her some food. What's all them ladylike rules o' yores gonna do fer her whilst she's a-layin' in her gawdang coffin!"

Peachy popped out of her chair and marched over to one of the sideboards. The servants quickly stepped aside for her. She grabbed a platter of moist turkey dressing, took it to the table and proceeded to fill Agusta's plate.

Agusta's eyes grew round with pleasure. But the slight nudge of her husband's elbow swiftly ended her delight. "Your Highness, I cannot eat—"

"Shore y'can," Peachy insisted. "Y'got my royal permission to clean yore plate. I'm yore princess now, y'know, so iffen I tell you to eat it, you gotta slap yore lips over ever' bit o' this good food, hear?

"'Course I ain't tasted nary a smidgeon of it," she continued, tossing a well-aimed glare at Seneca. "Don't seem to matter that I'm as hungry as a June crow, I ain't allowed to touch it. But you go on and eat on account o' it looks mighty good. Good enough to make yore teeth white, yore skin tight, and childbirth a pleasure."

Agusta bent her head, her napkin the only witness to her smile.

Her husband patted her shoulder, then cast a pleading look at Seneca.

Seneca rose. "Peachy—"

"You want some more, too?" Peachy asked the woman sitting next to Agusta. She held out the platter.

Callista Inger drew back. "No," she said icily, deliberately omitting Peachy's title, "I do *not.*"

Peachy stared at the woman. "Sweet Lord o' mercy, lady, what's the matter with you? Yore a-frownin' at me so hard yore teeth's the onliest things in yore face that ain't wrinkled."

Silence, like the eerie calm before a horrible storm, settled over the room. The king stood, his mammoth frame shaking with rage. "This meal . . ." he began, "this wedding— This preposterous and totally unseemly mockery of a dinner is over."

Every person at the table laid down their forks, patted their lips with their napkins, and rose to stand behind their chairs. The cake had yet to be served, the dancing had yet to begin. But King Zane had declared that the evening had come to a halt, and so it had.

Seneca glared at his father. It was true that Peachy was in dire need of discipline. True that she needed to be taught a great many things. But *he* would be the one to teach them to her. *He* would be the one to deliver the discipline.

His father had no right to cut short the festivities. Not only that, Senenca fumed, but his sire's announcement told one and all that Peachy was far from being in the king's good graces. And now every aristocrat in the room would adopt their sovereign's attitude toward her.

Unless Seneca could think of a way to dissuade them.

Shoulders back, chin lifted high, Seneca walked regally toward Peachy and folded her hand around his lower arm. Without so much as a look at Callista, he led his baffled wife to the doors and turned back to the crowd of people watching him.

"The princess has made it known to me that she would enjoy becoming better acquainted with each of you," he announced. "I'm sure you will all endeavor to satisfy her wishes. And now, your future *queen* and I bid you all a good night."

His sharp blue eyes met every gaze in the room. By emphasizing the word *queen,* he sought to remind everyone present that he would soon be king and that one day the royal favor they so desperately desired would be granted by *him.* He couldn't be sure if his parting words had had their desired effect, but he hoped that they had at least planted seeds for thought.

Ignoring the look of thunderous rage on his sire's face, he bowed, and led Peachy out of the silent room.

By the time he and Peachy reached the upper halls that led to his chambers, Seneca's wrath knew no bounds. True, he'd taken measures to salvage Peachy's reputation at the wedding feast, but not by any means had he forgotten or forgiven her for her behavior.

She *would* be accepted by Aventine's nobility. Not because he forced the aristocrats to do so, but because they would have no reason not to. No matter what it took, he would turn this wayward princess into a true lady.

Ignoring the custom that the bride prepare for her wedding night in separate chambers and then join her husband in his, he opened the door to his apartments, urged her inside, and shut the door.

Peachy saw rage flame in his sapphire eyes. It blazed forth with such startling reality she felt as though it was burning her. "So we're a-startin' our honeymoon with a cuss fight, huh, Seneca? Who gits to go first? Me or you?"

He stalked away from the door, crossed the spacious room, and stopped before a chaise lounge. There, he disrobed down to his shirt and pants. "I will be the one doing the talking, Peachy," he snapped, crushing his neckcloth into a tight wad. "You will listen."

She refused to be a part of a one-sided conversation. "Go fry some ice." She whirled toward the door.

Seneca reached it before she did. "Sit down."

She raised her gaze to him. "No."

"Sit down." He gave her an icy glare, counting on it to prevent her from talking back to him again.

"Yore a-contraryin' me, you airyfied-as-a-peacock varmint," she warned him, blatantly ignoring his plain-as-day fury.

Blast it all! he fumed. Was there anything at all that would keep her from talking back to him? "We will discuss your feelings as soon as you sit down. Indeed, we will be discussing many things tonight, Peachy."

She realized he wasn't going to back down. Well, she wouldn't give in, either. Besides, her feet hurt. She wasn't used to shoes with heels on them, and her feet had been cramped for several hours. "I'll go set down, Seneca, but not because you tole me to, hear? I'm a-settin' down on account o' my feet is a-miseryin' me something fierce. 'Sides that, I reckon I got as much right to grab *you* where the hair is short, jest like yore a-tryin' to do to me." She flounced over to a small satin settee by the blue-velvet-draped window and removed her shoes.

Seneca saw she'd hiked her skirts up to her thighs. Transfixed, he watched as she peeled off each of her stockings. Her slender legs were the same color as the creamy marble floor. The sight almost made him forget the lecture he was going to give her.

Later, he told himself. Later, he would have her. He could chastize her first. He would make it perfectly clear that she was under his authority and that she would never disobey him again. Then he would bed her. He would make love to her all night, and when morning came there would be no doubt in her mind that he was her master in all things and that she would submit to every demand he made of her.

With much effort, he tore his gaze from her legs and aimed it into her flashing eyes. "Your behavior today was nothing short of atrocious. What you did to your wedding clothes, your decorum at the wedding feast . . . You will *never* defy me again, Peachy. On the contrary, you will abide by my every word."

She rubbed her thumbs over the sides of her shoes. "That sounded like a order."

"It was."

"I cain't even obey *God*'s commandments. How the hell can I obey yours?"

Her thoroughly insulting reply caught him completely off guard. As before, he felt the unseemly, yet almost uncontrollable, urge to laugh.

Her ability to instantly make him lose control of his bearing angered him further. Jaw clenched, he stormed toward her. "You will guard that unruly tongue of yours at all times. You have a title now. You will live up to it and demonstrate the spotless behavior befitting the Princess of Aventine. And if you do not, you will answer to me."

She tightened her grip on her shoes and battled the temptation to bang him over the head with them. "Yore biggity as all git out. Got yore nose so high up in the air it's a gawdang wonder you ain't got a inch o' snow on it."

He went rigid. "Peachy!"

"Seneca!" she shouted right back at him.

"You—"

"Hesh up," she said, cutting him off, determined to have

her say. "I come here with ever' intention of a-fallin' in love with you, got that? But I reckon I might have better luck a-tryin' to lick honey offen a blackberry vine. I ain't gonna give up on you yet, but I'm a-warnin' you right here and now that you'd best change yore ways, hear?"

Absolute amazement filled him. *You'd best change your ways,* she'd said. Change his ways? He was the Crown Prince of Aventine, for God's sake! Since the day he'd come into the world he'd been fashioned and molded into a man who fit the royal title. And he wore that title now as snugly as he wore his gloves!

So just what did she mean by him changing his ways? He was everything his station in life required him to be! *She* was the one who needed to change!

He longed to dismiss her warning. It was ludicrous, of course. But it remained in his mind like a faraway sound he couldn't stop hearing, couldn't quite forget.

His eyes narrowed. "It's not your love I want, Peachy," he informed her curtly. "It's your obedience."

His words hurt her. It was almost as if they were tangible things. Sharp things, for they seemed to stab into her like so many needles and knives.

Knowing she was on the verge of tears, she didn't reply. Instead, she looked down at the shoes she still held.

Seneca had seen the shimmer of sadness in her eyes. An odd twinge passed through him. He was unfamiliar with the feeling, and it was a moment before he recognized it.

Guilt.

He tried to erase it. He had no need to feel guilty about anything he'd told her. None at all, and that was that. "You will cease feeling sorry for yourself, Peachy."

She gritted her teeth. Not only did the man think to tell her how to act, dress, and eat, but he thought to tell her what she could and couldn't *feel* too!

She jumped to her feet and poked her finger into his shoulder. "I've had me some wonnerful times in my life, but I'll tell you the truth, this ain't one of 'em. So let's jest let the milk down and git this whole dang thing done with, all right? I know yore riled, and I know why. But I fixed my weddin' dress on account o' the one you had maked fer me weren't my dream dress. You was real wrong to do that to me, Seneca. I had my whole heart a-set on the dress I drawed, and you knowed it. I wouldn't never have done that to you, not never, no how, no matter what.

"And I give Agusta that food on account o' it 'peared to me that she's on the go down," she went on, jabbing her finger into his shoulder again. "She's a-feelin' real puny-like, Seneca, and it jest weren't right fer all y'all menfolks to sit there a-greasin' up yore mouths and not let her eat, too. Iffen yore so gawdang worried about a-bein' manner-able, you cocky cuss, 'pears to me you orter set down sometime and *think* about what a-bein' mannerable really is."

"You—"

"What's more," she continued, "Agusta's fat ole husband, Veston, ain't a nice man. He's got thin lips."

"Thin lips? What in God's name—"

"And jest in case yore interested, I ain't too happy to-night. I'm s'posed to be happy fer whatever time I got left, Seneca. That ruby-throated hummin'bird said so. Yore a-messin' up the omen. And y'know somethin' else? I didn't sleep good last night. That's one o' the tipinosis symptoms. 'Pears to me that my time's a-gittin' shorter and shorter."

"Oh, of all the . . ." He rolled his eyes. "What bride *does* sleep well the night before her wedding, for God's sake! Forget about those ludicrous omens, do you hear me? I will not have you jumping to ridiculous conclusions over common, everyday happenings!"

"Y'cain't fight omens, Seneca. Y'gotta accept 'em and make the best of 'em. I'm a-dyin' and there ain't a gawdang thing nobody can do about it." With that, she picked up her skirts, swept past him, and headed for the door.

"And just where do you think you're going, might I ask?"

Her hand on the doorknob, she turned to face him. "I've enjoyed about as much o' this evenin' as I can stand, and I'm ready fer it to be over. I'm a-headin' fer my rooms. It's a dang shame, too. This a-bein' our weddin' night and all, I got a powerful hankerin' to git to know you real good, Seneca. Inside and outen."

As her words drifted through him, he felt his impatience and anger fade a little. She wanted to know him. Wanted to find out what made him who he was.

Once upon a time he'd tried to tell lots of people about himself. His father. His mother. Various servants. He'd been so desperate to tell someone, he'd even approached Lady Muckross. He'd had so many wishes and thoughts and plans he'd wanted to share.

No one had listened. No one had had time. No one had really cared.

"Seneca?" Peachy cocked her head, trying to understand the odd expression on his face.

He felt suddenly vulnerable, as if he'd allowed his mask of indifference to slip.

He shot her a cynical look and silently dared her to read his thoughts. At any rate, he no longer felt that childish need to reveal his secret desires, ideas, or aspirations. His boyhood was over. It was dead and buried, and he would not resurrect it just because *she* wanted him to. His expression hardened.

Peachy remained undaunted. "Y'hurt my feelin's when y'said you didn't want my love, Seneca. But y'know what I aim to do? I'm gonna offer up my hurt feelin's as penance. And y'want to know what else? I'm gonna love you anyway. I gotta *know* you first, though. We ain't had much of a chance to git acquainted real good yet, and I don't mind a-tellin' you that I was so excited about us a-jawin' together tonight that ever' time I thought on it, I got a quiver in my liver."

His astonishment was so great it widened his eyes and cut off his breath. "You— You thought to *talk* tonight? *Talk?*"

"Yeah, but I ain't gonna do it," she told him, tossing her hair off her shoulder. "I'm tired, hungry, and so agger-pervoked with you that it's all I can do to keep from a-flingin' these here shoes at you. I'm a good aim, Seneca, and iffen I set to knock you up side that empty head o' yores, that's exac'ly what I'll do. So don't you go a-illin' me no more tonight."

Seneca fairly exploded with all the emotions running

through him: Fury. Guilt. Amusement. Amazement. Bewilderment.

Desire. He still wanted the audacious spitfire! Even after she'd set him back on his heels, after she'd contested everything he'd told her, after *she'd* lectured *him* . . . after she'd threatened to throw her shoes at him, he still wanted her!

Indeed, he wanted her more than he'd ever wanted any other woman. There was something about her . . .

Whatever it was, it made him want her with a desire so fierce it was almost painful.

"We will most assuredly come to know each other tonight, Peachy," he informed her, his voice deep with unspoken insinuations. "Now, come here."

She shook her head. "I tole you I'm a-goin' to my own—"

"These *are* your rooms. We're married now, and we will sleep in the same chambers. Indeed, in the same *bed.*"

"Ha! I stayed in here with you that first night on account o' you wanted to keep me hided. But I ain't a-stayin' in here tonight. I tole you two weeks ago that it's too soon fer any o' that kinda stuff, and iffen you think you can keep me in here a minute longer, you'd best sneeze on account o' yore brains is dusty."

"Oh, really?" He practically tore off his shirt.

She squealed when she saw him coming toward her. There was a purposeful intent in his long-legged stride, and it filled her with the instinct to either fight or flee. She decided to fight.

Seneca's reflexes were superb. Right before her shoes hit his forehead, he caught both of them.

Peachy's last resort was to flee. But much to her dismay, the door was locked, the bolt jammed. Spinning back around, she had to lean her head back to see him, he was so close.

There was something strong, something powerful in his eyes. It made her feel all squishy inside.

"Peachy," he said quietly, huskily.

His deep, soft voice held a tinge of irritation. A touch of arrogance. A lot of impatience. And something else, too, something she could find no name for . . .

She caught his scent. Wine, she thought, that wonderfully mellow wine they'd sipped earlier. And warmth; the man smelled warm. Like the smooth stones around a hearth. Like that special kind of sunshine that comes after a rain, musky, steamy, inviting.

And masculine. He smelled masculine. And though she'd never been this close to any man, her instincts told her that there were no words to describe the smell of a man. It was, very simply, a male fragrance. A potent scent that aroused a woman's senses.

She stepped to the side. "Quit it. I done tole you I cain't fight what yore looks do to me. And when you commence a-talkin' in that low voice ... When you stare at me with them blue-as-mornin'-glories eyes o' yores— God Almighty, even the way you smell! What y'do to me, it's like— Like you got a spoon inside me and yore a-stirrin' up all my feelin's. They go round and round s'fast that I jest know I'm gonna fall plumb to pieces. So quit it." She reached for the bolt on the door again.

He closed his hand around hers. "I appreciate your honesty, Peachy," he told her in that same deep and sexy voice. "And I can assure you that I will use that bit of information to my best advantage."

She looked at his dark hand wrapped around her pale one. His touch made her feel as though her insides were full of hot sparkles.

"You're a maiden," he murmured. "You're afraid. I can understand that. But, Peachy," he said, his lips at her temple, his hard body leaning into hers, "I will not be denied."

His naked chest pressed gently against her breasts. His warm breath ruffled her hair. His lips grazed hers. Panic swept through her. "Seneca—"

His mouth smothered the rest of her words.

Chapter 4

S he felt his lips move lightly across hers, barely touching her at all. But gentle though his kiss was, its effect was dizzying.

The man was hard. From head to toe, and most especially in between. Peachy swayed, her loss of balance forcing her to hold on to him lest she fall.

She needn't have worried. Seneca felt her wobble and tightened the embrace himself. God, she felt so good next to him. And her scent, too, he thought. It was an odd fragrance, one he'd never encountered before. Lemon? Yes, lemon, but something else, too. Something he didn't recognize.

Her breasts pushed against his chest. He could feel her nipples stiffen. He wanted to free those lush orbs, see them, hold them . . . for the first time.

But he sensed her continued anxiety. Her lips were tightly pursed, making it impossible for him to give her the passionate kiss he yearned to give her. "Peachy," he whispered, his lips still clinging to hers, "open for me, Princess."

She heard him speak softly to her, but couldn't make out what he'd said. All she could comprehend was that she was letting him kiss her. After she'd just told him it was much too soon for this sort of thing! How could one kiss dissolve her resolution so quickly?

"Peachy, open for me," he whispered again. Slowly, he cupped her breast, his thumb sliding back and forth across the hardening peak beneath her satin gown. And then he deepened the kiss slightly, sweeping his tongue across her lips and finally between them.

Peachy stiffened. Not only had she heard what he'd said this time, she felt him attempting to bring his demands to fruition as well! With every bit of strength her slender body possessed, she pushed at his chest, then moved quickly away.

Seneca was taken off guard by her swift action. One moment she was in his arms, melting against him, and in the next she was standing several feet away, her green eyes spitting fireballs at him. "What—"

"I ain't a-openin' nothin' to you, you slicker'n a greased eel varmint! You— You put yore *tongue* in my mouth! What the hell kinda thing is *that* to do to—"

"Peachy—"

"And— And you touched Miz Molly, too!"

He frowned. "Miss Molly?"

She cupped her right breast. "*This* is Miz Molly. The other one's Miz Polly, and neither one of 'em is ever been touched like you—"

"I realize that, but—"

"But nothin'! I tole you it was too soon!" Deeply flustered, she raised her hands to her cheeks. They were hot; she knew she was blushing. "Why'd you kiss me, Seneca?"

"Because—"

"Did y'know that kiss maked me feel like I didn't have no more muscles in my body?" she yelled at him, her red curls bouncing. "Did y'know it give me a tickle betwixt my legs and maked me want to scrunch my thighs together?"

He folded his arms across his chest and leaned his shoulder against the door, contemplating her startling candidness once again. "I had a vague idea you were feeling something like that."

"Say yore sorry fer a-makin' me feel that way, Seneca. Say it!"

"Apologize for kissing and touching my own bride? I will not."

He saw two distinct expressions on her face. One was a look of deep anger, the other of intense determination. It was obvious that she had every intention of escaping his attentions. Indeed, clearly she had no doubt that she *would* escape them.

He'd had enough. She would submit to him, and she would do it right now.

He straightened to his full height. "Peachy, you will cease these delays. I married you this afternoon, and the time has come for us to consummate our union. Now take off your clothes and get in bed."

"What?"

"You heard me. Now do it."

"I— You— Low! That's what you are! *Low!* So gawdang low you could dive offen a dime!" She lunged for the jammed door bolt again.

His actions blurred, he caught her shoulders, spun her around, and swept her into his arms. Deaf to her loud objections, he carried her out of the sitting room and into his bedchambers, where he sat her on the bed. Quickly, he unfastened his trousers and began to peel them down his hips.

Peachy had just begun to fly off the bed when she saw what he was doing. Her gaze shot to the open vee of his pants.

It revealed a mat of thick, black hair. She could see no more than that, but it was enough. It was too much. Her senses spun; it was a moment before they returned to normal. "God Almighty, Seneca, what the hell do y'think yore a-doin'?"

The true panic he heard in her voice stilled him completely. "For God's sake, Peachy, do you think I won't go gently with you? That I will become some sort of savage monster while bedding you?"

She finally succeeded in tearing her gaze from the absolutely enticing sight at his opened pants. "No, I— It ain't that." She blinked several times.

"I know you're afraid of me, Peachy, but—"

"Afeared o' *you?*" she yelled. "I ain't afeared o' you!"

"Then what are you afraid of? Tell me!"

"Purgatory!"

"Purgatory?"

She crawled across the huge bed, grabbed a plump pillow, and hugged it to her breasts. "It's— It's all yore gawdang fault, y'know! I been here fer two weeks, Seneca, and durin' that time I bet we ain't said but a hunnerd words to each another. I been with them sewin' girls ever'day, and you been a-doin' whatever the hell it is you do all day. I ain't hardly seed hide ner hair o' you. Iffen it weren't fer Nydia and Ketty, I'd've been jest as lonesome as a ugly girl a-standin' unner mistletoe!"

"What has that to do with tonight?" he demanded. "And what bearing does Purgatory have—"

"Well, dang it to hell, Seneca, do y'think I'm gonna sleep with a complete stranger? God Almighty, iffen I was to do that, I prob'ly wouldn't even make it to Purgatory. I'd go straight to hell!"

He felt fury rattle his bones. "I'm your *husband!* How can it be a sin to sleep with your own—"

"It jest is! Fer me it is! You— I— I come up a-bein' larnt that iffen you think somethin's a sin, it *is* one! Iffen something don't feel right, it *ain't!* And— And— And *shame* on you fer a-tryin' to make me go agin' what I believe!" Her eyes never leaving him, she scooted off the bed and stood on the other side of it.

Frustration gnawed holes in his insides. He was at the point now where he didn't know what else to do but give in to her obnoxious beliefs. "What kinds of things do you want to know about me?" he shouted. "Ask them quickly, I'll answer them just as fast, and then you will take off your clothes and get in the bed!"

She scowled furiously. Here she was trying her hardest to keep her soul as clean as possible, and he was hell-bent on sending her straight to the devil! "You jest listen to me, mister, I—"

"I'm not a *mister!* I'm a *prince!* More important, I'm your *husband!* And as your husband, Peachy, I am telling you to take off your clothes and get in the bed!"

She gasped. "I don't even know what yore favorite color is!"

He stared at her. As if he had the power to read her every thought. Indeed, he wished he *did* have that power, for it seemed to be the only way possible to understand how that mind of hers worked.

"Let me see if I have this straight," he murmured, his quietly spoken words a direct contrast to the rage building inside him. "You have to know what my favorite color is before you'll get into my bed?"

"Well . . . Fer starters . . . Yeah." Struggling to tame the powerful yearnings the sight of his opened pants brought to her, she took a few deep breaths and thought about what she should do.

She really *did* want to know her husband. And who knew how much longer she'd have to see that important wish granted? She could die tomorrow, next week, or even within the coming hour. It was silly to waste whatever time she had left.

"All right, Seneca," she said suddenly, "I've decided to give you another chance tonight. I was gonna leave, but— Well, I reckon my weddin' present to you is another chance. But you mess this one up, and I'm a-leavin', hear? Now pull up yore britches and talk to me. Tell me about yoresef. You was a-gonna tell me what yore favorite color is."

He watched her sashay to the overstuffed velvet chair that stood between two windows. There, she sat, smoothed her skirts and her hair, folded her hands in her lap, and gave him an *I'm-waiting-for-you-to-begin* smile. She presented the perfect picture of a woman preparing for a long, pleasurable chat.

Surely this wasn't happening to him, he thought dismally.

"Well, Seneca? What is it?"

"What's what?" he asked absently.

"Yore favorite color."

"*Green!* All right? It's *green!* Now get in the bed!"

"You still ain't pulled up yore britches."

"Nor will I! Peachy—"

"Pull 'em up, or I ain't a-stayin' here a second longer. Pull 'em up, pull 'em up, pull 'em—"

"All right!"

She watched him yank them up and breathed a great sigh of relief. "My favorite color's red," she said, hoping with all her heart that they could finally have a real conversation. "But I gotta be real keerful about which red I

wear on account o' my hair. Some reds don't go good with
it, y'know. 'Course my hair ain't *pure* red, in case y'ain't
noticed. It's got some yaller and brown in it, too. Anyhow,
I like to wear the kind o' red that's the color of a tin
bucket that's been a-settin' in the rain and sun fer a few
seasons. Ever seed a bucket like that, Seneca? It's all
rusty-red."

He'd never seen a rusty bucket like the one she described. It was such a simple thing, and yet he'd never
seen one.

It angered him further that he was even thinking about
a stupid rusty bucket. He stormed to the windows, stopped
by her chair, and loomed over her. "Peachy—"

"Who's yore bestest friend?"

Her question jolted him. He had no friends. He'd never
had any. Especially not a best one. "Cease this interrogation, and get in the—"

"Which do you like the mostest, apple pie or cherry?"

"Lemon! Now get in the—"

"I didn't say lemon, Seneca. I said apple or cherry.
Sweet tater pie's good, too, but I ain't much fer pecan
pie. Iffen y'don't get ever' piece o' the shell offen them
pecans . . . Lord, them bits o' shells is bitter as all git out.
'Course, I reckon I'd like pecan pie withouten the shells.
It's jest that I cain't never seem to git 'em all outen. I give
up a-makin' pecan pies long ago."

She twiddled her thumbs for a moment. "My neighbor-
woman, Miz Mackintosh? Now, *she* knowed how to make
a good pecan pie. Ever' Friday, we'd go over to her cabin
and have us a party. Mr. Mackintosh'd play the banjo, and
Paw, he'd commence to a-blowin' on his jug. Paw loved
that ole jug o' his. Called it his angel tit. We'd eat, too.
Miz Mackintosh'd always serve up pecan pie and a mess
o' squirrel stew. I didn't never take ole Thurlow
Wadsworth McGee over there, on account o' it would've
sickened him plumb to death to see us a-eatin' his kinfolk.
Yeah, we'd have us a larripin' good time on them Fridays.
I'll tell you the truth, Friday nights at the Mackintoshes
was one o' the finer things o' life. So y'say you like lemon
pie, huh, Seneca?"

He stared at her so hard his eyes stung. Here he was

wanting to make love, and *she* was rambling on about mountain music and squirrel stew! He was too furious to even speak to her.

"All right, Seneca, fergit about pies. Iffen the smell o' vaniller and the smell o' roses was the only two smells in the world and you could only smell one of 'em, which one would it be?"

"God." He groaned miserably, closed his eyes, and sought one last shred of patience. "Roses."

"I'd pick vaniller. Can you and me run barefooted through them purty green fields tomorrer?"

"No."

"I'll ask again tomorrer, and maybe you'll say yes. Can you do birdcalls?"

He opened his eyes. "No!"

"I can."

For one fleeting second, he wondered which birdcalls she could do. But no sooner had the question entered his mind than he dismissed it. "For the last time, Peachy, get in the bed. *Get in the bed!*"

"Y'ain't never kilt no daddy longlegs, have you?"

He had to restrain himself from kicking the table next to the chair. "I don't even know what a daddy longlegs is!"

She could hardly believe that. "Well, Lord o' mercy, Seneca, it's one o' them spiders with real, real, real, real long legs."

He noticed she was looking at him with pity, as if he'd missed out on one of the finest things life had to offer. "I'll have you know, Peachy, that spiders aren't even *on* my list of priorities. And since I've never seen one of those long-legged spiders, I doubt very seriously that I have ever killed one. Satisfied? Now get in the bed." He reached for her hand.

Before he could get hold of it, she pushed it under her bottom and sat on it. Upon further thought, she sat on her other hand, too. "Good thing y'ain't never kilt no daddy longlegs, Seneca, on account o' iffen you do, the cows'll go dry. Yeah siree, a-killin' daddy longlegs is a bad omen. I maked me a animule hospital one time in a ole woodshed Paw didn't use no more. There was always nests o' daddy longleg spiders in there.

"Yeah," she continued smoothly, "when I was a young'un, I brung ever' keeled-up, got-down, pegged-outen animule I finded to my hospital. Cured most of 'em, too. With yarbs. I'm a yarb doctor. There's some folks who say the onliest kind o' medicines worth a-usin' is them fancified ones that certiffy-fied doctors give outen. But there's a lot to be said fer yarbs, Seneca. I brung a lavish o' yarbs here with me to Aventine. Iffen y'got any dwindlin' animules, I'll try to cure 'em.

" 'Course, I can cure people, too, but I don't like a-messin' with 'em much on account o' how they whine. Animules don't whine near as much as people. Yarbs work best when you give 'em with love, y'know. That's part o' the secret, y'see. Sometimes I wonder what's more powerful, yarbs or love. I reckon the two go hand in hand."

Seneca jammed his fingers through his hair. "I have no idea what *yarbs* are, I don't care to know, and if you don't get in that bed right now, I'm going to—"

"Yarbs is plants, Seneca," she told him sweetly. "I've heared 'em called *herbs,* too, but me and ever'body else in Possum Holler always called 'em yarbs. We'd have us some good ole times when we'd go a-yarbin'. How many times do y'chew yore food afore you swaller it?"

"For God's sake, Peachy! Why—"

"Paw always said to chew it twenty times, but I never do on account o' it turns to mush. I ain't much fer a-swallerin' mush. You reckon I've already tore up my insides by a-swallerin' food I ain't chewed twenty—"

"Peachy—"

"Paw's name was Duff," she quickly informed him. "Sometimes when he and me was a-foolin' around, I'd call him Duffers, and he'd call me Peachers."

Peachers? That was the most ridiculous nickname Seneca had ever heard.

Nickname. The word brought a long-forgotten memory to him. As a boy he'd wanted a nickname. He'd asked everyone to think of one to call him. But no one ever had.

His own rambling thoughts added to his already explosive anger. "I care nothing at all about spiders, and I care about nicknames even less. Now you have ten seconds to take off your—"

"Y'ain't never cut yore hair in March, have you, Seneca? Iffen y'cut yore hair in March, you'll have a year o' headaches."

He clenched his fists so hard his nails bit into his palms. "You are the worst headache I've ever had!"

"What works good fer a headache is a poultice o' horseradish leaves, turpentine, and beef taller. But the bestest cure o' all is to sleep with a pair o' scissors unner yore piller."

"I'd rather sleep with *you!*"

"Yeah, y'already maked that real clear, Seneca." Unable to help herself, she glanced at his pants again. Though he'd pulled them back up, he'd failed to fasten them.

She could still see all that hair. Between his hips. Set against his dark skin. Thicker and blacker than midnight.

She wanted to touch it. Wanted to slip her fingers through it. She wanted to know if it was as soft as it looked. Wanted to discover for herself what lay beneath it, what was totally concealed from her.

Heat enveloped her. Inside, outside . . . She felt like scrunching her thighs together again. Sweet Lord o' mercy, she had to get away from the man before she melted.

"What are you thinking about, Peachy?"

Her gaze flew to his face. The look in his eyes told her that not only had he caught her staring at that sensuous part of him but he was also fully aware of what the sight had done to her.

"I— I was jest— Jest a-settin' here, y'see," she stammered. "Yeah, a-settin' and a-thinkin' about . . . About what a comfortable hair this— I— I mean *chair!* This here *chair's* shore comfortable, Seneca! God Almighty, I ain't never set in sech a comfortable chair!"

As soon as the lie was out of her mouth, she regretted telling it. Surely the falsehood had added two hundred and thirty-seven more years to her Purgatorial stay. "I lied. Dang it to hell, Seneca, I lied, and y'know it. I weren't a-thinkin' about no chair. Yore britches— I—"

She sprang out of the chair and crossed the room to the fireplace. "I ain't never seed no nekkid man 'cept Paw," she said, wringing her hands. "Seed him a-warshin' once.

He was a mite withered, Paw was, but you, Seneca? Well, I ain't seed you nekkid yet, but I got it figgered that there ain't nothin' withered on yore whole body."

"And don't you want to see for yourself if your suspicions are true?" Not waiting for her answer, he started for her, but after only a few steps he slowed and finally stood motionless, his gaze embracing her.

Firelight shimmered all over her. As on the night he'd first met her, he was enchanted by the ethereal image she presented.

She wore white. Before the fire flames, it shone with a mellow luster. He'd seen her dressed like that before. He'd seen her thick red curls lying upon all that white. Somewhere . . . sometime.

Again, he was haunted by the feeling that he knew her, that he'd seen her long ago, that she was not of this world, but of another. He looked into her eyes and experienced that same powerful sense of tranquility. Something peaceful radiated from her beautiful green gaze. It seemed to fill a lonely void inside him.

"Peachy," he whispered.

She gasped softly at the look in his blue eyes, one of intense yearning and need. It made her want to hold him, kiss him, and murmur sweet words to him. She wanted to give him everything there was about her to give. And if she didn't leave, that was precisely what she would do.

She couldn't comprehend why she felt such emotions for a man she barely knew.

She held her hand up, trying to stop his advance before he took the first step. "Don't. Seneca . . . Y'jest cain't know how yore a-makin' me feel. Somethin's a-happenin' inside me. Somethin' so strong I cain't hardly hold it in. I cain't recall a-wantin' nothin' as bad as I want you. Sweet Lord o' mercy, I'm hotter'n a firecracker lit on both ends and a-poppin' in the middle right now. But . . ."

"But what?"

She wondered how to explain her fragile feelings to him. "I ain't got much time left to be alive," she said quietly. "I jest want ever'thing to be right afore I cain't never make it right again. Seneca . . . Cain't y'see how desperate I am to make shore and sartin that the last days o' my life'll be the best I can make 'em? I cain't go agin' what I believe, Seneca, on account o' I won't have enough time to mend my wrongdoin's. I gotta do ever'thing right the first time."

She paused, praying he'd understand what she was about to tell him. "I want our first time to be special. The mostest specialest it can be. And there ain't no way it can be special like that iffen I ain't shore what I'm a-doin' is right. I gotta be shore, Seneca. Shore o' who you are and how I feel about you. It cain't be no other way fer me. Jest cain't."

He took another step toward her. "Peachy—"

"Seneca— You— God Almighty, I cain't stay here a second longer."

He watched her scurry through the archway that led into the sitting room. In the next moment he heard the door slam. Its loud bang broke the strange spell that had held him captive.

He didn't go after her. He didn't try to stop her.

Every instinct he possessed warned him that unless he dragged her to his bed and tied her to it, nothing he did or said would get her there tonight. And though he wanted her with every fiber of his being, he would not resort to ravishing her.

He stood there staring at the empty archway for a long time before finally stalking to a small oak cupboard in the far corner of the room. He retrieved a bottle of fine brandy and a sparkling snifter from the cabinet and went to sit by the fire.

He began to drink, not stopping to appreciate the brandy's heady bouquet or smooth taste like he usually did, as he'd been taught to do. Irritated as he was, he would have consumed the liquor had it been rotgut.

His wedding night, he seethed inwardly, staring into the flames. He'd spent half of it fighting with Peachy and answering her pointless questions. He would spend the other half alone. Drinking.

Thinking.

During the time it took him to finish the first three glasses of brandy, he dwelled on his anger. By the fourth glass, he was wondering what daddy longleg spiders really looked like.

He threw his glass into the fireplace. Drinking from the bottle, he remembered catching a spider once. A small brown one he named Sylvester. He kept it in a small jar and gave it live flies to eat. Lady Muckross came across the jar one day, dumped Sylvester out, and stepped on him.

" 'The Crown Prince of Aventine,' " Seneca murmured, repeating his nanny's words, " 'will not entertain himself with insects. Such antics are for the peasant children.' "

He slumped in the chair. The memory of Peachy standing by the fire aglow with golden light floated through his mind. The mental image brought him a sense of tranquillity he hadn't felt in years.

Rusty-red buckets. Apple, cherry, and lemon pies. March hair trimmings, and dry cows. Best friends, and mushy food.

He wondered what Lady Muckross would have said if he'd slept with a pair of scissors under his pillow. "Go fry some ice, Lady Muckross," he muttered.

As drowsiness flowed through him, he thought of doors. *You'll be the door, see, and I'll slam you.*

He fell asleep.

And in his dream, he allowed himself to laugh.

As her nephew, Bubba, began rowing the dinghy away from the packet ship, Orabelle Hoggard tried to ignore her pitching stomach. The trip from North Carolina had been the worst experience of her life. Not only had she been seasick for the entire voyage, but passage for her and Bubba had cost her almost all the money she had left.

Anger overcame her nausea. It was all her cousin Duff's fault. The man had died and left her nothing. If he'd remembered her in his will, she wouldn't be shivering in a rickety boat on this freezing sea right now. The selfish man had left everything to his daughter. The land and it's gold-filled creek. It all belonged to Peachy.

Orabelle's anger climbed to rage. The stupid girl had left Possum Hollow to chase the ridiculous dream of marrying a prince. At least that's what her neighbors, the

Mackintoshes, had said. Her flight had forced Orabelle to follow.

Peachy was going to pay. Pay for her father's sins, pay for leaving North Carolina, and pay for making Orabelle suffer so needlessly.

Yes, the girl would pay the highest price of all.

"Uh ... The fog's goin' away, Aunt Orabelle," Bubba advised her, his beefy arms bulging as he moved the small craft over the white-capped waves. "Look at the land. We're almost there now."

"I can see that for myself, you idiot." Orabelle's pale gray eyes studied the mist-covered island. Somewhere on it was Peachy.

Her thin lips became thinner as she smiled. "Aventine," she murmured. "This is far enough, Bubba. I see rocks ahead, and you'll probably row us right into them. Carry me the rest of the way, and don't you dare let me get wet!"

Bubba tossed the oars into the foamy water and stepped out of the bobbing dinghy. The frigid North Sea sucked up to his waist. His huge body shook with cold. As carefully as he knew how, he lifted his Aunt Orabelle out of the boat. He held her and her heavy bag high, almost to his neck, and waded toward shore. His aunt's sharp nails dug into his thick, bare arms, but he ignored the pain and concentrated on keeping her from getting the least bit wet.

An especially strong wave ruined his efforts. As it crashed into him from behind, he lost his footing. He didn't fall, but he sank low enough into the water to drench his aunt's skirt.

Orabelle gasped with outrage. "You worthless imbecile! Can't you do anything right?" She began to slap him, her thin hand pelting his fat, chappy cheek like a pale switch.

"S-sorry, Aunt Orabelle," Bubba mumbled. He closed his eyes against the sting of both the salt water and his tears.

When he finally set her upon the white sand of the shore, Orabelle smacked him once more for good measure. When that was not enough to calm her fury, she gave him a swift kick in the shin, too. "I can't think of any word that describes your stupidity, Bubba," she ranted, trying to brush the clinging sand off her wet skirt.

His childlike mind searched desperately for the word she said she couldn't think of. He figured that maybe if he thought of a good one, she wouldn't be mad at him anymore. "Uh . . . Dumb?" he offered piteously.

"You are beyond dumb. Why do I put up with you?"

"You put up with me, Aunt Orabelle, cuz— Uh . . . Cuz y'need me to dig fer gold in Cousin Peachy's golden crick. Y'said we was gonna git that crick fer our very own. Y'said we was gonna be rich. Y'said—"

"I know what I said, you witless ass!"

Bubba cringed, knowing she was going to hit him again. She did, and it made him cry once more.

Orabelle paid his hurt feelings no mind at all. Instead, she dwelled on what she should do next. "Obviously," she began, speaking her thoughts out loud, "we must find out where she is."

"In— In the castle," Bubba sniffled, warm tears rolling down his cold-reddened cheeks. Blinking, he rubbed his numb hands over his arms. "She's in the castle, Aunt Orabelle, with— Uh . . . with the prince she come to marry."

Again, Orabelle ignored him. Bubba was a twenty-year-old man with the intelligence of a five-year-old. He demonstrated some kind of know-how with animals, but that was only because he was as dumb as they were.

Bubba's only real value was his massive body. He would, indeed, dig the gold from the McGee creek. Powerful as he was, he would do the work of three men. That alone was reason to continue putting up with him.

Gold, Orabelle thought, the word pumping excitement through her frail frame. People had been finding gold in those Appalachian hills for years. Oh, Duff had written a few years back and told her his own creek had all but dried up, but Orabelle suspected there was still a veritable treasure lying beneath the muddy creekbed. Duff had gotten gold dust from it, hadn't he? Anyone with a shred of intelligence knew that where there existed yellow dust, there also existed yellow nuggets. And maybe some of them were big. Big enough to be called boulders.

Big, small, whatever. They would all soon be hers.

A chill sea breeze swept past her, causing such a strong

shiver to run through her that she swore she heard her bones rattle. She tightened her woolen scarf more snugly around her neck.

His lips blue with cold, Bubba watched her bundle herself up. "Uh ... Y'said that when Cousin Peachy's dead I git a coat, Aunt Orabelle. Can I have a room in the house, too? When's she gonna git killed, Aunt Orabelle? Can I have a dog when she dies? Did y'know I got a secret, Aunt Orabelle? I got a secret, I got a secret, I got a secret, I—"

"Shut up, Bubba." God, she wished he'd stop telling her about his stupid secret. He'd been raving about it for years already. She began to walk, leaving him to follow with her heavy bag. Shortly, she found a small, tree-lined path that led inland. As she flounced down the sandy trail, her thoughts turned back to Peachy.

She'd never met the girl, but Dr. Greely had given her a detailed description. Orabelle was sure she would recognize the green-eyed, redheaded bitch instantly.

"Dr. Greely," she mused aloud.

Bubba's head snapped up. "Uh ... I 'member who he is, Aunt Orabelle. He's the one who tole Cousin Peachy she was gonna die. I 'member. He tole ever'body in Possum Holler she was dyin'. I 'member. You give him lots o' money to tell them lies. Yore real smart, Aunt Orabelle. Am I gittin' smart, too? I got a secret, Aunt Orabelle. Did y'know I got a secret?"

"It should have been so easy," Orabelle muttered, thinking of the plan that had failed. "So very easy."

"Uh ... easy?" Bubba asked before tripping over an exposed tree root and falling. "I falled down. Falled, Aunt Orabelle."

Orabelle didn't bother to turn around and see if he was hurt. In the next moment she heard him trudging behind her again. "Hurry up, Bubba."

"Yeah, hurry up, Bubba," he told himself. "But don't tell the secret." Examining his surroundings, he suddenly saw fields dotted with fluffy white animals. Joy burst inside him. "Dogs, Aunt Orabelle! Big white dogs! Can I have one o' them—"

"They aren't dogs; they're sheep! And you can't have one."

He stuck his bottom lip out. "When Cousin Peachy's dead, I'm gittin' one. I'm gitten one! I'm gitten one! I'm—"

"All right!" She grabbed a hunk of skin on his arm and pinched him cruelly.

He winced, then gazed longingly at the sheep in the distant meadow. "Come to make Cousin Peachy die. Uh . . . She's selfish. She won't share her gold with us. She was s'posed to stay in her cabin back home, huh, Aunt Orabelle? We was gonna visit her. We—"

"Yes!" Orabelle screeched, pinching him harder.

Gently, Bubba removed her hand from his arm. "You're mad at me cuz y'think I don't 'member, huh, Aunt Orabelle? That's why you keep pinchin' me."

"Bubba—"

"I *do* 'member. We was— Uh . . . We was gonna visit her. You was gonna feed her your special poison. You was gonna put it in her food. See? I 'member. Nobody was gonna take you to jail, huh, Aunt Orabelle? Ever'body was gonna think Cousin Peachy got killed by the disease the doctor maked up. And then the golden crick was gonna be ours, cuz you and me's the only kin she's got left. Did y'know I was that smart, Aunt Orabelle?"

He nodded vigorously, the fat under his chin rolling up and down. "But she didn't stay in her cabin, huh, Aunt Orabelle? We went there and she was gone. That man— That Mr. Mackintosh. He tole us she come here to git all her wishes to come true. Uh . . . she's Cousin Princess Peachy now. She wears a crown. Ain't that right, Aunt Orabelle?"

"Idiot! Do you really think a prince would marry a common mountain girl?"

Before he could answer, a moth alighted on his arm. He scooped it into his massive hand and freed it. "Uh . . . Maybe Cousin Peachy's purty. Maybe she likes animals. Why cain't I have another dog? My dog's gone! He d-died!"

When she saw his tears, she gave in to the urge to strike him. She hit him so hard her palm stung and her wrist ached. "You will stop your whining, Bubba Hoggard, or I'll send you back to the place you went to after your mother died! Do you remember the orphanage, Bubba? No one in the whole world will want you. They'll lock you up in a little room and you'll never get out!"

Bubba had no memory of that place, but she always described it as being so awful that the mere mention was sufficient to terrify him. And he'd figured out long ago that if he ever had to go back there, he'd never get another dog.

Noting the fear in his long-lashed brown eyes, Orabelle knew she'd frightened him enough to keep him quiet for the time being. She spun away from him and continued walking down the path. Before long, she spotted a group of children. They all held staffs, and one carried a lamb in her arms. Orabelle wondered why mere children had been given the task of shepherding so many sheep.

Quickly, she turned and whispered to Bubba. "You say one word while I'm talking to those children, and I'll . . . I'll poison every animal in Aventine. Do you see all the sheep, Bubba? Nice, soft, sweet little sheep. I'll kill them, all of them, if you say one measly word."

Terrified for the sheep, Bubba curled his lips between his teeth and bit down on them.

Satisfied, Orabelle approached the Aventine youngsters. She would accent her speech so they would have no idea where she was from. It simply wouldn't do for anyone to alert Peachy to the fact that there were other Americans on the island. If the girl knew, she would more than likely seek them out immediately.

And Orabelle needed time to plan the best way to commit the murder. She certainly didn't need the victim around while she planned it.

"Good day, children," she said, her speech as accented as she could make it. "My nephew and I have only just arrived to visit your beautiful island. I was hoping you might be able to tell me a bit about it. About your king. About what things we should see while here. I've already seen what fine sheep you have. Why, I imagine there have been other visitors here as well. Am I right?"

The oldest boy in the group, a lad of fifteen, answered.

"What is it you hope to see here, ma'am?" he asked, his young voice crackling with anger. "I am Asher, and I tell you there is naught but misery here. Our sheep suffer, and only the children are free to tend them."

Sorrow filled Bubba's tremendous frame. "Poor little sheep," he murmured, before remembering he wasn't supposed to speak.

Nodding, Asher dug the tip of his staff into the sand. "We try our best to guard the flocks, but—"

"That's all very interesting," Orabelle interrupted, trying to conceal her irritation, "but we would like to—"

"By the king's command, our parents must cultivate the paschal," Asher flared hotly. "But we are shepherds. We have been for centuries. Our only use for paschal is fodder for our sheep. Bah! Why do women buy the paschal blossoms to wear? While they cover their gowns with the flowers, our sheep wander, and if they don't become lost, they become wounded, sometimes fatally. We need our parents' help."

Orabelle cared nothing at all about the stupid peasants' troubles, but realized she had to humor the boy. "I'm sorry. How dreadful."

Asher shrugged and dug his staff deeper into the sand.

The girl with the lamb in her arms stepped forward. "There was a wedding in the palace yesterday, ma'am," she offered sweetly. "My name is Marlie, and I watched the line of coaches travel to the castle. The ladies were wearing jewels. But the guests didn't eat the cake. My aunt works in the kitchens, and she was able to bring a piece of the cake to me last night. I ate all of it."

Orabelle felt foreboding snake through her. "A wedding? Who was married?"

Marlie smiled again. "Prince Seneca. He's very handsome. I see him sometimes when he rides his horse. His horse is black. The prince jumps his horse over the highest fences and hedges in Aventine. No one has ever seen him fall. My uncle says Prince Seneca is sad. He says the prince never smiles."

Asher frowned. "He is not the only one who doesn't smile, Marlie," he reminded her sternly. "We do not smile either. We have nothing to smile about."

Marlie stuck her tongue out at him.

Her patience stretched tightly, Orabelle struggled to contain the urge to shake both children. "Who did the prince marry?"

"A lady," Marlie replied. "My cousin and I saw her one day by the river. She played with our sheep and caught a fish for us. Her boot fell in the water. We all tried to get it out, but it got swept away. The lady said maybe the trolls got it. She said trolls live by castles but that all they wanted is to steal boots. She said they were boot-filching trolls, and we laughed. We asked her to come visit us, and she promised she would. She said that someday soon she and Prince Seneca are going to have a picnic in the meadows and that maybe the king will come too. We've never seen the royal family in the meadows. The lady has a funny name. I wish it was my name because I like it."

"What's her name?" Orabelle demanded loudly. "What is it?"

"Peachy."

Chapter 5

As Seneca left his apartments, he saw one of the maids he had chosen to serve Peachy. "Advise the princess that I wish to speak to her immediately. I will await her in the blue drawing rooms."

Downstairs, he entered the blue drawing rooms. At his arrival, two maids curtsied and scurried out. Seneca noticed they held small paintbrushes and knew that Tiblock's order of the day entailed cleaning all the intricately cut woodwork in the palace. Seneca had often seen the maids working all day, whisking dust from within the tiny crevices of delicate knickknacks and ornate furniture.

As a boy he'd pitied them. As a man he still did.

But he could do nothing to ease their workload until he possessed the throne.

With a deep sigh of frustration, he accepted a cup of tea from a footman and settled into a luxurious blue velvet sofa to wait for Peachy. Next to him lay a small cream-colored pillow with red flowers embroidered around the edges. He picked it up, noticing that the blossoms weren't a true red, but a rusty red like that of an old bucket that had been left outside.

Like Peachy's hair. He wondered what was taking her so long.

"Seneca."

His father stood in the threshold.

The king took only three steps into the room before stopping. The grimace on his face betrayed his pain. "She will never be accepted here."

Seneca tossed the pillow back on the sofa and stood. "She will." With a nod of his head, he dismissed the footman from the room. He then set his teacup down, his eyes never leaving his father's.

The king stood his ground. "She won't. Even as queen, she will be hated."

"I am prepared to see that your prediction does not come to pass."

"You married her to defy me."

"It is you who suggests it to be so."

"I know you well, Seneca. You wed her only to oppose my wishes."

You do not know me, Father, Seneca shot back silently. *You've never wanted to.*

"So you deny marrying her to challenge my authority?" the king asked.

Seneca clasped his hands behind his back. "My reasons for wedding her are beside the point now, Father. She is my wife."

King Zane lifted a snowy eyebrow. "It's true that I couldn't prevent the wedding ceremony from taking place. I can, however, refuse to recognize the marriage. Indeed, it is possible that I can dissolve it."

Seneca struggled to maintain his outer calm. "You don't say," he drawled. "And how do you plan to do that, Father?"

The king took a long moment to wipe the nonexistent lint from his immaculate coat sleeves. "The one clause in the Royal Marriage Acts of Aventine that would have prevented you from marrying the girl was her lack of virginity."

"Ah, but the court physicians testified to the fact that she—"

"Don't be too quick to gloat, Seneca. She is *still* a maiden," the king stated bluntly, triumphantly. "Your union hasn't been consummated. And according to the Acts, a marriage ceremony only *begins* at the altar. It is not truly valid until the bedding has been accomplished. Therefore, you are not yet legally married to the girl."

Seneca felt a cold glitter come into his eyes. "What did you do, Father? Have my bed sheets examined?"

The king laughed spitefully. "I didn't have to resort to such medieval practices. The girl left your rooms shortly after having entered them. Actually, she *ran* out of them. And she was still wearing that revolting wedding finery of hers. She slept in her own chambers, and you remained in yours. I have only two eyes, but I own every other eye in the palace. All see what I do not."

Seneca refrained from commenting. He couldn't very well argue with the truth.

"I understand the fear a maiden experiences on her wedding night," the king continued. "Your mother was afraid, but she submitted to me. You were born ten months later. True, Arria never conceived again, but she succeeded in her responsibility of providing me with an heir."

"Father—"

"You are married in name only, Seneca. That is not sufficient. You are the crown prince, and as your title compels you to do, you must sire an heir to the throne. I can see no possible way for you to do that if the girl doesn't sleep in your bed. Callista would never have run from you. She would have embraced her obligations as the Princess of Aventine."

"Callista, however, is not the princess. Peachy is."

The king took a moment to admire the huge blood-red ruby in his ring. "Perhaps that girl you consider your wife isn't all that attracted to you," he suggested, rubbing the ruby on his sleeve until it shone. "It could be that she fled last night because she can't bear the thought of—"

"You are wrong, Father."

The dead seriousness in his son's voice made the king frown.

When his father lapsed into silence, Seneca studied him carefully, a new realization dawning on him. "The fact that I have not yet consummated my marriage to Peachy isn't the issue, is it, Father? You know full well that it's only a matter of time before the bedding takes place, but because you are desperate to destroy my marriage and have not yet found the means to do it, you are grasping at straws. You—"

"Consider this, Seneca! Everyone is aware of what transpired— Rather, what *didn't* transpire last night. You know how swiftly palace gossip spreads. And while I'm sure you will never see the ridiculing smiles or hear a strain of the taunting laughter, you may be certain that the nobility will be doing both behind your back. You will be seen as a fool. Indeed, you already are! You showed true stupidity by choosing the girl in the first place. You further proved your idiocy by failing to make sure that she dressed properly for her wedding. At the banquet, you allowed her to talk back to you, embarrass the Sherringhams, and insult Callista. And after all of that was said and done, you accepted her refusal to surrender her innocence to you. Now, having been reminded of all those things, what have you to say for yourself?"

Seneca knew an uncontrollable urge to release a scornful answer to his father's question. And because he felt the distinct suspicion that he had the upper hand, he decided to give in to his urge. "I can only say," he began, folding his arms across his chest, "that the depth of my patience is truly astonishing. *Think* of how much I have put up with, Father. Why, if not for Peachy, I might never have discovered the full measure of my endurance."

His son's very rare show of sarcasm shocked the king. In the next moment, his astonishment gave way to fury. He clenched his teeth and his fists so tightly his arms and head shook, the action causing him considerable pain. "Are you telling me that despite the fact that she has made you the laughingstock of Aventine, you will allow her outrageous behavior to continue?"

"I said nothing of the sort."

"You don't *care* that the nobility derides you?"

"If there were nothing I could do to alter their way of thinking, I would care very much. However, that is not the case." Without requesting leave of his father, Seneca began to walk out of the room.

"I will have the marriage annulled!" the king shouted as Seneca passed him. "And I have the grounds to do it!"

Seneca stopped at the door and turned around. "You have them now, Father, but you won't for much longer. Peachy will be my wife in every sense of the word, have no doubt about that."

"Ah, you will ravish her."

The very thought of abusing Peachy in such a way sickened Seneca. "No."

"And after you have forced yourself on her, you will dress her in satin and jewels. You will then sew her lips together so she cannot utter another repulsive word. That accomplished, you will tie her to a chair, where she will spend the rest of her life sitting like a lady."

Seneca stared at the ceiling, as if deep in contemplation. "A clever plan. If my own attempts fail, perhaps I will resort to yours."

"You truly believe you will succeed, don't you, Seneca?"

"I do."

The king rubbed his chin. "Care to make a wager?"

"Be careful, Father," Seneca warned. "The last offer you made left me with a bride of my own choosing."

"It was a stroke of luck that brought you the girl exactly when you needed her. You'll need more than mere luck this time. I stand no chance of losing this wager. Oh, and it will be kept between us, Seneca. A secret bargain. If you violate that secrecy, the wager is invalid."

Wary and curious, Seneca answered, "Indeed. What does this secret, no-lose wager entail?"

The king began to pace, stopping every few steps to rub his throbbing knees. "Proceed with the impossible task of transforming the heathen into a lady. Because I am a fair man, I'll give you one whole month. Your efforts will come to naught, of course, and then, Seneca, you will send the girl back to whatever godforsaken place she came from, ill manners intact. You will arrange for your marriage to be annulled, and when it has been dissolved, you will marry Callista Inger."

Seneca's face registered no hint of the tumult of emotions crashing through him. "I accept. And I will speak of the wager to no one," he added, unwilling to risk hurting Peachy's feelings by letting her know she was the object of a bet.

At his son's foolhardiness, the king laughed.

Seneca waited until his father's laughter faded to a quiet chuckle before continuing. "We didn't discuss what will happen when I succeed in turning Peachy into a lady."

"You expect to do the impossible? In *one* month?"

Seneca planned to have help. He would enlist the aid of his indomitable Aunt Viridis, a woman of impeccable manners. "It won't be impossible. And when I have proved that to you, you will give me the Crown."

"The Crown? Good God, you really *are* sure of yourself, aren't you?" Snickering over his son's absurd and groundless confidence, he waddled out of the room and down the hall.

Seneca followed him into the marble entryway, determined to force him to agree to his side of the wager. "Father—"

"Ah, there's the elegant princess now!" The king looked up the Grand Staircase.

Seneca felt cold anger come over him. There, at the top of the staircase, directly beneath the glass dome, stood Peachy, dressed in her homespun skirt and blouse. Her closets fairly burst with expensive clothes, yet she insisted on dressing as if she were ready to begin scrubbing the fireplaces!

God help her, he was going to wring her neck.

"Seneca!" she hollered down to him, her shout echoing through the vast foyer. "Y'look riled! I'm sorry I'm late, but I was buck-nekkid when Nydia and Ketty tole me y'wanted to see me. Wait right there fer me! I'm a-comin' down fast as I can!"

Without hesitation, she lifted her leg over the slick mahogany banister, Thurlow Wadsworth McGee clinging to her shoulder. As she began the long, winding slide down, the back of her multipatched skirt billowed over her head, exposing her lacy underwear to the two men who were watching her from below.

Seneca was too furious to speak, to move, even to breathe.

But King Zane was absolutely delighted.

She slipped off the end of the banister and landed in an upside-down, inside-out, thoroughly twisted heap, Thurlow Wadsworth McGee's muffled chattering coming from beneath her.

"Ladylike behavior at its finest," the king quipped, then chortled.

Ignoring his father's snide remark, Seneca watched Peachy stagger to her feet. Her squirrel had somehow become captured within the thick mass of her hair. The creature shrieked with irritation as Peachy tried to disentangle him.

King Zane laughed so hard his merriment overcame his physical pain. "Seneca, if— If within a m-month you perform the ... *miracle* of t-turning that wild female yokel into a true lady, the Crown is yours!" His chest heaving, he limped away.

"You are wearing rags."

Seated in the hard ladder-backed chair in Seneca's office, Peachy squirmed and crossed her legs in an effort to find a comfortable position. She ran her hand over her worn brown skirt. "I was a-tryin' to hurry, Seneca. These here clothes is easy to git on. Them dresses you had maked fer me take nigh on half a hour to git buttoned into. Hell, one of 'em's got a hunnerd and twenty-four buttons down the back."

He stared at her from behind his massive desk. God, even dressed in tatters, she was gorgeous. Her thick auburn hair tumbled over her slight shoulders in rich waves that sparkled and curled and tempted him sorely. Her beige blouse stretched tightly over her full breasts. Indeed, it seemed that if she took a deep breath, her buttons would pop and her breasts would spill forth.

The thought aroused him. There she sat, his virgin wife. And here he sat, aching with heavy male need. His fury swelled.

"I *do* have on purty unnerwear," she said, hoping her declaration would temper his anger. "I tuk the time to put a lacy slip on. Jest one, though. I don't like a-wearin' too much. Nobody cain't even see how purty my unnerwear is, but it makes me feel like a real princess."

"Oh? And I suppose when you stood at the top of the staircase and screamed out my name, you felt like a real princess. And when you announced you had been naked when I called for you, you felt like a real princess. And let's not forget when you slid down the banister. That must have made you feel like a *queen.*"

"I—"

"Silence!" He slammed his fist to the desk, causing a silver inkwell to rattle and a frightened Thurlow Wadsworth McGee to flee from the room, his bushy tail three times as big as usual. "What you did was totally unacceptable. A lady does not shout without very good reason, Peachy. Nor does she discuss the subject of nakedness. She doesn't speak about her body at all. And when descending a staircase, a lady skims her hand along the railing. She does not *ride* it!"

"Seneca—"

"Your manner of sitting in that chair is improper. A lady never crosses her legs. You will sit straight, legs together, feet flat on the floor."

"But this chair is—"

"And about your stride ... You bounce. As if there were springs attached to the soles of your shoes. You will cease to walk in that manner. A lady should give the impression that she is gliding across the floor."

He leaned forward, giving her a piercing gaze. "You will wear the clothes I had made for you, and you will spend your days in a quiet fashion. You may choose to amuse yourself with embroidery. That is a very feminine pastime. You might also learn to paint. As a royal, you may correspond with other royals, and—"

"Can I write to Queen Victoria?"

"You may. During the day, you may also sit and converse with your ladies-in-waiting, a group of women that I will personally choose for you very soon. One in particular I have in my mind is my Aunt Viridis. She is well versed on the subject of etiquette, and although she is rather stern, it is such strictness that you need. At any rate, Peachy, your ladies will endeavor to keep you entertained, and I hope to God they succeed."

Peachy scowled with confusion and ire. "But I already got me some friends. Ketty and Nydia—"

"Are your servants. You will pick your friends from among the nobility, but never forget that even the noblewomen are beneath you. You—"

"Well, yore my friend, too. I'll be your friend, Seneca. Yore noble enough, ain'tcha?"

"I am your husband."

"Y'cain't be my friend on account o' yore my husband?"

He wasn't sure how to answer her. "It is entirely within your rights to advise the noblewomen. They, in turn, should follow your advice. You are the princess, the only female royal. Therefore, once you have learned proper etiquette and earned their respect, it is possible other women will seek to imitate you. Think about that, Peachy. It is a goal you would do well to reach for."

"I—"

"You will learn to play a musical instrument. You—"

"I can play the jug. Paw larnt me."

"You may take walks in the garden, and visit your new friends at their respective estates, as well as invite them to call on you here. You may plan dinner parties and balls. You don't need a specific cause to hold such gatherings, but the nobility enjoys having their birthdays and anniversaries remembered by the royal family."

He rose and came to stand in front of the desk, continuing to glare at his hellion princess. "You might even organize specific charities. There is nothing wrong with endeavoring to help the less fortunate, and you have the authority to request that the aristocrats assist you with your efforts. Your request, Peachy, will be received as a command. Coming from a royal, the word *request* is merely a more polite word for an order. And you may be sure that I will see to it that the nobility takes you seriously."

"Seneca—"

"Before I agreed to marry you, you promised to learn to be a lady. Renew that promise now, and you may have your crown. You've expressed your wish for it several times, therefore I'm fully aware of its importance to you. Before you decide to fashion another homemade crown yourself, allow me to show you the one that was created for Aventine's princesses centuries ago."

He stalked out of the office, knowing her curiosity would lead her to follow. When he arrived in the queen's chambers, a small but luxurious sitting room designed especially for the queen and her ladies, Peachy was right behind him. "There it is," he said, pointing to the beautiful portrait that hung over the marble fireplace. "That is my great-grandmother, Diandra. She became queen shortly after this portrait was painted, but she is wearing the crown that I will give you should you agree to become a lady fit to wear it."

Peachy couldn't stop staring. The headpiece atop Diandra's shining black curls was the most gorgeous thing she'd ever seen. Thousands of tiny diamonds were set in dainty rows that built atop each other to make a three-inch-high circlet of dazzling beauty.

"The night I met you," Seneca continued, "you told me you needed a prince to grant you all your wishes. I am prepared to do that. Not only will I present you with the crown, but I will give you more jewels than you can possibly wear. Be it small, or be it grand, whatever luxury you desire will be yours. In return, all I ask is that you follow my instructions concerning ladylike behavior."

She licked her bottom lip. "Will y'give me a horse o' my own?"

Momentarily mesmerized by the pretty sparkle of excitement in her eyes, he paused before replying. "Done."

"I don't want no mare, Seneca. I want a stallion. A pure white one with a real long mane."

"A stallion?" He hadn't realized she was a skilled rider. "Very well."

"And a carriage? A gold one? With pink satin seats inside? I cain't *wear* pink on account o' my red hair, but I reckon I can set on it. And can I have some gold coins to throw to the peasants whilst I'm a-ridin' around in my coach?"

"Whatever you want, Peachy. Just give me your promise to follow my instructions, and I will provide you with a life of leisure and luxury beyond your imagination."

She tapped her chin with her finger.

"Do you or do you not want to be a *real* princess?"

"Well . . . Yeah."

"Then you must behave like one. Can you not understand that the very things you profess to want are the very things I am offering you? All you must do is learn the ways of a lady."

She thought of all the things he'd told her that ladies

were supposed to do. Dress in elegant clothes, sew, paint, write letters, give advice, and play music. Talk to ladies who waited on her, walk outside, sit straight, and glide across the floor. Remember birthdays and anniversaries and have dinner parties and balls. Visit the rich folks and help the poor ones.

She could do all those things. Why, she'd probably *enjoy* doing them!

What was there to think about?

"All right, Seneca." Smiling, she held out her hand. "Let's shake on it."

He recognized her suggestion as his first opportunity to further his endeavors to get her into his bed. "I would prefer to acknowledge the bargain with a kiss. It's a much more binding way to seal a deal."

His announcement made her knees wobble.

"Steady, Princess," Seneca murmured, clasping her about the waist.

Peachy felt those hot sparkles inside her again. The ones she'd felt last night. "But Seneca . . ."

He saw indecisiveness cloud her beautiful eyes and suspected her surrender was more possible this morning than it had been last night. Recalling her wish to know more about him, he said, "I am fond of Schubert's compositions."

"Schubert?" She'd never heard of Schubert, but it didn't matter. All that mattered right now was the sensual sound of his deep, husky voice and the desire in his blue, blue eyes. "Yeah, good ole Schubert," she whispered.

He drew her closer, his eyes locking with hers. Slowly, gently, he stroked the small of her back and concentrated on what else he could tell her. "I enjoy William Strode's *The Floating Island,* a political drama he wrote in 1655. I've read it four times."

"Four times," she repeated on a long breath. She didn't know who William Strode was either, but remained tantalized by Seneca's nearness.

"I like mathematics," he added, sliding his hand up her spine, then curling his fingers around the back of her neck. "I very much admire the Swiss naturalist Louis Agassiz, who is an authority on the movements and effects of glaciers. I would like to meet the English physicist James Prescott Joule. Several years ago, he determined the amount of work required to produce a unit of heat."

"Heat?" Lord o' mercy, she sure knew what *that* was right now.

He leaned down to her, his face a mere inch from hers. "And Peachy . . . I would like to kiss you now."

The urge to deny him disappeared as soon as it rose. "Um . . . Jest one kiss, Seneca. And I ain't a-openin' nothin'. Ain't, hear?"

"I hear," he murmured right before he settled his mouth upon hers.

Peachy melted against him, giving in to all the feelings he'd stoked within her last night. God's truth, she wanted this kiss as much as he did. She wanted it so badly that she'd thought of little else since leaving his rooms last night.

Still though, she kept her lips tightly pursed, deciding that a closed-mouth kiss was surely regarded as one of innocent friendship. And there certainly wasn't anything sinful about that.

Seneca set about changing that determined mind of hers, and moved his hands to the sides of her face. Slowly, he threaded his fingers through the red silk of her hair and tilted her head slightly. He moved against her, allowing, indeed, *forcing* her to feel how much he desired her.

He knew he'd succeeded when she scrunched her thighs together. "Peachy," he murmured, his mouth moving upon hers.

He spoke her name in that low, smooth voice that so affected her. "Seneca," she whispered in return. "Quit it now."

He almost smiled, for there wasn't a shred of conviction behind her demand. "No."

He ain't gonna quit, God, she said silently. *What's a girl to do?* Having made sure her Maker was aware of the no-win situation she was in, she surrendered to the tingling feelings Seneca created inside her.

Like a flower bud seduced by the warm and insistent rays of the sun, her lips parted slowly.

Seneca experienced a surge of wild pleasure. Desire

spilling through him, he entered her mouth and knew her sweetness. God, what sweetness it was. Wanting more of it, he began a deep and thorough exploration of her mouth and groaned softly when she allowed him his quest.

At the sound of his low moan, Peachy felt his fingers moving down the front of her blouse. Before she could understand what he was doing, she felt his warm hand cup her bare breast and realized he'd unfastened her buttons. While she summoned the will to make him stop, tickles coursed through her, prompting her to scrunch her thighs together again.

Gently, Seneca kneaded the lush treasure he held. Her nipple hardened in his palm just as she emitted a small squeak. Knowing he could take no more from her without infuriating her, he reluctantly removed his hand from inside her blouse.

He straightened, pulled the cuffs of his sleeves, and stepped away. "The deal is sealed. You will keep your end of it and stay out of trouble today." With that, he strode from the room.

When he was gone, Peachy looked down at her open blouse. Fingers trembling, she slipped her hand inside, just as he had done, and fondled the same breast he had. Her action intensified the sweet ache he'd begun. It felt so good, she forgot to be mad at him.

She wanted very much to go to heaven when she died. But there was heaven to be had on earth as well, she realized.

And the man who offered her that worldly paradise was Seneca.

Several hours after having agreed to Seneca's bargain, Peachy strolled through a lush meadow. She'd started her walk in the palace garden, as he'd told her she could, but had felt confined within the tall hedgerows that encircled it. "Well, a walk's a walk, Thurlow Wadsworth McGee," she told her squirrel, who scampered along beside her. "Ladies are s'posed to walk, and I'm a-walkin'. And I'm dressed real fancy-like, too, boy. Seneca's gonna be happy that I'm a-doin' what he tole me to do."

She ran her hand down her midnight-blue velvet cape

and the skirt of her sapphire-blue satin gown. Her thoughts remained on all the things Seneca had instructed her to do, until a small sound captured her attention. She realized it was someone crying. Following it, she soon came upon a little boy. He was bent over a prone sheep, his slight shoulders shaking as he sobbed.

"Well, what in the world's a-matter, little man?" Quickly, she knelt beside him, her knees sinking into a sticky puddle of chilled mud.

"My sh-sheep," he tried to tell her, his head still buried in the animal's thick wool. "He got in the marshes, and when I finally got him out he was real sick. Papa's going to be so upset! He trusted me to take care of his flock while he and Mama worked in the paschal fields! This— This is the only ram we've got, and if he dies—"

"Hesh up now, and let me look at him," Peachy told the boy. Bending over the ram, she saw its breathing was shallow. Truly concerned, she lifted one of its closed eyelids and saw that its eye was glazed and motionless.

A terrible suspicion almost sickened her. Frantically, she did a more thorough examination, not an easy task, for its wool was extraordinarily thick and difficult to part. After many long moments, she found what she'd hoped she wouldn't.

Two puncture wounds near the ram's neck.

Snakebite.

She scrambled to her feet. "What's your name, darlin'?"

"Tivon," he sniffled.

"Well, I need your help, Tivon," she said.

She snatched off her velvet cape, then together she and Tivon carefully rolled the ram onto it. Her heart hammering with worry and exertion, Peachy pulled the cape across the meadow, careful to drag her heavy burden over the smoothest ground she could find. When the soft grass gave way to pebbled earth, she left the ram and Tivon and scurried toward the castle. There, at the gates before the river, stood two uniformed guards.

She screamed at them to come to her, and was furious when they did not obey. Picking up her skirts, she sped closer to the gates. As she ran, her gown snagged on a dense mass of briars. She tugged at the satin until it finally tore apart. Unmindful that a large piece of her dress remained within the tangled thorns, she dashed toward the guards again, yelling at them. "What the hell's the matter with the two o' y'all? Didn't you hear me a-callin' you?"

"Your Highness," one of them began nervously, "we are not allowed to leave our posts."

"Yeah? Well, I becomed yore princess yesterday, and I'm a-givin' you a order! Go git that ram over there and carry it into the castle!"

"Your Highness!" the other guard exclaimed. "We cannot bring a sheep into the—"

"You git that ram right now, or I'll tell Seneca that you didn't do what yore princess tole you to!"

Neither of them moved.

Peachy glared at them, her mind spinning. "All right, I'll carry the ram inside mysef! It's real heavy, and it'll prob'ly hurt me real bad to carry it. I'll faint dead away from the pain inside me. The doctor-men'll examine me and tell Seneca that I won't never be able to give him no babies. They'll say that when I toted the ram I messed up my baby-makin' innards. That can happen y'know."

The guards began to shuffle uneasily.

"Well, I reckon there won't never be another King of Aventine after Seneca," Peachy went on, shaking her head. "And all on account o' y'all wouldn't hep me when I asked. But that's all right. Y'all jest stay right there a-guardin' them dumb gates, and I'll go ruin Aventine's chances o' future kings. Bye." She turned and charged back toward Tivon and his ram.

The two guards arrived before she did. One of them lifted the ram and hoisted it over his shoulders. In only a few more moments, the determined princess, hopeful shepherd boy, fearful guards, and sick ram made their way over the bridge, through the castle entry court, past the carriage porch, and finally entered the grand entryway of the palace.

Peachy silently thanked all of heaven when she saw Nydia preparing to ascend the grand staircase. "Nydia! Fetch me my bag o' cures! And tell Ketty to git a bowl o' hot water, a onion, some salt, a piece o' fatty meat, and a spoon!" Her orders delivered, she set about looking for a place to nurse the ram.

Seneca's arrival into the entryway cut short her search. His eyes widened at the sight before him. Two of Aventine's men-at-arms stood near the doors, one of them with a sheep wrapped around his shoulders, the other holding a filthy velvet cape. A small peasant boy wept beside them, his hand stroking the ram's foot.

And Peachy . . . Good God, it was only noon, and she was wearing an evening gown! A *ball* gown! A muddy ball gown! *Half* a muddy ball gown! he amended furiously, noticing the large hole in the skirt. Half a muddy ball gown whose bodice exposed a generous amount of her lush, dirt-splotched bosom!

He seethed. Had it really only been a few hours since he'd given her instructions on proper etiquette? How *could* she have forgotten the lessons so quickly!

Peachy watched the rage explode in his eyes. "You hesh up, Seneca!" she demanded before he could say a word. "Jest hesh right up, hear? I got me a ailish ram to doctor, and I ain't a-takin' no sass offen you!"

She turned toward the guard who held the ram. "Take it in there and put it on the sofer," she instructed him, pointing to the blue drawing rooms.

"Remove that animal from the castle immediately!" Seneca barked at the guard.

The guard started for the door, but Peachy reached it first, blocking it with her body and outstretched arms.

Seneca wasn't about to let her win. "Peachy, you will move away from the door and let the guard pass. Barnyard animals do *not* belong inside the castle!"

"Here's your bag of cures, Peachy," Nydia said, panting as she raced into the foyer.

Seneca was so outraged he didn't know which outrage to address first. "Nydia, you dare to call your princess by her first name?"

Nydia paled, but before she could answer Ketty arrived. "I brought all the things you asked for from the kitchen, Peachy."

Seneca could not believe his ears. "Ketty—"

"Oh, hesh up, Seneca," Peachy hissed. "I tole 'em to

call me Peachy, and they have to do what I say." She looked at the guard with the ram again. "Take it to the sofer in that room," she repeated, pointing to the drawing room again.

"You will *not* take it in there," Seneca snapped. "You will take it back outside where it belongs."

Peachy opened her mouth to argue, but was silenced by Tivon's small voice.

"Please, Your Royal Highness," the boy squeaked through his tears. "The princess is going to try to make my papa's ram well again. We only have one ram, sir, and if it dies, we'll have no more lambs. We've already lost four ewes. I'm— I'm only seven, and I ... I can't take care of the whole flock by myself! I need my papa to help me, but he has to go to the fields! He—"

"Hold your tongue, boy!" one of the guards admonished. He threw a nervous glance at the prince.

Seneca stared at the boy, watching huge tears slide down the lad's freckled cheeks. Silence filled the room as everyone waited to see what the prince would do.

But the tension was soon broken by the king's booming voice as His Majesty prepared to exit a nearby room. Peachy's disheveled state in mind, Seneca acted quickly. He crossed to the doors and took her elbow. Leading her out of the entryway and into a long hallway, he tightened his hold on her arm when she tried to escape. Tivon, the ram-toting guard, the guard with Peachy's cape, Nydia, and Ketty all trailed along behind.

"Seneca!" Peachy blasted as he took her farther down the corridor. "Dang it, the last time I seed somethin' like you, it was a-sheddin' its skin! A *snake's* what you are!"

"Peachy—"

"I was only a-tryin' to hep little Tivon's ram! But you? Well, you shore as hell won't never git dizzy from a-doin' no good turn fer nobody, huh, Seneca?"

"You will cease your struggles," he ordered, releasing her arm and taking her by the waist. "You will apologize for calling me a snake, and then you will be quiet."

"Ha!" She renewed her battle to get away from him.

He was much stronger than she was, and had no difficulty restraining her. "Do you or do you not want a place in the castle for the ram?"

His question gave her pause. "A place? Y'mean yore gonna—"

"I am, but only if you stop acting like a wild woman. You agreed to our bargain, did you not?"

She swallowed hard and calmed down instantly. "I'm sorry."

"Very well." He continued taking Peachy and her followers through the long, dim hallway. He passed the billiard room and the deed room. He marched past the gun room, the footman's room, and Tiblock's room. Down the corridor he went, passing the servery, two pantries, and finally the kitchen court. At the end of the hallway was a plain wooden door. He opened it and proceeded up a long, winding set of stairs. The odor of mildew was strong, the network of spiderwebs thick. He brushed the filmy webs aside, continued up the stairs, and didn't stop until he reached the top, where another door opened into a tower room.

The dim ray of sunlight that crept through a small crack in one of the shuttered windows was the only source of illumination. "Open the windows," Seneca instructed Nydia and Ketty.

Sunshine poured in, and Peachy saw that everything in the room was buried under at least three inches of dust. The only furniture was a large wooden trunk. Suspended from one of the ceiling rafters hung a thick rope.

Listening to the scuffling of fleeing mice, Peachy took immediate objections to the room's filthy condition and whirled on Seneca. "This is the worstest place I ever—"

"Nevertheless, you will make the best of it," he declared. "Or you will take the animal outside. The choice is yours."

Muttering under her breath and swiping flying dust away from her face, Peachy took her velvet cape from the guard who held it and laid it on the cleanest part of the floor she could find. "Put the ram here."

Tivon, the guards, Ketty, and Nydia knelt around her as she examined the sheep. It was still alive, but its breathing was even more shallow than before. With her ear to its chest, she listened to its slow, faint heartbeat.

The ram wasn't going to live. Her cures would be useless. She knew it.

"Tivon," she whispered, her throat clogged with regret, "yore ram . . . he's real far gone, darlin'. He needed hep hours ago."

Tivon began to cry again.

Ketty wept also. "Isn't there anything we can do?"

"Surely Your Highness could *try* the medicine," one of the guards suggested, his deep voice a bit shaky as he stroked the dying ram.

Peachy looked at the expectant faces around her. Only Seneca's registered understanding. She realized he knew the ram was going to die and that nothing she could do would save it.

Nevertheless, she began to prepare the remedy, wanting Tivon to know that everything possible had been done. She peeled and cut the onion and dropped it into the bowl of warm water along with the piece of fatty meat and a handful of salt. After poking at the concoction for a moment, she removed a piece of the onion and the meat and placed them on the snakebite site, then instructed Tivon to hold them there.

Next she threw pinches of her herbs into the water. "Pokeberry powder. Yaller root and cherry bark. Wild ginger, willer leaves, and cow's horn scrapin's." She stirred the mixture well and commenced to feed the animal spoonfuls of the herb medicine.

The liquid ran down the beast's throat, but he didn't swallow it. Nor did he choke. His reflexes were completely gone.

The ram was dead. Peachy sat back on her heels, her vision blurred with tears. "Oh, Tivon," she murmured. "I— He . . . It was a snake, darlin'. Yore ram—" Overcome with regret, she could say no more.

Seneca took over. "Your ram is dead, Tivon, but you will thank your princess for trying to save it."

Tivon could barely manage the words. "Th-thank you," he whispered, tears rolling over his lips.

Seneca helped the boy to his feet. "The guards will

carry the ram's body outside and help you bury it. And then you will return to the meadows and tend to the rest of your flock, as I'm sure your parents have instructed you to do."

Sobbing, Tivon shuffled to the door. But before leaving, he turned to Seneca. "Maybe you'll throw me in prison for saying this, sir, but I hate your father. I—"

"Be silent, boy!" one of the guards commanded, horrified.

"I *do* hate him!" Tivon shouted, his chest heaving. "I hate him so bad that sometimes I wish he would *die!*"

Ketty and Nydia gasped. "Oh, Tivon," Nydia whispered. Both girls waited in fearful expectation of what the prince would say or do.

It seemed to Peachy that the tension in the room was thicker than the blanket of dust. She rose from the floor. "Tivon, y'don't hate the king. Y'don't really want him to die. Tell Seneca y'didn't mean to say them things."

"No," Tivon said. "I *did* mean them. I— I wish a snake would bite the *king!*"

Peachy looked straight into Seneca's eyes. "He don't mean it," she told him. "He's only seven years old, Seneca. Young'uns ... They're too innocent-minded to unnerstand what they're a-sayin'."

Seneca's piercing gaze never left Tivon's defiant one. "Your princess defends you, Tivon. I would know if you are truly worthy of her defense. If you are, I will pardon you. If you are not, you will be punished."

Peachy took Seneca's arm. "Seneca—"

"Tivon, do you realize that expressing a wish for the king's death is considered an act of treason against the Crown of Aventine?" Seneca asked.

Tivon nodded and lifted his small chin high. "Aye, I know it, sir."

"Then you are not as innocent as your princess claims. You are not worthy of her defense, therefore you will be punished. By my own hand. But until I am prepared to mete out your punishment, you will do as I commanded you to do and return to your flock immediately. Go."

Tivon fled from the room, his footsteps echoing down the stairwell.

Seneca looked at Ketty and Nydia. "You will not repeat a word of what the boy said. If you do, I will hear of it. Now, leave us."

The maids nodded, curtsied, and hurried from the room.

Seneca then addressed the guards. "You will keep silent as well. Go assist the boy in burying the animal."

When the guards left with the dead ram, Seneca turned to Peachy and was fairly blinded by the rage flashing in her eyes. And with each angry breath she took, her breasts pushed at the low-cut bodice of her gown. Her fury hinted at the seething passion that dwelt within her beautiful body. It seduced him so thoroughly, it was an effort not to succumb to the unseemly urge to take her on the dusty floor of the tower room.

He swallowed, forcing himself to concentrate on the situation at hand. "You would do well to understand that what Tivon said was not only morally wrong but under Aventine law also illegal. Nothing you say will sway my decision to punish him."

"What are you gonna do to him? Y'ain't gonna hurt—"

"It was never my intention to hurt him, Peachy."

She wrung her hands. "I— I couldn't save his ram," she squeaked. "Now his family won't git no more lambs."

Seneca saw the sparkle of tears in her eyes. Her sorrow made him feel distinctly undone. "You did what you could."

She nodded and dried her eyes. "Why does Tivon hate yore paw?"

She was back on ground he knew well. "That is none of your concern."

"I don't like you very much right now."

Her announcement bothered him immensely. And the fact that it bothered him bothered him even more.

"And I don't like not a-likin' you," she added. "It gives me a case o' the weary dismals inside."

He wanted to ask her why she felt bad about not liking him. "Your feelings are irrelevant to me," he said instead, then stalked to the door. There, he waited for her retort, knowing it wouldn't be long in coming.

"There must be a lot o' good in you, Seneca, on account o' don't none of it ever come outen."

He had known the comeback would come, and come it had. He gave her his most fierce glare.

She outdid him with a ferocious one of her own. "Yore tougher'n stewed owl, but I'm tough, too, and you'd best mem'ry that. When you kissed me this mornin' ... It's true you make my britches twitch, but I'm a-thinkin' that ain't enough fer me. I maked up my mind to have me a heaven on earth, and I know yore the one who can give it to me. But the way I see it, that kind o' thigh-scrunchin' heaven'll be better iffen love's got a part in it, too.

"I really want to be yore friend, Seneca. And like I done tole you last night, I'm hell-bent on a-fallin' in love with you, too. Lord knows y'ain't a-makin' it easy, but I ain't a-givin' up till I figger outen how to do it. There's gotta be *somethin'* about you fer me to love, and I aim to find it."

She looked around the filthy room. "You a-lettin' me bring the ram up here to this tower's a start, I reckon. Y' could've maked us go outside, but you brung us up here. Weren't the nicest thing y'could've done, but it weren't the meanest, neither. I'll plant that like a seed and hope that friendship and love commence to sprout outen it."

Something tender tried to come to him. He felt it tempering his anger. But he wanted to be angry right now. The situation demanded it. "I thought I made it clear to you, Peachy, that it's not your love I want. It's your obedience, and my mind is closed on the matter."

She stared at him for a long time. "I've heared it tole that there ain't nothin' harder to open than a closed mind."

"Then I suggest you don't bother trying to open mine."

"I won't."

"A wise decision."

"I'll work at a-openin' yore heart instead. The way I see it, once yore heart's open, yore mind won't have no choice but to foller."

He saw no logic at all in her hypothesis. "Peachy—"

"Don't spit no more tacks at me, Seneca. I'll do my dangdest to give you the obedience yore so all fired up to git. But afore I die, yore gonna git my love, too. I might not never git yores, but yore a-gittin' mine jest as soon as I start a-feelin' it fer you. And it'll be strong love on account o' when I set outen to do somethin', I don't never do it halfway. 'Sides that, it's *my* love, and I can give it to whoever the hell I want to. And it's my *life,* too. I'm a-livin' the little bit of it I got left to the very fullest I can. And y'know? A life withouten love ain't no gawdang kind o' life a'tall."

He resisted every soft emotion it was possible to feel. "Are you quite finished?"

"Jest fer the time bein'."

"Very well, watch your mouth, go take a bath, and put on something more suitable than a satin ball gown. I will forgive you your improper behavior this time, but be forewarned, Peachy, that I will not excuse it again."

Why was he forgiving her for trying to help a sick animal? she wondered. It didn't make a bit of sense to her. She studied him intently, trying to understand him.

Seneca didn't care for the way she was staring at him. "And I'll thank you to cease looking at me as though I were a perfect idiot!"

"Nobody's perfect, Seneca."

Her sarcasm caught him completely off guard. A tide of fury coursed through him.

But so did a hint of amusement. A shred, but it was there all the same.

He didn't know what to do with such opposite emotions. Scowl and shout? Smile and laugh?

The devil take her for doing this to him.

He kept his expression still. "You will spend the afternoon quietly, Peachy. I am to dine with my father's advisors tonight, so you will take your meal in your rooms. However, I will expect you in my chambers at precisely nine o'clock. Do not keep me waiting."

His mask of indifference firmly in place, he spun and stormed down the steps of the tower.

Chapter 6

In an effort to get warm, Bubba buried his huge body in the mounds of hay. He couldn't see his aunt in the dark loft of the abandoned barn, but her mumbled cursing assured him she was nearby. Reaching into the pile of hay beside his face, he stroked the soft head of the bird he'd found when Orabelle wasn't looking. It had a broken wing. Bubba wished he knew how to fix it.

"I tole you, Aunt Orabelle," he said, squinting when a piece of hay poked him in the eye. "Uh ... Didn't I tell you Cousin Peachy was a princess? Are you proud I guessed right? Did I do good? Aunt Orabelle—"

"Shut up!" Orabelle yanked her cloak over her bony shoulders, enraged that she had been reduced to sleeping in moldy hay. Bugs crawled on her face. From the far corner of the drafty loft, mice squeaked. Something sounded like it was clawing its way up a wall. And the smell ... Orabelle was sure she was breathing in every revolting odor in the world.

The fury she'd felt upon learning that Peachy was now the Princess of Aventine had not abated. It had increased and joined with a hatred so bitter Orabelle could taste their rancid flavors. She'd thought about returning to North Carolina and simply taking over the McGee cabin and gold-filled creek, but who was to know whether or not the girl would ever return to her land? It was entirely possible that she would one day want to visit those ignorant neighbors of hers, the Mackintoshes.

No, the girl had to die. There was no other way.

"Aunt Orabelle?"

Orabelle sighed impatiently. "What is it now?"

"What about that prince Cousin Peachy's married to?"

"What *about* him!"

Bubba continued to stroke his bird, hoping real hard it wouldn't chirp loudly enough for Orabelle to hear. She didn't like animals. "That prince, Aunt Orabelle. When Cousin Peachy's dead— Uh ... maybe he'll want her golden crick. We gonna kill him, too?"

Orabelle swiped at the bugs on her face, pondering Bubba's comments. The prince wouldn't get the land even if he wanted it, which was highly doubtful. Duff McGee's will was ironclad. In it, he'd expressed in no uncertain terms that only blood relatives would inherit. *Ever.*

"Aunt Orabelle, I got a secret. A big secret. I—"

"For God's sake, shut up and go to sleep!"

Bubba didn't want to go to sleep. He'd just thought of a real smart idea. "Aunt Orabelle? Y'know what I was thinkin'? Uh ... Now that Cousin Peachy's the princess, maybe she don't want the golden crick no more. She lives in a castle, and she prob'ly has some princess gold. If I lived in a castle and had some princess gold, I wouldn't want no cabin or no muddy crick. Y'know what I'm gonna do tomorrow? I'm gonna go to the castle and knock on the door. When Cousin Peachy answers it, I'm gonna ask her straight out if we can have the cabin and the golden crick. I'm—"

"Idiot!" Orabelle yelled, her shout causing the mice to squeak more loudly. "She's got riches here *and* riches in North Carolina!"

"So?"

"Bubba, who in their right mind wouldn't want it all? Why would *anyone* willfully give up a speck of wealth?"

Bubba took a moment to try to comprehend his aunt's logic. "*I* would, Aunt Orabelle. If I already had a lot of gold, I wouldn't want no more."

"That's because you're stupid, Bubba. Imagine someone not wanting as much gold as they could have! You are the dumbest creature in the world. And you have bothered me so much tonight that you aren't having any breakfast in the morning. You can go hungry, Bubba."

He started crying.

She heard him sniffling, but didn't care one iota. Instead, she turned her thoughts back to Peachy's death. The killing would be more difficult now since the bitch would probably be surrounded by armed guards at all times. But it wouldn't be impossible.

After all, accidents happened.

The girl could trip and break her neck. She could fall into the river and drown, or get in the way of a hunter's bullet. Why, she could smother beneath her pillow, or choke to death on a chicken bone!

She might even eat poisoned food.

Death could strike at any given time. It was a diverting challenge to think of all the ways it could happen.

Orabelle's imagination began to soar.

Peachy awakened with a start. The gentle light of dawn had chased away the night shadows, casting a strawberry-pink hue over the furnishings. Thurlow Wadsworth McGee sat on the windowsill, chattering softly.

Peachy sat up, her satin sheets falling away from her bare breasts. Disoriented, she rubbed her numb feet and looked around the room. After only a few seconds, her memory came back to her.

These were her chambers, she recalled. She was married to Seneca.

She yawned deeply and felt the numbness in her feet go away. They began to prickle uncomfortably. Frowning, she massaged them harder.

But her hands soon stilled. Her heart skipped beats.

She'd forgotten where she was. And her feet were tingling, as if a thousand pins were stuck in them.

Lapse of memory and tingling feet. Two of the tipinosis symptoms Dr. Greely had told her to watch for.

Pain bolted through her. She gritted her teeth and swallowed the sob that rose in her throat. "I'm dyin' more," she whispered, bowing her head. "Sweet Lord o' mercy, I ain't got long now." Tears filled her eyes; she began to rock from side to side.

A very long while passed before her sorrow began to lift. Thoughts of the ruby-throated hummingbird omen filled her mind, reminding her that her last days were supposed to be happy ones. "I ain't gonna spend my last days a-cryin'," she told her squirrel.

Forcing the vow deeply into her heart, she finally felt a hint of peace whisper through her.

But the sight of a yellow velvet dressing robe at the end of her bed dispelled her tranquility. The robe, she thought. She'd been going to wear it for her visit with Seneca last night.

She shook her head in her hands. "God Almighty, Thurlow Wadsworth McGee, I was s'posed to meet him at nine! I laid down fer jest a jag, and I must've gone to sleep. Dang it, I sleeped clear through the night!"

Seneca was going to be riled. She hadn't meant to fall asleep, but he'd give her a lecture anyway. He'd go on and on about obedience and how she never gave him hers. He'd yell, she'd holler right back, and the fight would cost her several thousand years in Purgatory. It was a sin to do battle with your husband. It was a sin to war with your wife, too, but Seneca never appeared worried about his own Purgatorial stay. Just because he wasn't Catholic didn't mean he wouldn't go there. She'd pray for his sin-blackened soul while she prayed for her own.

"But fer right now, boy," she said, hopping out of bed, "I'd best do somethin' that'll merry him up some. That way when he commences a-hollerin' at me later on, I can tell him about the good things I done today. Yeah, that's the plan, little feller."

Swiping the red curls away from her eyes, she crossed to her desk and looked down at the list of activities Seneca had demanded she include in her life as a princess. She'd drawn up the list yesterday afternoon so she wouldn't forget anything he'd told her. "Sew," she read to her squirrel. "Paint, dress purty, write letters, play music, visit the noble folks, give parties and dances—"

She smiled. "Visit. Well, good Lord, I *love* to go a-visitin'! This ladylike stuff ain't gonna be hard a'tall, boy. And when I git back from a-callin', Seneca'll be so proud that I done what he tole me to do."

Thrilled with her plan of salvation, Peachy entered her spacious closet. She spied many beautiful gowns, but they all had a multitude of buttons. There was no earthly way she could get into one of them without Ketty's or Nydia's help. And the maids worked hard all the time. No, she wouldn't call them right now. She'd let them sleep.

Unable to find anything in her closet, she began rummaging through her dresser and withdrew a beautifully feminine gown of champagne silk. The cuffs were of frothy ivory lace, and tiny seed pearls formed a lovely border around the scooped neckline.

"Well, looky here, Thurlow Wadsworth McGee!" she exclaimed, holding the gown up for the squirrel to see. "This here dress ain't got one dang-blasted button on it! It's the slip-over-yore-head kind, and it's so *purty!* Seneca's gonna be happier'n a hog with his head in a slop bucket when he sees me today. He— Lord o' mercy, boy, he might even give me my *crown!"*

The head groom led the prince's huge black stallion, Damascus, out of the immaculate barn. Careful to keep his eyes glued to the princess's face, he stopped before her. Her clothing was certainly none of his business, but in all his years of working for the royal family, he'd never seen a gown quite like the one Princess Peachy was wearing this morning. For that matter, he'd never known a gentlewoman who rose so early. It wasn't even seven o'clock yet.

"Much obliged, Weeb," Peachy said sweetly, admiring the gorgeous stallion. "Where can I hang my bag?"

Weeb lifted a flap on the saddle and tied the strap of the bag to a metal loop. Just as he finished, the bag moved. Weeb let out a startled shriek.

"Ain't no need to be afeared." She opened the bag. "It's jest ole Thurlow Wadsworth McGee in there, see? He ain't never rid no horse afore, so I thought I'd take him fer a ride this mornin'." She patted her squirrel's soft head and closed the bag again. "Will y'hep me up, Weeb?"

Weeb shrank back. He wasn't *about* to touch the prince's bride. Rumor had it that the prince hadn't touched her yet, either, and though Weeb cared naught for gossip, he still wasn't going to lay his hands anywhere on the virgin princess. "There's a mounting block there, Your Highness." He pointed to a smooth block of sparkling white granite.

As Peachy led Damascus to the block, the horse tried to bite her. He didn't get his teeth around her skin, but he managed to tear a bit of lace off the cuff of her gown.

"Shame on you!" Peachy yelled at the horse, snatching the lace out of his mouth. "That's one o' the meanest things I ever seed anybody do!"

Weeb paled. "Please, Your Highness. Let me select a gentler mount. That devil is—"

"Go soak a rag in vinegar, Weeb. Don't wring the rag. Bring it to me real wet, hear?"

He hurried to obey and returned with the vinegar-soaked rag. Peachy found a long stick and wrapped the smelly cloth around it. "My paw had him a mule once," she told Weeb. "That mule had him a reservation in hell the day he was borned. He was the bitin'est thing who ever walked this earth. Bitin'er even than Damascus. Anyhow, Paw had him a trick he used on that ole mule, and it worked. I aim to see iffen it'll work on Damascus." Holding the stick tightly, she stepped closer to the wild-eyed stallion, near enough for him to bite her again.

He tried, but Peachy made sure he got a mouthful of vinegar instead. Damascus let go of the rag-wrapped stick, coughing, snorting, and shuddering.

Peachy shook the stick at him. "Now, don't you go a-bitin' me again. Jest to make shore and sartin you don't, I'm a-keepin' this here stick with me, hear?" She led him back to the block. It wasn't easy to mount, what with having to deal with her long silk skirts and velvet cape, but she managed.

When Damascus began to throw his head and prance sideways, Weeb took hold of the bridle, trying desperately not to look at his princess's exposed legs. She rode astride, like a man, her silken skirts bunched up around her thighs. And though she wore a long, fur-trimmed cape, she was sitting on most of it.

Settled on the horse, Peachy wished she'd thought to wear her buckskin breeches beneath her gown. She tugged her skirts down and tucked the delicate fabric around her legs to keep them from becoming chafed by the saddle.

Watching her touch her legs, Weeb feared his heart would fail him at any moment. He noticed that Damascus didn't like her fidgeting much either. The horse was giving snorts of warning. "I beg Your Highness once again not to take Damascus. The prince himself must use all his expertise to manage the stallion. Let me saddle a tamer mount."

Peachy patted Damascus's silken mane. "I don't want a tame mount, Weeb. I want a fast one, and you said Damascus was the fastest horse in the kingdom."

Weeb sorely regretted giving his princess that bit of information. But when she'd asked which horse was the swiftest, he'd had no idea she planned on riding it! "The prince will have my head if anything happens to Your Highness."

Peachy thought for a moment. "He cain't fault you over somethin' I maked you do, Weeb, so don't you go a-frettin' that he's gonna chop offen yore head or nothin' like that, hear? 'Sides that, iffen you hadn't saddled up Damascus fer me, I'd jest've done it mysef. Now, will y'answer a few questions fer me?"

He gave a weak nod.

Peachy gifted him with another brilliant smile. "When I want Damascus to go, what do I do?"

Weeb almost swallowed his tongue. "Ride . . . Your—Your Highness can't ride?"

"Well, shore I can ride, Weeb. Jest tell me how."

Weeb's knees buckled, forcing him to lean on the mounting block for support.

"Iffen you don't tell me, I'll jest try a jag o' ever'thing," Peachy warned merrily.

Weeb realized that no amount of pleading was going to get the new princess off the black devil of a horse. And even if he awakened one of the stable lads and sent the boy to the palace with a message for Prince Seneca, the princess would surely be gone before help arrived.

The only thing he could do now was give her a verbal riding lesson. "Your Highness should p-press in with her heels, keep her elbows by her sides, and not give Damascus too much head. K-keep the reins tight, but not too tight. Stay on by squeezing him with madam's . . . *legs*." He blushed scarlet, embarrassed deeply that he'd had to mention a body part to his princess. "Keep madam's b-back straight, and move madam's— Er ..." God, he couldn't say it.

"Move my what, Weeb?"

He wanted to die. But he didn't want the princess to do the same, so he forced himself to explain. "Her Highness must move her ... *lower region* to the rhythm of his gait."

"My lower region? Oh, y'mean my bottom? Move my bottom along with the way Damascus moves his body?"

"Yes," Weeb whispered, utterly mortified.

"And what about when I want him to turn?"

Hands shaking, he showed her the correct way to hold the reins. "Madam must pull the left rein when she wants to go left, and the right when she wants to go right. Damascus will feel the pull in his mouth and respond accordingly, but only if Your Highness goes gently with him. He will react violently if—"

Peachy laughed. "Weeb, there ain't a animule in the whole dang world that I cain't unnerstand. Me and Damascus is gonna git along jest fine. All's we need is some time together to talk."

"T-talk?"

"Yeah, him and me's gonna do us some a-geein' and a-hawin'. After that, we'll be friends. You'll see."

When she pulled on the reins, Weeb let go of them. He watched her urge the stallion toward the meadows. "But what will I tell the prince when he asks me where Your Royal Highness went?" he shouted desperately.

Peachy looked over her shoulder. "Tell him I went a-callin' on my neighbors. He'll be real glad, Weeb, so don't go a-worryin' about nothin'."

Worried did not begin to describe how Weeb felt. His forehead broke out with beads of sweat when he saw Damascus begin to trot. Within moments, the stallion quickened his pace into a fast canter, then a full gallop, his polished hooves beating up earth in great clods that flew all around his royal rider. Numb terror slid through Weeb's frame.

His last thought before he fainted was that he'd forgotten to tell Princess Peachy how to stop.

* * *

As Damascus sped through the meadows, Peachy savored the feeling of the cool wind as it whipped through her hair. The air smelled of sea, and grass, and morning sunshine, and good, fertile soil.

Laughing, she leaned low over the stallion's neck. Weeb hadn't told her to do such a thing, but it felt right. She'd also figured out how to slow the steed down. She'd discovered the secret accidentally when she'd been about to fall off. In the hope that pulling on the reins would help her find her balance, she'd tugged on them hard. Amazingly enough, her action had slowed Damascus from a gallop to a canter, to a trot, and finally to a walk, whereupon she'd commenced to tell him stories that he'd liked very much. Just as she'd predicted, she and the stallion had become friends.

Now she had a visit with Agusta Sherringham in mind. Thoughts of the thin, unhappy woman continued to plague her. Agusta was the first noblewoman she hoped to befriend.

She had no idea where the Sherringham estate was located, but hoped to encounter someone who could give her directions. The countryside was dotted with small villages; she'd seen many of them while atop a high hill a short while ago. They were scattered along the winding path that led to the palace. It wasn't long before she came to one such village.

Shock hit her so unexpectedly it almost knocked her out of the saddle. The hovels were barely fit for animals, much less human beings. Some of them were little more than shacks made of sticks and wads of straw. God Almighty, she'd had no idea the people lived like this!

Her dismay thickened into anger. She began to understand why Tivon hated the king. It was apparent that the sovereign did little to ease the hardships of his people. And what of Seneca? she wondered hotly. Surely he could do something about the poverty. Why hadn't he?

"Mornin'! Anybody here?"

Her shout disturbed one scraggly rooster, but there was no other sign of life in the village. Baffled, Peachy sent Damascus cantering down the curving road again. The next village she came to was as dilapidated as the first one and equally deserted. So was the third.

She couldn't understand where all the people were. Thoroughly confused, she kept Damascus on the path and was relieved when she finally spotted a young boy and girl watching over a huge flock of sheep. She waved to the children.

The girl waved back. "It's her! Gervase, it's Princess Peachy!"

Peachy watched the girl come running. After a moment, she recognized her to be Marlie, the girl she'd met by the river the morning after having arrived in Aventine.

"Your Highness!" Marlie squealed.

"Keerful, Marlie," Peachy said, tightening her hold on the reins. "This here ridin' critter's kin to a rattler on his paw's side and a black widder spider on his maw's. And a-seein' as how you ain't tole him no stories, he prob'ly won't take too kindly to you. Don't git too close, hear?"

Marlie took a step away from the huge stallion. "Will you be having lunch in the meadow with the prince and the king today?"

Peachy smiled down at the friendly girl. "Not today, Marlie, but soon. Real soon. Who's yore friend?"

Marlie turned to her companion, a boy of twelve. "This is my cousin, Gervase."

Peachy nodded at the boy, "Who's yore furry friend?"

Marlie held up the tiny calico kitten. "This is Rainbow. I don't usually take her out with me, but she's sick and I didn't want her to be alone."

"Lemme see her." Marlie handed her the kitten, and it took Peachy only a few seconds to make a diagnosis. "She's wormy. Ain't nothin' serious. Bring her to the palace and I'll fix her up fer you."

"Are you a doctor?"

Peachy grinned again. "I'm a yarb doctor. I used to have a animule hospital back home."

Marlie was awed. "My big brother, Mintor, has a sick dog. And my friend, Yola, has a pig who won't eat. Do you have an animal hospital in the castle?"

Peachy considered the dusty tower room. "Um . . . Yeah, I got one. Bring Rainbow, the sick dog, the dwindlin' pig, and whatever other ailish animule that needs a-tendin'.'"

"Oh, thank you!"

Peachy nodded and looked out over the meadow, noticing a few of the sheep wandering away from the flock. "Y'all outen here all by yoresefs? Where's yore folks?"

"They're in the paschal fields," Marlie replied. "We watch the sheep while they tend the crops. But sometimes we don't do very well. I lost a lamb yesterday. I looked all over for her, but I never found her. When my father came home from the fields, he was very upset. I thought he was upset with *me*, but he said it wasn't my fault."

" 'Course it weren't yore fault, Marlie," Peachy cooed. "A-takin' keer o' a big flock o' sheep ain't no easy task fer nobody, 'specially a little'un like you."

Marlie smiled. "That's why Gervase is with me today. Last night our parents decided to combine our flocks so Gervase and I could watch them together. Papa said that two shepherds are better than one. Papa misses being with the sheep, though. He's been very sad."

Gervase elbowed Marlie and shot her a look of warning.

Peachy didn't miss the gesture. "Got a secret, Gervase?"

He shook his head and stared at the ground.

Marlie pulled at one of her long braids. "We're not supposed to speak of how we feel about the paschal fields. Our parents hate working in them, but they don't want to get in trouble, so they don't say anything."

"Trouble?" Peachy repeated. "Who'd git 'em in trouble? And iffen they ain't much fer a-workin' in the fields, why do they do it? 'Pears to me that iffen they're shepherds, they orter be outen here with the sheep."

When neither child answered her, Peachy realized something was wrong. Very wrong. "Marlie? I'd be much obliged iffen you'd answer me, darlin'. I swear on God and His Holy Maw that I won't git yore folks in trouble."

Marlie's hesitation began to fade when she heard her princess's vow and saw her warm, caring smile. "The king makes a lot of money sending the paschal flowers in sailing ships. That's why he ordered us to plant big fields of paschal. Somebody on the other side of the sea buys a lot of it. But Papa said that while His Majesty gets richer and richer, we get—"

"Marlie!" Gervase whispered.

Marlie quieted immediately.

Not wanting to upset the children any further, Peachy decided to stop prying. She wasn't nearly finished with the matter, however, and intended to understand the whole of it as soon as possible. "I'm a-gittin' sorter tired o' jawin' about fields and flowers, y'all," she fibbed, hoping her little white lie would relieve the children's worry and not get her too much time in Purgatory. "What I really need to know is where the Sherrin'ham house is."

Gervase relaxed visibly. He pointed to a small knoll in the near distance. "It's right over that hill, Your Highness. I deliver kindling to the house sometimes."

Peachy bid the children a good day and set off toward the hill. As she neared it, she passed a man and a woman who were walking along the path. "Mighty fine mornin', ain't it, y'all?" she called to them. Smiling, she waved and continued on her way.

Orabelle stared after the black stallion. "Y'all," she whispered, realizing the word was not one common to Aventine. "She said *y'all*. She had red hair and wore a velvet cape. Rode a fancy horse, too."

"Uh . . . fancy horse?" Bubba repeated, rubbing his empty stomach. "Aunt Orabelle, please lemme have somethin' to eat. I'm hungry, Aunt Orabelle. Can I have some—"

"She'll be back," Orabelle murmured. "This is the only road that leads to the castle."

She withdrew a pistol from her bag and looked up at Bubba. The boy was brainless, but he knew how to shoot a gun. It was a good thing, too. The gun held only one bullet. "Yes, you do look hungry, Bubba," she told him, forcing compassion into her crackly voice. "How would you like a tall stack of hotcakes with honey, some fat sausages, and a big glass of cold milk?"

Bubba drooled. "Y'know where we can git that breakfast, Aunt Orabelle? Oh . . . did you go to the market while I was still sleepin'?" He slipped his hand into his pocket and rubbed his hurt bird.

"Oh, yes, I did, Bubba. And I bought all those things for your breakfast. But before I make it for you, you have to do me a little favor. Will you?"

Bubba nodded and jumped up and down in the sand.

Smiling, Orabelle placed the pistol in his huge hand.

His stomach growling loudly, Bubba listened attentively to her instructions.

Lamorna, the Sherringham cook, and Rula, the housekeeper, stood in front of the kitchen wall that was covered with hanging pots and pans. They'd been ordered not to carry on with their work right now. Overcome with bewilderment and disbelief, they watched the issuer of those orders.

Dressed in the most shocking manner the servants had ever seen, her Royal Highness, Princess Peachy, stood before the huge stove across the room. A gray squirrel on her shoulder, she was busy making breakfast for Lord and Lady Sherringham, who were both still abed and therefore oblivious to the fact that the newest member of the royal family was preparing their morning meal.

Rula and Lamorna had never witnessed such an outrageous thing in all their lives.

Blithely unaware of the servants' consternation, Peachy placed the fried ham on a silver platter. "What sorter vittles do y'usually make fer Agusta, Lamorna?"

Wringing her hands in her apron, Lamorna glanced at Rula. "I— She— Lord Sherringham insists that she— That is to say, he's very careful about what she—"

"For breakfast Lady Sherringham has a small bowl of fruit and a cup of tea," Rula explained, patting Lamorna's trembling shoulder. "Her midday meal is a clear broth and water. Teatime consists only of tea and no food. Her last meal of the day is usually more fruit and a bit of meat."

Peachy was stunned. "And what does ole Veston eat?"

Lamorna cast another worried glance at Rula. "His lordship is a big eater, ma'am. He consumes four full meals a day and enjoys a hearty snack before retiring."

Peachy remembered Veston's thin lips, the sure sign of

inborn meanness. "He eats all that, huh? There his wife is, so skinny she prob'ly has to run around in a rain shower to git wet, and there he is, so big he could model fer a gawdang shipbuilder!"

Pondering the situation, she decided that what Veston and Agusta needed was some advice. After all, Seneca himself had told her that giving counsel to the nobility was the ladylike thing for a princess to do. Lord o' mercy, she'd certainly found a lot of problems to solve since leaving the palace this morning.

She took off her apron and crossed to the huge chopping table, upon which were spread plates of all the food she'd cooked. "Well, here it all is. A mess o' scrambled eggs, and bacon biscuits bigger'n cat heads. Agusta'll need both hands to hold 'em. Fried ham, corn puddin', and little gingerbreads with raisins in 'em. I'll serve it all up with a bottle o' that French likker called champagne and a smidgeon o' them fish eggs called caviar. That'll make the breakferst more elegant, y'see, and Seneca says I gotta commence a-bein' real fancy-like. Will y'fetch me some French likker and caviar, please, Lamorna?"

Lamorna hastened to obey.

"Your Highness," Rula said, eyeing the meal, "it looks simply delicious. But— Lord Sherringham . . . He prefers beef steak, creamed potatoes, and freshly baked bread for breakfast. He doesn't care for eggs."

"Yeah? Well, ain't that jest the most pitiful pity? Look, Rula, the man's already big enough to go bear huntin' with nothin' but a stick, and he don't need no huge breakferst. I'm a-givin' him Agusta's fruit plate."

Ignoring Rula's soft gasp of incredulity, she quickly prepared two bowls of fresh fruit, one for Veston and one for Thurlow Wadsworth McGee. By the time she finished, Lamorna had returned with the champagne and caviar.

Rula hurried to the door. "I'll go awaken them now. They'll need time to dress before coming downstairs."

"Naw, let 'em rest. I'll carry their breakferst up."

Rula's knees knocked. "But Your Highness, Lord and Lady Sherringham— They . . . Well . . . They're in the same room, ma'am." She blushed deeply.

"Well, that's all right, Rula," Peachy said, picking up

the heavy tray and balancing it atop her head. "I'll serve 'em in bed. A-eatin' betwixt the sheets is a real life-o'-luxury thing to do, and me a-totin' breakferst up fer 'em's real nice. Seneca'll be powerful happy that I'm a-bein' so neighborly. Oh, and won't ole Veston and Agusta be surprised?"

Seneca stormed through the bright morning sunshine that pooled on the floor of his office. He arrived at the window and snatched at the gold tassels that held back the white velvet curtains.

Peachy hadn't come to his rooms last night. While he'd waited for her, her maids had come to tell him she'd fallen fast asleep at around eight, but that knowledge hadn't lessened his desperate urge to be with her. He'd gone to bed angry and disappointed, and his dark mood had kept him awake for hours.

His temperament was even more foul now. Not five minutes ago, Ketty and Nydia had come to him with another bit of infuriating news. Peachy was nowhere to be found. According to the maids, she hadn't been in her rooms when they'd arrived to assist her with her morning toilette at seven.

Seneca knew Peachy was an early riser, but the fact that she'd been gone before seven proved that she had left her chambers before dawn! That alone told him that whatever it was she was doing was going to enrage him.

"Your Highness?"

He turned and saw Nydia. The maid's hands were clasped so tightly her fingers were as white as her apron. A shred of foreboding crept through her. "Did you find her?"

"No, sir. But the head groom— He— He's come to see Your Highness."

"Weeb? Whatever for?"

Nydia hated to tattle on her mistress, but fear for Peachy's safety induced her to do so. "He— He says he was with the princess early this morning."

Seneca's foreboding deepened. "Bring him."

In only moments, Weeb shuffled into the office. He kept his gaze riveted to the stark white carpet. "Your Highness, the princess— The devil b-bit the princess!" he stammered, wiping his sweaty palms on his pant legs.

"Weeb, get hold of yourself and tell me what you know."

Weeb nodded. "The princess— Madam gave him vinegar. Had me s-soak a rag. I tried to tell Her Highness how to ride, but— It was the fastest riding lesson I ever gave! I didn't touch the princess, sir. Honest to God, I didn't. Madam mounted unassisted. I begged madam to take a tamer mount, but— I didn't know the princess couldn't ride. Madam didn't tell me in time!"

"She can't ride? And she's out riding?"

"Yes, sir, and I f-forgot to teach the princess how to stop. Fainted ... I fainted with fear, Your Highness, or else I'd have c-come with the news sooner."

Seneca had to force himself not to shake the hysterical man. "Where did she go?"

"V-visiting. Madam— Madam said Your Highness would be glad to know that." He looked up from the rug, anxious to see if the prince really *was* glad to know the princess was out visiting. One look at the prince's face dashed his hopes. "Her Highness— Madam took Damascus, sir."

"*What?*" Seneca pushed his fingers through his hair several times. Peachy couldn't ride, and she was on Damascus, who was half horse, half demon!

As his worry mounted, his imagination took wing. What if the monster threw her? Even now she might be lying on the ground somewhere. Cold. Maybe bleeding. Frightened.

And the marshes were infested with adders.

And, God, what about the dense forests? Those thickets sheltered not only wild animals but sometimes foreign criminals as well. And what of the peasant men? Peachy had never ventured far from the palace grounds, and it was possible that the workmen wouldn't recognize her as their princess. Her breathtaking beauty would entice them, and they'd take full advantage of the fact that she was alone.

The thought of his bride in the hands of lust-crazed men or murderous villains sent black waves of fear and anger rolling through him.

Peachy. His heart somersaulted as he invisioned her.

Copper hair. Pale jade eyes. Magnolia skin and pink lips that tasted sweet and spoke outrageously.

I'll be yore friend, Seneca.

Something strong took hold of him, squeezing him, pulling at emotions he didn't recognize.

His body taut with tension, he raced out of his office. He met Tiblock at the end of the corridor. "I want every soldier assembled," he snapped at the servant. "And each one is to be well armed and mounted."

Tiblock was about to protest that such orders were supposed to be delivered to Medard, the captain of the guards. But one look at the rage on the prince's face sent him scurrying to obey.

Twenty minutes later Seneca mounted the white stallion he'd planned to give to Peachy and led Aventine's men-at-arms through the palace gates. Each soldier was ready to confront any danger that threatened the safety of the princess.

But no man was more prepared than Prince Seneca. Not only would he defend his bride . . .

He vowed to kill any man who dared to touch her.

Her right hand holding the breakfast tray steady on her head, Peachy knocked on the bedroom door with her left.

"Leave us!" an angry voice shouted from inside.

Peachy knew it was thin-lipped Veston who had yelled. "It's me! Princess Peachy! I got yore breakferst!"

She heard frantic scrambling from within the room. "Y'all decent yet?" she asked after a few moments. "Iffen y'ain't, you'd best hide, on account o' I cain't hold this heavy tray no longer."

She opened the door and walked inside, the tray still balanced on her head. Veston and Agusta were dressed in long robes and standing by the bed. "Well, I was gonna serve y'all in bed, but a-seein' as how you ain't in it no more, I'll serve it over here." She took the tray to a table by a big window and opened the curtains. Streams of warm sunshine lit up the chill and gloomy room. "Y'all come on over here and eat afore it gits cold. It ain't as good as Maw could o' maked, but I reckon it'll fill empty holes."

Veston stared at her gown, his eyes widening to such an extent that they began to sting. Struggling to keep his composure, he took his wife's hand and kept her close to his side. "Your Highness, this is most embarrassing. Tell me, does the prince know of this visit?"

Scrutinizing him, Peachy felt her temper rising. Though he'd spoken in a soft tone of voice, his real feelings were reflected in his small gray eyes. The man was about to explode with fury.

She didn't care. Agusta was the one she was worried about. God Almighty, the poor woman looked worse now than she had at the wedding. Her brown hair hung in lifeless strings around her gaunt face and thin shoulders. And she was so white. Even her lips were pale.

Peachy glared at Veston. "As a matter o' fact, Seneca's who tole me to come a'callin'. Iffen y'got a problem with that, you'd best take it up with him. Or I could tell him when I git home. What's yore druthers?"

Agusta bent her head and pretended to tighten the sash on her robe. Her lips trembled with a smile.

"Well, Veston?" Peachy pressed.

Veston shifted his huge frame from foot to foot. He most assuredly *did* have a problem with the princess bursting into his bedroom. But he hadn't forgotten the thinly veiled warning the prince had given at the wedding feast. It wouldn't be long before Seneca claimed the throne, and Veston had no desire to jeopardize his chances of winning the favor of the future king. Especially since he desired a position as one of Seneca's advisors.

He didn't know what else to do but make the best of the awkward situation. With a false smile on his lips, he led Agusta to the table, stopping when he saw a gray animal perched upon it. The creature was gnawing a bit of apple.

"This here's Thurlow Wadsworth McGee," Peachy explained, rubbing the squirrel's back. "He ain't never rid no horse, so I brung him along."

Veston curbed the urge to frown in distaste. He seated Agusta and placed one of the fruit plates in front of her.

Peachy took it away. "This ain't hers, Veston. It's yores." She put the plate back on the table.

"But— But she always has fruit for breakfast, Your Highness. She enjoys it. Isn't that right, Agusta?"

Agusta nodded meekly.

Smiling triumphantly, Veston pulled out another chair. "Please, join us, Your Highness."

Brow raised high, Peachy sat down.

So did Veston. "Here's your fruit, Agusta." He gave the fruit plate back to his wife.

"I done tole you, Veston, that the fruit ain't fer her. This ain't no formal dinner party, so Agusta can eat as much as she can hold. Seneca says the noblewomen should imitate me. The first thing I want Agusta to copy is my appetite. Seneca also tole me that iffen I request somethin', yore gonna see my request as a command. I'm *a-requestin'* that Agusta eat what I want her to eat."

Veston dared to pretend he hadn't heard her comments. He helped himself to generous portions of the fried ham, bacon biscuits, corn pudding, and gingerbreads. He also dipped out several heaping spoonfuls of caviar and poured himself a glass of champagne. "I don't care for eggs, but the rest of the meal looks delicious. And the champagne lends a very festive air."

"Festive?" Peachy echoed, her eyes narrowing to mere slits. "Y'mean like in *celebration?*"

"Splendid idea!" Veston raised his glass, still battling his rage over the stupid girl's ill manners. "Yes, let's celebrate, shall we? To Your Highness, with much gratitude for the breakfast and the visit. Oh, and be sure to tell the prince how much we appreciate the call."

Peachy paid him no mind. Instead, she watched how Agusta's hand shook as the girl lifted her glass for the toast. "I ain't in no mood fer a-makin' merry, Veston." Peachy took his overloaded plate away from him, added eggs to it, and placed it before Agusta. "All right, Agusta, there's yore breakferst. Cram it in with ever' finger, and stomp it down with both feet. When you've done et ever' crumb, then we'll celebrate." She gave Agusta a big, reassuring smile.

Her eyes lighting up, Agusta picked up her fork.

Veston almost choked on his fury. How dare the yokel usurp his dominion over his own wife! "Agusta, my dear," he murmured, determined that she understand his will, "have I told you lately how much your delicacy pleases me?"

Agusta put her fork back down and swallowed her anger.

Peachy realized Veston had warned his wife not to eat. Sudden comprehension came to her. "It ain't that Agusta don't got no appetite, is it, Veston? It's that you don't *let* her eat! She's so skinny she has to stand twice to make a shadder, but that's how you like her, ain't it?"

Veston was hard-pressed to keep his violent anger at bay. "Agusta is a proper lady, Your Highness," he said, still smiling his fake smile. "She is well aware of the importance of pleasing her husband. That is, after all, a wife's duty, is it not?" He gloated inwardly, recalling the gossip he'd heard concerning the fact that the princess had refused to allow the prince to consummate the royal marriage.

Peachy noted the taunting gleam in his eyes. "And yore real big on proper stuff, huh, Veston? A-puttin' on them airs and a-struttin' yore okra like y'ain't second to none. But did y'know that dirt shows up best on the cleanest cotton?"

"I— Pardon me?"

"Y'can load gold on a mule, but it's still a mule."

He didn't care at all for what she was insinuating, and promptly returned to the subject of his wife. "I— It's true that I do not want Agusta to be — Eh . . . shall we say *too round?* I prefer fragile women. Agusta has been my wife for only six short months, but after only a few weeks of my tutoring, she demonstrated unmitigated obedience to me. Of course, I'm certain Your Highness is already aware of the value of a submissive, rule-abiding wife."

"The value?" Peachy repeated, her voice shaking with anger. "Like in a valuable horse? A valuable dog? Any sorter valuable piece o' goods?"

Veston shrugged and reached for the full plate of food.

Peachy could control her temper no longer. "Why, you high-headed, uppity as a mountain goat, mean ole *varmint!*

I knowed them thin lips o' yores meaned you was cruel! Yore so fat that iffen you falled down, you'd rock yorsef to sleep a-tryin' to git up, and yet yore a-starvin' poor Agusta to death!"

"I—"

"Let me tell you somethin', Veston. I don't keer a dang what sorter women you like! Iffen Agusta don't commence a-eatin' more, she ain't gonna last any longer'n a paper shirt in a bear fight, hear? And iffen you think I'm gonna stand still whilst you kill her, then yore so wood-brained that I reckon ever' time you scratch yore head you git splinters in yore fingers! Now git outen this room!" She balled up her linen napkin and flung it at him, hitting him square in the face.

Veston stood. The king would hear of this, he swore vehemently. If the prince couldn't handle the barbaric princess, then maybe His Majesty could! Veston would word his message carefully so as not to anger the prince, but the palace *would* hear of the princess's shocking conduct. Indeed, he would compose and send the missive immediately!

Struggling to keep from scowling, he patted Agusta's frail hand. "I'm to meet Lord Ritting Tavens shortly, my dear. He and I will be hunting for a few hours this morning. While I am gone I shall keep the image of your fragile beauty in my mind." He gave her a meaningful look, willing her to understand his unspoken demand.

Peachy rolled her eyes.

"Good day, Your Highness." Shuddering with deep rage, Veston stalked out of the room.

When he was gone, Peachy handed Agusta a fork. "Eat."

Agusta ate a tiny bite of egg.

"More."

Agusta consumed a goodly amount of corn pudding.

"Smile."

Agusta smiled.

"Do y'ever talk, Gussie?"

Warmth streamed through Agusta's thin frame. "My father called me Gussie. He was the only one who did."

"Yeah? My paw called me Peachers. Do y'mind iffen I call you Gussie? I'll quit iffen you want me to."

Agusta didn't have to think before answering. "I don't mind **at all**, Your Highness."

"Call me Peachy. Or Peachers. Or Peach. Or . . . Well, I was gonna say Pea, but that ain't the purtiest nickname I ever heared."

Agusta laughed, the sound of her own laughter sounding very strange to her.

Peachy raised her glass of champagne and touched it to Agusta's. "Friends?"

Agusta's smile broadened. "Friends."

"Eat."

Agusta devoured everything Peachy had made for her.

Peachy's temper was still simmering as she rode back to the palace. "Dang this country, Damascus," she flared, directing the trotting stallion down the path that led to the castle. "The young'uns have to tend the sheep whilst their folks grow pink flowers. The king gits richer, and the people git poorer. The menfolks eat whatever and whenever the hell they want, and the women ain't barely allowed to eat a'tall. I ain't never in my life seed the beat of it, and I'm a-tellin' you right here and now in this day and time that I aim to make rimptions o' changes."

She would speak to Seneca. If he dared to lecture her, she'd ignore him and then talk to the king. That the king hated her was obvious; he'd never spoken one measly word to her and went out of his way to avoid her. But she'd confront him even if it meant sneaking into his rooms in the middle of the night and holding the discussion on his bed! No matter what she had to do, she wasn't going to let either of the royal varmints keep her from correcting the wrongs she'd been made aware of this morning. Good manners were high on the list of their priorities, but they both needed to learn what *real* manners were! That thought uppermost in her mind, she urged Damascus into a canter.

Just as he'd quickened his pace, an explosion of gunfire shattered the quiet morning. It happened so quickly Peachy had no time to understand, no time to scream.

She simply crashed to the ground.

Chapter 7

A s the white stallion rounded the bend in the dirt road, Seneca heard the unmistakable crack of gunfire. Only moments later, he spotted Damascus racing toward him.

The horse had no rider on his back.

Seneca's stomach constricted into a tight knot. Lying low over his mount's thick neck, he sent the horse into a ground-battering gallop, Aventine's soldiers following closely behind. After swerving around another curve, Seneca saw her just ahead.

Peachy lay in the road unmoving.

He was unprepared for what the sight did to him. In a mere second, he felt himself lose all control.

"God, no." He didn't even wait until his horse had reached a full stop before jumping off his back.

He landed on his feet, then knelt beside Peachy. Vaguely, he heard Medard, the captain of the guards, giving orders for the area to be thoroughly searched, but he could concentrate on nothing but her, his bride.

Peachy. He couldn't tell if she was breathing. Deeper fear raged through him. He couldn't think rationally. Memories trickled through his apprehension.

Dried up creeks, hummingbirds, and lilac leaves. Swapping spit and doctoring ailing rams. Purgatory and breasts that had names. "Peas in feather beds," he whispered soundlessly.

Afore I die yore gonna git my love.

"Die?" Seneca whispered. "Peachy?" Gingerly, he placed his palm upon her cheek.

Medard knelt next to him. "Is the princess . . . all right, Your Highness?"

Seneca had no answer. As carefully as he knew how, he lifted Peachy into his arms, almost panicking when her head lolled to his shoulder. "Peachy," he murmured, his face close to hers. "Peachy." *Wake up,* he demanded silently.

She stirred. Slightly at first, then with more strength. Finally she squirmed vigorously.

Seneca was hard-pressed to keep her from wiggling back to the ground. Relief almost overcame him. "Peachy—"

"Seneca?" Blinking, she brought his image into view.

"You fell . . . off Damascus. Are— Are you hurt?" Each word was an effort to speak. He drew her closer, trying to believe she was unharmed and trying to get hold of himself.

Peachy shut her eyes and remembered the accident. "He standed up on his hind legs. I slipped right outen the saddle and slided over his back. I—"

Seneca saw her eyes widen with what could only be terror. "What is it?" he demanded.

"Oh, God, Thurlow Wadsworth McGee's in a bag on the saddle! He—"

"Damascus will return to the mews. Weeb—"

"Mews?"

"The stables. Weeb will see to the squirrel. Are you hurt?" It was all he could do not to hug her tightly to him. The knot in his stomach hadn't loosened one bit.

Relieved about her pet, Peachy moved her limbs and torso. Other than a sore bottom and a slight headache, she felt no pain. "I ain't hurt. Now, lemme git up."

Seneca remained unconvinced. "But you were unconscious."

"Yeah, well I'm awake now. 'Sides that, I think all's that happened was that I got the breath knocked outen me."

Seneca felt like ripping her clothes off and looking for injuries himself.

Peachy didn't miss the doubt in his wide blue eyes. "Lord o' mercy, Seneca, all's I done was fall offen a horse.

And I falled in this here soft sand. I ain't no liar, so iffen I say I ain't hurt, I ain't hurt, hear?"

He'd never known a woman so unconcerned about the possibility of being hurt! Most women he'd met would be in tears right now, hysterical over what might have happened. That, or they'd have fainted soon after having gained consciousness.

And what of his own panic? Even if Peachy was hurt, it was obvious that her injuries weren't serious. So why couldn't he rid himself of the cold dread that continued to pump through his veins? "But— Peachy, I heard a shot."

She sat up, pushing curls from her face. "Yeah, I heared it too, but—" She broke off, suddenly remembering not only her spill off Damascus, but memories of the entire morning as well.

Struck instantly by a bolt of fury, she grabbed Seneca's shirt. "You low-down, no-'count *varmint!* Means's what you are! So mean I reckon yore maw had to feed you with a gawdang slingshot!"

Rendered speechless by her sudden and inexplicable ire, Seneca could only stare down at her and wonder what terrible thing he'd done to deserve her wrath.

Peachy jerked out of his arms and staggered to her feet, oblivious to the nearby contingent of guards. "The people around here's so poor it wouldn't surprise me nary a jag iffen I finded outen that all's they got to eat is bread dipped in fried water! *Shameful's* what it is, and iffen you and yore paw ain't gonna do nothin' about it, I *will!*"

His gentle feelings of only moments ago fled. He stood, well aware that Medard and every other soldier could hear her. Not only were they listening, they were staring at her scandalous garb as well. Staring *through* it, he amended. His hands tightened into fists; his gaze touched every barely concealed curve of her body.

That his men were also enjoying the gorgeous sight of her turned his irritation into hammering anger. He stepped directly in front of her and jerked the edges of her cape together. "Peachy," he whispered, "now is not the time to discuss—"

"When *is* the time then?" she hollered, slapping his hands away. "Will we talk about it after the people and their sheep is all dead and buried? What the hell kind o' country would Aventine be then? All's you'd have here would be the rich folks, but I'm a-tellin' you right now, Seneca, it's the *poor* ones that keep this here island a-goin'! They're—"

"Your Highness," one of the guards said as he rode up. "We found Lord Tavens and Lord Sherringham in the forest, sir. They've been hunting."

Seneca watched the two noblemen emerge from a thick grove of sycamore and maple trees. Both held rifles.

"Your Highness," Ritting Tavens said to Seneca, bowing his head. He glanced at the princess, relieved when he saw she appeared to be unharmed, but not a little shocked by her unconventional attire. "I'm most dismayed over what has happened. Lord Sherringham and I were hunting for rabbit. We'd separated in order to cover more area, but I swear we had no idea the princess was near. I'm afraid either mine or Lord Sherringham's shots must have frightened Her Highness's mount. But since we'd parted, I cannot know which of us fired the shot that caused the accident."

"Please accept our deepest apologies," Veston added. "We take full responsibility, Your Highness." He curbed the temptation to look at the princess, for he knew full well that he would be unable to conceal his fury with her.

"Very well," Seneca said.

"Git any rabbits, Veston?" Peachy flared.

He shuffled his feet. He would be utterly humiliated if she lashed out at him in front of the prince, the soldiers, and Ritting Tavens. "Er . . . Yes, Your Highness. We have caught three. And I do believe that I will have my cook prepare the meat for Agusta."

Peachy saw right through his lie. "Yeah, I jest bet."

Seneca sensed Peachy's and Veston's anger with each other. He would interrogate Peachy about it later, but he refused to allow their hostility to continue. "You and Lord Tavens may proceed with your hunt," he told Veston. "Good day." He turned to the soldiers who'd conducted the search. "You found no one else about?"

"No, sir. Only footsteps. Lord Tavens informed us that there were two shepherd children out here as well as two peasants. Lord Tavens believes that perhaps they were as startled by the gunfire as Damascus."

"I concur, Your Highness," Medard said.

Satisfied that Peachy's fall had been, indeed, an accident, Seneca led her to the white stallion. "I'd planned to give you this horse this afternoon. I was under the impression you could ride. I've a good mind now, however, to provide you with a hobby horse."

"I rid Damascus real good. All's I had to do was tell him stories, and then him and me—"

"Be silent." Effortlessly, he lifted her into the saddle and positioned her so that she sat as a proper lady should. He then mounted behind her, his fluid motions belying his strength and expertise.

Angry as she was, Peachy tried not to notice her husband's masterful touch and muscled thighs. She attempted to ignore the way he felt against her back as well.

She failed miserably. A warm tingle flowed through her as his nearness and masculine fragrance enveloped her. Lord o' mercy, her attraction to him was growing. Becoming deeper and harder to resist. She couldn't understand it. How was it possible to still want the varmint she was so mad at? She tried to move away from him.

Seneca pulled her closer, cradling her in his arms. He remained thoroughly irritated with her, however, when he noticed her garment again. "You are wearing a nightgown," he growled into her ear, and urged the stallion into a brisk trot toward the palace. "Yesterday you wore rags, and today you wear sleeping attire. What will you do tomorrow, go naked? You've a closet full of beautiful clothes, yet you—"

"This ain't no nightgown, and quit a-holdin' me so close." Once more, she tried to wiggle out of his arms, her pulse skittering when he tightened his sensuous hold on her. "Dang it, Seneca, yore a-givin' me them hot feelin's again! Yore all hard and warm, and y'smell that . . . way. That man way that makes me want to nuzzle into yore neck."

Seneca refused to dwell on the desire her confession unleashed. He put the stallion into a canter. "This *is* a nightgown, I won't stop holding you close, and while I appreciate your yearning to nuzzle my neck, I'm afraid you will have to wait until it can be done in private. You will not dare to reproach me in front of anyone again. Shouting at me about the peasant situation while the men-at-arms were listening was an extreme breach of etiquette. It is not your place to advise me about the dilemma with the peasants, and I—"

"Dilemma?" she yelled, twisting in his arms so she could glare into his eyes. "It's more'n jest a *dilemma,* you cold hearted—"

"Keep your voice down, and do not call me names." He took the stallion from a canter into a loping gallop, hoping the pounding of the steed's hooves would drown out Peachy's loud arguing.

He couldn't wait to get back to the palace and give her a thorough dressing-down! He would stand for no more of her tosh, and if she thought for one second that he was through with her, then she was daft. Her outrageous conduct had gotten her into a very tight place indeed.

"Jest wait till we git back to the castle, Seneca!" Peachy yelled, trying to be heard over the horse's thundering hooves. "Iffen you think fer one gawdang minute I'm finished a-cussin' at you, then yore calf ain't suckin' the right cow. Yore in a powerful heap o' trouble, mister!"

He saw her lips moving. He couldn't hear her, but he suspected she was cursing him. He didn't bother to respond. What good would it do him? She'd just lash back at him. He ignored her and fell into deep thought, remembering the way she'd looking lying in the road, so still, so helpless. He could have lost her today, he mused, his stomach pitching at the possibility.

He turned his head slightly and felt her wind-blown curls caress his face. She smelled of lemon. And cream. And she felt so soft in his arms. He'd never held her for this long before. It felt so good.

He could have lost her today.

The thought weighed heavily on his mind all the way back to the palace. By the time he directed the stallion to the royal mews, his emotions were so completely unraveled he felt like shouting.

He dismounted swiftly and reached up to assist Peachy.

But she was off the stallion before he could help her. As soon as her feet hit the ground, she raced toward Damascus, whom Weeb had tied to a post. Opening the bag attached to the saddle, she withdrew a very loquacious Thurlow Wadsworth McGee.

"Your Highness!"

Peachy turned to see Tivon. The boy was so covered with white paint he looked as though he'd bathed in it. In one hand he held the paint bucket, in the other a large, dripping paintbrush. "Tivon, whatcha y'doin', darlin'?"

"I'm painting!"

Peachy noted the bright sparkle in the boy's big eyes. "And who's a-tendin' yore sheep?"

Seneca moved to take her arm. "You may talk to the lad later, Peachy," he murmured quietly. "Right now, go to your rooms and stay there. I will join you shortly."

She glared at him. "Roses is red, some trees is mossy. Let go o' my elbow and quit a-bein' *bossy.*"

As he listened to her ridiculous rhyme, a spurt of amusement leaped through his anger. So that she wouldn't see his mixed emotions, he looked at Tivon. "You have only finished painting three stall doors. I told you that you were to be completely finished before evening. If you do not succeed, I will find yet another punishment for you tomorrow. Indeed, Tivon, you will continue to be punished until I am satisfied with your work. Is that understood?"

"But can I tell the princess one more thing, sir?"

"One more, and then you will return to your work," Seneca agreed, unable to resist the hope in the boy's voice.

"Princess, my mother sent you a sweater! It's a thank-you gift for trying to save our ram. She made it herself from our own sheep's wool! It's right outside, hanging on the fence." He walked back to the stall door. Dipping the brush into the bucket, he filled it with paint and began slapping it on the door.

Watching him, Peachy almost laughed. "Seneca, yore a-punishin' Tivon by a-makin' him paint?"

He heard the astonishment in her voice and suspected she was appalled by the harsh punishment. He squared his broad shoulders. "Yes, and I advise you to give up any in-

tention you might have to change my mind on the matter.
I realize painting so many stall doors is hard and tedious
work, but the boy did wrong and must be made to suffer
the consequences of his actions. Now, you will obey my
instructions and go to your rooms."

Because she was on the verge of laughter and realized
her amusement would only further infuriate Seneca,
Peachy left the stable. As she walked out into the bright
sunshine, she spotted a flock of sheep enclosed within a
large, grassy paddock that normally held horses.

Milling about with the sheep were three healthy rams.

She stopped. Never having seen sheep directly on the
palace grounds before, she wondered who they belonged
to. In the next moment, she spied the sweater Tivon's
mother had sent her. It hung on a post of the paddock
fence.

Sudden understanding filled her. Profound tenderness
folding around her heart, she turned to Seneca. "Them's
Tivon's sheep. You let him bring 'em up here so's nothin'd
happen to 'em. And you had them rams give to him, too,
huh?"

He'd never heard her voice so soft. And her eyes . . .
The sweetness in them made him feel she was pleased
with him. Unfamiliar with the odd contentment that feeling brought to him, he pretended to remove a piece of lint
from his sleeve. "The boy's flock is none of your concern,
either." He didn't speak as harshly as he'd intended to.
"Get your sweater and go."

She retrieved the sweater, and was astonished by its
thick, rich texture. The wool was the finest and softest
she'd ever felt. "Seneca, this here sweater's—"

"For the fourth and final time, go to your rooms."

The tenderness she felt for him induced her to obey. As
she meandered toward the castle and into the royal gardens, Thurlow Wadsworth McGee and the extraordinary
sweater cuddled in her arms, she dwelled on the fact that
Seneca had replaced Tivon's dead ram with not one, not
two, but *three* lively ones. Deliberating upon the compassion, kindness, and generosity he'd shown to the boy, she
felt a wonderous realization blossoming in her mind.

Only yesterday she'd sworn to find things about Seneca to love.

Today she had found them.

After Nydia and Ketty divested her of her dusty garments, Peachy examined the wool sweater again, marveling anew over its excellent quality. She'd seen and worn lots of wool in the Blue Ridge, but never any like this. She wondered what it was about the Aventine sheep that caused them to produce such splendid fleece.

Lost in thought, she didn't at first realize her maids were suspiciously quiet. Normally the girls' chatter rivaled Thurlow Wadsworth McGee's.

She put the sweater down. 'Y'all riled at me?"

Nydia shook her head, walked behind a silk screen, and began to fill the tub with numerous buckets of hot water that several servant boys had lugged up to the room.

But Peachy had already gotten a good look at her face. "What's that red mark on yore cheek, Nydia?"

"I— Nothing," Nydia said from behind the screen. "Um . . . An insect bit me there this morning."

Puzzled by the odd tremble in Nydia's voice, Peachy looked at Ketty, hoping the other maid would give her a more truthful answer.

Ketty carefully avoided her mistress's eyes and bundled up the soiled nightgown and velvet cape. She placed them by the door, intending to take them to the laundress later.

Deliberating over the girls' strange behavior, Peachy stepped behind the screen and sank into the steaming water. "Wouldja fetch me my sack, Netty?"

Netty knew exactly which plant-filled pouch Peachy wanted. Quickly, she brought her mistress the little bag.

Peachy opened it and sprinkled dried magnolia petals into the water. At once, the familiar scent of the flowers permeated her senses. Picturing the big creamy blossoms in her mind, she breathed deeply of the sweet and lemony fragrance. "Shore would be nice iffen I had somebody to talk to whilst I'm a-warshin'. And it shore would be nice iffen two o' the onliest friends I got wasn't riled at me."

Nydia poured water on Peachy's back. "We aren't mad."

"But we've been frightfully worried," Ketty blurted.

She waited as Nydia finished wetting Peachy's hair, then began to wash and rinse the long, sand-filled red curls. "We couldn't imagine where you had gone so early. And when we finally learned that you'd taken Damascus, we were beside ourselves. Master Tiblock put us to work straightaway, but we couldn't stop thinking about you."

"Snort-Face put you to work? Yore *my* maids. What the hell right does he got to put you to work! What did he make ya'll do?"

"He had us doing what we used to do before becoming your maids," Ketty explained. "We washed, dried, and stored dishes. Cleaned, peeled, and chopped vegetables, then scrubbed the kitchen floors. It's not that we minded the chores, but it wasn't easy for us to keep our thoughts on what we were doing while fretting over your welfare." She glanced at the red mark on Nydia's cheek.

"And you should have seen the prince," Nydia added, rubbing her thumb over a spot of dirt on Peachy's lower arm. "When he learned what you had done this morning . . . Well, I've never once witnessed His Highness lose control of himself until today. Within mere minutes he had an entire contingent of soldiers assembled. His Highness led them, and it was as if they were off to battle an enemy army."

So, Seneca had been fearful for her safety, Peachy thought to herself. She closed her eyes for a moment, picturing how he must have looked as he led the men-at-arms out to find her. She shivered with pure delight at the romantic notion.

Of course, she regretted having caused him such apprehension, and made a mental note to apologize. But she would never forget what he'd done. She would keep the memory sheltered in her heart always.

"There now," Nydia said, picking up a thick white towel. "Out with you before you catch cold."

Peachy smiled. Nydia always said the same thing after assisting with the baths. Peachy decided Nydia would collapse and die if she knew her princess was actually more accustomed to bathing in cold creeks than in hot-water-filled, magnolia-scented tubs.

She donned the silken robe Ketty held out to her and sat

on a velvet stool before the fireplace while the girls brushed her hair.

It was still damp when a knock sounded at the door.

Peachy shot to her feet. "Seneca," she whispered, a thrill speeding through her.

Nydia answered the door. A footman and two guards stood in the hallway. The servant held a large black velvet box.

"His Highness the Prince instructed me to deliver this to the princess," the footman said.

"One moment," Nydia said. She turned and looked at Peachy. "Get behind the screen. That robe is fairly glued to you."

When Peachy slipped behind the screen, Nydia allowed the servant to enter. The footman set the box on a table by the door. "Inform the princess that although the box was to be delivered yesterday, its contents were in dire need of cleaning. I'm afraid it took a bit longer than we expected. Indeed, we have not yet completed the task but will endeavor to deliver the rest by tomorrow. Please extend my most humble apologies to Her Highness."

As soon as she heard the man leave, Peachy popped out from behind the screen and hurried to the box. It was quite heavy. She held it close and ran her hand over the luscious black velvet.

Her heart told her what was inside. So excited she could barely get her fingers to work, she reached for the gold clasp that held it closed.

A second knock at the door kept her from lifting the lid. "Dang it, who the hell is it now?"

Again, Nydia moved to answer the door. But before she reached it, Seneca stepped into the room. "You are dismissed," he told the maids. When they scurried out, closing the door behind them, he turned his attention to Peachy.

She wore a silky green dressing gown. It was the same green as her beautiful eyes. A soothing green, serene yet vibrant. The robe clung to her body, hiding everything . . .

Hiding nothing.

His chest tightened. That special lemon-cream scent of hers caressing his senses, he felt almost overwhelmed by the temptation to take her into his arms, reassure himself that she was unharmed, and hold her close for a long time.

Instead, he ignored every emotion he felt except the one he was most accustomed to feeling around the little hoyden he'd married.

Anger.

He stepped closer to her, willing her to recognize his wrath. He wanted her to breathe it, taste it, feel it.

His nearness awakened every nerve Peachy possessed. "Seneca," she whispered, drinking in the sight of him.

He was still dressed as he had been earlier. His snug buff pants hugged every muscle and manly curve in his lower torso. Even his black boots molded to his thick calves. His white shirt stretched tightly over his broad chest. The first four buttons were not fastened, giving Peachy an enticing view of his smooth brown chest.

Having admired his physique, Peachy gazed at his face. His midnight hair curled rakishly around his neck and temples, and several locks fell over his forehead, one touching the corner of his left eye.

It did nothing, however, to detract from the stony expression in his eyes.

God, she thought, *he looks like he wants to kill me.* "Yore— Yore a-starin' at me like you wouldn't like to do nothin' better'n put me to bed with a pick and a shovel."

He said nothing, merely turned and locked the door.

Peachy saw he held a piece of paper. She was about to ask him what it was when his fingers turned white around it.

Lord o' mercy, the man was beyond mere irritation. " 'Pears yore plumb scunnered, Seneca."

"I have told you before not to use those bizarre expressions. Why don't you ever listen to me?"

He may as well have spit ice at her, for she felt a deep chill whisk through her. "Scunnered," she whispered, "means disgusted as all git out."

"Disgusted does not begin to describe how I feel."

"But— But what about the romantic thing y'done?"

"I beg your pardon?"

"You rescued me! You went a-chargin' outen into the countryside a-huntin' fer me."

"Had I known exactly what you were up to this morning, I might have left you out there to fend for yourself!"

She clutched the velvet box to her breasts, her wariness and confusion intensifying. *Why* was he in such a rage? And dang it, why did a fight have to start brewing now when all she wanted was to tell him she'd found things to love about him?

"I'm sorry I maked you worry, Seneca."

Was that *all* she was sorry for? he seethed. What about the other hundred and one transgressions she'd managed to commit since dawn? "Peachy—"

"And I'm sorry fer a-cussin' at you earlier. I still don't know the whole knock-me-back story about the people and their sheep, but— Well, I'm purty shore that I shouldn't've faulted *you* fer it. Y'ain't the unfeelin' varmint I was a-thinkin' y'was."

He felt the caress of her words just as surely as if she had stroked him with her hand.

"Paw? Well, he always tole me to keep my words soft and sweet on account o' one day I might have to eat 'em. He was right, o' course, but that don't make it no easier to do. Paw said I come into the world able to cuss bacon into a sizzle, and I ain't slowed down nary a jag. Sometimes I wonder iffen I shouldn't jest give up a-hopin' that I won't have to stay in Purgatory ferever."

Seneca didn't reply, but the thought of cussing bacon into a sizzle pricked his sense of humor.

He didn't smile, though. He intended to give her a stern dressing-down, and smiles could have no part of it. "Peachy—"

"Purgatory," she repeated shakily. "Seneca . . . I got more symptoms this mornin'. Waked up and couldn't mem'ry where the hell I was. And the bottoms o' my feet? Well, they was a-pricklin' somethin' fierce. Now, I ain't a-tellin' you this so's y'won't be mad no more. It's jest that— Well, you a-bein' my husband and all, I reckon y'got a right to know that it ain't gonna be too much longer afore you'll be a widder-man."

He closed his eyes, seeking patience that didn't exist.

She suspected he was saddened by her news. "Oh, Seneca, don't be sorrerful. We cain't be a-cryin' and a-carryin'

on over this, darlin'. I'm a-doin' all I can to be happy, and
that's what you gotta do, too. So don't be sad about them
symptoms, hear?"

He opened his eyes, wondering why he'd sought patience when fury was more appropriate. "I am not sad!
Those so-called symptoms— You were disoriented when
you awakened. That is *not* a warning of impending death!
And there isn't a person in the entire world who hasn't felt
his feet fall asleep! You and your ludicrous death signs . . .
For God's sake, Peachy—"

She clucked and gave him a sympathetic smile. "I know
yore a-tryin' not to believe what's a-happenin' to me on
account o' it's jest plumb too hard to take. It's all right,
Seneca. Iffen it heps you to pretend I ain't dyin', I
unnerstand." Bowing her head, she looked down at the
velvet box she still held.

He took the box from her and stalked to the bed. There,
he opened the box and spilled its contents over the mattress. They fell into a dazzling, multicolored heap. "I am
keeping my end of the bargain, and will continue to do
so," he snapped, tossing the empty box to the bed. "When
may I expect you to begin keeping yours?"

Mute with wonder and trembling with excitement,
Peachy ran to the bed and stared at the mountain of flashing beauty on her bed. Her diamond crown, the one
Seneca's great-grandmother was wearing in the portrait
downstairs, lay in the middle of the gleaming pile. Beside
it was a delicate tiara of diamonds and sapphires as well
as a fragile diadem of emeralds and more diamonds. Besides the three headpieces there was so much jewelry that
Peachy didn't know how in the world she'd have time to
wear it all.

She would, of course, find a way. She'd wear everything
at once if she had to, but she *would* enjoy every single
piece of it.

Joy bubbled from her on a high-pitched giggle. She
reached out to pick up her princess crown.

Seneca stayed her hand. "I asked you a question. When
are you going to start keeping the promises you made to
me?"

His sharp voice brought her gaze from her glittering

jewels to his glittering eyes. "Seneca ... You— I don't unnerstand. I *have* been a-keepin' my promises. I been a-tryin' to do ever' thing you tole me to do."

His hand still wrapped around her wrist, he turned her so she faced him. "When did I tell you to go gallivanting around the countryside alone, mounted on a horse whose sire was Satan himself?"

"I won't never leave the palace alone again. I won't—"

"And I did *not* tell you to visit the Sherringhams at the break of dawn. I didn't tell you to make their breakfast or serve it to them—with your squirrel—in the privacy of their bedchambers while they suffered the humiliation of being in your presence in their nightclothes. But of course since you were wearing your nightclothes as well, I imagine it was a rather quaint get-together!"

"Seneca—"

"Nor did I tell you to compare Veston Sherringham to a mule or give him instructions on how to treat his own wife. And I most assuredly did not tell you to throw a napkin at his face!"

Her buoyant mood plummeted. The way he described what she'd done this morning made her activities seem like crimes. He wasn't angry only because she'd left the castle alone; he was furious over every single thing she'd done!

Lord o' mercy, she mused dismally. She thought she'd done so well. Thought for sure he'd be pleased with her.

She began to wonder if there was any pleasing him at all. " 'Pears I mommixed ever' single thing I tried to do."

"Mommix?" he queried loudly.

"I— Means I messed up real bad."

"Messed up is putting it extremely lightly, Peachy," he snapped.

She resisted the tears that stung her eyes. "When— How'd you find outen about what I—"

"I learned of your scandalous conduct only moments ago." He showed her the paper in his hand. A flick of his wrist unfolded it before her eyes.

Peachy scanned the words, not an easy task as the handwriting was cluttered with elaborate swirls and scroll-like designs. But she got the gist of what the letter said. "Dang that thin-lipped varmint! I'd like to have a two-hit fight with him!"

Seneca frowned again.

"A two-hit fight," she explained quickly, "means that I'll hit Veston, and . . . and he'll hit the ground. His wife— Seneca, I done decided I want Agusta to be one o' them ladies you said yore gonna git fer me. I want her with me so I can feed her, hear?"

Seneca could hear nothing but his thundering anger. He crushed the letter into a wad. Peachy had been the third person to read it. He'd been the second.

His father had been the first. Upon handing it to Seneca, the man had almost collapsed with glee. Recalling the scene now, Seneca could still hear his sire's taunting words: "She— She made them eat her rustic meal while they were still in their nightclothes!" the king had sputtered. "And with her—her *squirrel* dining *with* them! Right at the *table* with them no less!"

His father's eyes had gleamed with triumph; his laughter had vibrated with victory.

Peachy watched Seneca's eyes brew a terrible storm. "I didn't mean to break my promises," she murmured. "I was a-tryin' to *keep* 'em. I went a-visitin' like you said. I give advice like you said. I looked real elegant, too. Jest didn't know that dress was a nightgown, is all. I'm sorry iffen I didn't do none of it right, Seneca. Ain't shore exac'ly what I done wrong, but I'm sorry."

The pure sweetness in her voice curled through him, trying to touch parts inside him that he didn't want touched. He stiffened, refusing to be softened. "You have misinterpreted every instruction I gave you. I am sorely disappointed in you, Peachy, and I wonder if I will ever find a way to get through to you!" He clenched his jaw again and waited in tense silence for her to blast into him like she always did.

"I didn't mean to," she said very quietly. An ache spreading through her, she hung her head and stared at the floor. "I'm jest the sorriest kind o' sorry, Seneca."

With her head bowed so low and her voice squeaking with submissiveness, she looked and sounded like the epitome of humility. Her docile attitude was so contrary to what he knew her to be, he felt unsettled by it. He was puzzled by his own feelings. Wasn't this passiveness what he wanted from her? Wasn't it precisely what he'd been demanding from her since the very beginning?

"Look at me," he ordered.

She lifted her head and blinked several times.

"You say you aren't sure what you did wrong. Very well, tell me this, Peachy. How could you not know that throwing things in a person's face is wrong? Would you have me believe that such behavior is acceptable in your town of Possom Hollow?"

"No," she whispered, "it ain't acceptable a'tall."

He raised a brow, waiting for her to meekly admit that what she'd done was terribly ill-mannered and that she would never do such a thing again.

"It ain't acceptable," Peachy continued, "on account o' it wouldn't't've been enough. Iffen I'd been back home, I'd've filled ole lard ass's ass with buckshot!"

It took a moment for her unexpected statement to register. Seneca inhaled sharply, stunned surprise jolting him. "Peachy! You— How *dare*— That is totally—" Unable to find words, indeed, to finish a single sentence, he spun on his heel and crossed to the window, his back to Peachy.

Her declaration continued to bounce through his mind.

He wasn't going to smile. He *wasn't*.

He tried with all his might to retrieve his anger.

But he couldn't find it.

Blast it all! What *was* it about the impudent little wench that got to him the way it did? And how was it possible that one moment she was so meek and humble, and in the next she was threatening to shoot someone in the ... er, the *ass?*

Apparently the outlandish hellion in her wasn't at all defeated; she'd returned with a vengeance.

Lard ass. Good God, he couldn't begin to imagine what Veston Sherringham's reaction would be if he could hear the insulting title Peachy had bestowed upon him.

It did fit the man, though, Seneca mused, his lips twitching.

"Seneca?"

He didn't answer; even now he felt the unseemly laughter almost upon him and it was only with extreme will-power that he was able to stifle it. He hoped and prayed that she wouldn't say another outrageous word. If she did, he would lose all control.

When he didn't answer, Peachy approached him, stopping directly behind him. "Please don't be riled at me no more. I jest hate it when yore mad. I— It makes me real nervous. Nervous as a ole maid in a asparagus patch."

As her indelicate expression hit his ears, he bit down on both lips.

But his inappropriate mirth would not be subdued any longer. He leaned on the windowsill and shut his eyes as strong gusts of silent laughter whipped him.

Peachy saw his shoulders shake. Lord o' mercy, she thought, the man was so furious he was literally quaking with rage. She wondered if a change of subject was in order—one to make him a little happier.

Tentatively, she placed her hand on his broad and trembling shoulder. "Seneca? About Tivon's rams ... What you done fer that boy larnt me more about you than a thousand questions could've tole me. It was a powerful kindly thing you done."

His laughter faded; he listened attentively.

"Yore a generous man, Seneca. Compassionate, too. Them things is deep important to me, and I'm plumb proud and tickled to death to know they're a part o' who you are. O' who my husband is."

He didn't reply. He didn't know what to say.

"And the other day whilst we was in that room that has yore granny's picture in it, y'tole me y'like dramas on floatin' islands, and—"

"William Strode's *Floating Island* is a political drama."

"Yeah, and y'tole me y'like a-figgerin' numbers, and y'like movin' glaciers, and y'got a hankerin' to meet that feller who makes heat over there in England. And y'like that shoemaker named Bert, and—"

"Schubert, Peachy. Schubert. And he's not a shoemaker. He's a composer."

"Well, yeah, that's what I meaned to say, Seneca. You— Um ... Y'know? Y'shore ain't as much of ... of a stranger to me now as you was afore."

At her hint, fervent hope shot through him like a geyser. "Indeed," he murmured. Raising his head, he stared out at the emerald landscape and the distant sea, seeing no part of them. "And dare I believe what I suspect you might be trying to tell me?"

She said nothing for a long time. "I . . . Today I finded some things to love about you," she whispered.

He closed his eyes again. *Peachy.* He wanted to say her name, but it seemed to him that the only part of his being that was working was his heart. It beat so wildly, so loudly, he felt as though there were thunder in his veins.

It's not your love I want, Peachy. It's your obedience. He recalled telling her those words.

He couldn't make himself say them again.

"Seneca?"

He opened his eyes.

"Y'seem . . . Well, more like my husband now. And I feel more like yore wife. Don't y'think that we— Well, what I mean is— 'Course, maybe y'changed yore mind and don't want to no more. Yore deep-down mad at me. And when folks is mad, sometimes they don't want nothin' to do with the folks they're mad at."

"What do you want to do, Peachy?"

She moistened her lips. "Seneca— More'n anything, I want to please you."

Her announcement alone pleased him. "And how will you do it?"

"Well, 'pears to me that it might be a good time to commence with some o' them husband-and-wife things. You know— Them thigh-scrunchin' things. Do y'think— I— Would that make you happy, Seneca?"

Swallowing hard, he managed a jerky nod. He felt her take her hand off his shoulder and then heard the swish of fabric. Was she undressing? His breathing became ragged.

"Y'done meeted Miz Molly," she said softly. "Meet Miz Polly, too."

His heart lurched. Desire stirring, he turned slowly and saw her.

She'd slipped her arms out of the sleeves of her robe, unveiling her full breasts. He could see no more than that; the robe was still tied around her waist. But it was enough.

It was almost too much. "Peachy." He held out his arms.

She walked into them.

He enfolded her in his embrace, groaning at the feel of her naked flesh beneath his hands. Bending down to her, he pressed his lips to the sweet hollow of her throat, gradually taking his kisses up to her mouth.

Peachy parted her lips for him immediately, a surge of warm happiness taking hold of her when he accepted her invitation. Timidly, she touched her tongue to his, then drew away. "Y'know? Afore I meeted you, I never in my life would've touched tongues with somebody. Jest the thought is icky. But it ain't icky, Seneca. Ain't icky a'tall. In fact, it makes me feel even closer to you. Let's keep on a-doin' it, want to?"

"Yes, Peachy," he said softly, savoring the way her bare breasts felt upon his chest. "I want to."

"I do, too. Let's—"

His kiss quieted her.

Peachy did everything he did, kissing him exactly as he kissed her, copying every movement he made right down to the irregular rhythm of his breathing.

Seneca groaned again when he felt her enter his mouth and imitate his own actions. Deepening the kiss even further, he slid his hands down her back, then up again, and finally around to the front. For a short moment, he kept them still beneath her throat.

And then he moved them. Downward, to cup the treasures he'd wanted to touch for so long. They filled his cupped palms, and he felt her nipples stiffen against his skin. Her obvious desire increased his own. "God, you're so beautiful, Peachy."

His words made her blush with delight; his touch was a hint of heaven. His hands were so warm upon her breasts, so gentle. And while her body pulsated with pleasure, her mind swam with thoughts.

She pondered her handsome prince. His soft lips, warm hands, and hard, hard body so full of muscle and skill. She thought of sheep, too, and rams, three of them. And a sweet little boy elated by his punishment of painting.

Suddenly, she felt happy all the way to the very core of

her being. Curling her arms around his neck, she kissed each corner of Seneca's mouth before sliding her lips to his cheek and then to his temple. "A-gittin' to know you . . . A-findin' outen things about you little by little, bit by bit— Us a-commencin' to be friends . . . It gives me good feelin's, Seneca. The bestest kind o' feelin's. I ain't never knowed the beat of 'em."

Her sentiment set his senses aflame; her kisses set his loins afire. He swept her into his arms, into his heat.

She cuddled next to his chest and placed her hand on his cheek, her fingers slipping into his thick midnight hair. "Yore the first man who ever seed my nekkid boobies. And y'know? It don't make me feel nervous that yore a-seein' 'em, Seneca. It don't feel like a sin no more. It feels . . . Feels real right now."

God, it felt right to him, too. So right that he could wait no longer. With powerful strides, he carried her to the bed and carefully lowered her to the mattress. Her jewels lay scattered on the other side of her. They sparkled, but not as brightly as her eyes.

"Seneca?" The pink satin coverlet felt cool against Peachy's bare back. It made her miss his warmth. She held out her arms to him.

Seneca took a moment to enjoy the richness of her beauty. Another rush of desire washed over him.

"Seneca?"

He heard her questions in the sound of his name. In answer, he stretched out beside her.

He'd married her at the altar, he mused, gathering her close. And today . . . Now . . . In this bed . . .

Finally he would make her his wife.

Chapter 8

His movements tightly controlled, he placed his hand across her throat, the tips of his long fingers sweeping over the side of her neck. When he heard her miss a breath, he began pressing soft kisses to her ear, then flicked his tongue over its delicate curves. "Once more," he murmured, his breath ruffling her hair, "tell me what you want."

"To please you."

He traced her cheekbone with his thumb, his eyes caressing the softness in hers. "And I would like to please you as well, Peachy."

Rich sensations flooding her body, she nodded. " 'Course I ain't got this whole thing figgered outen real good yet, but seems to me that iffen I please you, I'm gonna be pleased too, on account o' it'll give me pleasure to see you pleased."

He perceived the gist of her twisted hypothesis. "How right you are, Princess. The pleasure will be all the greater if we share it."

She smiled an agreeable grin, but then frowned suddenly. "Onliest thing is, though, I ain't rightly shore who does what first. I ain't never—"

"I know you haven't," he whispered, smoothing his hand down her chest to hold her breast again. "But soon you will."

Unaware of her own actions, she cupped her other breast, her hand copying Seneca's slow and sensual movements.

154

Seneca almost smiled when he saw what she was doing. It was obvious to him that she wasn't willing to wait for the pleasure she'd spoken of. "Impatience—in this instance—becomes you, Peachy."

He lifted her hand from her breast, brought it to his lips, and kissed the back before turning it over and kissing her palm. He slid his tongue up each of her fingers, then took her ring finger into his mouth.

Peachy felt as though it were encased in soft, warm velvet. And when he began to suck on her finger, the tingles inside her deepened, swirling through her womanhood. "Seneca, I never knowed fingers had s'many feelin's in 'em. Whoever would've thought that a-gittin' my fingers sucked on would make me want to scrunch my thighs together? Strange how I feel them finger feelin's down betwixt my legs, huh?"

Seneca saw nothing strange about it. He nipped gently at her knuckle before withdrawing her finger from his mouth.

Her heart raced when he drew the tip of his tongue from her wrist to her shoulder, across her collarbone, up her neck, and then traced the outline of her lips.

"Tongues. Good Lord, I always thought they was jest fer a-tastin' and a-talkin'. I didn't never know there was s'many pleasure-givin' things you could do with 'em."

He realized that lovemaking with Peachy would not be a silent procedure. She'd talk her way through every part of it.

"Yeah, tongues is real useful, huh, Seneca?"

"They are," he answered softly, smiling inwardly as he thought of yet more sensual things one could do with them. Soon he would show her those wonderful things, too.

Surrendering to the drugging feelings Seneca evoked, Peachy slipped her arms around his neck and turned in to him, in to the hot, hard shelter of his body.

It was all the urging Seneca needed. She was ready for more now. His desire heightened. "Peachy," he whispered, peppering her lips with lighter kisses and more whispers.

Tantalized, she watched him move his head to her chest.

Bursts of pleasure shot through her when he circled kisses around the peak of her breast.

"Sweet," Seneca murmured, relishing the taste and texture of her. "So sweet."

She not only heard his deep, husky voice; she felt it vibrate upon her sensitive flesh as well. She gasped with surprise and delight, and the desire for something she couldn't understand. "I want . . ." Her voice trailed away; she slid her fingers through the thick black satin of his hair. "Seneca, I want—"

"I know, Peachy. I know." He took her nipple into his mouth, suckling her.

An involuntary moan escaped her, and she thought how primitive it sounded. "Lord . . . Oh, Seneca . . . The feelin's . . ."

He moved his attentions to her other breast and began smoothing his hand softly over her flat belly. "Feelings?" he coaxed softly. "What about them?" His hand journeyed up and down the curve of her side.

"They're good. Don't stop. Please don't stop."

Her plea fairly rendered him senseless with sensual need. "I won't." Shifting his position, he nuzzled his face into her warm, moist neck and moved over her so that she was on her back and the upper part of his chest was upon her. The rest of his body he kept beside her, close to her. He wanted her to feel him, to become accustomed to his weight and to begin to sense what he was going to do to her.

Peachy felt the slabs of muscle in his chest press into her. He was heavy; she didn't mind. He was hard; she loved his hardness. Sweet feelings ebbed all through her and made her want more of the man who sired them. "Your shirt," she whispered. "I'm a-thinkin' I might really like the way yore skin feels on mine. So can I take offen yore shirt?"

Did she really think she had to ask? he wondered. For that matter, did she believe for one second that he'd refuse her? God, it was all he could do not to rip it off himself.

When he rolled to his side to make the task easier for her, Peachy fumbled with the fastenings, then slid the garment off his powerful shoulders. In a moment, his chest was as bare as hers.

She glided a slender finger across a swell of muscle. "Yore so strong, Seneca. How'd y'git so strong?"

He leaned over her once more and kissed the soft valley between her breasts. Her lemon-cream scent swirled into him, arousing him further. "Swordplay, I imagine."

Her lashes flew upwards. "Y'know how to fight with a sword?" she asked, thrilled by the romantic notion.

"I do."

Thinking how he might have looked when he'd left the palace in search of her this morning, she pictured him with a sword in his hand as well. An entire play unfolded in her fertile imagination. "There's a long line o' criminals jest a'waitin' to git me, Seneca," she told him suddenly, pointing to a nonexistent line of blackguards across the room. "They're full o' hate and evilness and plans to ravish and hurt and kill me!"

He glanced in the direction in which she pointed. "What—"

"I'm plumb terrified!" she shouted, covering her cheeks with her hands. "Thurlow Wadsworth McGee comes a-scamperin' up to save me, but the little darlin' ain't no match fer them bloodthirstin' bushwhackers. But— But— What's this? Oh, sweet Lord o' mercy, here *you* come now, Seneca! Yore muscles is a-bulgin' outen all over you, and yore eyes is a-shinin' with courage. 'Seneca!' I cry outen as loud as I can. 'My dearest beloved!' And you holler back at me, 'Don't y'go a-fearin' nothin', Princess!' "

She sat up, swinging her arm as a swordsman flourishes his sword. " 'Take that!' you yell at the first varmint you kill. And y'swish yore sword this way and that way, and all around, a-cuttin' down ever' one o' them no-gooders!"

As he watched her stab her invisible sword through the thin air, he was forced to dodge her waving arm. "Peachy—"

"Y'kill 'em all, Seneca, but jest when y'think yore done . . . Oh, God, no! The *dragons* come at you! Flames come a-roarin' from their nostrils! The heat drives you back, and back, and back some more, but then you press on and on, bravery a-oozin' outen ever' part o' you whilst them dragon flames keep a-snappin' at you. Yore sword gleams as y'wield it around, and y'finally kill all them fiery monsters. They fall at yore feet, a-shudderin' fer a minute afore a-takin' their last quiverin' breaths. And then . . . Then y'git on Damascus, pull me into yore strong arms, and we ride away into the horizon. Me, you, Thurlow Wadsworth McGee, and yore trusty sword."

The emotions aroused by her fantasy were still sweeping through her when she looked at Seneca. "Y'saved me, my most dearest beloved. It was a real hero thing y'done, Seneca. Yore a true champion through and through."

He wondered if she'd lost her mind. Hadn't they been consumed by the throes of passion mere moments ago? He longed to be back in those throes. "Peachy, would you mind if we continued what we were doing before—"

"I'm all shivery inside now," she whispered, placing her palms upon his cheeks. "My sword-totin' prince. My handsome conqueror. Oh, Seneca, ain't it romantic?"

Her eyes smoldered with excitement. When her lips met his, he felt amusement and tenderness at once. God, she was a batty bit of female, he thought. By means of a medieval fantasy, she'd just seduced her own self!

Still, if her silliness led her back into his arms, he certainly wouldn't object. He pulled her atop his chest and held her close.

She kissed the tip of his nose. "Will y'let me watch you do yore sword stuff sometime, Seneca?"

He considered what swordplay did to her. The glow of desire lingered in her eyes. "You may do so at any time, Princess."

She leaned farther down to him, bestowing kisses all over his face.

He wanted more, much more. And he wanted it now. He slid his hands down her back, and farther downwards until he cupped both cheeks of her bottom.

Peachy's gay and relaxed mood shattered into shock. "Sen— You— Yore a-feelin' my *bottom!*" She began to squirm away from him.

Instantly, he caught her shoulders and held her still, both with the command in his eyes and the strength in his body.

"Peachy, you asked me not to stop. I promised I wouldn't. I'll keep my vow and make you my wife." Gently, he eased her to her back and moved over her again.

"Wife? I— I *am* yore wife," she told him, bewildered. "Don't y'mem'ry our weddin'? I don't unnerstand—"

"I know you don't. But I'm going to teach you. I'm going to show you what I mean."

She watched his burning gaze sweep over her breasts, down her belly, and down, down . . .

Seneca saw her thighs squeeze together. Determined that they would soon open for him, he glanced at the sash tied around her tiny waist. The silken robe was his only hindrance, for he knew she wore nothing beneath it.

With unhurried motions, he reached out to unveil the whole of her beauty. "Princess," he whispered as his fingers closed around the sash.

When she saw what he was doing, the mist of confusion in Peachy's mind cleared instantly. Wariness spread through her. Quickly, she rolled to her belly, stilling his hand by lying on it.

Frustration skimmed through him. "Peachy—"

"God Almighty, give some people a inch, and they take three hunnerd and ninety-seven miles. I tole you to meet Miz Polly! I didn't tell you to shake hands with Guinevere!"

He didn't have to think to realize who Guinevere was. He resisted the temptation to roll his eyes.

He resisted anger, too. It had gotten him nowhere on their wedding night, and his instincts warned him it would get him nowhere now, either. With heroic effort, and because he had high hopes that he still stood a chance of sensual success, he summoned every shred of patience he possessed. "Peachy," he began, pulling his hand out from beneath her, "let's talk about this, shall we? Exactly what did you have in mind when you said we could do those husband-and-wife things?"

She remained on her belly so he could see nothing but her head and feet. "Well . . . I had in mind exac'ly what we done. 'Course I didn't plan on all that suckin' stuff you commenced to do. It ain't that I didn't like it, but you'd best know right now, Seneca, that you got away with more'n you was s'posed to git. And as iffen that weren't enough, you had the gawdang nerve to try and git more! Here I ain't even hardly used to *touchin'* yet, and there you are ready to git a wagonload o' gravel fer yore goose!"

He reminded himself he was supposed to be frustrated and aggravated, not amused. Still, it was hard not to crack a smile at her unseemly description of what he'd done and what he still wanted to do.

"And y'ain't gotta look at me like I don't know what them husband-and-wife things is, Seneca. I *do* know. Ain't never done 'em, but I know about 'em."

"I see." Slowly, he rolled to his back and pulled her into his arms, tightening his hold when she struggled. "Stop it. All I'm doing is holding you."

She stopped fighting. Not because he told her to, but because her wiggling only succeeded in moving her closer to him. "Seneca—"

He forced her silence with a soft and leisurely kiss, and continued to kiss her until he felt her relax in his arms. "These husband-and-wife things you know so much about," he murmured, picking up her hand and holding it tightly. "How is it that you possess such knowledge of them if you've never experienced them?"

"Miz Mackintosh—"

"Merely *told* you about them. You cannot know about them, Peachy, until you do them."

His husky voice was nearly her undoing. "I *do* know," she snapped, determined to ignore the sensual power he had over her. "Miz Mackintosh explained ever'thing real good."

"Ah, then I suppose she told you about this." He moved her hand to his thigh, then eased it to his groin.

Peachy felt his hardness beneath her palm. Only his snug pants separated her hand from the very essence of his masculinity.

Fear zigzagged through her. She tried to yank her hand away, but Seneca wouldn't let it go. "Dang you—"

"I thought you knew everything about this, yet you're acting as though you know nothing. If you possessed the knowledge you claim, you'd realize that your touching me like this isn't going to hurt you. Moreover, I've never harmed you before, and I've no intention of doing so now."

She tried to rid herself of nervousness. But his maleness felt so hot. So big. She hadn't known it would feel that way and wondered why it did. Mrs. Mackintosh had certainly never said anything about its ability to grow.

Seneca swore he heard her mind clicking. Insistently, he moved her hand up and down the length of his manhood. "Tell me what you know," he pressed, keeping her hand firmly to him. "Tell me what we're to do with this."

When she realized what he meant by "this," she gasped. "Well, good Lord, Seneca, ain't y'got a dang bit o' modesty?"

"Not in bed, and I wish you didn't, either. Now, tell me what we're going to do with this."

Trapped within the curves of his body and thoroughly imprisoned by his devastating sensuality, Peachy could not escape him physically or emotionally. She could only lie there, completely at his mercy. "We ain't a-doin' *nothin'* with it! Yore a-goin' too fur. This weren't one o' the things I thought we could do today. Now let me—"

"No. Answer my questions."

She had no recourse but to submit to the royal rogue. Glaring into his eyes, she prepared to prove that she knew everything there was to know.

Of course, she had to guess at some of it. "Well . . . You . . . You git it real long and hard like this, y'see. Then— And you shore as hell didn't have no problem a-gittin' it all long and hard like that, huh, Seneca?"

"You're a very beautiful woman. I don't imagine it will ever be a difficult task to accomplish." He pressed her hand more firmly to him. "Continue, please."

It seemed to her he was hotter now than he'd been before. She was sure that if she looked at her hand, she'd see that it was on fire. The thought made her go all melty.

"Peachy," he urged, "what else?"

"Um . . . Well, it has to go inside, y'see. It gits in there . . . and then y'wiggle it around some. When you've done wiggled it fer as long as y'can wiggle it, you commence to shudder some. You'll prob'ly sweat, too, because that wigglin'll wear you outen. And you'll moan and carry on, too. You'll do that on account o' all that wigglin' will've maked y'feel good. It's a wearin' outen kind o' wigglin', but it's a good feelin' kind, too. Then I reckon I git to a-feelin' good right along with you. When neither one of us cain't take no more wigglin' or feelin' good, you take it outen and ever'thing's over."

He didn't smile because he believed that such a gesture would embarrass her. "You said it goes inside? Inside where?"

"Me."

"You? Where inside you?"

"You know."

"Oh, I do indeed know, Peachy. But I'm wondering if you do."

"It goes in Guinevere, all right?" she yelled.

He thought her indignation enchanting. "All right. Now, about that wiggling you described. What, precisely, does it entail?"

She felt a blush creep across her cheeks. "How the hell should I know?"

Blushing became her, he mused. God, she was so incredibly gorgeous. "I thought you knew everything, and I believe I've told you to stop cursing. Are you admitting ignorance, Princess?"

"No, but I ain't no man, Seneca, so there ain't no way I can know what all kinds o' wigglin' you men do. Now let go o' my hand. It's near 'bout burnt up."

He kept it exactly where it was. "While I'm moving inside you, are you supposed to move too?"

"Well, *that's* the dumbest question I ever did hear! How the hell could I move with you a-layin' on top o' me? God Almighty, it'll prob'ly be all I can do to breathe!"

"You'll be able to move. And you will. Not because I ask you to, but because you'll want to. And there are other ways of making love, Peachy. I assure you that I won't always be on top."

She didn't reply, but wondered about the other ways.

"This good feeling you mentioned," Seneca continued smoothly. "What sort of pleasure did Mrs. Mackintosh tell you it was? Did she describe it?"

"Look, pleasure's pleasure, hear? If somethin' feels good, it jest plain feels good. There ain't no two ways about it."

"Peachy," he whispered, "let me show you how very wrong you are."

His unspoken promise of mysterious pleasures pulled her more deeply under his spell. The tender plea in his voice tore her apart. "Seneca— God Almighty, y'jest cain't know how much I want to. It's the strangest thing that's ever happened to me. My woman parts . . . They say yes, yes, yes. But my mind? It—"

"Says no, no, no," he finished for her.

His bitter disappointment didn't escape her. On the contrary, it sent a pang of guilt into her. And no matter how she tried to ignore it, it wouldn't go away.

Guilt. "I larnt that it comes from yore conscience," she muttered. "Larnt that you shouldn't never ignore yore conscience on account o' it ain't never wrong."

That thought in mind, she began to wonder if denying Seneca, denying them both, was as virtuous as she'd thought.

God, what was right?

"Peachy?"

"For the very first time," she mumbled, "I feel wishy-washy over my own beliefs, Seneca."

"Wishy—"

"I'm a-doubtin' my own sef. I didn't think I'd ever feel that way. I was so all-the-way shore that what I thought was the right way to think."

Disturbed by the tremble in her voice, he turned to look at her. "What do you mean?"

The soft glow in his black-lashed blue eyes deepened her guilt. "I thought I was right to want to know you inside and outen afore our first time. I believed it was good to want our first time to be as special as it could be. But now . . . Now, I ain't so shore. I cain't stand a-seein' you upset with me. I hate it. I tole you I wanted to please you, and I ain't come near to a-doin' it."

"Peachy." Gliding his fingers through her thick hair, he touched his lips to hers.

He'd never kissed her so gently before; her senses spun.

She felt the desire, but longed to feel security as well. Sweet Lord o' mercy, she wanted to trust Seneca. Yearned to place herself in his hands, in his care, and know in her heart that he would do right by her.

She whispered against his lips. "I don't know what to do. I cain't think good, Seneca. I cain't unnerstand what's right no more. It's like I've gone all to pieces inside and I cain't git them pieces back together again."

His lips a breath away from hers, he waited in anxious silence for her to tell him what she wanted to do.

"Seneca?"

"Princess."

She loved when he called her that. "There's only one thing I can think of to do." She turned to her side and laid her arm across his chest.

"And what is that?" Anticipation pumped through him.

"Well, since I cain't think good right now . . . Since my thoughts is all twisted and knotted . . . I— 'Pears to me that the onliest thing I can do is trust you. I'll confidence in you on account o' I know now that you ain't no unfeelin' varmint. So iffen y'think the time's right . . . then I'll believe you, Seneca. Iffen you think it ain't right, I'll go along with that, too."

He was too surprised to speak. Excitement shot through him. The time was right. Oh, it was definitely right. He reached for the sash on her robe again.

"Yeah, I'm gonna confidence in you, Seneca," she murmured again.

He thought he heard the tiniest hint of a tremble in her voice. Ignoring it, he pulled at the sash, his heart hammering when it came completely undone. Slowly, he moved to open the robe.

Peachy felt his hand on her thigh. She realized what he was doing and couldn't suppress a soft squeak of anxiety. Nor could she control her shiver. "Sp-special," she managed to tell him. "You'll make it special, Seneca."

His gaze moved from her hips up to her eyes. "I'll make it special, Peachy," he whispered in return.

She gave a slight nod, struggling to subdue her nervousness. "My very first time . . . It'll be jest the way I've prayed so hard fer it to be. We'll— We'll both have them wonnerful feelin's a-runnin' ever'where inside us. Not jest the body kind, but the heart and soul kind, too. You'll make it like that fer us, Seneca. You will."

His hand remained on her thigh, his fingers still wrapped around her robe. *You'll make it like that fer us, Seneca.* He glanced downward, groaning inwardly when he saw how close he was to seeing and touching the heart of her feminine splendor.

We'll both have them wonnerful feelin's . . . He gave another silent groan, knowing full well what sort of feelings she referred to. She wanted the sensual pleasure, yes, but she wanted emotional pleasure, too. The kind she would have if she loved him.

The kind she would sense if he loved her in return.

He'd promised to make her first time special for her, and she trusted him to keep that oath.

He understood now that he couldn't.

Y'shouldn't never ignore yore conscience on account o' it ain't never wrong.

He rolled to his back, stared at the canopy, and damned his conscience for interfering.

"Seneca? What's the matter? Why are you . . ." She paused for a moment, a shred of comprehension coming. "The time . . . The time fer us to make love— It ain't right yet, huh?"

"No." Even as the word left his lips, he couldn't believe he'd said it. He got out of bed and retrieved his shirt.

Peachy watched as he put it on. "Yore a-leavin'?"

His fingers flew over the buttons. "I no longer have a reason to stay."

There was an odd tightness in his voice. "Yore riled at me again."

"If I thought anger would do me a shred of good, I would fly into a rage this very second."

He was too mad, she thought, sitting up. "You've done give up on me, huh?" she whispered.

What he'd given up on was trying to understand himself. He couldn't believe what he'd just done. He'd had the opportunity to bed her properly; and he'd let that chance pass by. He'd never done anything like that in his entire life. Blast it all, what had come over him? What was it about her that was more powerful than his own sexual desires?

He wasn't going to allow it to interfere again. This afternoon was over, and it hadn't gone well. But tonight was yet to come, and he had every intention of making sure it would be a night to remember.

Conscience or no conscience.

He eyed her sternly. "We will dine together tonight in my chambers, Peachy. Seven o'clock." He turned to leave.

"Seneca?"

Her small, sweet voice had all the power of a deafening shout. It stilled him instantly. He stopped at the foot of the bed and turned to face her.

"I have somethin' fer you." She slipped her arms back into the sleeves of her robe and retied the sash.

He watched her get out of bed and retrieve a clear glass jar from the top of her dresser. When she pressed it into his hand, he noticed a piece of paper tied around the opening, punched with tiny holes.

He held it parallel to his eyes and saw it held a spider.

"It's a daddy longlegs," Peachy explained. "I finded it in the gardens a while ago and catched it fer you. You said you ain't never seed one, and I couldn't hardly believe that. Dumb as it sounds, I feeled bad fer you. Ever'body should see a daddy longlegs sometime durin' their lifetime on account o' ... Well, they jest should, is all. Spiders is one o' the real fine things o' life."

And as he observed the spider, he thought of all the many gifts he'd received in his lifetime. Expensive gifts, all of them. Of gold, of silver, of jewels.

But none with meaning.

It was such a simple gift. Only a spider.

But it touched something deep, deep inside him.

"Seneca? Do you— Do y'like him? I been a-wantin' to give you somethin', y'see. But since I ain't got no money, it had to be somethin' I could git fer free. When I seed the spider in the gardens ... Well, I thought it'd be a good present fer you."

"It's— It's a good— It's quite nice. Thank you."

"No, thank *you*."

He gave her a puzzled look. "For what?"

She cupped his cheek in her hand. "Thanky fer a-knowin' it weren't the right time fer us yet."

He thought of his sensual plans for later that evening. Guilt nagged at him. He wondered how he could make it go away before tonight.

"And thanky fer my crown, too." She reached across the bed, picked up the crown, and placed it on her head.

He thought the diamonds looked beautiful against her burnished copper curls.

She smiled up at him. "Can I wear my crown to supper tonight?"

He slid his thumb over the edges of her smile. "You may."

"Can we have stewed backbones, and black-eyed peas, and turnip greens with hog jowl, and fried green 'maters, and squash muffins, and strawberry jam cake?"

"I doubt it." He ambled to the door and opened it.

"Seneca?"

He looked at her.

"Would y'do somethin' fer me?"

"What is it?"

"Spread yore lips. I ain't never seed you do it."

He quirked a brow in question. "I beg your pardon? Spread my lips?"

"Smile. Will y'do it?"

He wasn't at all accustomed to smiling on demand. Indeed, he was only just becoming used to smiling in secret. Besides that, she was standing there staring at him, waiting for him to do it.

God, if he didn't know any better he'd think that the feeling that suddenly welled within him was shyness. *Shyness?* The very thought was absurd!

He lifted his chin. "I shall see you at seven."

She performed a curtsy. "And I shall meet up with you at seven, too," she agreed in the most sophisticated voice she could muster. "And maybe tonight you shall smile."

He ignored her hint and concentrated on how the front of her robe parted as she curtsied. He got a glimpse of her full breasts.

He couldn't get out of the room fast enough. As he strode down the hall and ascended the staircase that led to his rooms, he thought of the frigid North Sea and how close it was. If it wasn't such an unseemly thing to do, he'd go jump in it right now.

As he arrived at his apartments, Latimer emerged from the bedchamber. "Prepare a bath," Seneca ordered.

"At once, Your Highness," Latimer said, scurrying toward the door. "I shall see to heating the water immediately."

"No."

Latimer stopped. "No, Your Highness?"

"Don't heat one drop of it."

"But— But it will be very cold, sir."

"Indeed it will, Latimer."

The three court physicians helped the king into his huge canopied bed. One of them drew a sheet over His Majesty's bare legs.

"We have much confidence in this new remedy, Your Majesty," Sir Bramstill said, holding up a small brown bottle for the king to see. "It's a complicated mixture of several unusual ingredients and has taken us weeks to concoct. We feel sure it will ease Your Majesty's pain."

The king eyed the bottle. "Am I to drink it?"

Sir Grishire shook his head. "That one is a salve that will be massaged into Your Majesty's knees. This one is to be consumed." He held up another flask. "It, too, is composed of a variety of rare and potent herbs."

The third physician, Sir Treece, lifted the sheet over the king's feet to expose the royal knees. "With Your Majesty's permission, we will begin. And Your Majesty will endeavor to remember that the medicine must be applied firmly?"

The king tried to prepare himself for the intense pain the massage would cause. "It had better work. I have lost count of how many medicines the three of you have invented. I've swallowed them, bathed in them, been oiled with them, and inhaled them. None of them have helped, and my confidence in you is quickly waning."

The physicians shot nervous looks at each other before beginning the therapy. Sir Grishire poured a large spoonful of medicine and held it toward the king's mouth. "We've sweetened it thoroughly, Your Majesty."

The king swallowed the liquid, nodding in appreciation of its sweetness. "Very well, proceed."

As gently as possible, the physicians smeared the salve over the king's swollen knees and reddened skin.

The king didn't bother trying to subdue a scream of pain. When he didn't feel immediate relief, but instead experienced deeper pain, he beat the mattress with his fist. "You're rubbing too hard! It doesn't work! It hurts worse now than before! You've failed again!"

"Your Majesty must be patient," Sir Treece advised. "We've yet to rub it into the skin. Please—"

"Out! Imbeciles! Get out!"

The doctors practically ran to the door.

In their extreme haste, they knocked Peachy to the floor just as she raised her hand to knock on the door. "Well, dang it to hell! What—"

"Your Highness!" Sir Bramstill exclaimed, horrified to see that the princess had fallen. He helped her to rise and hurried to join his fellow physicians, who were already at the end of the long corridor.

Huffing, Peachy smoothed her lavender silk skirts, adjusted her crooked crown and the jewels she'd put on after Seneca had left the room, and clapped her hands. Thurlow Wadsworth McGee sprang into her arms. Cuddling him, she turned back to the king's room.

From his bed, he glared at her. "Leave!"

"No." A glance at the clock told her she had an hour before she was to meet Seneca for supper. She'd use every second of that time if need be, but she *would* accomplish her mission.

She set down the squirrel and locked the door. "I come in here to give you some thunder and lightnin'."

"Thunder—"

"Come to cuss you outen. Don't nobody never do that, huh? You a-bein' the almighty god o' Aventine, folks is too afeared to tell you what they really think about you."

The king didn't know how he could escape the wild chit. Not only were his lower legs bare, but he knew from experience that these attacks of pain prevented him from being able to walk. As best he could, he tried to draw the sheet over his calves. When he failed, his anger rose. "I am not decent, and I demand that you leave!"

She walked across the opulent room and stepped up the red-velvet-covered steps of the dais. "Yore right. You *ain't* decent. Yore the mostest *un-decent* ole goat a-walkin' this earth. And I ain't a-talkin' about yore nekkid legs, neither. Is there anybody on this entire island who likes you? What do y'do when y'want a friend, anyway? Tie a pork chop around yore neck and call the dogs?"

"Tiblock!"

"Snort-Face is downstairs. I passed him on my way here. He cain't hear you. 'Pears it's jest me and you and Thurlow Wadsworth McGee."

The king tried to reach the scarlet bell pull that hung near his bed.

With one quick toss, Peachy threw it atop the canopy.

Despite the terrible pain flowing through his tremendous frame, King Zane attempted to heave himself out of bed. He vowed to *crawl* from the room if necessary, but he was *not* going to remain in the hellion's presence.

Peachy pushed him back onto the mattress. "Ever since I got here, you been avoidin' me the way a drunk avoids a swamp at midnight. Till today, I ain't keered nary a jag that I didn't never see you. But now I—"

"Get your hand off me!" He moved to yank her hand off his chest.

Thurlow Wadsworth McGee screamed a high-pitched warning and sprang to sit on the king's chest.

"Iffen I was you, I wouldn't go a-illin' Thurlow Wadsworth McGee," Peachy advised. "I've knowed him to be meaner'n sour owl piss. Y'ain't a-fergittin' what he done to Rupert-Dupert-Figgymoopert, are you?"

The king stared at the chattering creature perched atop his chest.

"You ever tried to crack a hickernut? Them things is harder'n lightard knots. You ever seed a lightard knot? It's the middle of a pine stump, y'see, and it's full o' pine pitch. There ain't nothin' harder'n the dried pine pitch of a lightard knot. 'Cept hickernuts. And Thurlow Wadsworth McGee cracks hickernuts like they weren't nothin' but hollered-outen cotton bolls. Imagine what he could've did to old Snort-Face's hand iffen he'd had him the mind. And y'know? *Yore* hand's mighty close to him right now."

His eyes never leaving the squirrel, the king dropped his arm back to the mattress. "Get him off," he whispered.

Peachy snapped her fingers. Her squirrel moved to the king's pillow, his bushy tail swishing across the king's forehead.

Peachy ignored the king's agitation. "You jest lay there and listen to what I got to say, hear? Iffen y'don't, I'll tell Thurlow Wadsworth McGee to hep himself to yore ear. He won't eat it, but he'll shore as hell shred it up some."

"You—"

"Shet up."

He gasped in outrage. "You dare to—"

"What is it with you royal folks and dares? Seneca's all the time askin' me how I can dare to do stuff, too. I'll tell you the truth—the two o' you'd best unnerstand that I ain't never backed down from no kind o' dare in my whole life."

He stared at her for a long moment, vowing that he wouldn't back down either. He was the king, for God's sake! "What do you want?" he thundered.

"I want to know why yore so gawdang selfish and tight-fisted! Hell, I bet you wouldn't pay a dang penny to see the Resurrection! Shameful's what it is!"

"I have no idea what you're talking about. What's more, I don't care. Now get out of—"

"I'm a-talkin' about yore people! And they don't *want* to raise yore stupid paschal! They ain't *farmers,* got that? They're *shepherds!*"

"And *I* am the sovereign! As such, I have complete and total power over every person in Aventine!"

"Yeah, I done figgered that outen all by mysef," she replied, crossing her arms over her chest and tapping with the tips of her fingers. "When Seneca leaved my room earlier, I thought long and hard about it. I feel real bad that I didn't figger it outen afore I laid into him. I was powerful riled at him, but he ain't no unfeelin' varmint, so I know that iffen he could do somethin' fer the people, he'd do it quicker'n a winter wind can lift a dead leaf. As it is, you don't *let* him do nothin', huh?"

The king didn't comment; he was too busy pondering the fact that Seneca had been in the girl's bedroom. He wondered if his son had succeeded in consummating the marriage.

"Y'want to know what else I figgered outen? There's one person on this here island that you ain't got nary a jag o' power over."

Her statement got his undivided attention. "Who?"

Peachy smiled. "Me. S'what I come in here to tell you. Oh, and there's somethin' else, too." She leaned closer to him, staring right into his eyes. "I cain't hardly believe they let you be king. Anytime you git a idee, you got the whole thing in a nutshell. Dumb's what you are. Them sheep y'got here in Aventine? Their wool's the best wool I ever feeled in my whole life. I ain't figgered outen what it is about Aventine sheep that makes their wool better, but whatever it is, it's real special. 'Pears to me that instead o' sendin' them stupid paschal flowers all over the world, you should—"

"Apparently *you* are the one without sense! Wool is plentiful all over Europe! Why, England alone—"

"Yeah, I've feeled English wool afore. My neighbor-woman back in Possum Holler, Miz Mackintosh, had her a wool blanket from England. She traded her bestest hog fer it. But I'm a-tellin' you that Aventine wool's better, and I think the whole world should know it. I'm even a-sendin' a Aventine wool sweater to Queen Victoria over there in England. Iffen she's got a jag o' sense, she'll realize that Aventine wool is—"

"You know nothing at all about the wool industry! I—"

"I know you'd make a lavish o' money on Aventine wool! A zillion times more'n y'make on them dumb pink flowers! And the shepherds'd make money, too. You'd buy the wool from 'em, y'see, and then—"

"Get out! Out! Out!" Having worked himself into a frenetic rage, the king began kicking his feet.

Peachy gasped when she saw his legs. "God Almighty, yore legs is as red as a bear's ass in pokeberry season!"

Frantically, the king tried to pull the sheet back over his

bare legs. But pain and his huge belly prevented him from having much success. He collapsed back to the mattress, heaving with exertion.

In spite of her profound dislike for the man, Peachy couldn't help but feel true concern over his condition. Bending, she examined his legs more closely.

Her nose twitched. "Chestnut bark?"

The king opened his eyes and peered over his belly to see her sniffing his knees. "Get away from me!"

She paid him no mind; her nose continued to twitch. "Milkweed? Horsehair and persimmon root?" Frowning, she straightened and looked at the king. "You ain't got no warts on yore knees."

"What—"

"Why'd y'put wart medicine on yore knees?"

"Wart medicine?"

"A salve o' chestnut bark, milkweed, horsehair, and persimmon gits rid o' warts. But you ain't got no warts. You've got crippled-up joints and bad skin. I've seed this sorter skin afore, and I hear tell it hurts." She glanced at his bare legs again, then placed a finger to a blotch of redness on his calf.

Though he tensed in preparation for the pain her touch would bring him, he felt none at all. He lay very still, watching her.

"Y'know what causes this kind o' bad skin?"

"What?"

"Orneriness," Peachy replied flatly. "There's all sorts o' reasons folks git bad skin. But the kind you got comes from a-bein' mean and grouchy all the time."

His anger returned full force. "Get out! Get—"

"What's this?" she asked, picking up a flask from beside his foot. Sniffing at its opening, she frowned again. "Do you wet the bed?"

"What?"

She smelled the bottle once more. "This here's elderberries and red sumac with a heap o' honey added. Elderberries and red sumac cures folks o' bedwettin'. A-wettin' the bed ain't nothin' to be ashamed of, y'know. The onliest time it's plumb shameful's when y'do it awake jest on account o' y'was too lazy to get to the pot in time."

His face purpled. "I do *not* wet the bed!"

"Then why're you a-takin' a bedwettin' cure?"

His fingers closed around handfuls of the sheet. "My physicians prepared the remedies for me, and they are *not* for warts or bedwetting!"

"Yeah, they are."

"Are you saying you know more about medicine than my own doctors?"

"Iffen they tole you these here medicines would cure you o' what's ailin' you, then yeah, I'm a-sayin' I know more'n they do. What you need is crippled-up joint medicine, grouch medicine, and a blood-richin' tonic to take ever'day. I like you about as much as I like a stomachache, but doctors cain't go a-lettin' their feelin's git in the way o' their sworn duty. I'll—"

"*You* are not a doctor."

"Yeah, I am. I'd ruther work with animules instead o' crotchety ole grandsirs like you, but 'pears I ain't got no choice right now. I'm gonna fix y'up enough medicine to last you fer a month. Oh, and y'need a cane, too. You prob'ly wouldn't have to use it fer long, though. Jest till the medicines kick in real good."

"A cane?" He shook with rage. "I will *not* use a cane!"

"Why? Afeared it'll make y'look old and broke down?"

He sucked in such a deep breath he almost choked. "I— You— Get out!"

"You *are* old. Near about old enough to have been a waiter at the Last Supper. And yore plumb broke down, too. There ain't nary a thing y'can do about a-bein' old, but y'ain't gotta be broke down. The right medicine and a cane'd take keer o' that.

"Let's see," she murmured, tapping her chin with her finger. "The cane should be o' ash wood. Could be white oak, but I'm partial to ash. Y'all got any seasoned ash around here?"

"I do not concern myself with woodpiles!"

She shook her head at him. "That's yore problem. You concern yoresef with all the wrong things and don't pay nary a jag of attention to the important ones. It ain't jest the woodpiles in yore kingdom that you should know about; it's other things, too. Like the way Aventine grass feels unner yore bare feet. The way sheep and sun-warmed young'uns smell. Y'should know what them little villages look like and maybe spend the night in one of 'em so's you'll realize how cold the night wind can be when it blows inside.

"I bet you don't even know the *sounds* o' Aventine, huh? The swish o' the waves down at the seashore. The squawk o' the seabirds and chirps o' the songbirds. The silent sound the Aventine clouds make whilst yore a-layin' on yore back a-watchin' 'em float by."

"The royal family does not lie about on the ground!"

"Yeah, I know, I know. And I'm a-knowin' more with each passin' day. Poor Seneca didn't even know what a daddy longlegs looked like."

"Daddy—"

"Money and power's all you keer about, huh? You must be the most unhappiest man in the whole world, and iffen I didn't dislike you s'much I'd feel powerful sorry fer you."

She bundled her squirrel into her arms and stepped down the dais. When she reached the door, she faced the king. "You orter take up whittlin' fer a hobby. I could git you some wood and a good knife and show you how to—"

"I do *not* want to whittle!"

"Well, that's a dang pity. It calms folks down, y'know. Oh, and I meaned what I tole you about the people here. I—"

"I forbid you to interfere with my—"

"*Ferbid?*" She laughed. "You cain't ferbid me from a-hepin' folks who need hep. And iffen I was to let you do it, it'd be the most gravest kind o' sin there is. And iffen you think I'm gonna let you send me to hell, then yore so dumb a mind reader'd only charge you half price. 'Night."

When she was gone, it took the king a long while to calm his anger. When it faded, he picked up the medicine flask and pondered the possibility that his physicians really *had* given him cures for warts and bedwetting.

What would the little heathen have given him?

As fresh pain flooded his body, he couldn't help but wonder.

Chapter 9

Ketty sighed in relief when she saw Peachy descending the marble stairway. "Where have you been?"

Peachy stepped off the last step and set Thurlow Wadsworth McGee down. "I been to see His Majesty Varmint," she said, adjusting her crown and patting the three diamond necklaces that glittered between her breasts. "Now I'm on my way to Seneca's floor. Why does ever'body gotta have their own floor? This floor, that floor— The red room, green room, yaller room ... Lord o' mercy, a person could wear hersef plumb outen jest a-goin' from floor to floor and a-tryin' to keep all them colored rooms straight."

She looked at the wrapped package in Ketty's arms. "Is that the sweater fer Queen Victoria? The Aventine wool one I wanted to send to her?" She pointed to the bundle.

Ketty nodded. "I was preparing to have it shipped to her when ..." She looked around to assure herself no one else was near. "The animals are here!" she whispered loudly.

"Animules? What animules?"

"The guard at the east gate of the castle sent you a message. He's the same guard who helped you with Tivon's ram. There is a little girl and a young man waiting to see you. They have a multitude of sick animals with them, and the little girl says you told her to bring them here!"

"Oh, that'd be Marlie," Peachy said with a smile. "And I reckon the man who's with her is her big brother, Mintor. He has a ailin' dog and Marlie's kitten's got worms. Yeah,

176

I tole 'em to come. Did they bring a pig, too? There's some pig who won't eat."

"The dog, the cat, the pig, a rabbit, a turkey— Dear God, they even have a *cow!*"

"A cow? Y'reckon her milk dried up?"

"The guard says she's coughing."

Peachy frowned. "I better go see her." Lifting her skirts, she reached for the gleaming banister.

Ketty caught her elbow. "But Peachy, what about the prince? You're to dine with him in ten minutes!"

"Dang it, that's right. All right, go tell Seneca I'm a-doctorin' ailish animules and that when I'm done, I'll go meet up with him in his rooms. We'll jest have to git the supper hotted up again, is all."

"Oh, *please* don't ask me to do that! He'll be so angry!"

Peachy caressed Ketty's pale cheek. "He won't be riled at you, Ketty. He'll be riled at me. But y'know? I don't think he'll be riled a'tall. He's who tole me to hep the poor folks. And y'know what else? Today I larnt what a softy he really is. He give Tivon three rams to make up fer the one that died. I cain't see why he'd want me to turn them dwindlin' critters away, can you?"

Ketty was hesitant to answer that sensitive question. "Where you will be—if His Highness demands that I bring you—"

"I'll be in the tower room."

"You're going to take a *cow* into the tower? Oh, dear—"

"Ketty, I won't bring the cow to the tower. She'd have too hard a time a-cloppin' her way up all them stairs. I'll see the cow outside afore I bring the others up to the tower. Can y'git Nydia to fetch me my yarbs? And I'll need her to carry some lamps up to the tower. And soft blankets. And a broom, some soap, and a pile o' cleanin' rags. I'm gonna have to clean that room iffen I'm gonna use it fer the hospital, and I'll need you and Nydia to hep me iffen it ain't too much to ask. Are y'too tired to hep me tonight, Ketty?"

Ketty gave a warm smile. Princess Peachy never demanded anything of her maids. She always asked. "We'll be there," she promised.

"One more thing. I'm gonna need some lard, whiskey-likker, sugar, camphor, soot, and a couple o' pieces o' flannel fer the cow. Ask Nydia to bring them things to them eastern gates. That's where I'll be with the cow. And don't fergit to mail the sweater to Queen Victoria."

Ketty scurried to obey. And as she ran, she thought about the whiskey Peachy wanted for the cow.

"Oh, Peachy," she murmured. "A drunk cow. Dear God, I hope the prince is truly the softy you claim him to be."

With pale moonlight and three small lamps her only sources of illumination in the dark shadows by the palace gates, Peachy rubbed a thick mixture of lard, soot, and camphor into the cow's chest. While she worked, she was forced to sidestep the indignant animal's stomping hooves. "Keep ole Wilma still, y'all. And see iffen y'can hold her head up so's Mintor can git more o' the cough tonic down her."

The castle guard, Marlie, Nydia, and Ketty took hold of Wilma's halter and attempted to quiet her. Mintor managed to pour a generous amount of the whiskey-and-sugar medicine into her mouth.

Marlie noticed the tremendous shudder that passed through Wilma's body. "She got a lot of whiskey that time. Won't she get drunk?"

Peachy swiped at a fly and absently wiped her greasy hands on the front of her silk gown. "Yeah, she'll git plumb snockered, Marlie. Y'all are gonna have to lead her home real slow-like on account o' she'll be right limber-legged. Mintor?"

Brushing the hungry flies away, Mintor bowed his head. "Yes, ma'am?"

Peachy smiled at the young man. His hair was a mop of blond curls, and his blue eyes shone with compassion for the cow and other sick animals he'd brought to the palace. Indeed, it was his love for the beasts that had endeared him to her instantly.

"Wilma's gotta have the tonic twice a day. And y'need to git her to eat some onions and garlic. They're real good blood richeners. She won't have the sweetest breath in the world after a-eatin' them onions and garlic, so y'might not want to kiss her or nothin' like that. And keep on a-rubbin' the lard mixture into her chest, then cover her chest up with a double layer o' flannel. Like this."

She picked up the two thick pieces of dark blue flannel Nydia had procured for her.

Mintor's mouth dropped open when he saw them. "Ma'am— Both pieces are embroidered with Aventine's royal crest! His Majesty the King—"

"Well, ain't they purty," Peachy said, examining the elaborate designs. "I reckon the king had 'em sewed on. These is his nightgowns. Ole Wilma can wear 'em jest like he does. He's jest about as big as Wilma, so these here gowns orter fit real good."

Oblivious to Mintor's startled expression, she shook out the gowns and, as if she were dressing a person, she pulled the garments over Wilma's head and slipped the cow's forelegs into the sleeves. That done, she buttoned the gowns closed over Wilma's chest. As she predicted, the sleeping apparel fit the cow perfectly.

"Y'can tie the front parts o' the gowns into a knot so's Wilma won't trip and fall down over 'em." Quickly, she knotted the fronts of the gowns together. "There now, Wilma, ole girl, I know y'feel a mite drearisome, but you'll be perted up in jest a few days."

Wilma began to weave. If not for Mintor's immediate assistance, she'd have fallen to the ground.

Peachy smiled. "Well, Mintor, Wilma's so high now that I reckon iffen you smelled her breath you'd git a nose-bleed. Tie her to the gate and let's take the other critters up to the tower."

Slapping biting flies off his neck, the guard stepped forward. "I'll— I'll watch over the cow, Your Highness."

"Well, ain't you jest the kindest man in the whole world. What's yore name?"

"Diskin, ma'am."

"Y'like animules, do you, Diskin?"

"I do, ma'am. I have several of my own, and I was wondering . . . I was impressed with madam's attempts to save the boy's ram a few days ago, and . . . Well, I have a goat. She has the hiccups. The problem is that she's had them for almost a week, and they haven't gone away."

"Everlastin' hiccups, huh? Can y'bring her in tomor-rer?"

Diskin shuffled his feet. "I was hoping Your Highness could see her tonight. She's over there beside that shrub-bery." He pointed to a darkened area in the near distance.

Peachy peered into the night, making out a shadowed form. "Well, Lord love her, there she is. Go git her."

"Oh, yes, Your Highness!" Diskin gushed, bowing his head. "Yes, I will! Thank you!" He ran to retrieve his goat, then helped Mintor secure Wilma to the gate.

The cow taken care of, Mintor picked up the turkey and the dog. Marlie carried her kitten, Nydia held the piglet, and Ketty took charge of the rabbit.

Her sacks of cures bundled in her arms and Diskin's goat trotting along beside her, Peachy led them all over the bridge and into the castle.

Diskin watched until they disappeared. As he turned back to his post, he was startled to see an old hag standing beside Wilma. "What business have you at the palace?"

Quietly sniffing the oddly familiar odor in the air, Orabelle drew the hood of her cape more tightly about her face. "Curiosity brought me here, sir," she answered, her voice thickly accented. "Nothing more. That beautiful girl who tended the cow ... Is she the princess?" She knew full well the girl was Peachy. And the bitch had been wearing enough jewels for ten women. The very thought of the girl possessing such wealth enraged Orabelle.

Diskin gave a jerky nod. "That was Her Royal High-ness, Princess Peachy. Now, be on your way."

Orabelle ignored the command and concentrated on the cow. "Her Highness has a way with animals, I see," she commented, patting the cow's neck. "I noticed she took a few into the castle. They are unwell?"

"They are. Now leave the grounds immediately, or I shall be forced to—"

"The princess will cure the animals inside the castle?"

"Although it is no concern of yours, yes."

Orabelle took a short moment to deliberate. "Kind sir, do you think it would be possible for me to bring my bird to Her Highness? The poor thing broke its wing."

"Another time. The princess will not be disturbed any further tonight. Off with you now."

Satisfied, Orabelle shuffled off the palace grounds and into the shadowed grove of trees where Bubba awaited her. She realized he was crying. "Stop your snivelling, Bubba. You've been at it all day."

"But— It st-still hurts, Aunt Orabelle." Gingerly, he touched his swollen, blood-encrusted nose and winced with pain.

"Well, of course it hurts! It's *broken,* you imbecile! But you should consider yourself lucky that you ended up with nothing but a broken nose, Bubba. I had a good mind to break your empty head!"

His feelings hurting as badly as his nose, Bubba hung his head. She'd hit his face with the butt of the gun he was supposed to have killed Peachy with. She'd never hit him so hard before. He wished so badly that he could make her understand why he'd done what he'd done.

He wrung his hands. "I couldn't do it, Aunt Orabelle. Uh . . . I tole you I seed a squirrel in her bag. What if I'd shooted the sweet little squirrel instead?"

"Well, shooting at the sky certainly didn't accomplish our goal, did it, you dolt! And then you lost the gun! Now we've no weapon at all, and no money to buy one. Did you know that I spent the very last of our funds on supper?"

Miserable, he shook his head. "I ain't never tellin' you about my secret. It's *my* secret, and you don't know what it is, Aunt Orabelle. I got a secret, and—"

"Do you still have that bird with the broken wing?" Orabelle demanded.

Bubba eyed her suspiciously.

"I'm not going to hurt it, Bubba. I'm going to take it to Peachy. She cures hurt animals."

"She— Uh . . . She does? I got him right here, Aunt Orabelle. Here he is." Carefully, he withdrew the tiny sparrow from his pocket. "Can we take him now? Huh, Aunt Orabelle? Will Cousin Peachy fix his wing all better now? Will she—"

"Soon, Bubba. Soon. Now, come along."

She set off down the narrow path that wound through

the windswept meadow and led to the barn she and Bubba had been staying in. She soon heard Bubba trampling along behind.

She understood now that Peachy felt the same obnoxious compassion for animals as Bubba did. For that reason, the bitch would not turn her away when she showed up at the palace with the hurt bird.

The mountain princess, however, would get more than a simple thank-you for curing the bird. Such kindness deserved a gift.

A deadly one.

Orabelle laughed all the way to the barn. Before much longer, she'd be heading back to North Carolina.

Possum Hollow, North Carolina, where beneath the shallow waters of a humble creek lay an inestimable fortune in gold.

Seneca stormed up the dank stairwell that led to the tower. The sumptuous supper he'd had prepared lay cold and untouched in his apartments. The candles had all melted down, the blazing fire had died, and the chilled champagne had warmed.

His unruly bride had erred again. God, would anything *ever* go according to plan when she was involved?

Muttering under his breath, he climbed the last few steps and reached for the tower doorknob. He had no idea what outrageous scene would meet his eyes when he opened the door, but if it was anything like the ludicrous sight he'd witnessed at the palace gates, he knew it would madden him completely.

He opened the door.

Mintor bowed. Marlie, Ketty, and Nydia curtsied.

Seneca ignored them and approached Peachy, who sat on the floor struggling to hold an angry turkey. As he neared her, he caught the strong scent of whiskey and another odor, perhaps camphor. Camphor and whiskey?

Had Peachy been drinking some strange mountain brew?

He glared down at her. After a moment, her appearance overcame his hostile interest in her fragrance. Her lavender gown was thickly coated with black grease and animal hair. Her diamond crown hung off one side of her head, and the only reason it didn't fall off was because a tangle of curls was caught around it. From every suitable part of her body diamonds glittered. Indeed, she was wearing what looked to be every piece of diamond jewelry he'd given her, more than enough for a bevy of women.

He felt the beginnings of true anger. There were so many reasons for his ire he didn't know which one to address first. "There is an intoxicated cow at the gates who is wearing my father's sleeping gowns," he finally said.

With the back of her hand, Peachy pushed a few red curls out of her face. "Yeah, well, you'd be snockered too iffen you'd had to drink a whole bottle o' whiskey-likker by the gulp-and-shudder method."

"I beg your pardon?"

"Most times likker should be sipped, but we maked Wilma drink it straight down. That's the gulp-and-shudder method. And them gowns she's a-wearin' was the onliest things o' flannel that Nydia could find on sech short notice. She finded 'em in the laundry, and Wilma needed 'em real bad. Wilma's pert near, but she ain't plumb, which means o' course that she's only a little bit sick but not such a little bit sick that she didn't need no tendin' to."

"I see," Seneca managed to say. He glanced around the dim room. What he could see sparkled with cleanliness. Even as he inspected the room, Nydia and Ketty continued to scrub the walls.

"This is my new animule hospital," Peachy informed him as she released the irate turkey and got to her feet.

"Come here." Grasping her hand, he led her to a corner where he could talk to her without being overheard. "What, may I ask, have you done to your gown?"

She looked down at herself. " 'Pears to me I got it dirty."

"It is beyond dirty, Peachy. It's— It's—" He couldn't even think of a word to describe it.

"It's jest soot, Seneca. And camphor. And lard. I didn't really want to use hog lard. What works best in a chest poultice is polecat fat. But I don't got none, and I didn't have time to go hunt down a polecat, and maybe y'all don't even have any polecats in Aventine. Do you?"

"I have no idea what a polecat is. Moreover—"

"It's a skunk, Seneca. Do y'got skunks here in—"

"I haven't the faintest notion. But what I do know, Peachy, is that you reek."

"Reek?"

He bowed his head for a moment, trying to control his anger. "Your fragrance is less than pleasant."

"Oh, y'mean I stink. Well, iffen y'think hog lard stinks, y'orter smell polecat fat. Lord o' mercy, now *that's* a smell that'll even drive buzzards away. It's good medicine, though. Iffen y'can stomach the smell. So what do y'think about my hospital?"

He glanced around once more. The goat bleated at him. "Peachy, you cannot keep the animals here. It is totally un-acceptable, and—"

"Do y'know of a better place, then? Maybe one that ain't so high up? It ain't that I mind a-climbin' all them stairs, but I'll be a-comin' and a-goin' from here right much, and— Oh, Seneca," she murmured, laying her palm on his shoulder and giving him a small smile, "I done finded a way to hep the people."

He wasn't blind; he saw the tender joy in her smile. "I— Uh, yes. It's commendable that you've found a way, but—"

"And it makes me happier'n a wettin' dog with a mile o' tree trunks ahead of him," she added, her smile broad-ening. "I'm gonna do ever'thing I can to make things bet-ter fer the folks here, Seneca. Cain't do ever'thing at once, so I'm a-startin' small, y'see. Firstest o' all's them animules. Why, I've already done give Marlie's kitten, Rainbow, the cure fer worms."

Seneca had no desire to discuss worm-ridden felines. His desires were of a completely different nature, and he had no intention of trying to accomplish them here.

Nevertheless, he looked in the direction Peachy pointed to and saw a ball of white, orange, and black fur rolling around on the clean floor. The lively kitten appeared to be very soft. For a brief moment, Seneca wondered just how soft it really was.

"Worms ain't hard to cure, y'know. All's y'need is some crushed-up, hard-baked-till-they're-brown-and-brittle eggshells, a little merlasses, and some butter. Y'mix all that together and git yore patient to eat it. Rainbow likes butter, so she lapped it up real good fer me."

"Peachy—"

"Them brittle eggshells cut the worms to pieces, y'see," Peachy continued. "It sounds icky on account o' it *is* icky. But it really works."

"You've no idea how relieved I am to know the kitten will recover. Now, if you will please—"

"And as fer that little pig . . . I ain't never in my life seed sech a nervous pig. He watched his sister git kilt fer sausage, y'see, so now he thinks he's next. He's even got hives on his little pink belly. Catnip tea'll take keer o' them hives in jest a few hours. Catnip tea works on people, too, so iffen y'ever git hives, lemme know."

Seneca looked at the small pig, who lay very still upon a mound of soft blankets. "The pig has hives?" The poor animal, he thought, recalling the tormenting case of hives he'd had as a child. His skin had itched and stung for days, and none of the remedies the physicians had given him had worked.

"And y'know what else? The people shore know a lot about sheep, but they don't know a dang thing about how to raise pigs. These Aventine pigs is the scrawniest critters I ever laid eyes on. Paw knowed more about pig-raisin' than anyone in the Blue Ridge, and he larnt me ever'thing he knowed. So what I'm gonna do is pass on what he larnt me. 'Course yore a-wantin' to know about the goat, huh?"

"The goat? Actually, I—"

"A-seein' as how she belongs to yore guard, Diskin, yore worried about her, ain't that right? Hot apple cider got her shed o' them hiccups. Ketty went and fetched the cider from the kitchens, bless her heart. The goat drank it right up. You know how goats is, Seneca. They'll eat anything. Miz Mackintosh has a billy goat named Judd who et all her unnerwear whilst it was a-hangin' on the clothesline. Miz Mackintosh, it tuk her a week to git more sewed, so fer them seven days she had to go withouten a stitch o' unnerwear on her whole body. We didn't let on that we knowed on account o' she'd've been embarrassed, but I mean to tell you, Seneca, she was mighty keerful when she was a-walkin' in a strong wind."

Seneca's mind spun as he tried to keep up with her.

"Anyhow, that little rabbit over there?" she continued, pointing to the rabbit. "Well, all's he had was a sore on his ear. Fixed that right up with yaller root, pine resin, and a smidgeon o' lard. And the onliest thing wrong with Mintor's dog, Hildegarde, is she's old. A-goin' on fourteen. But iffen she chews sang root she'll feel young again."

"Sang?"

"Its real name is ginseng, but *sang's* easier to say. Hildegarde could have it as a tea, but you know how dogs is. They love to chew on stuff. 'Course, Hildegarde don't have many teeth left, but I reckon she'll manage all right."

Seneca studied the dog. Age had turned her face stark white, but her big brown eyes sparkled and her long black tail thumped the floor rhythmically. Though he wasn't familiar with dogs, he could sense Hildegarde's gentleness. "Perhaps if you boiled the ginseng root to soften it, it would be easier for her to chew," he suggested without realizing it.

"That's a dang good idea, Seneca."

He felt proud that he'd thought of it. "And maybe she'd lap up a bit of the tea after having chewed the—" Abruptly, he broke off, remembering himself and what he was doing here. Lifting his chin, he brought his gaze back to Peachy. "I did not come up here to discuss the animals. It's a wonderful thing you're doing for them, but—"

"There ain't nary a need to thank me, Seneca," she whispered, moved by his obvious gratitude. "I'm only a-doin' what's right. But I will tell you that I'm powerful happy y'ain't riled. I didn't think you would be, a-seein' as how y'ain't no unfeelin' varmint, but you and me *did* have us some special plans fer this evenin'. I said a quick prayer that you'd unnerstand, and I reckon my prayer got heared. We can eat them vittles later, jest as soon as I figger outen what's wrong with the turkey. Will that be all right, darlin'?"

He noticed how her eyes glowed with her sweetness and her compassion and the tremendous enthusiasm she felt for her animal project. He glanced at the menagerie of sick beasts again. Frustration weaved through his anger, indecisiveness in its wake. Struggling with the irritating emotions, he shoved his fingers through his hair.

"Your Highness!" Mintor called.

Marlie began to cry. "The t-turkey's not breathing!"

Peachy spun on her heels and saw that the turkey had keeled over beside Hildegarde. "Oh, Lord!" She raced back across the room and knelt beside the turkey, Seneca at her side. Frantically, she swept her hands over the bird's twitching body, but felt nothing unusual. "What the hell's the matter with him?"

"Maybe he fainted from pain," Nydia said.

"Is he dead?" Ketty asked.

"Right before he fell, he was making a strangled sound," Mintor announced. "It was a rattling sound."

Peachy's gaze riveted to the turkey's closed eyes. "What was wrong with him afore? Why'd y'bring him to me in the first place?"

Mintor continued to caress the bird. "His voice— It— His gobble wasn't right."

"His gobble?" Instantly, Peachy opened the turkey's beak. "Hold the lamp close to his face, Mintor." Light shining down the turkey's mouth, Peachy saw a small object lodged in the back of its throat. "Well, God Almighty, he swallered a rock!" As carefully as possible, she inserted her thumb and index finger into the turkey's mouth. "Dang it, I cain't reach it!"

Seneca grasped the turkey's legs and held the bird upside down well above the floor. "Mintor, position the lamp so that it shines up into the turkey's throat, then hold the bird's beak wide open," he ordered with princely command.

Peachy understood immediately. As soon as Mintor followed Seneca's instructions, she knelt beneath the bird and tried again to remove the rock. The turkey's upside-down position made the task easier.

A collective sigh filled the room when she brought forth the offending pebble. "It's a yaller rock. I reckon he thought it was a piece o' corn and swallered it right down."

Gently, Seneca laid the turkey back on the floor, whereupon Peachy began a vigorous massage of its neck and chest. In only a moment, the bird gasped for breath and began flapping its wings. Soon it was on its feet and strutting, its loud and healthy-sounding gobble echoing throughout the room.

Peachy looked up at Seneca. "Real smart how y'thought o' hangin' him upside down. The rock slipped down fur enough so's I could reach it. You . . . Yore quick thinkin' saved his life, Seneca. Yore a hero."

Her warm praise cloaked him with contentment. He thought about what he'd done to deserve it and decided it really was rather heroic. Smugness playing over his features, he glanced at Mintor, Marlie, Nydia, and Ketty, and noticed they were watching him.

Suddenly, he felt exposed, as if every person in the room was seeing him without clothes . . .

Without his mask.

He stiffened, deeply piqued that his feelings had been witnessed and chastizing himself for becoming emotional over a stupid turkey. His actions as dignified as possible, he brushed a few turkey feathers off his chest, pulled at his cuffs, and strode to the door. "You will come with me now, Peachy. The rest of you are dismissed, as are your animals."

Peachy joined him under the threshold. But before leaving, she turned to Mintor. "You and Marlie'd best take a few o' them blankets to cover up with whilst y'walk home. God's a-fixin' to pull the cork, and it's gonna sizzle sozzle here fer nigh on all night long."

"Sizzle sozzle, ma'am?" Mintor asked. "Rain?"

Seneca glanced out the open window. A clear, star-sprinkled night sky met his eyes. "There's not a cloud in sight."

"Don't differ none. The flies is a-bitin' tonight. It's a omen. Means a power o' rain's a-comin'."

Without further question, Mintor and Marlie retrieved two thick blankets from the floor.

At their blind faith in Peachy's ludicrous beliefs, Seneca rolled his eyes. Taking her hand, he led her down the stairs, Thurlow Wadsworth McGee springing along beside them.

As they stepped off the last step, the deep roar of thunder reverberated throughout the palace. When they reached the marble entryway, lightning flashed in every window. Seconds later, rain pelted the glass dome above the grand staircase.

Peachy tossed her husband a smug smile. "I ain't gonna say that I tole y'so, but I *did* tell y'so."

He threw back his shoulders. "Coincidence, Princess. Mere coincidence."

As they reached the ornately carved door to Seneca's rooms, the palace clocks struck nine o'clock. Seneca knew he had to speak to Peachy about bringing animals into the palace, about concocting strange cures outside in the dark, about wearing all her jewelry at once . . .

But the lecture could wait. All he wanted to do now was kiss her.

Unable to postpone the moment a second longer, he drew her close, seeking and finding the sweetness he'd craved all afternoon, all evening.

Peachy had no time to prepare herself for the current of warm desire his sudden kiss brought forth. Her sacks of herbs fell to the floor as she lifted her hands to his shoulders. Her fingers curled around solid muscle.

"Peachy." Seneca spoke against her lips.

His voice was a velvet murmur, rich, inviting, and it lulled her more deeply into his aura of sensuality.

Seneca felt her weaken in his arms. "The hour is early yet," he hinted softly, his hands trailing down her back, his whispery kisses moving to her cheek.

It could have been three in the morning, and Peachy wouldn't have cared. She did, however, remember her disheveled state. "I'm so dirty, Seneca."

He pressed a kiss to the top of her head, his lips grazing the diamonds in her crown. "*Filthy,* I think, is a better word."

"Yore filthy now, too," she whispered. Tilting her head back, she gazed into his vivid blue eyes. "Y'helt me close, and I got Wilma's chest poultice all over you."

He cupped her chin, his thumb caressing her cheek. "It would seem a bath is in order. For both of us."

She gave a slow nod and reached up to slip her fingers through his thick midnight hair. "I'll go git mine, and I'll be back as soon as I—"

"You may bathe in my rooms, Peachy."

She took a deep and quivering breath.

"In my big gold tub you admired the night you arrived in Aventine," he added.

"With you?"

Her question shot the fire of passion through his veins. He imagined her in his bath. Naked and wet and warm. "Is that what you want, Princess? For me to bathe with you?"

Mesmerized by the soft and compelling flicker of light in his steady gaze, she licked her bottom lip.

The sight of her pink tongue sliding slowly over her full and rosy lip drove him wild. God, how he wanted her. Close to him. Holding him. Beneath him and sighing with the pleasure he so longed to give her.

"Peachy?" He touched the lone tear that sparkled from the corner of her eye. It trickled down his long finger and moistened his palm. "What—"

"The turkey."

"Turkey?" He groaned inwardly. Here he was trying to seduce her, and she was crying over barnyard fowl! "The turkey is alive. Why are you weeping?"

"Because he didn't die and because you keered enough to make shore he didn't. And y'done it withouten a second's worth o' dawdlin'. Y'commenced a-snappin' outen orders that saved his life. Y'got on them fancified prince clothes, and you was real clean and real royal jest like y'always is. But y'helt that smelly ole turkey right next to yore chest."

She smiled a whisper of a smile. "I know withouten nary a doubt that you ain't never done nothin' like that in all yore born days. I tole you one time that y'orter think about what a-bein' mannerable really is. I said that afore I knowed y'good. Now I unnerstand that I shouldn't orter a-said it. It was a mighty mannerable thing y'done fer that turkey, Seneca."

He pondered her words. He was the crown prince, a

man with impeccable social manners. And she was more impressed by his help with a choking turkey.

He could barely understand that. Even so, her sincere gratitude and the sweetness of her sentiments played a gentle melody upon his heartstrings. So touched was he, he could think of no words with which to answer her.

Moving his hands to her waist, he pulled her to him again and held her. Simply held her.

Wrapped in his heat, in his strength, Peachy sighed. "Yes," she whispered.

"Yes?"

"I'll take my bath in yore golden tub."

He couldn't breathe while waiting to hear if she would say the words he yearned to hear next.

"With ... with you, Seneca," she murmured.

She'd said them.

No music he'd ever heard had sounded so beautiful. His eyes never leaving hers, he opened the door to his chambers.

Peachy walked inside.

Seneca retrieved her pouches from the floor and joined her in his rooms. Quietly, so as not to startle her, he shut the door.

And he vowed it wouldn't open until morning ...

Chapter 10

As was his custom each night, Latimer knocked on His Highness's door and entered the royal apartments. He stopped so suddenly he almost lost his balance. There stood Prince Seneca, his princess in his arms. "Your— Your Highness, I had no idea that the princess— That is to say . . . Please f-forgive my intrusion, sir." He spun and grappled for the doorknob.

"Latimer, have a bath prepared," Seneca commanded.

Still struggling to calm himself, Latimer bowed his head. "A cold one again, sir?"

Seneca's gaze raked down Peachy's soft form. "No, Latimer. A very hot one."

"Very good, sir. I shall see to it straightaway."

"Latimer?"

His princess's small voice still him instantly.

Peachy gave him a beautiful smile. "Can y'please ask one o' my maids to bring me a nightgown? It's a-gittin' late, and I don't feel like a-puttin' on more clothes again."

"Peachy," Seneca whispered. "Remember yourself."

"Mem'ry mysef?" she asked, puzzled.

"Never mind," Seneca said, glancing at his red-faced valet.

"Would y'do that favor fer me, please, Latimer?" Peachy asked, still trying to understand what Seneca had scolded her about.

A few moments after Latimer left, Ketty and Nydia arrived with Peachy's night attire. Both maids scurried into the bedchamber. Seneca watched them from where he stood.

He smiled inwardly when he saw them lay out Peachy's night garment upon his bed. The maids were apparently trying to assist him with his evening plans; they'd selected a nightgown so sheer it might as well have been made from whispers.

The maids then entered the bath. They turned down the bright lamps in the mirrored room and lit a multitude of tall white tapers instead. They also started a fire in the marble fireplace across from the tub. Seneca imagined how the soft, flickering candlelight and tranquil flames would complement the slow and gentle seduction he planned for Peachy.

He made a mental note to reward the maids for their excellent service.

As Ketty and Nydia were leaving, a brace of footmen arrived with hot water for the bath. With utter haste, they performed the task of filling the gold tub. Then they, too, hastened away.

Peachy peered up at Seneca. "All right, what was I s'posed to me'mry? I said please to him."

He wished he didn't have to scold her right now. But perhaps he wouldn't have to do so again. In two days, his Aunt Viridis would arrive at the palace to tutor Peachy and the matter of her discipline would be taken from his hands.

"Seneca?"

"It was unseemly for you to mention something as intimate as a nightgown to him. The proper thing would have been to have him summon your maids. When they arrived, you would have mentioned the nightgown to *them.*"

She wondered if she would ever learn all the many rules. Talking about a silly nightgown didn't seem like such a terrible thing to her. "Sorry."

He caressed a lock of her silken hair; it curled around his finger. "An easy way to remember that bit of etiquette is to recall that there is only one man in your life with whom you may speak about such intimate matters as your clothing." He touched her sleeve, fingering the soft silk. "Your toilette." He gestured toward his bath. "Or your body." His large hand cupped her breast. "I am that man, Peachy."

Her knees wobbled. "I— We're alone now."

"So we are." He stepped out of his shoes and, while unbuttoning the top three buttons of his shirt, he saw her examine her nails. He saw also that she tried to act casual about it, and wondered if she was aware that her whole hand was shaking. "Peachy—"

"Breaked three nails a-riding' Damascus today," she blurted. 'I reckon these here nails o' mine ain't never gonna git all the way long and purty like I hoped."

Her rambling worried him. "I wish you wouldn't be afraid of me, Princess."

Her gaze centered on his chest. "I— I ain't afeared o' you, Seneca. But I'm . . . Well, I'm a jag nervous over us a-gittin' buck-nekkid together. It's sorter—sorter—"

"New?"

She nodded, trembling all over when he slowly led her into the mirrored room that held the exquisite bathtub. Looking into the steaming tub, she took a deep breath. "That there water shore is clear, ain't it? I reckon it won't hide too much of us whilst we're in it."

His mouth twisted with irritation when she left the bath and swept into the sitting room. He stalked after her. She wasn't going to get away from him tonight no matter what trick she tried.

She was already returning to the bath when he met her in the bedchambers. From her wrist swung a small pouch. "Herbs?" he asked.

"Magnolia petals. I like to put 'em in my bathwater. Is that all right, Seneca?"

As long as she got into the tub with him, he wouldn't care if she poured polecat fat into the water. "As you wish, Princess."

His shoulder against one of the four marble pillars that rose from each corner of the tub, he folded his arms across his chest and watched her sprinkle the dried petals into the water. Soon the warm room filled with that same lemon-cream scent that so captivated him. Now he understood that Peachy's sweet fragrance came from the magnolia flowers she bathed in.

She turned to him, her gaze darting around the room while she twisted the skirt of her gown around her hands. "I— I reckon the time's come now."

He bit back a grin. "Perhaps you'd welcome a blindfold?"

"A blindfold?"

"You look and sound as though you are preparing to face a firing squad. I believe such executions are performed while the victim is blindfolded."

His gentle barb loosened slightly the knots of her anxiety. She let go of her wrinkled gown. "That's the very firstest time you've ever teased me."

So it was, he mused. And if not for her showing him how, he'd probably never have learned to do it. "It would seem tonight is a night of firsts."

His unspoken meaning did not escape her. "Yore jest about as subtle as a garlic sandwich."

He closed the space between them. "And you, Peachy," he began, curling his hands around her waist, "are the most beautiful woman I have ever known." Slowly, he pulled the sash of the bow at the small of her back. The lengths of lavender silk flowed to her sides. "Is this one of the gowns that has the hundreds of buttons?"

She felt as though she were drowning in the sapphire pools of his eyes. "Yeah, and you'll have to undo 'em on account o' I cain't reach 'em."

"I assure you that no task would give me greater pleasure." He walked behind her, swept her luxurious mane of hair to the side, and reached for the silk-covered button at the nape of her neck.

Because the room was walled with mirrors, Peachy could see his every action. His long, dark fingers had but to touch the buttons and they opened for him. " 'Pears y'know jest how to git a girl's dress offen her, Seneca," she couldn't resist saying. "How'd y'git so good at it?"

Finished with the buttons, he slid a finger across the soft curve of her jaw and endeavored to think of an answer. He certainly wasn't about to share his past sexual experiences with her. "I used to play with dolls."

His reply both surprised and amused her. "Liar," she said, and giggled.

Seneca thought the silvery sound of her laughter made the room seem even warmer, and realized that his attempts at teasing were having a relaxing effect on her. He tucked that bit of knowledge away for future use.

Hands at her shoulders, he peeled the top of her gown down her arms, then released it. It swished down the lacy ruffles of her undergarments and flowed to the floor, creating a pool of lavender at her feet.

Peachy ran her hand down the front of her petticoat and tried to stem her nervousness. "I— Ketty and Nydia had about twenty-five million o' these here slips fer me to put on, but— Seneca, yore a man, so y'cain't know how agger-pervokin' they can be. And I cain't stand that thing they try to lace me into, neither. How's a girl s'posed to breathe with that squeezin' contraption on?"

"Perhaps I should remove the torturous garments, then?"

Quivers raced over her skin. Her stomach twisted in apprehension. Her mind spun.

Seneca sensed her tension and reminded himself to go slowly. "What are you thinking, Princess?"

He stood behind her; she gave his mirrored reflection a timid smile. "I was a-tryin' to think of a reason why I shouldn't let you undress me."

"I see." The words were a growl. "And did you think of one?"

"Not nary a one, Seneca. In fact, I'm real ready fer you to do it. I'm a little bit afeared fer you to see me all the way nekkid, but I reckon I'll git over it as soon as you commence a-touchin' me. When y'touch me, y'see, them thigh-scrunchin' feelin's feel s'good that I fergit to be nervous. You *are* gonna touch me, ain'tcha, Seneca?"

She was dead serious. He almost laughed. "I'll touch you, Peachy. I give you my solemn word."

Nodding, she closed her eyes. The only sounds in the room were those of the crackling fire, the soft beat of the rain upon the windows, and Seneca's deep breathing. The sounds drifting through her, she waited in tense expectation for him to begin.

Seneca's experience at unfastening buttons was trivial compared to his expertise at divesting women of their undergarments. That, coupled with his raging desire to unveil the whole of her womanly splendor, enabled him to remove the silken, ruffled, and lacy things with little problem. And while he did, he found himself glad that Peachy had refused to don the multitude of petticoats her maids had wanted her to wear.

He kept his head bent low while removing the last of her undergarments, a thin chemise. His loins pulsed with heat as he watched it skim down the length of her naked body to join the frothy mass of underthings at her feet.

He swallowed. Slowly, he raised his head and caught sight of her beautiful reflection in the mirror.

She wore nothing but a fortune in diamonds.

A groan rumbled in his throat. Her bare skin glowed in the golden candlelight. The soft glimmer of the fire highlighted each of her delicate curves.

His breathing became shallow; he could see nothing in the room but her. A spark of recognition came to life inside him, becoming one with the blaze of desire. Bits of memories shimmered through him, beautiful memories that brought him a rare serenity. As had happened twice before, he experienced the profound feeling that he knew her. That he'd been close to her.

That he'd loved her once upon a time.

"Seneca?"

Her voice lured him back to the present, prompting him to slide his hungry gaze down her body once more. He knew in his soul that Peachy was the most enchanting woman God had ever made. "Peachy." He groped for more words, finding none to express his wealth of emotions.

Peachy watched his features tighten as though he were in pain. "Seneca? You all right?"

"Fine." His whisper ruffled her hair. Lifting his hands to the back of her neck, he unfastened each of her three diamond necklaces and dropped them one by one into the lavender pool of her gown. He did the same with her glittering earrings and the four bracelets she wore on each delicate wrist. The rings he left on her fingers, but he did move to take off her crown.

"Please— I want to keep it on."

He pressed an airy kiss to her shoulder. "Very well." His palms itching to touch her, he settled his hands on her hips and rotated his thumbs on her bottom, the feel of her warm satin skin causing him to moan once more.

"Yore— Yore a-seein' Guinevere, huh?"

Her question aroused him to such an extent he ached. "Yes, Peachy." The words were torn from his chest.

She lifted her hand and trailed a slender finger down the curve of her breast. "Do— Do y'like me? No man 'cept Paw ever seed me nekkid, and I was only a little girl when he did. Seneca, yore the first man who ever seed me since I becomed a woman. All nekkid like this . . . I— Am I shaped all right? The way men like?"

The tenderness her innocent worry evoked within him transcended passion, and he knew a heartfelt desire to soothe her. His hands still at her hips, he turned her to face him and kissed her more gently than he ever had before. "Princess, your beauty challenges the very definition of the word *beautiful*. In truth, I cannot think of a word that describes how much you please me."

She wrapped her arms around his waist and leaned into him. "Oh, Seneca, y'ain't never said sech purty things to me afore. Say some more."

"I'd rather *show* pretty things to you, sweetheart."

"Sweetheart?" The pet name sent elation exploding through her. "Oh, say that again!"

Her excitement took him aback. Cupping the firm, white cheeks of her bottom, he urged her against his throbbing hardness. "Sweetheart," he whispered, kissing the fragile slope of her neck. "Sweetheart," he whispered again, taking his kisses to her shoulder.

His deep-timbred voice and the feel of his warm, gentle hands weakened the last shreds of her reservations. "Seneca, I want to see you now. See the man, not the prince. I want to see my husband the way God maked him."

See the man, not the prince. The words rang through Seneca's mind a thousand times, playing through him like a song he'd only just learned but would never forget.

Tilting Peachy's chin, he settled his mouth over hers, willing her to feel every emotion he attempted to put into the kiss.

Her lips parting for his sensual entry, Peachy unfastened his shirt. When the last button opened in her fingers, she stepped away, savoring the sight of his smooth brown chest. "Seneca." She whispered his name simply because she liked the way it sounded.

So preoccupied was she with his chest, Seneca decided she'd forgotten all about taking off his shirt. He did it for her and dropped it to the creamy marble floor.

Softly, she laid her hand on the swell of muscle beneath his nipple. "Hard," she whispered. "But soft, too. Like a piece o' wood with a little bit o' pillow on top."

Her touch was almost his undoing. Though her hand was only on his chest, pleasure began to flow through his manhood. And the only reason he could fathom for such an odd occurrence was that he'd never wanted a woman as badly as he wanted Peachy.

He covered her hand with his own, stilling her caressing fingers before she managed to sever all his control. "You've no idea what your touch does to me."

"What does it do?"

In answer, he pressed her hand to his rigid masculinity, as he'd done that afternoon. And then, to test her, he let go of her hand, waiting to see if she would take it away.

She didn't. Instead, she slid it up to the fastening at the top of his trousers. In a moment, she pulled the pants apart so they formed a vee between his hips. "There it is," she whispered. "All that hair that maked me so hot on our weddin' night. It's blacker'n midnight. I wanted to touch it then, but I was too afeared. Tonight . . . I ain't afeared no more, Seneca."

Clenching his jaw against the aching throb of desire, Seneca looked down and saw her small white hand lying upon the thick black mat of hair at his groin. If he was midnight, she was magnolias, he thought. "Peachy," he whispered.

"I know," she whispered in return.

Seneca allowed his head to drop back over his shoulders as she removed his pants, undergarments, and stockings.

He was naked now. He waited for her to speak. To touch him.

She said nothing. Did nothing.

But he could feel her warm breath whispering upon his thigh.

He raised his head and looked down at her.

She was kneeling before him. Staring. Her eyes were wide. With awe and a bit of apprehension.

He swore he could *feel* the caress of her intent gaze. Deeper pleasure engulfed him. He slipped his fingers through her hair; his thumbs smoothed across the blush on her cheeks. "Tell me what you're thinking."

She swallowed and licked her lips. "I— I was jest mem'ryin' somethin' Paw used to say all the time."

"And what is that?"

Her big, round gaze slid up and down the hard, thick length of him. "Paw said ... Said it was nigh on impossible to fit two pounds o' rocks into a one-pound bag."

It took a moment for Seneca to comprehend what she meant, and then he had to battle the urge to laugh out loud.

He won control, however, because he understood her worry. *Go slowly,* he reminded himself while helping her to rise. Lifting her into his arms, he cradled her as he would a child, and, without a word, he stepped down the marble steps that led into the tub. When the water rippled to his thighs, he lowered himself into it, Peachy still cuddled against his chest.

He sat and, keeping her in his lap, began to pour warm water over her creamy shoulders. She felt so good, all wet, and warm, and soft. The delicate scent of magnolias surrounded him. The fragrance brought his desire to a fever pitch.

He'd wanted to go slowly. Had had every intention of making this evening a leisurely one.

Now he wondered if he could. "Peachy, I've given a lot of thought to what happened between us this afternoon."

"Me too," she whispered.

Watching water droplets glisten between her breasts, he doubted she'd had the same thoughts he had. "I ended our encounter earlier out of deference to your wishes. I understand your desire for your first time to be a special one, and I assure you that I will not toss you to the bed and ravish you. But," he added, pulling her closer, "I am not made of stone."

His turgid maleness pressed hotly against her side, a staff of fire burning her skin. She nodded mutely.

"I want you, Peachy," he continued, his voice simmering with hot desire. "I haven't forgotten about— The special feelings you want . . . I'll try . . . to go slowly, sweetheart, but— I can't wait forever."

Unable to look at him, she stared at the wall ahead. No matter where she looked, he was there in the mirror, surrounding her with his reflection, his dark and potent sensuality.

She closed her eyes. His image came into her mind. She couldn't escape him.

She didn't want to.

Turning in his arms, she hugged him tightly, her breasts flattening against his corded chest.

At her unexpected display of passion, Seneca lost all control of himself. As if she weighed no more than one of the bubbles floating on the water, he lifted her and positioned her so that she straddled him. Holding her tightly against him, he began to move his hips. Slowly. Rhythmically. Warm waves of water splashed gently around him, around her.

The feel of his rigid masculinity sliding up and down her belly caused Peachy to gasp with a yearning she had no idea how to satisfy. The rock of his hips, the slow and sensual cadence of his movements, beckoned to some alien part of her she'd had no idea existed. A soft moan sounded in her throat.

Seneca's pleasure heightened, and he realized his end was near. He could wait no longer to bury himself inside her. Hands around her waist, he lifted her again. Her legs were still spread, making it easy for him to position himself for a swift, deep entry. "Peachy."

He probed at the most intimate part of her, his hotness melting through her. She shuddered with need and wonder.

And uncertainty.

"I reckon— You . . . The time's right? Righter'n it was this afternoon, huh, Seneca?" She whispered so quietly, she could barely hear her own words.

Seneca could hardly hear them either, but they were loud enough for him to understand. That same prick of guilt needled him. Gritting his teeth against every emotion except desire, he lowered her onto his hot, pulsing shaft and felt her sweet opening stretch and encircle the tip of him.

Peachy squeezed the swell of muscle at the top of each of his shoulders. She tried to swallow the fear that rose from the pit of her belly, tried to believe in the man in whose hands she'd placed her trust. "Will it fit?"

He kept her poised above him, and slid deeper, slightly deeper, stopping before he met her maidenhead.

Her virginity. One quick thrust would rip right through it.

Rip. God, he hated the way that sounded. "Peachy—"

"It's all right. I'm . . . I tole you I tr-trust— The time must be right. I'm ready."

He heard her uncertainty in each word she stammered out. He heard other words, too, ones she'd spoken earlier.

Y'shouldn't never ignore yore conscience on account o' it's always right.

His loins burned. The promise of pleasure skimmed through him. He wanted more, all of it, and no amount of willpower erased his hammering need.

But God help him, he would have it without betraying her confidence in him. Without ignoring his conscience.

A hoarse moan of wild and absolutely uncontrollable desire escaped him as he lifted her once more and felt himself slide out of her soft, tight sheath. He settled her in his lap again; her slender legs curved around his back. He held her tightly to him and began to move as he had before, ramming himself between them with slick, urgent thrusts.

He didn't want it to be this way.

But he couldn't stop.

Nature ended what he could not. The splashing waves of the bathwater washed away all evidence of his loss of control.

But even as his physical pleasure peaked, his anger mounted as well. Fury and ecstasy. He hated the confusion he felt at such contradictory emotions.

He buried his face in the red curls lying upon Peachy's

slight shoulder. Her special scent permeated his senses, reminding him of her purity and her sweetness.

He yearned for her to embrace him and tell him it was all right. That she understood his lapse of restraint.

But of course she wouldn't. She couldn't. She was too innocent to even understand what had happened.

He loosened his embrace and heard her take a deep breath. More guilt sluiced through him when he realized how tightly he'd been holding her. "Peachy, I'm sorry. I'm so damn sorry."

The swear word he'd muttered revealed to her the depth of his dismay. But it did nothing to help her comprehend the reason for his apology. "Seneca, I don't unnerstand what—"

"I know you don't." He kept his face buried in her silken hair.

"But . . . Well, ain'tcha gonna tell—"

"No."

He chin propped on his shoulder, she stared at her reflection in the mirror and saw her own confusion. "Yore a-hurtin' my feelin's," she murmured. "I trusted you. And now y'ain't even gonna tell me what's a-botherin' you."

God, he groaned inwardly. If only she knew what lengths he'd taken to preserve the trust she'd placed in him. He took her face between his hands and kissed the tip of her nose. "I'm sorry for holding you so tightly. It dawns on me now that perhaps you were unable to breathe."

"What— Seneca, what happened jest now?"

"I was enjoying the way you feel when I hold you, Peachy," he explained simply. "It gave me great pleasure to move against you the way I did."

"I'm thrilled near to death that I was able to make y'happy, Seneca. I done tole you this afternoon that I wanted to do it."

Her joy filled him with the kind of inner warmth only she could make him feel. What mattered most to him now was that he'd kept himself from hurting her. He'd remembered her trust in him even while desire had pounded through him.

And for that he was glad because in spite of what she

said, she wasn't ready, and he knew in his heart that he would wait until she was.

"The water is getting cold, Princess," he told her, surprised by the tenderness in his voice.

"I love when y'talk soft to me like that, Seneca."

"You do, do you?" He reached for a bar of soap and rolled it around in his wet palm until a rich, thick lather seeped through his fingers.

He began to wash her. Slowly, as if he had not only tonight but the rest of forever to complete the task.

She squeezed her thighs together when his hand neared her hips. He moved his hands to her back and slid them into her hair. Soap twinkled brightly through her rich, red mane. Finally, he rinsed her clean.

When he was finished, Peachy took soap in hand and washed his upper torso and hair, loving the way the creamy white suds looked against his dark skin and midnight curls. She almost hated to rinse it away. "Stand up now."

Her order surprised him, but he obeyed. He looked down and watched her smooth the soap over his legs. And then she stopped. Stopped and stared at the sable triangle between his hips.

"It ain't as fearsome lookin' now. Afore, it was a-standin' straight up like a soldier at attention. What happened to it?"

He didn't answer, for in explaining he would have to admit what he'd done. Instead, he sat back in the water and rinsed the soap from his legs.

Peachy purred with happiness when he picked her up and lifted her out of the tub. The air cooling her, she snuggled up against him, one corner of her smile pressed against his chest.

Seneca carried her into his bedchambers, uncaring that his footsteps left puddles upon the marble floor. "Do you want your nightgown?" he asked, glancing at the sheer garment lying on his bed.

"What fer? That's the uncoverin'-est thing I ever seed in all my life. I might as well wear air."

"That's what you *are* wearing." He settled her upon the plush dark blue rug before the fire. "Stay here."

When he returned from the bath, he was carrying a stack of thick white towels.

The golden light of the fire shimmered over her. Her luxurious red hair glowed with a beautiful richness that seemed almost heavenly to him. And her eyes ... They pulled him into their pale green depths, making his heart turn over with a longing for more. The tranquil sight of her awash with fireshine brought back those same haunting yet elusive memories.

It dawned on him then that he always felt this way when she was near a fire. The realization bewildered him.

"Seneca?"

Her voice penetrated the spell surrounding him. He sat down beside her and covered her wet shoulders with one of the towels. He laid another across her moist legs.

She, in turn, performed the same service for him. "All warm now, darlin'?"

She spoke so sweetly. And she said such caring things. He pulled her into his arms, laid her across his legs, and supported her head in the crook of his elbow. He wanted to hold her all night long. "Stay with me tonight, Princess."

She realized that his words were not an order but a request. Tears filled her eyes.

"You— You don't have to," he added, disturbed by her tears.

"I want to."

Joy poured through him. "And do you always weep over things you want to do?"

She smiled and dried her tears with the back of her hand. "Y'didn't *command* fer me to stay here. You *asked* me. There ain't jest a *world* o' difference in that, there's a whole dang *universe.*"

He stared at her for a long moment. She was right; he *had* asked. He'd meant to demand. Now he was glad he hadn't. "I see. So you're saying that if I *request* your co-operation instead of *demanding* it, you'll acquiesce?"

"Acquiesce?"

"To accept. Comply. To yield passively."

She grinned at him. "Means all that, huh? Well, Seneca, I ain't a-sayin' I'll do ever'thing withouten a bit o' argufyin', but I'd be more willin' to try and see yore side o' things iffen y'didn't try and force me to it."

He pondered that. "So if I had *requested* your presence in my bed on our wedding night, you would have complied?"

"Nope. Can I sleep with my crown on?"

"No."

"Why?"

"Because it will—"

"Please?"

"Peachy—"

"Purty, purty, purty please?"

"Oh, very well." He couldn't believe he'd agreed to her ridiculous request.

She slipped off his lap and stretched out before the fire. The towels slid off her body, but she didn't care. "Y'want to gee and haw fer a while, Seneca?"

"Gee—"

"Talk. Or do y'want to play a game?"

As long as she stayed with him, he didn't care what they did. "What is this game?" Shedding his own towels, he lay down beside her. Her skin felt like heated satin next to his body.

Peachy wiggled her toes. "It's called the First Word That Comes to Your Mind game. I say a word, see, and you tell me the first thing y'think of."

He'd never heard of that game. "All right. I'll go first."

"No, ladies first."

He gave her a questioning look. "Are you a lady?"

"I swear to be one tomorrow."

"Just like that?" He snapped his fingers. "And how do you plan to accomplish such a feat?"

"It's simple, Seneca. I won't talk about nightgowns to Latimer."

"Peachy, there's much more to being a lady than—" He broke off when he saw her smile and realized she was teasing him. Well, he could tease, too. "I get to go first because I'm a prince, and you're only a princess. Indeed, I am heir to the throne. I outrank you. Moreover, I am truly a royal, and you merely married into royalty."

She giggled at his arrogance. "Y'know, Seneca? You

could make a fortune a-rentin' yore head outen as a hot air balloon. It's *my* game, so *I'm* a-goin' first."

He could think of no argument for that. Nor could he stop thinking about her comparison of his head to a balloon. His lips quirking with amusement, he gathered her into his arms and held her close. "Begin your game."

"Paint."

"Paint?"

"That's yore word."

The word was so unrelated to the sensual mood of the evening that it took him a while to concentrate on it. "Paint ... Tivon."

She knew he'd say that; it was the opening for what she'd been wanting to tell him. "Weren't much of a punishment y'give that boy, Seneca."

His embrace loosened; he scowled. "Painting every stall door in the barn wasn't a good punishment?"

"Nope."

"But it's hard work."

"Not iffen yore a little boy, it ain't. Paintin's fun. It's one o' them real fine things in a young'un's life. Don't y' mem'ry that?"

How could he remember? he wondered. Besides a bowl of fruit on an empty canvas, he'd never painted anything in his life.

His silence spoke volumes to Peachy. It was just as she suspected. She wondered what else he'd never had the chance to do in this great big palace he'd grown up in. "Yore turn."

A while passed before he could stop dwelling on the highly peculiar idea that painting was fun. "Thighs," he blurted, watching her alabaster leg sway back and forth upon the dark blue rug.

"A-scrunchin' 'em."

He knew she'd say that. And it made him feel kind of good that he'd known.

"My turn," Peachy said. "Um ... Game."

"Hide-and-go-seek."

"Did you play that when you was little?"

"No, I ... No, I didn't."

His voice sounded hollow to her. "Well, how do y'know about it?"

He forced himself to sound nonchalant. "The peasant children used to play it. I'd watch them from the window."

"Oh." She felt sad for him. "Yore turn."

"Food."

"Hungry."

He had a feeling she'd say that; neither of them had eaten tonight. Leaving her for just a moment, he retrieved a loaf of bread and a covered platter of cheese from the tray of food that was supposed to have been their evening meal. From the cabinet across the room, he withdrew a bottle of fine, red wine.

"It's your turn," Seneca reminded her while they feasted upon the simple food.

"Turn?" God Almighty, she thought. His robin's-egg eyes looked so good against his dark skin and raven hair. And she liked the way his long, thick fingers looked around the fragile stem of the crystal wineglass.

"The game, Peachy. It's your turn."

A red-gold curl fell across her face; she caught the scent of magnolias. "Magnolias."

"Midnight," he answered immediately.

"Midnight and magnolias?" She sipped the wine, savoring its mellow smoothness. "What do midnight and magnolias got to do with each other?"

He summoned the memory of how her pale hand had looked against his darkness as she'd learned intimate things about his body. "Nothing . . . and everything."

His answer didn't help her understand at all. Seneca was certainly a mystery, one she was determined to unravel. "Can I have another turn even though it ain't my turn?"

"It would be rather unchivalrous of me to deny you." He lay down on the rug again.

Peachy slipped into his open arms and looked around the room while trying to think of a word. It didn't much matter what word she gave him; his answers always revealed a bit more of who he was. "King," she said, noticing a small portrait of some crowned man.

"Father."

She took his hand and intertwined her fingers with his. "Why do y'always call him 'Father'?"

With his other hand, he massaged the slender stretch of muscle in her thigh. "He's my father."

"Well, yeah, but ... Y'could call him 'Paw.' Or 'Daddy.' Or 'Papa.'"

Seneca felt a wave of sad nostalgia. Truth was, he *had* attempted to call his parents 'Papa' and 'Mama.' Once, long ago, when he'd still been young and foolishly hopeful ...

"Yore paw," Peachy began, squeezing his hand, "he didn't never let y'call him nothin' but 'Father,' huh, Seneca?"

"My turn," he whispered without answering her. He tried to find a word, any word, but could concentrate only on 'Papa' and 'Mama.' "I can't think of one right now. You go ahead."

"Book."

"Gold strips."

She turned her head and looked at him. "Strips o' gold?"

"I use a thin strip of flattened gold as a bookmark."

"I don't use bookmarks."

He drew his hand down the soft curve of her waist. "How do you keep your place in books, then?"

"I jest bend down the page."

He stiffened, her statement taking him back some twenty-five years. He'd been seven. He'd folded the corner of a page in a book he was reading. A book about ... He couldn't remember.

But he recalled Lady Muckross's fury when she discovered what he'd done. She came up silently behind him, ripped the book from his hands, and spanked him with her paddle.

That paddle. God, he'd felt its horrible sting from the time he was a tiny boy until the time she'd finally broken it on his leg when he was twelve.

He'd never, not once, folded down the page of a book again.

"Seneca?" She watched a darkness come into his eyes. It made her think of sad things. Like flowers picked before they could bloom and stories without happy endings. "Lord o' mercy, darlin', what's the matter with you?"

He banished his dismal memories and stared into the fire, watching the blue-centered flames twist around each other. "You shouldn't fold the pages down in books, Peachy."

"I didn't used to. When I was little, I used a scrap o' paper to keep my place. But one time I seed Paw fold down a page in the Bible. I tole him he orter not do that. He smiled. He had a real tender sorter smile, Seneca. The kind that's barely there, but it's full o' nice thoughts y'ain't got to say 'cause they're all there in yore smile. Anyhow, he tole me he liked to fold down book pages on account o' all them folded-down pages maked the book seem real special. Like it was a much-loved book. After he said that, I thought o' folded-down pages in a real different way."

A much-loved book, Seneca mused.

"And now that I'm growed, I see ever'thing like that. Iffen y'cain't really enjoy the things y'got, why do you have 'em? I try to much-love ever'thing I have. Don't make no kind o' sense not to. Some folks? They— Um . . ."

"What about them?"

"I— Nothin'."

"Tell me."

She saw the genuine interest in his eyes. "Almost ever'thing y'all got in this castle's locked up."

He brushed his finger across the tips of her long, thick lashes. "For reasons of security. I told you that before."

"Well, yeah, but . . . Seneca, the other day I was a-wantin' to hold a tiny little lady that's in a cabinet in a room downstairs. She's so purty. Maked o' porcelain, I think. I went to open the cabinet, and it was locked."

He saw nothing unusual about that. "The figurine is breakable, Peachy. It's locked up so—"

"Then she ain't much-loved."

"She *is.* That's why she's kept safe."

"No, Seneca. Iffen she was much-loved, she'd be outen where folks could hold her and look at all sides of her. I would've much-loved her iffen I could've got her outen the cabinet. As it was, I couldn't do nothin' but look at her through a piece o' glass. I don't unnerstand that."

"Peachy—"

"I used to have a blanket when I was a young'un," she began to explain, tracing his collarbone. "It was really a piece o' scarlet velvet. My maw, she traded two dozen of her handmade baskets fer that piece o' velvet. See, where I lived folks always had more yearnin's than earnin's, so we traded fer stuff. Anyhow, I weren't more'n a arm young'un when Maw brung that velvet home, but I—"

"Arm young'un?"

"A arm young'un's a kid who's still gotta be helt in arms. There's lap babies, too, who ain't got enough strength to be offen their maw's laps. Knee babies is a jag stronger and can sit on knees. Then there's porch young'uns. Porch young'uns is kids old enough to play on the sweeped porch but not outen in the yard yet. They're still in that put-ever'thing'-y'see-in-yore-mouth stage, and they're little enough so that the nasty stuff they eat can hurt 'em some. After a-bein' a porch young'un, y'git to be a yard young'un. That's when you can finally eat dirt and yore maw won't bother you none about it."

"I see." It was an odd explanation, but it made perfect sense to him. He decided he was beginning to think more like she did. God help him.

Peachy finally went on with her story. "So I was a arm young'un, y'see. And Maw? Well, when she brung that piece o' red velvet into the cabin, I throwed a hissy fit to have it. 'Course, I ain't got nary a mem'ry o' that fit, but Maw and Paw tole me about it later on when I was old enough to unnerstand words. Maw, she was gonna make herself a bonnet outen that velvet, but she give it to me instead. Good ole Maw. She had a heart softer'n summer butter."

Seneca recalled his own mother. "And how would you describe a person with a cold heart?" he asked without thinking.

She couldn't help but wonder why he'd asked, and finally decided he was referring to his father. Maybe his mother, too, although she couldn't be sure. "Colder'n a man's pecker whilst he's a-pissin' in a blizzard. Colder'n biscuit weather."

It was a moment before his amusement faded sufficiently for him to speak. "May I remind you to watch your tongue? Now, what is biscuit weather?"

"Oh, Seneca," she said softly. "The bestest time to eat hot biscuits is when it's a-snowin' outside. That's biscuit weather. Y'set inside next to the fire, a-soppin' up merlasses with fresh, steamin' biscuits ... It gives you sech a cozy feelin' inside."

He found himself wishing he could have shared one of those cozy nights in her cabin with her. Even with all the fires lit, the palace was always cold.

"I love snow, Seneca," Peachy murmured, closing her eyes and remembering those snowy Appalachian times. "We'd git a lot o' snow in the Blue Ridge. I mem'ry one time about three or four years ago. Well, it snowed fer nigh on three weeks withouten a-stoppin'. Lord, there was s'much snow we near about had to sit on a rifle-gun and shoot oursefs up the chimney to git outen the cabin."

He smiled into the softness of her hair. "I imagine that would have been rather uncomfortable."

She giggled and nodded. "Anyway, about my velvet blanket, Seneca. I toted that thing around till it falled plumb apart. Maw, she could o' tole me I couldn't have the piece o' velvet, Seneca. She could o' thought on how expensive and fine velvet is. But she didn't. Even when I drug that velvet around in the mud she didn't say nary a word. She jest warshed it and give it back to me. It was much-loved, y'see. Much-loved things is fer usin'. Fer a-holdin'. Fer a-makin' you happy."

Turning, she pressed feathery kisses along his jaw. "You make me happy, Seneca. And like I tole you in the tower that day, I'm gonna love you. I'm gonna much-love you till the end o' my days."

He wanted to ask her how much closer she was now to loving him. She said she'd found some thing to love *about* him, but that wasn't the same as truly loving him.

But he didn't ask. He was afraid she'd ask him the same question. And he didn't have an answer to give her.

He lapsed into deep thought. Long minutes passed before he noticed Peachy was fast asleep. He carried her to the bed, thinking her creamy body looked even more beautiful against the dark blue satin sheets.

He lay down beside her. Her soft breathing and the gentle splash of the rain outside made him drowsy, but sleep wouldn't come. After a moment, he retrieved a book from his bedside table. He held it for a long time.

Finally, he opened it to the place marked by a long, thin strip of solid gold. With one flick of his wrist, he threw the bit of gold away; it skittered several feet upon the polished marble floor.

His fingers curled around the top corner of the page. He grasped it firmly and studied how the bit of paper looked between his fingers.

He folded the corner down. For good measure, he pressed his thumb along the fold to make a sharp crease.

Highly pleased with himself, he placed the book back on the table and pulled Peachy into the curve of his body, smiling when her diamond crown grazed his cheek. Warm, content, and wrapped in the luscious lemon-cream scent of magnolias, he waited for sleep to close his eyes.

"Seneca?"

He felt badly at having wakened her. "I'm here."

"Y'shore it'll fit?"

He knew precisely what she meant; her question made him wonder if she'd been dreaming of lovemaking. "I promise you it will, sweetheart."

"When the time is right. When we're both ready fer it to happen. When we both know it'll be special. Seneca?"

"Peachy."

"How'd it feel?"

He frowned slightly. "How did what feel?"

"How'd it feel to bend down that book page?"

He realized she'd watched him do it.

"Did it feel good, Seneca?"

"Go to sleep." He closed his eyes.

But Peachy opened hers. What she saw sent her heart spinning with happiness.

Seneca was smiling.

Chapter 11

When Peachy opened her eyes the next morning, she saw the space beside her was empty. A glance at the ormolu clock on the mantel told her it was nine o'clock. God Almighty, she'd never slept this late in all her life! She threw off the covers and started to sit up. A sharp pain stabbed into her neck, making her wince and hiss in a breath between her teeth.

Her eyes widened. She'd slept ... late. Her neck ... it ached.

Her mind swam with a dismal realization. *Excessive sleepiness. Neckache.* Two more of the tipinosis symptoms.

Slowly, she lowered herself back to the soft mattress, lying very still and trying to hang on to her fragile control. Her eyes stung; with a trembling hand, she brushed away the lone tear that puddled at the corner of her eye. She took several deep breaths and, little by little, she felt inner strength creep back into her.

God, she had so little time left now.

She wanted Seneca. Here, lying beside her and holding her in his arms. She had to find him. She hadn't much longer to be with him.

"Hummin'bird," she whispered. "Be happy, Peachy." Determined to ignore a lingering trace of sorrow, she began looking for her crown and finally located it under the blankets in the middle of the bed. With the crown on her head, she headed for the sitting room. Her hand was al-

214

ready on the doorknob before she remembered her nakedness. "Dang it to hell."

She hurried to the bath, looking all over for the soiled gown she'd been wearing the night before. When she couldn't find it anywhere, and saw that Seneca's clothes had disappeared as well, she guessed that maids had already tidied up the chambers.

She finally left the apartments wrapped in a satin bedsheet. If she hurried, maybe no one but a few upper-floor maids would see her. And if she asked them not to tell on her, they wouldn't. As she swept down the red-carpeted corridor, she did, indeed, hear young female voices. But the girls weren't talking, she realized with a start.

They were crying.

Quickening her pace, she turned a corner, then stopped. And stared. And felt instant fury burn inside her.

A short distance down the hallway stood Tiblock, two little maids cowering before him. He struck one, then the other. Both fell back against the gold-satin-covered wall.

"Jest what the hell do y'think yore a-doin'?" Clutching her sheet, Peachy raced forward, halting only when she stood between Tiblock and the frightened maids.

Tiblock stared at her bare shoulders and the satin sheet that clung to the rest of her body. Her hair cascaded around her face in a mass of tangled red-gold curls, and he couldn't help thinking that it appeared as though she wore a burst of fire flames on her head. She looked more like a common doxy than a member of royalty. Indeed, only the glitter of the priceless diamonds in her crown served to remind him that she was the Princess of Aventine. "Madam—"

"Yore so low you'd have to git up on a stump to kiss a snake's belly!" Turning, she helped the two maids to their feet. "Y'all all right, darlin's?" Her fury swelled when she caught sight of the red handprints on their pale cheeks.

"The bumbling chits dropped His Majesty's towels, Your Highness." Snorting, Tiblock gestured toward the pile of stark white towels lying on the scarlet carpet. "Now the linen must be laundered again."

Peachy glared at the towels. "Why didn't you hep pick them towels up instead o' mellerin' these here girls the way y'done?"

His nostrils flared. "Your Highness, that is *their* job. I have been in service to the royal family for twenty-one years and know precisely how to oversee the duties of each and every member of the castle staff. I assure madam that I am more than qualified to—"

"I thought you was the king's go-and-fetch man."

At the irreverent title Tiblock shuddered distastefully. "I am His Majesty's personal attendant. However, since I have been here longer than any of the other employees, I do my utter best to manage the running of the household as well. Supervising the staff is the least I can do for His Majesty, who has no time to worry about ignorant maids such as these two."

"I don't keer *how* long y'been here, Snort-Face. Y'ain't got no kind o' right to run all over the castle a-beatin' up on all the other servants! You—" She broke off as she remembered the suspicious red mark she'd seen on Nydia's cheek yesterday. "Y'hit my maid, Nydia, huh?"

"The clumsy girl broke a teacup."

"And you slapped her jest fer that?"

"It was utter carelessness on her part. A firm hand must be used when dealing with the lower classes."

Enraged, Peachy lunged toward the wall behind him and yanked down a long and wicked sword from the decorative collection. One hand holding the sheet together and the other brandishing the sharp weapon, she whirled on Tiblock. "Nydia ain't no low-class person. *You* are, you sorrier'n a suck-egg dog varmint!"

The point of her sword at his throat, Tiblock swallowed hard.

"What kind o' man goes 'round a-whackin' on women? You ain't no man, Snort-Face. And since y'ain't, you don't got nary a need fer them Tiblock jewels!"

Tiblock began to quaver with fear when she swished the sword down to his crotch. "M-madam—"

"Peachy!" Seneca's shout shot down the corridor.

Peachy saw him storming toward her, lightning in his eyes and thunder in his steps. Nydia and Ketty followed him, carrying the clothes they'd been about to bring to her in Seneca's chambers.

Upon arriving at Peachy's side, Seneca quickly divested her of the sword. His fingers turned white around the hilt when he saw how she was dressed.

"Your Highness," Tiblock said, "the maids spilled the linen to the floor, and I was merely chastizing them for—"

"Don't be a-pissin' down Seneca's back and a-tellin' him it's rainin'! Tell him the *truth* about what you was a-doin', you slimier'n cold snot son of a bitch!"

Struggling with a potent mixture of ire, shock, and totally inappropriate amusement, Seneca took hold of Peachy's arm. "Peachy, go to your rooms, and—"

"Ole Snort-Face was a-bangin' up on these girls, Seneca! All's they done was drop them gawdang towels! And he smacked Nydia yesterday fer a-breakin' a dumb *cup!* He's s'posed to be a-waitin' on the king, but he's got that onion nose o' his in ever' goin'-on in this here castle, a-flingin' orders ever' which way jest on account o' he likes a-bossin' folks around!"

Tiblock snorted loudly. "Your Highness, I have tried to explain to Her Highness that I am quite capable of running the—"

"Oh, shet up, Tiblock! Yore the conceitedest varmint I ever laid eyes on! Gawdangit, iffen you could ever git anybody to love you as much as you love yoresef, it'd be history's greatest romance!"

Tiblock stared at the hellion princess, his eyes growing big.

Seneca stiffened with rage when he saw that Peachy's sheet had slipped to reveal a glimpse of her lush cleavage. And the pompous servant had the audacity to stare! Instantly, he pulled Peachy behind him, his own body hiding her from Tiblock's view. "Ketty and Nydia, please accompany the princess to her rooms."

"But I ain't finished with that snortin', woman-beatin'—"

"You are finished, Peachy," Seneca cut her off sternly, his eyes never leaving Tiblock. "And the two of you are dismissed as well," he told the maids who'd dropped the towels.

Peachy watched the young girls as they began to gather the towels from the floor. "Leave 'em there. Snort-Face's gonna pick 'em up. And since he's so gawdang worried that they're dirty, he's gonna warsh 'em too." As the two maids disappeared down the hall, Peachy glowered at Tiblock from behind Seneca's broad back. "I *ain't* finished with you, Rupert-Dupert-Figgymoopert. You—"

"Peachy, please," Seneca warned.

She paid him no mind. "I aim to have it outen with you, Tiblock, and when I do? Well, when I do, you ain't gonna have no more of a chance than a one-legged man at a ass-kickin' contest, hear?"

"Peachy!"

"I'm a-goin', Seneca." Throwing one last look of warning at Tiblock, she sashayed down the corridor, her blue satin sheet and her maids trailing behind her.

Seneca took one long step toward Tiblock. "If I ever again see you look at the princess in the manner you looked at her a moment ago, I will happily run you through." Lifting the gleaming sword, he positioned its point at Tiblock's chest. Four flicks of his wrist cut four buttons off the shaking man's shirt.

The polished pearls peppered Tiblock's shining shoes. He gasped with obvious fear and hidden anger.

Seneca lowered the point of the sword to the floor and snagged a towel. He lifted it level with Tiblock's face. Staring at the man's twisted features, he decided Peachy had described him perfectly. Tiblock *was* a slimy son of a bitch.

He deposited the towel over Tiblock's bony shoulder. "I suggest you follow the princess's commands. Take these towels downstairs and wash them."

Tiblock's rage surpassed his fear. "Your Highness, I am His Majesty's—"

"There is not a person in this palace who is not aware of the fact that you are my father's personal attendant," Seneca snapped. "But you overstep the boundaries of your position, Tiblock, and I assure you that your days in the palace are numbered. You have earned the disdain of your future queen, and— Indeed, you have always had mine. Now go and launder the towels."

Tiblock retrieved the towels from the floor and stalked down the hall. Quaking with fury, he resolved to bring this matter before the king with all haste. His Majesty had the right to know that his favored servant had been commanded to become little more than a lowly slave in the laundry rooms, sweating over boiling pots of soiled linen. He had the right to know that the hellion princess ran around the castle dressed in nothing but diamonds and a sheet, threatening to mutilate men's bodies. And he most assuredly had the right to know that the crown prince had taken up the barbaric pastime of slashing shirts and threatening the wearers with death at the point of a sword.

Oh, yes, Tiblock thought as he scurried up the marble staircase that led to the king's personal apartments. The towels could wait.

Tattling to His Majesty could not.

The door to Peachy's room opened.

Ketty and Nydia took one look at the prince's face and couldn't leave the room fast enough. He barely had time to step out of the threshold before they raced through it.

Watching him shut the door, Peachy braced herself for the stern lecture she knew was coming. But no matter what he said, she wasn't going to apologize for what she'd said and done to Tiblock.

Turning from the door, Seneca caught and held Peachy's wide-eyed gaze. "Come here."

She remained by the pink-velvet-draped window. Bright sunlight poured over her, warming her, but not with the same intensity as did Seneca's eyes. His piercing gaze burned straight through the cream silk dressing gown she was wearing. Heat waves shimmered over her bare skin.

She lowered her thick lashes and studied him surreptitiously. He wore black. All black. Like midnight shadows, the sable color clung to him, encasing his hard, muscular form in such a way that left nothing and everything to her imagination.

"I ain't never seed y'dressed like that."

He held her gaze. "I've been fencing. All morning. And while I practiced, I remembered the story you told me about my killing all the bushwhackers and dragons. I couldn't keep my mind on the match, and for the first time in years, I lost. Perigrie, my opponent, beat me soundly."

She fiddled with the sash on her robe. "Y'riled at me fer that?"

He shrugged.

She wished she understood his mood. Dang the man for being such a master at concealing his emotions. "You don't look nothin' like the Prince o' Aventine, Seneca," she murmured. "All the black— Y'look like . . . danger."

"You're afraid of me, then?"

His deep voice filled the room the way dark clouds fill the sky before a storm. She half expected him to fling a bolt of lightning at her. "No. I ain't afeared o' you."

"You should be. But then, you've never done what you should."

"I always do what I should."

His slight smile had nothing to do with amusement. "You should obey me, should you not?"

She didn't answer. A sixth sense warned her she was about to be trapped.

"I've demanded your obedience time and time again. You will demonstrate it for me now."

She wondered what she was supposed to do. He hadn't given her any orders to obey. Her wariness heightened.

"Take off your robe."

She was too surprised to move, to speak. His unexpected command filled her with an intoxicating mixture of apprehension and desire.

"I told you to take off your robe."

"This . . . ain't got nothin' to do with Tiblock, huh?"

At her mention of the bastard's name, Seneca experienced the same explosive fury as he had when confronting the man. Though he'd never been given to violence before, he certainly was now.

Peachy was involved. That made all the difference.

His eyes narrowed to mere slashes. "First things first. Now, are you going to take off your robe, or shall I do it for you?" Without waiting for her reply, he moved toward her, slowly but with all the purpose and intent of a panther stalking its prey.

Peachy met him halfway.

He saw the cream silk of her robe flow around his black-clad legs. *Midnight and magnolias.* The words came to him again, reminding him of last night. "Peachy . . ." A growl of wild hunger for her rumbling in his throat, he crushed her to him and took her lips in a kiss that held every savage desire he'd battled to control all night, all morning. And while his tongue mated with hers, he slid his hands down her back, cupped her bottom, and pushed her into him. He wanted her with a fierce passion, and he wanted her to know it.

He knew she did when he felt her scrunch her thighs together.

"Good Lord, Seneca," she murmured, his rigid masculinity throbbing against her. "It shore don't take much to git you a-goin', huh?"

"It wouldn't take much for you either, and I truly believe the time has come for me to show you what I mean. Indeed, I have thought of little else since last night."

She shrieked with startled delight when he lifted her off the floor and carried her to the bed. There, he removed her robe and, when she was naked, quickly divested himself of his own clothes.

As bare as she, he stretched out beside her and pulled her into his embrace. Fingers beneath her chin, he lifted her face to his and settled his mouth over hers once more.

His long and drugging kiss turned Peachy into a captive who longed to remain with her captor. His tongue slid into her mouth, then out again, repeatedly, and some innate knowledge within her told her that this was the rhythm, the motion of lovemaking.

She inhaled softly when he pressed her hand to the top of his powerful thigh.

"You wanted to know me, Peachy. Know me now." He nudged her hand higher.

Those familiar tingles came to life inside her. A pulse began in her womanhood, prompting her to obey his sensual command. She drew her gaze down his sleek torso and saw her small, pale hand lying upon his dark skin. The contrast aroused her further.

Slowly, she inched her hand toward the base of his masculinity, which was fully erect against his flat belly. She grasped him gently, her fingers closing around him. The hot, hard feeling of him was strange and wonderful at once. It filled her with sweet awe. "So this is it. This is the feel of a man."

He waited to see what she would do.

She slid her hand upwards and ran her thumb around the tip of him. Her eyes widened when he moaned in response. The sound was one of pleasure, she realized, and for the very first time, she understood her power as a woman.

She glided her hand down again, then cupped the warm, soft pouch beneath his staff. It felt good in her hand. Felt nice to hold and caress, and again, her actions made him moan. "Feels good? When I touch you?"

His hand closed around hers; he caught her smile. "Do you find something humorous in this?" he asked, anxious to know what she was smiling about.

She continued to stare at his long, hard manhood. "I was jest a-thinkin' about names."

"Names?" What on earth did names have to do with what they were doing? he wondered.

Peachy giggled softly. "You orter have a name, too, Seneca. Iffen I'm Guinevere, you could be . . ." She smiled into his eyes. "Well, y'could be King Arthur or Lancelot. What's yore druthers?"

Her outrageous suggestion struck him mute. Profound amusement swept through him.

"King Arthur's a more royal-soundin' name," Peachy went on. "You a-bein' the prince who'll one day be king and all, maybe y'want to be King Arthur. But there's jest somethin' about *Lancelot*. It has a sartin ring to it, Seneca, don'tcha think? 'Course it's yore body, so which name do y'like the bestest?"

A huge grin curled over his lips.

Peachy noticed how it softened his features and lit up his startling blue eyes. "God Almighty, yore handsome, Seneca. And jest when I think y'cain't git no more handsomer, y'up and do somethin' that makes y'more handsome. Y'orter smile more often, y'know."

His amused smile fading to a tender one, he pulled her down to the bed and sat up beside her.

The sparkle of mirth in his eyes had given way to twin flames of passion. He'd said he was going to show her something. Tension and excitement sizzling through her, she quivered all over as she waited to see what it would be.

"You'll trust me, Peachy," he commanded. He placed his hand on her belly. Slowly, he glided it downward, stopping it over her femininity.

Peachy scrunched her thighs together.

"Open for me."

"Open? Why— You— Are you gonna *touch* me—"

"I was considering it, yes."

"But—"

"Open your legs, Peachy."

The thought of what he planned to do created a warm heaviness within her, causing her to tighten her thighs once more.

Seneca doubted they could be pried apart with a crowbar. "I understand why you squeeze your thighs together, Peachy, but those feelings that prompt you to do it can be heightened. And when they peak, you will feel them not only between your legs but all over your body. Can you trust that I'm telling you the truth?"

She nodded, filled to the very brim with trust in him.

"Very well, Princess, open for me."

Inch by inch, she obeyed.

Seneca slid his hand downward, his fingers delving into the outer softness of her womanhood.

"Seneca!" She squirmed, squeezing her legs together.

"Peachy—"

"But I never—"

"I know you haven't."

"I didn't know—"

"There are many things you don't know, sweetheart. But if you'll trust me, I'll teach them to you."

The meaning of his words, the softness in his voice, and the tenderness in his gaze helped her to relax. She became still again, her legs opening for him once more.

Seneca continued caressing her, his fingers gliding over the moist entry to her body.

A sense of wonder took hold of Peachy when an elusive

pleasure began to wander through her nether region. Like a spark not yet grown to a flame, it came and went, a bit stronger each time.

Seneca watched her lashes flutter upon her flushed cheeks. "This," he murmured, "is but a small sample of what lovemaking is all about."

She arched her hips completely off the bed when she felt his sensual invasion. "Seneca! Y'put yore finger—"

"Yes, I did."

"But that ain't . . . You ain't s'posed to—"

"How would you know? You've never done this before. Now, relax and stop fighting me." He slipped a second finger into her dewy softness. God, she was tight. *Too* tight. "Peachy, you must let go, Princess," he cooed. "Don't concentrate on the oddness of what I'm doing to you. Instead, dwell on how it feels. Think of my promise. I promised you pleasure. Remember?"

"I'll . . . try."

"I'll help you to remember. Like this, Peachy. Like this." He began to circle his thumb lightly over the hidden swell of flesh that he had every intention of bringing to life for the very first time.

Peachy closed her eyes and concentrated on the feeling of his fingers inside her. It felt strange, but it wasn't painful, not unpleasant. Moreover, the elusive pleasure was elusive no more. It tricked through her in rivulets that soon became waves that threatened to drown her. Though centered in the depths of her womanhood, it radiated throughout her entire body, prompting her to writhe and yearn for what she sensed was a culmination.

And Seneca sired it. Mastered it. And the pleasure rose, so strong now she wondered if she could stand it when it reached its summit. "Stop. Yeah, stop. No, don't. Hurry. Oh, Lord, somethin's a-happenin'. Make it—"

"I will."

"Seneca." She moaned his name, but could say no more.

She didn't need to. He began to caress her more quickly, his fingers continuing to pump deeply into her.

Ecstasy blossomed. Melted through her. Like flames speeding along a designated course, it heated and engulfed each part of her, leaving her weary with joy of it all, yet desirous for the last flickering pleasure that could be gotten.

Seneca didn't disappoint her, but continued to caress her until her body ceased to tremble, until she took a deep breath and became utterly still. Slowly, he withdrew his fingers, but he left his hand upon the warm, wet center of her womanly splendor. "And that, Princess Peachy," he began on a husky whisper, "is a hint of the wonders of love-making."

Her eyes still closed, she smiled but didn't comment.

"Peachy? Tell me what you're thinking."

Her smile widened. "About gravel. And gooses. What you jest done . . . That was it, huh, Seneca?"

"Yes." He lay on his side, pulled her into his arms, and positioned her so that her back nestled snugly into the curve of his body.

"It felt real good, Seneca."

"I told you it would."

" 'Pears I orter listen to you better."

"But you won't."

She smiled. "Seneca? What about you?"

"What about me?"

"Well . . . You didn't git no gravel fer *yore* goose, did you?"

"No." He waited in tense silence to see if she would ask him to make love to her.

She didn't, but he knew in his soul he could take her right now and she wouldn't object. She wouldn't fight him, nor would she question him.

But he didn't want to *take* her, and that realization stemmed straight from his heart. He didn't want only to *have* her.

He wanted her to *give* herself to him. Freely, and without a shred of reservation or inhibition. He wanted her to long for him with all the joy she was capable of feeling.

She'd yet to do that. He wondered how much longer he'd have to wait for her to reach that point.

And God, he wondered if he had it in him to wait. Patience had never been one of his virtues.

It was sheer hell learning it now.

"Seneca?"

"Princess."

"Thanky."

"You're welcome."

"Y'never did tell me which name y'liked best, King Arthur or Lancelot."

Smiling broadly, he looked down at himself and saw that he was still hard and thick with unappeased desire.

Laughter bubbled inside him. "Lancelot," he decided. "Definitely Lancelot."

She turned to face him. "I knowed y'say that, Seneca. Miz Mackintosh, she tole me about how men set sech a store over their man parts. So I jest knowed y'wouldn't be able to resist a-pickin' outen the biggest-soundin' name fer yoresef."

He could no longer contain his vast amusement. It escaped him on a loud burst of laughter.

Peachy joined him in his mirth. For a long while they lay in each other's arms, listening to the harmonious mingling of their laughter.

When the laughter finally faded, Seneca took Peachy's chin between his thumb and finger, and attempted a stern look, a difficult feat to accomplish with amusement still pumping through him. "I haven't forgotten the scene with Tiblock, Peachy."

Her lighthearted mood tightened into one of apprehension. She braced herself for the harsh lecture, wishing it didn't have to come now. Not now, when she and Seneca had been having such a good time.

Watching an expression of dread come into her eyes, Seneca readied himself to give her the dressing-down she deserved. "Don't do that again."

She frowned slightly. "That's it? Don't do that again? That's all yore gonna say?"

Lazily, he drew tiny circles around her nipple, thinking of the outrageous cursing she'd given Tiblock. Truth be told, he admired and envied her unique talent for verbal battles. He couldn't help but wish that once, just once, he could know what it felt like to be so free with emotions.

It seemed almost wrong to reprimand her over one of the things that so enchanted him about her.

Still, it had to be done. The wager with his father, his need to make her a lady fit to be queen, demanded it.

And he definitely didn't want her running around in a sheet again.

He raised a sable brow at her. "I would like to believe that it would be a waste of breath for me to say more than that. I'm hoping that you *know* your behavior this morning was unseemly. Moreover, I'm hoping you will never, ever sashay around the palace in nothing but a sheet. You are mine, Peachy. And I won't share so much as a glimpse of you with any other man. When Tiblock looked at you . . . I wanted to drive the sword straight through his black heart. You belong to *me,* only me, every silken inch of you. Do you understand?"

"You should've gone on and stabbed him. He—" Abruptly, she stopped speaking.

You are mine, Peachy.

You belong to me, only me . . .

She stared at him without blinking once, astonished by his possessiveness and the feelings of deep joy it brought to her.

"I asked you if you understood, Peachy."

She nodded, too overcome with emotion to speak.

"Very well." He got out of bed and dressed quickly. "Call your maids, have them assist you into something suitable for an outing, and meet me in the queen's chambers. I've four surprises for you, although God knows your improper behavior this morning should keep me from giving them to you. My advice, then, is that you would do well to hurry, lest I change my mind."

"Surprises?" She flew off the bed. "What—"

"Get dressed." With that, he quit the room, anxious to escape before she succeeded in coercing him to tell her.

Walking down the corridor toward the staircase that led to his floor of apartments, he thought abut the time he'd just spent with Peachy. True, he hadn't made love to her. Even now his sensual needs remained unfulfilled. But he *had* done something he'd never expected to do. Something he hadn't done since he was a small child.

He'd laughed out loud.

It felt almost as good as lovemaking.

* * *

"She threatened to make a eunuch out of you, Tiblock? My, what a ladylike thing to do!" The king laughed uproariously. His huge frame shook the mattress.

Tiblock snorted delicately. "Am I to understand that Your Majesty *condones* the prince's and princess's behavior?"

Grimacing with pain and smiling with amusement, the king shook his head. "With each outrageous antic the heathen commits, she brings herself closer to that Carolina mountain home of hers. Although it would appear that Seneca has succeeded in finally consummating the marriage— The yokel *was* wearing his bedsheet, didn't you say?"

"Yes, Your Highness."

"That would indicate she spent the night in Seneca's chambers. But her behavior this morning is proof that he has been unable to smooth even *one* of her many rough edges. The repulsive hoyden will soon be gone from Aventine." Finger to his chin, he deliberated for a moment. "I have learned that Callista Inger has fled to Paris. Broken heart, or some such malady, I believe. However, I am certain that if I summon her back to Aventine for her marriage to Seneca, she would return with all haste."

Tiblock scowled. "I beg Your Majesty's pardon, but I— Your Majesty, I am completely bewildered."

The king explained the terms of the wager he'd made with Seneca. "And so, you see, Tiblock, we mustn't discourage the little savage from proceeding with her natural inclinations. Don't you agree?"

It took Tiblock only a few seconds to understand the king's hint. "Oh, yes, Your Majesty. We shall give her every chance to be herself. And should I see an outlandish situation brewing, I will endeavor to further it along. Why, I feel certain that with a bit of intervention on my part, not even Lady Elsdon will be able to—"

"Viridis?" The king snarled the name. "What has she to do with this?"

"His Highness has summoned her to tutor the princess. I believe she will arrive tomorrow, sir."

King Zane didn't care for that information. Viridis

Elsdon had earned the title Matriarch of Etiquette, and with good reason. If one person on the entire earth could get through to the mountain spitfire, it was Viridis. And though Viridis was a distant relative of the royal family, King Zane detested her and always had.

He couldn't, however, refuse to allow her into the palace. She was well-loved by Aventine's nobility, and any objections to her on his part would besmirch his reputation among his subjects.

Deep foreboding filled him. "You must do everything you can do to disrupt the girl's progress with Viridis, Tiblock. Seneca *cannot* win, do you understand? I won't allow it!"

"I will do exactly as Your Majesty commands."

King Zane tried to calm himself. "You're a loyal servant, Tiblock. For twenty-one years, you have served me well."

Tiblock beamed with pleasure and genuine fondness for his king. "There is nothing I wouldn't do for Your Majesty. Nothing at all."

And he meant what he said.

When Peachy entered the Queen's Chambers, Thurlow Wadsworth McGee perched on her shoulder, she didn't see Seneca anywhere.

But it didn't take her long to notice the vast array of porcelain figurines scattered throughout the room. Why, altogether there had to be almost five hundred of the fragile knickknacks!

She understood immediately that the beautiful objects were one of the surprises Seneca had promised her. He'd listened carefully to her explanation about the pretty lady locked in the cabinet, and he'd taken her dismay to heart.

Profoundly touched, she picked up a hand-painted figure of a shepherd girl. The intricately designed sprigs of flowers on the girl's skirt amazed Peachy. Not to mention the perfection of her tiny facial features. Peachy held the figurine tightly, smiling as it warmed in her hand.

"Is she the lady you saw and wished you could remove from the locked cabinet?"

At the deep, familiar voice, Peachy turned to face her

husband, realizing he'd been sitting in the corner of the room all along. When her gaze joined his, she blushed, thinking of the sensual things he'd done to her earlier. "She's even purtier'n the one I seed. Seneca—"

"Come along," he said, going to the door. "You may admire the figurines later. There are still three surprises I've yet to give you."

He watched her place her squirrel on the floor. "What is that thing on his head?"

Peachy grinned. "It's his crown. I figgered that since I'm the royal princess now, he's the royal squirrel. So I maked him a crown outen that blue satin dress I teared up the day I was a-hepin' Tivon and his ram. Used a few little beads from my weddin' dress, too."

Seneca stared at the headpiece atop the squirrel's head. One row of small crystal beads encircled a burst of shiny blue satin. Peachy had attached the crown to the squirrel's head by means of a gold ribbon that was tied under its tiny chin.

"Don't he look cute, Seneca?"

Seneca had never seen anything so absurd in his entire life. Shaking his head, he walked out of the room.

Her curiosity and excitement rising, Peachy hurried after him. He escorted her out of the palace, through the sumptuous royal gardens, and toward the Mews.

As he strode upon the white quartz walkway, he glanced at her gown. "You're wearing a satin ball gown again, Princess. It's not even noon yet, and bright purple doesn't strike me as a morning color for a respectable woman. And is it necessary to wear so many jewels at once?"

She heard no anger in his voice, but suspected he was a bit dismayed over her choice of gowns. "I know it's a ball gown, Seneca. Ketty tole me so. But I— It's so purty. I love this color purple. Maw used to grow petuniers this same color. I jest wanted to much-love the dress." She touched the shimmering masses of emeralds at her throat, ears, wrists, and fingers, and patted her diamond crown as well. "And I want to much-love my jewelry, too. I jest cain't stand the thought o' havin' purty things and not enjoyin' 'em all the way."

Her soft, sweet voice and her obvious pleasure in the

gown made him wonder if it really mattered that she wore purple satin in the morning. And what harm was she doing by wearing every emerald she owned? Even if the dark green jewels *did* clash with the purple gown, she was happy.

He liked her happy. That thought in mind, he dismissed her gown and jewels and started for the mews again.

When he offered no comment about what she'd told him, Peachy wondered if he was still irritated with her. "Seneca, I ain't got much time left to enjoy these here things," she tried to explain, stumbling in her haste to keep up with his long-legged strides. "I weren't gonna say nothin' to you about this ... but— Well, I ain't never in my life slept as late as I done this mornin'. And when I waked up? Well, I mean to tell you, my neck was a-miseryin' me somethin' fierce."

He knew she was referring to symptoms she believed would ultimately lead to her death. He stopped once more and gave her a good frown. "Peachy, for the time being, I will endeavor to be patient with your bold way of dressing, but I will not stand for your morbid belief that you're dying."

"But Seneca—"

"You were up late last night. You slept in this morning because you were tired. As for your painful neck ... For God's sake, Peachy, you slept with your crown on. I watched you. As if you were perfectly aware that any movement on your part would cause the crown to fall off, you slept as stiffly and motionless as possible. Anyone would have an aching neck after a night like that. Now, no more talk of dying, do you understand?"

"Y'still cain't face the fact that the chill o' death's a-fixin' to pass over me, huh, darlin'? I'm a-tellin' you that I seed a turkey buzzard fly over my cabin, and that's a shore sign o' death. And Dr. Greely—"

"Dr. Greely? You've never mentioned a doctor before. Who is this doctor?"

She took a moment to pick a pink rose and sprinkle the petals on top of Thurlow Wadsworth McGee's back. "Dr. Greely was a-passin' through my neck o' the woods and kindly stopped by to give me a goin'-over. He's who figgered outen I got tipinosis."

Seneca comprehended immediately that she'd been examined by some mountain quack. Maybe some con artist who'd hoped to bilk her out of money she hadn't even possessed. "And you believed every word he said."

"He had a black bag and ever'thing."

Seneca rolled his eyes. "And his black bag, combined with the flight of the turkey buzzard, convinced you of your approaching death."

"I—"

"You are *not* dying. You've but to look in a mirror to see that you aren't even *sick*. Indeed, you are more than likely the healthiest person in Aventine."

"You ain't no doctor, Seneca. Yore only a *prince!*"

"*Only* a prince?"

"You—"

"I will discuss this no longer, nor will I allow you to broach the subject again. You are a young, beautiful, and vigorous woman with no need to worry about death right now. And you would do well to know that I do not care for the fact that you are constantly dwelling on such a gloomy subject. It strikes me as not only ridiculous but also rather morose. Now, come along."

Following him, she reminded herself that his unwillingness to face the truth that he would soon lose her to the Grim Reaper was probably a normal reaction. But she was sincerely worried. If he didn't accept the dismal situation soon, her death would be a blow that he might not ever get over.

So deep in thought was she, she failed to notice that he'd stopped. She ran right into him.

Seneca righted himself immediately. "Peachy, may I remind you that a lady *glides?* She does not clomp along and plow into people."

"Sorry."

Seneca remembered that Viridis Elsdon would be arriving in the morning. The thought reassured him. "Very well. Now suppose you tell me what you think about the second surprise?" He raised his hand, gesturing toward where he wanted her to look.

Peachy's knees buckled, prompting Seneca to grab her arm to keep her from falling. There, right before her eyes and gleaming brightly in the strong morning sun, was the Imperial Coach of Aventine. Her heart fairly pounding its way out of her chest, she approached the glittering coach, unable to believe that what she was seeing was real.

It appeared to be made of solid gold. Its framework consisted of eight upright lions which supported the elaborately scrolled roof. Upon the tiered roof four cherubs knelt, their chubby arms and hands raised to hold a massive replica of the Imperial Crown. Smaller crowns and more angels adorned the sides of the doors and all four sides of the sparkling windows were edged with intricately cut tracings of frosted glass.

Six matched grays made up the team, their manes plaited and adorned with slender gold ribbons. Each fine horse wore elegant state harness composed of dark blue leather decorated with gilt. The near-side horses were driven by two postillions dressed in the royal livery of burgundy breeches, tall black boots, and dark blue jackets embellished with gold braid. The riders' shiny black hats featured large burgundy feathers that swayed in the gentle North Sea breeze. Similarly dressed and seated at the back of the coach were two grooms.

Warmed by Peachy's obvious delight, Seneca escorted her to the coach door. "Would you care to see inside?"

"I know what's in there," Peachy whispered, overcome. "Pink satin seats."

"Ah, but that's not all, Princess. I present the third surprise." Smiling devilishly, Seneca opened the door.

Peachy's mouth fell open. There, sitting demurely upon one of the pink satin seats, was Agusta. *Gussie!* Oh, Lord o' mercy, Seneca, it's Gussie!"

Seneca felt a tad of envy over the fact that Peachy had given a nickname to a woman she barely knew. She'd yet to give *him* one.

He squared his shoulders, quelling his childish thoughts. "You did say you wanted Lady Sherringham as one of your ladies, did you not? She'll be with you during the day and return to her husband's estate in the evenings." He almost smiled, recalling Veston Sherringham's curtly worded message of compliance to Agusta's royal summons to the palace.

Whirling to face him, Peachy threw her arms around his neck and planted loud kisses all over his cheek. "Seneca, thanky! Thanky so very, very . . . The veriest o' much!"

He could feel her legs next to his and realized that if she wore any underwear at all, it consisted of nothing more than one thin slip. God, how he loved the feel of her thighs scrunching together.

He couldn't, of course, allow her improper demonstration of affection to continue. "Shall we go for a ride?" he asked, knowing his question would lead her to practically throw herself into the coach.

To prevent her from doing so, he handed her inside himself, dismissing the services of the footman who stood ready to assist her.

As soon as she was seated beside Agusta, Peachy took the woman's frail hand and gave it a tender pat. The bones in Agusta's hand felt like brittle sticks, prompting Peachy into sudden action.

She leaned out of the coach door and spied the footmen nearby. "Can y'all git us somethin' to eat, please? Don't matter what it is as long as it's more'n plenty."

Unaware that Seneca had echoed her command with a nod of his head, Peachy was enormously pleased by the footmen's instant obedience to her wishes. They soon exited the mews with a basket of food.

Peachy smiled in approval when she saw the basket held crusty breads, jams, and hard-boiled eggs. She handed it to Agusta. "Eat now, darlin', all right?"

Grinning, Agusta had to curb the urge to throw her thin arms around Peachy. She was thrilled to have been chosen to become one of the princess's ladies, and was looking forward to spending wonderfully diverting days with the vivacious mountain girl. Still grinning, Agusta lifted a piece of bread to her mouth and began to chew.

Peachy nodded in satisfaction. "Gussie don't talk much, Seneca, but she's a real sweet girl."

"I imagine you will talk enough for the both of you."

Agusta gave a timid smile to the prince. "The princess has a lot to say, Your Highness. And I so enjoy her conversation."

Seneca heard the truth in her words and understood that Agusta was very fond of Peachy. He'd never paid much attention to Agusta Sherringham in the past, but he decided now that he liked her.

"What about my fourth surprise, Seneca?"

"My, but you're greedy," he answered with a smile. "It's there, under your seat."

She leaned down and retrieved a small but heavy velvet pouch. It was full of gold coins.

"You asked for gold to throw to the peasants," Seneca reminded her.

"Yes! Oh, Lord o' mercy, yes! Seneca, thanky!"

"You're welcome. But Peachy, I will warn you now that I will not provide you with bags of gold whenever you feel the urge to fling it out of your coach window."

Hugging the gold to her chest, she nodded. "I promise not to ask fer more'n two or three sacks a week."

Seneca sighed.

And the coach rolled forward, heading for the countryside.

While Agusta began to eat, Peachy considered her plans to distribute the gold and deal with Aventine's scrawny pigs. She didn't have her cures with her, but she could certainly perform a few examinations of the kingdom's swine. Looking out the window, she thought about the many things her father had taught her about pigs.

Seneca didn't miss the bright twinkle in her eyes. She was up to something, and he had the distinct feeling he wouldn't like it.

He tried to quell his suspicions, reminding himself that his wayward wife was safely esconced within a closed coach. Opportunities for creating some sort of havoc were few. All they would be doing this afternoon was to take a quiet ride through the countryside.

He settled back against the pink satin seats, desiring nothing more than to sit across from his princess and relish her happiness and lush beauty. The ride would be slow, relaxing, and long, providing him with the perfect opportunity to grant his own wishes.

Yes, it was going to be a tranquil afternoon indeed.

Chapter 12

～♦～

An outrageous spectacle, that's what it was!

The Princess of Aventine, dressed in satin and emeralds and diamonds, stood beside a stack of wood in the small village square. Clasped within her bejeweled fingers was an ax handle. She'd chopped the wood herself, and short of dragging her back to the coach by her hair, Seneca could find no way to dissuade her from continuing to chop wood.

It had taken her only fifteen minutes to split a tall stack of logs. If Seneca wasn't so angry, he might have been amazed by her skill, however unseemly it was.

If only he'd suspected *why* she'd requested he stop the coach at the village. He'd thought she merely wanted to give her gold away, and sorely regretted not paying heed to his earlier suspicions. He should have realized that a closed coach wouldn't hinder her from causing chaos. He doubted that even the castle dungeon could hold her.

He glared fiercely at her. "Are you quite finished?"

She leaned the ax against the woodpile, adjusted her lopsided crown, and patted Thurlow Wadsworth McGee, who sat beside her slurping on a berry one of the villagers had given him. "Yore riled, huh, Seneca?"

Seneca stared at the elderly and the children of the village, his stony gaze coercing them to retreat toward their branch-and-mud huts. He glowered at Augusta, who waited under the shade of a chestnut tree, perched upon a piece of wood Peachy wanted to take back to the palace. Augusta tactfully turned her back.

Only then did Seneca answer Peachy's question. *"Riled?"* he repeated. "No, Peachy, I'm ecstatic. You've no idea how utterly thrilled it makes me to see you chopping wood. In fact, the only reason I married you was because I knew in my heart that you were the one person who could do something about Aventine's shortage of firewood."

He anticipated her caustic rejoinder. He was ready for it, fully prepared to come back at her with another biting reply. She'd taught him the fine art of forming stinging retorts, and he would show her what an apt pupil he'd been.

For a moment, Peachy only stared at him. She'd never heard him speak in such a manner. For a man unaccustomed to sarcasm, his mockery was wonderful, she mused proudly. She doubted she could have done better herself.

Amusement twinkled through her; she burst into loud laughter.

Her mirth led the peasants to believe all was well. They began drifting back toward her.

Their arrival forced Seneca to swallow the scathing reprimand he'd been about to deliver. Indeed, he couldn't even see her, for the villagers had surrounded her completely. After a moment, he heard a collective sigh among the people, and knew she had finally gotten around to distributing the gold.

She soon emerged from the crowd and bounced toward an assortment of enclosed pens on the outskirts of the village. Seneca gritted his teeth when he saw that the pens held hogs.

Dust floated around him as he stalked after her, passing the group of awed peasants, who bowed as he walked by them. "Peachy," he called as loudly as he dared.

She turned, but continued walking backwards. "I aim to see to the pigs, Seneca. It's why I wanted to stop here. I weren't gonna chop the wood, y'see, but when I seed it needed choppin' . . . Well, I been a-choppin' wood since afore I could drool. I knowed it wouldn't take too long to do. Y'want to know why the wood weren't chopped? The strong men's all outen in yore paw's flower fields. So's the able-bodied women. These here old folks cain't chop it, and neither can them young'uns."

She was right, and he knew it. He still didn't condone her unladylike performance of chopping wood, but he decided to dismiss it. However, he would *not* allow her to work among the pigs. "You are not going to mingle with swine." He moved to take her hand.

She snatched it away from him. "I ain't a-leavin' till I see to them pigs, Seneca."

"Get back in the coach. Right now."

"No. You'd have better luck a-tryin' to dig a ditch in the ocean than you'll have a-gittin' me to leave these here folks who need me."

He took a deep breath, struggling to conceal his fury from the villagers, who watched from a short distance away. "Peachy, you are the princess of Aventine, for God's sake. You *cannot* go wallowing in the mud with hogs."

She continued toward the pens. "I ain't gonna go a-wallerin' in mud, Seneca. Lord o' mercy, this is one o' my favorite-est dresses! Do y'think I'd go and git mud all over it?"

He tightened his hands into fists. Apparently, she hadn't noticed the damage she'd already done to her skirts while chopping wood.

He seized her arm, forcing her to a halt. "You will *not* tend the swine. It was one thing for you to see to one small pig in the tower, but it is quite another for you to wade among an entire herd of them. Now for the last time, get in the coach."

"*Yore* the one who tole me to hep the people. I'm a-hepin' 'em, and now yore a-pitchin' a gawdang fit over it. You beat all, y'know that, Seneca?"

He fixed his face into a mask of granite. "I am not given to pitching fits. There are other ways to help the—"

"The best way to hep 'em is to jest come outen here and *hep* 'em. I cain't do nothin' a'tall fer 'em whilst I'm a-settin' in the palace, Seneca. They need hands-on hep, and iffen you cain't unnerstand that? Well, iffen brains was ink, you wouldn't be able to dot an 'i.' "

He clamped his lips together as Agusta and the peasants gathered around. No matter how upset he was with Peachy, he would not allow anyone to know it.

Peachy took full advantage of his predicament and

swept toward the hog pens. The villagers waited for Seneca to join her before they followed.

It took Peachy only a short while to understand why the swine were doing poorly. "Y'ain't feedin' 'em right," she announced, scooping up a tiny piglet before the mother sow could protest. "They need more'n corn. Y'gotta give 'em meat scraps, all sorts o' vegetables, dried fish, oats, and flour. Give 'em lots o' bread. Fruit. Milk. Don't matter what kind o' milk, neither. Fresh milk, buttermilk ... Hell, they even like clabber. But what they need the mostest is mast. Y'got a whole forest on this island, and I can tell you right now in this here day and time that there ain't nothin' like mast fer hogs. Them woods over yonder's plumb full o' mast."

Agusta looked toward the forest. "Mast?"

"Nuts," Peachy explained to her and the peasants. "What y'all gotta do is let these here hogs go outen and forage, y'see. They won't go too fur, and they're right easy to bring home. Git 'em used to a sartin kind o' call, and they'll come a-runnin' whenever they hear it. And iffen y'cain't come up with no good calls, lemme know. We used to have hog-hollerin' contests back home in Possom Holler. Folks'd come from miles around to holler into them hills. The bestest hollerers got a brass pig fer their fireplace mantel and a side o' bacon fer their bellies. I winned last year. It was the bestest day o' my life, 'cept fer the day I wed up with Seneca. Them contests ... I mean to tell you, we'd have us a heap o' hilarity."

Seneca stared at her. A true lady never raised her voice. And Peachy had won screaming contests. He rolled his eyes.

An elderly woman stepped forward. "What kind of nuts should we prompt the hogs to eat, ma'am?"

Peachy scratched the piglet's ears, smiling when he grunted with pleasure. "You'll git the sweetest meat iffen the hogs eat chestnuts. The onliest thing is, though, chestnut-eatin' hogs'll give you dark oil instead o' fine white lard. And acorns'll make the meat bitter as all git out. So what y'do, see, is call in the hogs about a month afore y'slaughter 'em. Feed 'em anything but mast fer that month, and that'll git the meat shed o' bitterness. It'll make the hog fat good and soft, too, which'll mean better lard."

Seneca listened carefully to her explanation. Aggravated though he was, he couldn't help but respect her knowledge. Nor could he help noticing the villagers' deep worry over their swine. He glanced down at the pigs and realized they *did* appear rather unhealthy. He found himself hoping the diet Peachy had prescribed would work. And when he looked up, he saw that his hope was echoed in the villagers' eyes.

Indeed, their gazes shone with faith and adoration. One woman kept reaching out and timidly caressing Peachy's arm.

He'd never seen the people so happy.

His anger began to dissipate. He could no longer hold on to his belief that she shouldn't concern herself with swine. He certainly didn't want her sloshing around in their mud pools with them, but there was nothing wrong with her sharing her experience with the villagers. Indeed, he began to wonder what else she could teach them.

"And don't never slaughter hogs in front o' the baby pigs." Without thinking, Peachy handed the squealing piglet to Seneca. "It makes 'em nervous and gives 'em hives. Then they won't eat. Now, y'all be shore to pass on to the other villagers ever'thing I tole you today, hear? Seneca, what in the world are you a-doin' with that pig?"

He held the wiggling animal out before him. "I—"

"Don't hold him like that, darlin'. Yore a-makin' him afeared on account o' he thinks yore gonna drop him."

Exasperated with the fidgeting pig, Seneca handed it to a startled Agusta, who immediately cuddled it to her flat bosom. He then turned back to Peachy.

But she was already springing back to the village square to greet the men and women who were just arriving home from their day in the paschal fields. Seneca saw how each person kissed her hand.

Peachy kissed *their* hands, too! It didn't matter to her that the hands were rough and soiled.

She was much-loving the peasants he realized. They, in turn, were much-loving her. Like a beautiful figurine taken out from behind the glass doors of a cabinet, she was being held and touched and enjoyed on all sides.

The princess and her people, he thought. Though a thick layer of dust clung to her diamond crown, he couldn't remember any other of Aventine's royal headpieces ever shining as brightly.

As the afternoon wore on, Peachy, with Agusta close at her side, discussed the proper way to make soap, and how to weave baskets so tightly that they could hold water without a drop escaping. She reviewed various types of wood and told the people what each kind was best used for. She explained how to forecast the weather by watching animals, insects, and plant growth, and talked about the art of preserving vegetables and fruits and all sorts of meats. She described how to find wild plant foods, promising the plants would add flavor to the bland meals they were accustomed to eating.

And last, she demonstrated her talent at woodcarving. Using a sharp knife and small chisel that one of the village men provided, she began whittling a sturdy piece of ash she'd found earlier. Before long, she had the preliminary makings of a cane.

Only Seneca understood why she'd made it. Her thoughtfulness toward his sire touched him deeply. The king had mistreated her ever since her arrival, yet she'd chosen to overlook his cantankerous behavior and make him a gift.

Her innate kindness humbled him. In his mind, he stepped off his pedestal. His feet touched solid ground.

And it was a good feeling.

He smiled when she looped her arm through his. "Are you ready to return to the palace, Princess?"

Tired but satisfied, she nodded and allowed him to lead her toward the coach. A little boy handed her a bouquet of flowers.

"They're paschal flowers, ma'am. They grow in Aventine because of a miracle."

Peachy looked at the bright pink flowers. "A miracle?"

An old man in rags stepped forward, his cloudy eyes squinting to see the princess. His bare feet disappeared into a patch of bright yellow buttercups. "The miracle happened centuries ago, Your Highness."

Peachy wished she'd saved some gold to give the poor man. After a second of pondering, she removed the biggest of her emerald rings and placed it in his withered hand. Upon further thought, she gave him all the rings she wore with the exception of her diamond wedding band. "I know you'll share them jewels with the rest o' yore village, ain't that right?"

Too stunned to speak, he gave a slow nod.

Seneca was a bit shocked himself. Peachy had just given the man enough wealth to support the entire village for over a year. Not only that, but the emerald rings had belonged to Seneca's mother.

His mother. Pondering her, he remembered how she'd fawned over those very emeralds. How lovingly she'd gazed at them and caressed them.

She'd loved her emeralds more than she'd loved her own son.

That fact made Seneca suddenly glad that the old man had the jewels. Dismissing them from his mind, he moved to hand Peachy into the coach.

As his princess prepared to leave, the old man said, "Bless you, Your Highness. I don't believe anyone has done anything like this for us since Saint Paschal performed the miracle of the flowers. If madam has a moment, I will tell the story."

Peachy turned to Seneca. "Can we stay fer a minute? I love miracle stories. Must be the Catholic in me."

He couldn't resist the plea in her beautiful green eyes and gave her an indulgent smile.

"Centuries ago," the man began, his voice softening, "the sheep of Aventine were dying. Nothing the people did for them made them well. The people began to pray to Saint Paschal, the patron saint of shepherds. Saint Paschal heard their prayers. Soon, a strange plant began to grow on this island. No one had ever seen it before. It was a dainty plant, but a hearty one, and the sheep began to eat its bright pink blossoms."

He paused to cast a look of gratitude to the heavens. "The result was a miracle. Not only were the sheep cured of the ailment that had sickened them, but they thrived. The shepherds named the plant paschal after the benevolent saint who sent it to them. Many scientists and other men of learning have since come to study it. Some have tried to grow it in other countries, but to no avail. It grows nowhere else in the world. Our sheep continue to consume the paschal. We give it to them as fodder, and still they thrive, just as they have since Saint Paschal performed the miracle."

Peachy wept unabashedly, her tears dripping onto her gown until Seneca pressed a silk handkerchief into her hand. "I believe that's the purtiest story I ever did hear."

The old man smiled up at his prince. "Thank you, sir," he said, his voice quivering with emotion.

Seneca felt confused; he'd done nothing for this man. "Why do you thank me?"

The man smiled a toothless smile. "For bringing the princess to help us."

Seneca frowned slightly. Is that what the people believed?

"We've been managing poorly," the old man continued. "As our ancestors before us did, we have prayed for help. Our prayers have been answered, just as they were centuries ago. Then, they were answered with paschal. Now, they have been answered with the princess. The princess ... All the people are calling madam the 'Angel Princess.' "

Angel Princess, Seneca mused. For some odd reason, the word *angel* struck a note of recognition in him. He couldn't understand why, but he felt that he, too, had called her his angel.

Once upon a time ...

"I know that this day will long be spoken of," the man continued. "Down through the centuries parents and grandparents will sit around the fire and tell the tale of Princess Peachy. Her kindness will never be forgotten. Nor will yours, sir. Thank you for visiting us. Your Highness has done us a great honor."

Inspired by the man's heartfelt gratitude, Seneca reached out and laid a warm hand on the man's bony shoulder before helping Peachy into the coach. Agusta, assisted by one of the royal grooms, entered the coach as well, and Thurlow Wadsworth McGee sprang in behind her.

Seneca noticed that the squirrel was still wearing the tiny crown. Grinning, he stepped into the coach.

The vehicle lurched forward. The men and women of the village hurried ahead of it, ridding the road of any rocks that might jolt it. The children ran alongside it, shouting Peachy's name and tossing paschal flowers at her window. And the older villagers hobbled along as best as they could, waving their gnarled hands and flashing their toothless smiles.

As Seneca watched the poignant scene, he tried to remember if the people had ever done such a thing for his mother when she rode through the country. He'd been allowed to accompany her on only a few occasions, but as he thought of those times now, he couldn't remember a single instance when even one peasant had glanced her way.

He turned from the window and looked at Peachy. Dirt smudged her cheeks and chin; there was even a smear on the end of her nose. Wood chips clung to her flaming curls. Her tattered satin gown was covered with dust, and grass, and straw, and her dainty slippers were coated with mud.

She was the filthiest, most disheveled person he could ever recall seeing.

He felt very proud of her.

"There," Peachy said, giving the homemade remedy a few more stirs with the spoon.

Sitting in a chair by the window in Peachy's rooms, Seneca watched her mix the medicine she'd made for his father. She sat on the floor in front of him, her vast array of cures spread all around her.

They'd only just returned from their afternoon in the village and, despite his suggestion that she bathe and rest for a while before supper, she had insisted on preparing the herb potion and poultice as soon as Agusta had departed.

"What I done, y'see, Seneca, is I mixed the orneriness medicine in with the medicine fer his pain. This here bottle," she said, holding up a large flask, "is powdered rhubarb, crushed alfalfa seeds, rattleroot, sang, red corn root, wild cherry bark, golden seal root, and white likker. That's the part that'll shed him of his miseries. The grouch remedy ain't nothin' in the world but violet blossoms, and I put that right in, too. He has to swaller some in the mornin' and more at night. Yore paw's a mean ole goat, but don't nobody deserve to suffer. It's my sworned duty as a yarb doctor, y'see, to ease folks' miseries."

"Your kindness is much appreciated, Dr. McGee," Seneca replied, taking the bottle from her. He would do as Peachy asked and take the medicine to his father, but he entertained no hope that his sire would consume one drop. A pity, that, he mused, because if anyone needed an elixir to alleviate grouchiness, it was King Zane of Aventine.

Seneca laid the bottle on his lap and, while he waited for Peachy to finish preparing the poultice, he caught sight of something bright red in his chair seat. Upon pulling it out, he saw it was Peachy's red sock.

"I meaned to throw that thing away. I losed the other one, so it don't make no kind o' sense to keep that one."

Seneca rubbed his finger and thumb over the sock. "Is this wool?"

Peachy sprinkled a brown powder into the poultice mixture. "Yeah, from Miz Mackintosh's sheep. She only has one, so she don't git enough wool to make a lavish o' stuff, but she gits enough to make plenty o' socks. I declare, half the folks in the hills wear Miz Mackintosh's homespun socks. They'll be a-writin' Miz Mackintosh up in the Possum Holler hist'ry books one o' these here days."

Seneca continued to feel the sock. It was soft, yes, but his own wool stockings were much softer. He put his hand inside the sock and discovered that although it was warm, his own stockings were warmer.

"All right now, Seneca, I'm done with the poultice. Listen real good so's y'can tell yore paw real straight-like, hear? This jar o' mess is wildcat oil, pokeroot, mutton taller, turpentine, mashed Gilead buds, and yaller root. He's gotta rub this in three times a day."

"Fine," Seneca muttered, still concentrating on the inferior quality of Peachy's sock. *Wool,* he thought. *Sheep. Aventine.*

Paschal.

Realizations burst into his mind like so many exploding stars. He rose from his chair so quickly the bottle of medicine fell to the floor and hit Peachy's knee.

"Well, dang it to hell, Seneca! What—"

"Peachy, I must see my father. The wool— It's our sheep, you see. The paschal— Nowhere else in the world . . . It doesn't matter that other countries— Wool is produced everywhere, but not Aventine wool. You were right."

"Seneca, what—"

"I'll be back later." He raced for the door.

"Wait! You fergitted the medicines!" She scurried to press the cures into his hands. "Tell yore paw that I'll make him more when he runs outen."

"Yes, I will."

"He has to—"

"I know, Peachy, I know." He pressed a hasty kiss to her forehead and dashed down the corridor. He hoped to God he'd find Latimer in his chambers, and thanked all of heaven when he did. "Fine me something made of wool."

"Wool, Your Highness?"

"English wool. Irish wool. Australian . . . It doesn't matter as long as it's not Aventine wool."

Latimer retrieved a wool scarf from a bureau. "Your Highness purchased this scarf while in Paris last year."

Seneca took the scarf. He smiled. It was no softer than Peachy's sock.

He tore out of his chambers and soon reached the staircase that led to his father's apartments. And as he ascended the steps three at a time, he prayed that for once in his life his father would listen to him.

"Feel it yourself, Father. *Feel* it!" Seneca thrust Peachy sock toward his father's hand.

The king shifted his huge frame; the mattress groaned. "You are shouting at me, Seneca, and I will not have it. Nor do I want to feel the girl's absurd red sock!"

"Very well, then feel *this.*" Seneca held out the woolen scarf. "I bought this in France. Feel it."

The king pushed Seneca's hand away. "Wool is wool."

"You're wrong."

King Zane yanked the sheet up to his chin and glared at his son. "I am never wrong. I am the king."

"Your possession of the throne does not make you infallible. You *are* wrong about the wool."

"Bah!"

Frustrated, Seneca stepped off the red-carpeted dais and stalked to the middle of his father's huge bedroom. "It's not the paschal you should be exporting, Father, it's the wool. It will bring a much higher price than dried flowers. As it is now, the paschal is being used for purely decorative purposes. The world can certainly survive without pink flowers on its tables and clothes. But wool . . . Father, wool is a much more important commodity, and I am telling you that Aventine wool is—"

"I will hear no more from you! You are not king yet, Seneca, and I demand that you cease ordering me about!"

Seneca thrust his fingers through his hair. "I am not ordering you to do anything. I'm trying to make you understand that it's the *paschal* the sheep eat that makes their wool superior! You know as well as I do that paschal grows nowhere else in the world. What other reason explains the quality of Aventine wool? What—"

"I am making a veritable fortune on the paschal, and I see no need to—"

"You see nothing but what you choose to see."

The king gasped in outrage. "What? How *dare* you speak to me in such a fashion!"

Seneca raised his chin a notch. "I dare to do it, Father, because this time you go too far with your unreasonable stubbornness. I cannot stand idly by—"

"You will do exactly that until you are crowned. I—"

"The exportation of Aventine wool will benefit everyone in the kingdom. You will still make your fortune in export, and the people will be allowed to return to their sheep. They—"

"Ah, it's the people, then," the king taunted. "Why *are*

you so concerned about a bunch of peasants, Seneca? You would do well to forget the ignorant—"

"*You* are the one showing your ignorance, Father."

The king lost a breath as rage exploded in his barrel-like chest. After choking for several moments, he glared at his son. "You have never in your entire life shown me such disrespect. It's that . . . that savage you married, isn't it? She's turned you into a—"

"She is not a savage, and I will not allow you to—"

"Not allow me?" The king managed a surly smile. "What can you possibly do to prevent me from doing as I wish?"

One defeated step at a time, Seneca returned to his sire's bedside. "I had hoped to find some shred of logic in your mind, Father. Perhaps a bit of decency in your heart. I have found neither, and I understand now that I was sadly mistaken to have believed that you might listen to what I had to say to you. But then, you never have. Not ever."

With a deep sigh, he withdrew from his coat pocket the medicines Peachy had prepared. "Because she believes that no one should suffer as you do, the *savage* I married has seen fit to supply you with these remedies. She sends you the message that she will make more whenever you ask."

The king watched his son place the cures on a small table. "Take them away. I want none of her obnoxious—"

"Very well, then, don't use them. Leave them here on the table, lie in your bed, and suffer the pain." Seneca stepped down the dais and approached the door.

"Seneca?"

He stopped, but didn't turn.

The king smiled. "My room is quite chilly. There must be a lack of firewood in the palace. Perhaps your ladylike wife could chop some? Oh, and do tell her that I would appreciate it very much if she could finish the chore soon. After all, she'll be back in her barbaric homeland before much longer, and I doubt seriously that Callista would consent to ruin her hands by wielding an ax. She'll be too busy filling her role as the elegant Princess of Aventine."

Seneca stiffened at the realization that someone had seen Peachy in the village and had reported her activities to the king. It was true; his father had eyes all over the kingdom.

"Well, Seneca? Will you ask your lady to chop wood, or won't you?"

Seneca left the room. As he walked down the corridor, his father's cruel laughter followed him. Only one thing finally drowned it out.

And that was the thought of Viridis Elsdon.

"Seneca!" Peachy exclaimed as he opened the door to her rooms. "Lord o' mercy, I been as jumpy as a cockroach on a hot griddle, a-waitin' on you. Did y'give yore paw the cures? Did he take 'em? What—"

"I gave them to him, Peachy." He shut her door, bolted it, and walked into the room.

She noticed he'd bathed and changed his clothes. She'd done the same, and was ready for an intimate evening.

But while pondering the expression on his face, she wondered if the night would end up the way she hoped. "Seneca, 'pears to me you got a overdose o' woe, darlin'. What dropped the bottom outen yore harmony?"

He smiled and shook his head, unwilling to answer her. Tonight was their own, and he saw no reason to bring his father into it. He would forget his sire and concentrate on his wife.

Bride, he amended mentally. She wouldn't truly be his wife until he'd bedded her. That goal ever on his mind, he strode over to where she stood in a pool of silver moonlight by the window.

"I— I had vittles brung up," she stammered, recognizing the smoldering look in his eyes and anticipating what it meant. "I done et, though, on— On account o' I was hungrier'n a woodpecker with a headache. Hope y'don't mind none."

Her lemon-cream scent drifting through his senses, he slid his arms around her waist, locking his fingers behind her back. His hunger was not for food.

He glanced down at the bodice of her gold silk gown. At the sight of her lush cleavage, he grew warm with the beginnings of desire, and smiled a slow, meaningful smile.

The languid spread of his lips . . . the gradual uncovering of his straight, white teeth . . . and the way his gaze burned into her . . . made Peachy feel dizzy with longing.

He tightened his hold on her, pulling her closer. "I didn't expect you to be dressed upon my arrival, Princess. Rather, I was hoping you would be wearing that gossamer nightgown . . . or nothing."

She scrunched her thighs together. "I ain't got a stitch o' nothin' on unnerneath this here gown."

He'd already deduced that by the feel of her legs against his. Drawing his hand up beneath her heavy mass of hair, he unfastened the top button on her gown. The second button was already open, as was the third and the fourth. He smiled again when he realized she had fastened only every fifth button. "You weren't anxious for this evening, were you, Princess?" he teased.

"Anxious?" She shook her head. "This evenin'll prob'ly be as excitin' as a-watchin' wet paint dry. Let's hurry and git it over with so's I can finish a-countin' how many hairs Thurlow Wadsworth McGee's got in his tail. Mighty interestin' pastime, hair-countin' is."

He loved the mischievous twinkle in her beautiful eyes. "Yes, let's make haste. I've a book about the feeding habits of the Mongolian spotted beetle that I've been eager to study. I can hardly wait to get to it."

Lord o' mercy, how she loved it when he teased her.

Hands at her shoulders, he pulled her gown down over her breasts, and noticed how her rosy nipples stiffened beneath his hungry gaze. "Mistresses Molly and Polly are certainly anxious even if you and I are not. It would be an extreme breach of etiquette on my part to deny them my attentions, don't you agree?"

She placed her hands beneath her breasts, lifting them in sweet offering. "And you a-bein' a prince and all, yore always s'posed to do the mannerable thing."

"I guess Thurlow Wadsworth McGee's hairs and my beetle book will have to wait?"

She feigned a look of dismal resignation. "I reckon so."

"Well, what must be done, must be done." Bending, he took her left breast into his mouth, circling his tongue around its rigid peak. He then performed the same ministrations to her right breast, continuing until he heard Peachy's low moan of desire.

He straightened and took hold of her gown again, which rested on the gentle curves of her hips. "I wonder if Guinevere is as anxious as the Mistresses Polly and Molly?"

Peachy could barely breathe, much less speak.

Seneca gave a knowing smile and let the gown rustle to the floor. His burning gaze never leaving Peachy's, he cupped the warm mound between her legs, his fingers sliding into the folds of her femininity.

He heard his own groan. God, she was hot, he thought. Wet. He slipped a finger inside her, another groan escaping him when he felt how tight she was. "Guinevere shows definite signs of anxiousness. I suppose, Peachy," he whispered next to her ear, "that I should attend to her wants as well."

Peachy melted against him.

Seneca steadied her instantly. "Princess," he murmured right before his lips met hers.

His kiss sought, found, and brought forth every hidden trace of desire her body held. She writhed in his arms, some primitive impulse inside her urging her to push her hips forward. Into male heat.

Into Seneca.

Her actions, made so innocently, almost drove Seneca to the brink of madness. "Peachy."

She was struck by the raw need in his voice. It beckoned to the maiden inside her, and she understood then that that was the ancient way of things. A virgin knew nothing; a man's desire wooed her and taught her.

She stepped out of his embrace. "Y'ain't gotta wait, Seneca. I don't want y'to wait no more."

She heard his sharp breath and watched as he quickly disrobed. When he was naked, she saw his powerful body quake and knew he trembled for her, for what she could give him, for the passion and pleasure they would soon share.

She walked purposefully toward the bed. Before, he'd always carried her to it. She wanted him to understand that it was her own desire that carried her there tonight.

She reached for the satin coverlet, gasping with surprise

when he shot out his hand, stilling hers. "Seneca, I only wanted to git the bed all ready fer—"

"It will take too long."

She listened to the growl of his voice. The dark and brooding roughness of it. He watched her with heavily hooded eyes that devoured every part of her.

Gone were all traces of the proper Prince of Aventine, she realized. Standing before her now was a man who wanted his woman with every raw fiber that made him who he was.

And she was that woman. She belonged to him. The thought made her feel wonderfully weak. She yearned to place herself at his mercy, and hoped he wouldn't show her a shred.

"I'm hot," she whispered, her voice sounding like the rustle of a flame. "Hot enough to melt diamonds, Seneca. What the hell are you a-waitin' fer?"

A moan rumbling in his chest, he fell to the bed, hauling Peachy with him. His dark hands swept up and down her sides, while his mouth ground down on hers with an urgency he could control no longer.

And Peachy gloried in his wild need. It was her own, and she understood it as well as she understood that tonight was going to hold all the specialness she'd ever dared to wish for. "Now, Seneca. The waitin's over, darlin', fer both of us."

His body turned to stone by driving need, he rolled atop her, his weight pushing her deeply into the soft mattress. With his knee, he spread her legs slightly, gladdened to his very soul when she took over from there and opened them wide for him.

He shifted his hips so that his thick, rigid manhood caressed the slick entry to her body. And he teased her with shallow thrusts that stopped just short of the thin barrier that shielded her virginity. Bursts of fire licked at his loins as her tight sheath enfolded him.

Innate feelings induced Peachy to arch her hips up to his. Her nails dug into his back when she felt him slip inside her again, more deeply this time. Her body struggled to stretch and accommodate his thickness; a shimmer of pain eased through her.

Seneca felt her stiffen beneath him. "I'm sorry, sweetheart."

"I ain't no virgin no more, huh?"

He wished it were that easy. "You are, Peachy."

"But— But yore inside—"

"I must be buried completely inside you before you cease to be a maiden."

She shifted slightly, again feeling him slide within her. "It'll fit . . . right?"

"I promise you it will."

She lay still, thankful when Seneca made no movement, either. The pain faded some, but enough remained to remind her that there was more to come. "Y'didn't tell me it was gonna hurt."

He clenched his teeth, then exhaled a deep, pent-up breath into her fragrant hair. His fragile thread of control was slowly unraveling. "I didn't want to frighten you."

She felt him pulse inside her. "I ain't never been afeared o' no kind o' pain, Seneca, but I like to know when it's a-comin'."

"Very well," he whispered. "This is going to hurt you, Peachy, and there's nothing I can do to keep it from happening. But the pain . . . Only this time, Princess. When I bed you again— The next time we come together there will be no pain."

She bit her bottom lip. "Will I bleed tonight?"

"Yes."

"A lot?"

God, he hoped not. "Some."

"But after the pain . . . There's the pleasure, right, Seneca? The thigh-scrunchin' kind y'give me this mornin'?"

Her sweet search for reassurance dredged up feelings of warm tenderness inside him. "Yes. I swear, Peachy, I'll give you the pleasure again. And again. As many times as you want it."

She knew he meant what he said. He was telling her the truth, and that truth drew trust from her. Tentatively, she lifted her hips higher, throbbing with an ache she trusted him to ease.

But the tense way she held herself told Seneca of her

lingering fear. "Not yet," he told her, his voice half moan, half whisper. "Not yet."

"But Seneca . . ." She tried to hold on to him when he moved downward, but he slid easily out of her hold. Anger and desperation mingled with her desire, creating a profound frustration. "Seneca—"

The rest of her words died on her lips when she felt his mouth on the heart of her womanhood. At the unexpected sensation, astonishment burst within her. "Seneca!"

He only continued to caress, taste, and love her in a way that he'd not done before. She was sweet, God, she was sweet. She was warm and wet, and he made her wetter, and that fact nearly drove him senseless with a desire so deep he knew not from where it came.

He knew only that he wanted her to experience the bliss in this way before he gave it to her in the way that would cause her pain. He understood full well that he wouldn't be able to keep from hurting her when he claimed her innocence, but he wanted her relaxed and sated when he took it.

He as her husband, she as his wife.

Striving to arrive at those long-awaited ends, he quickened his loving pace with her.

Peachy responded with a hoarse cry of delight. His tongue . . . his lips . . . his warm, warm breath . . . His every touch shot rapture through her trembling limbs. She surrendered to it wholly, clutching at the midnight satin of Seneca's hair, keeping him to her, and arching her hips to him as he guided her to paradise.

And as the ecstasy flowered inside her, his presence filled her mind. Seneca. Her mental image of him heightened her pleasure, and she understood at that moment the feelings that dwelled in her heart. "I love you," she breathed. "I love you."

The waves of bliss began to soften and melt into sweet tremors that sang through her. "Seneca, I love you."

Her softly spoken words hit him like a ton of stone. He lifted his eyes to her and saw the joy shimmering from her luminous gaze.

Seneca, I love you. Her declaration weaved through him, leaving a trail of intense astonishment in its wake.

"Peachy . . ." His own voice startled him. The shock of her announcement left him without words.

The emotions he felt overcame passion. His fierce desire melted away, a sense of powerful wonder taking its place.

He eased himself forward, stopping when the mound of her femininity pushed into his chest. He felt the pulse of her sensual fulfillment mesh with the beat of his heart.

His gaze locked with hers.

Peachy lifted her hands to the sides of his face, her fingers parting his raven hair. "I been a-feelin' powerful feelin's, but I jest weren't shore what they was till tonight. Whilst you was a-makin' me feel so good jest now? Well, yore face . . . ever'thing I know about you come to me then, y'see. They sorter turkey-tailed all through me, a-meetin' up with the pleasure, and when that happened it was like I didn't know about nothin' else in the world but you. Jest you, and only you, my dearest beloved."

He tried to swallow. His throat wouldn't cooperate. Nor could he speak yet. He had no words to tell her.

" 'Pears this night's a-turnin' outen jest as special as I always dreamed it would be, huh, Seneca?"

He saw a glow of expectation in her pale green eyes. She wanted something from him. And she was hoping with all her heart that he would give it to her.

His own heart told him exactly what it was.

His love.

Peachy . . . She made him laugh. She made him think about things he'd never thought of before. He admired her in many ways. She touched something inside him, and sometimes he felt as though he knew her and always had.

But that wasn't love. Love was . . .

He didn't know. And that was what convinced him that he didn't love her. If he did, he would know. One didn't fail to recognize love.

It would glitter. Like diamonds, it would blind him with its brilliance.

He wasn't blinded by anything right now. He saw everything clearly, and nothing dazzled him.

Except Peachy's trusting smile.

He rolled off her.

"Ain't'cha gonna say nothin' about me a-lovin' you?"

When he didn't answer, she studied the look on his face. It certainly wasn't a happy one.

Maybe he didn't want her love. Maybe—

It's not your love I want, Peachy. It's your obedience. The memory of what he'd told her broke into her thoughts. She swallowed. On their wedding night he'd tried to convince her that he didn't want her love. She hadn't listened; she hadn't wanted to believe him.

She didn't want to now, either.

Sitting up, she tossed her hair over her shoulders. "The onliest way you'll ever broaden yore mind, Seneca, is iffen y'put it unner a gawdang train. Love ain't somethin' y'can turn on and offen. I love you, and that's jest plain it, hear?"

He got up and began to dress.

"I ain't never in my life meeted nobody who needed love more'n you do."

He slipped into his shoes.

"Y'don't love me, huh, Seneca?"

He stared at her, then thrust his fingers through his hair. Why was she asking to hear words that would hurt her?

His silence spoke louder than words. "Well, I reckon that answers my question. Y'don't love me."

He walked to the door, anxious to leave before she asked him more questions he didn't want to answer.

"Don't hurt as much as I thought it would, you not a-lovin' me. Y'want to know why?"

He stopped at the door.

"On account o' I'm purty shore y'don't hate me. Iffen y'don't hate me, y'must like me. And iffen y'like me, maybe one day you'll love me. Love commences with like, y'know. I liked you afore I loved you. I'll think on that ever' time I git to a-feelin' upset that y'don't love me. I cain't git sad, y'see, on account o' I'd be a-messin' up the hummin'bird omen."

He opened the door.

"I love you, Seneckers. 'Night."

He left quickly. In the corridor, he leaned against the closed door, his heart beating so loudly he swore he heard the sound bouncing off the walls.

Seneckers. She'd called him Seneckers.

In the same night, she'd given him two things he'd never had in his entire life.

Love and a nickname.

Chapter 13

Bright morning sunlight glinted off the chandeliers in the luxurious Audience Room, the sparkles shining on Viridis Elsdon's silver hair as she walked toward the most uncomfortable chair in the room.

Seneca watched his Aunt Viridis sit, noticing she did not allow her back to touch the chair. He wondered how long it would take her to teach Peachy to sit in the same manner.

Peachy. God, he'd paced until dawn, trying to name what it was he felt for her.

"Seneca?" Viridis's voice sounded like a banner snapping in a strong wind.

Pulled from his thoughts, Seneca selected a chair across from her. It wasn't easy to dismiss Peachy from his mind, but he forced himself to concentrate on Viridis.

He wondered what Peachy would think of her.

Viridis began the niceties. "How is your father?"

She'd asked the question as if each word left foul-tasting venom in her mouth, Seneca mused. She detested his father, and because of her dislike for him, Seneca knew she wouldn't cease the lessons even if his sire showed his disfavor. She'd continued with them just to spite the king. That, of course, was a plus. "Father has taken to his bed. The pain is growing worse."

"I'm sorry to hear that."

"I'm sure you are. I do appreciate your agreeing to a position as one of Peachy's ladies, Aunt Viridis."

She gave an almost imperceptible bow of her head. "I

259

suggest that you keep the number of ladies to a bare minimum for now, Seneca. One more would be sufficient. A large group will only hinder me in my efforts with her."

"I have invited Lady Sherringham."

Viridis smiled. "I'm certain that Veston is thrilled."

"To the point of bursting." Seneca returned her smile.

"Agusta Sherringham will be fine. She is well-mannered and should prove to be an excellent influence. Now, has the princess been given any instruction since the wedding? I must say that her behavior during the wedding feast was nothing short of shocking."

"She was unaccustomed to our ways then."

"You are defending her?"

Seneca realized he was, indeed, defending Peachy. "I am reminding you that she was very new to Aventine then. And please call her Peachy. You are family, Aunt Viridis."

"She is named after a fruit. Do you know if she has a more proper name?"

Seneca felt a flash of irritation. He liked Peachy's name. "To the best of my knowledge she has only one."

"More's the pity. Suppose you enlighten me as to what form of instruction she has already received. It would help me to know what she has already been taught."

Seneca remembered the stern lecture he'd given Peachy the day she'd slid down the staircase banister. *The banister.* The memory of her outrageous descent almost made him smile. "I . . . You will be happy to know that she doesn't ride the staircase railing anymore."

Viridis scowled.

"Beyond that, I have revealed to her what is expected of her. My explanation, however, was brief."

"And what was the outcome of your brief explanation?"

Seneca met her stare. "I only recently gave it to her."

"I take that to mean she is still quite . . . shall we say, *unrefined?*"

Seneca decided he didn't care for the word *unrefined.* "I think *unconventional* is a better word."

Viridis shook her head. "Unconventional? Is that how you would describe her behavior in the village yesterday? I have learned that she chopped wood and played with pigs."

"She did not *play* with the pigs. She instructed the villagers on how to feed them."

Viridis eyed him intently. "And feeding pigs is one of her duties as the Princess of Aventine?"

His irritation grew a tad deeper. "What Peachy did yesterday . . . Whatever she has done since her arrival in Aventine is over and done with. You are here now. And have I forgotten to mention that you have only a month?"

"A month?"

"Actually a bit less." He refused to explain the one-month period. The wager was between him and his father.

"I suppose we should begin immediately. Where is she?"

He wondered if she was still in bed. *Bed.* God, she'd been so sweet last night in bed. So soft and willing and wonderful.

"Seneca?"

He squared his shoulders. "She retired late last night. It could be that she is yet asleep. If you will be good enough to wait, I will have her maids—"

"Nonsense. I've no objection to climbing stairs." She rose regally. "I have already said that I would like to begin now. If in fact she is still abed, I shall awaken her myself. Where might I find her?"

"In the pink rooms."

"Very well. This will give me the opportunity to give her her first lesson in the art of dressing properly. Oh, and I warn you now, Seneca, that I will not stand for your interference. You will leave Peachy in my hands and allow me to perform the service for which you have summoned me, will you not?"

He inclined his head.

"I will go gently with her." With that, Viridis glided out of the room.

Her last words stayed with Seneca. Perhaps Viridis would endeavor to go gently with Peachy.

But would Peachy go gently with Viridis?

Encased within what felt like a thousand yards of underwear, Peachy squirmed in the ladder-backed chair by the window and watched Seneca's aunt fuss over a drawer full of gloves. "I'm hotter'n a desert rat's armpit, Aunt Vardis."

Viridis looked up from the gloves and frowned. "My name is *Viridis*. And physical comfort has nothing whatsoever to do with dressing correctly. What's more, you will cease to talk in such an utterly repulsive fashion. A lady does not speak of . . . *armpits*."

She turned back to the gloves. "My, but Seneca has done well by you. He has spared no expense on your wardrobe."

Seneca, Peachy thought. Aggravated though she was with Viridis, she smiled at the memory of her night with Seneca. She wasn't finished with Prince Seneca of Aventine. She was going to love him whether he liked it or not. She'd show him her love at every opportunity and in any way that presented itself. And she would do anything she had to do to win his love in return.

After all, she wasn't dead yet. And until she was, she had a lot to live for.

"Peachy!"

Startled, Peachy looked at the woman. "What?"

"A lady does not daydream when someone is speaking to her. Now, sit up straight. Your back is not to touch the chair. Feet flat on the floor, if you please, and do not fidget. Hold your chin up. Up, my dear, up. You are a princess Peachy and you must learn the royal bearing."

Anger made Peachy want to huff. She tried, but couldn't take in enough air for a respectable huff. Despite Peachy's heated objections, Seneca's aunt had laced her into the hateful squeezing contraption. Not only that, but she'd forced her to don nine petticoats over some sort of round thing that looked like a trap one might use to catch a wild boar in.

Because of the woman's age and the fact that she was Seneca's aunt, Peachy had refrained from arguing about the insufferable underwear. She wished now, however, that she'd put up a fight the likes of which the woman had never seen.

She threw a look of desperation to Ketty and Nydia, who stood silently against the wall. She flung another to Agusta, who sat in a chair in front of the other window.

Ketty and Nydia lowered their gazes to the floor; Agusta wrung her hands. It looked to Peachy as if her friend was about to say something but didn't quite know how to say it.

So much for their help. Shifting in the hard chair Viridis had made her sit in, Peachy pondered her situation and wondered what Seneca would say when she told him that she'd decided to decline his aunt's services.

"You are daydreaming again," Viridis declared. "And you are squirming. A lady never squirms, Peachy."

Peachy felt like sticking her tongue out at the bossy woman. "Look, Aunt Verdis, I—"

"*Viridis.*"

"Vesdis. I'm all fer a-larnin' how to be a lady on account o' I sweared to Seneca that I'd be one. But—"

"Well, you are not trying hard enough." Viridis glided into the middle of the room, her chin held high, her hands clasped at her waist. "Your behavior in the village yesterday— Utterly shocking! Peachy, how *could* you have indulged in the unladylike task of chopping wood? Moreover, it was terribly uncouth of you to mingle with pigs!"

Agusta raised her head. "Excuse me, Lady Elsdon, but Peachy didn't mingle with the swine. She merely—"

"Agusta, you will stay out of this. Peachy's decorum in the village yesterday was highly improper, and she must be made to understand that."

Peachy gripped the seat of her chair. "I wouldn't't've chopped the wood or tuk keer o' them pigs iffen the able-bodied folks was there to do them chores theirsefs. But they was gone, Aunt Vridin. Gone to them gawdang flower fields to make money fer King Varmint."

Viridis shook her head. There was no love lost between herself and the king, but she would not allow her young charge to interfere with royal decree. "For the last time, my name is *Viridis*. And I must insist that you have a care with that wayward tongue of yours. A lady never curses. And Peachy, you will leave matters such as the peasants to His Majesty. *He* is the sovereign, and you must never call him names again."

"The peasants ain't *matters*. They're *people*. And the king's—"

"Eat your meal while I select your gown."

Huffing as well as she could, Peachy resigned herself to putting up with the woman until she could talk to Seneca. "I'm a-wearin' my red satin today. It's the rusty-red bucket kind that goes good with my hair. And I'm a-wearin' my sapphires with it. Weared my diamonds the other day, my emeralds yesterday, so today I'll wear my—"

"You will not wear red satin in the morning. The dress you describe is a ball gown, and I'm quite sure it would show an indecent amount of bosom."

Peachy thought about that. "Y'mean it's all right fer me to show my boobies at night at a big party, but it ain't right to show 'em in the daytime?"

Viridis nodded, glad that Peachy understood that bit of etiquette but dismayed by the word *boobies*.

"Well, that don't make a bit o' sense to me. Women don't got boobies when the sun's out, but they grow some when the moon's in the sky. Dumbest thing I ever did hear."

"Nevertheless, you won't forget it. Nor will you continue to say *boobies*. You may say *bosom*, but only in the presence of your maids and ladies."

"I call mine Miz Molly and Miz Polly."

It took Viridis a moment to absorb that bit of outlandish information. "That is quite the most childish thing I have ever heard. Silliness has no place in your role as princess. And if and when you do wear the red ball gown, Peachy, you will not accessorize it with sapphires. You will wear diamonds and pearls."

Watching the women march into the dressing room, Peachy stuck her tongue out, then took a vicious bite of bread.

"Oh, and the crown you're wearing—Queen Diandra's crown—is for formal occasions, and unsuitable for daytime or casual evenings," Viridis called from the dressing room. "You may wear a small diadem if you are on a very special outing or receiving important visitors during the day, but Queen Diandra's crown will be reserved for formal occasions. Take it off now, and I will see that it is taken to the crown room, where it will be locked away. You will not keep your valuables in here."

Peachy's bite of bread stuck in her throat. She tossed the roll back on the tray, patted her crown, and fumed in silence. She *would* wear the big princess crown, and she *would* keep all her jewelry in her rooms. She much-loved the beautiful things, and no uppity aunt of Seneca's was going to forbid her to enjoy them the way she wished.

"Here we are," Viridis announced as she joined Peachy again. "This is a lovely gown and quite appropriate for morning wear."

Peachy frowned when she saw the ugly dove gray silk gown. Hideous black butterfly appliqués adorned the skirt. The high neckline was trimmed with stiff black lace she knew would scratch her throat. And the long sleeves looked tight. She hated tight sleeves; they didn't allow her to bend her arms well. "I ain't a-wearin'—"

"Yes, my dear, you are."

"No, m'dear, I ain't. That thing's ugly enough to skeer a maggot offen a pile o' dog—"

"Peachy!" Viridis clasped her hand over her heart.

As the indomitable Lady Elsdon paled with shock, Agusta let out a delicate giggle.

The timid woman's mirth gave Viridis a second shock. "Agusta! I thought you would be a good influence over Peachy. And yet it would seem that *she* has influenced *you!* Have you no shame?"

Peachy saw fire. "Y'can fling whatever kind o' sass y'want to at me, Aunt Vrisdin, but when y'go to talk to Gussie? Well, I'm a-warnin' you right now in this here day and time that you'd best keep yore words sugarcoated. Iffen I hear you a-shamin' her again, I'll—"

"A true lady does not make threats," Viridis snapped.

"She does when her friends is a-gittin' shamed fer no good reason. Gussie ain't got nothin' to be ashamed over." She turned to Agusta. "Yore a-comin' outen yore quiet little shell. It's a nice world outen here, ain't it, Gussie? Maybe soon you'll have enough guts to give ole Veston what's fer. Y'done real good, Gussie. Now, eat yore breakferst. I had them apple tarts sended up 'specially fer you. They're s'good they'll set yore lips to rejoicin'."

Viridis shook her head. "Peachy, if you are finished with your meal, we will begin your toilette."

Peachy glanced at the ugly gown again. "I done tole you that I ain't—"

"And when you are dressed, we shall find Seneca and ask his opinion."

Sure that Seneca would see her side of the situation, Peachy hung on to what little patience she had left. For an hour and a half, she forced herself to comply with each and every one of the fussy woman's demands. Her sole consolation was that Viridis would soon be gone.

And then she could forget frivolous subjects such as ribbons, hairpins, hand creams, and skin whiteners.

Then she could get down to the all-important business of loving Seneca.

Viridis stood in the threshold of Seneca's office. "Here is your princess now," she announced, stepping into the room and gesturing toward the doorway.

Anxious to see what his aunt had done, Seneca rose from behind his desk and waited for Peachy to enter the room.

When she walked inside, he frowned. She wore gray; he hated the color on her. It made her look pale, unhappy, almost sick. Her beloved crown was absent from her head. Instead, her long and beautiful hair was swept up into a tight circle of what looked to be intricate knots. And she stood stiffly, as if her spine were made of stone.

Viridis smiled at Peachy. "There now, my dear, do you see? He is absolutely speechless, overcome with admiration and delight." She turned back to Seneca. "I have explained to her that because you are the crown prince, she must stand by your side like a valuable and beautifully adorned object. Don't you agree, Seneca?"

Seneca stared at Peachy's billowing skirts, realizing she wore the layers of underwear she hated. She was laced into a corset, too; he could tell by the way she was breathing in short pants. He understood then that it was the corset that forced her to stand and move so rigidly.

"Isn't it so that a woman's attire says much about her husband's position, Seneca?" Viridis pressed, irritated that he'd yet to agree with her.

Peachy took a few more steps into the room. "I don't want to be no object, Seneckers," she murmured.

The nickname created a deep contentment inside him. But when he saw the hurt in her beautiful eyes, his pleasure faded. "Peachy, you aren't an object," he said softly.

"Peachy," Viridis said, kneeling down to smooth the back of Peachy's skirts. "It is unseemly for you to call your husband by such a vulgar name. He is the crown prince, for heaven's sake, and as such he deserves your utmost respect. Seneckers, indeed. And as for your being an object, you must simply *act* like one when you are on display." Still bent over, she smoothed another wrinkle out of Peachy's skirts.

"Display?" Peachy turned, her skirts swiping Viridis directly in the face.

"Peachy!" Viridis exclaimed. "Do have a care with—"

"I ain't no object, and I ain't much fer a-bein' on display, Aunt Vudin!"

"My name is *Viridis*. And if you will allow me to continue to explain—"

"You been *explainin'* fer nigh on two and a half hours! What did yore maw raise you on? Tongue sandwiches? God Almighty, lady, you got enough wind in you to keep a windmill a-goin', and I git hoarse jest a-listenin' to you!"

Seneca bent his head and pretended to examine the hideous appliqués on Peachy's skirts. It was only with much effort that he managed to erase his smile. "Aunt Viridis, may I have a word with Peachy alone?"

Viridis clucked. "Only for a moment. She and I have much to discuss. By tonight, I hope to have succeeded in making her understand the vital importance of keeping a civil tongue in her head. Peachy, Agusta and I shall await you in the Queen's Chambers."

When his aunt and Agusta were gone, Seneca picked up Peachy's hand. "Why is your hand so cold? It's never felt like this before."

She lifted her other arm. "It's these dang sleeves. They're so tight, I cain't hardly bend my elbows."

"Then why are you wearing this dress?"

"General von Vardis says it's the right dress fer mornin's. I wanted to wear red satin with my sapphires, but she— Seneca, I unnerstand that you want her to be my lady. I know she's yore aunt and all, but I cain't git along with her. I'm a-tellin' you, iffen she got to heaven, she'd ask to see the upstairs. There jest ain't no pleasin' her."

He smiled. "Peachy—"

"It weren't gonna hurt nobody iffen I weared my red satin and sapphires. Why does it differ what I wear? Could y'please tell yore aunt that we don't need her?"

He laid his other hand on her shoulder and missed the mane of soft hair that used to be there. Something else was missing, too. After a moment, he realized what it was. "Your scent . . . It's different today. You're no longer bathing in the magnolia petals?"

"I tried to, but Varmint Visdris tole me that jasmine is a heap more elegant. She put it in my bathwater, then splashed more on me whilst she was a-dryin' me offen. Send her home, Seneca."

"Peachy, she's here to teach you—"

"Please, Seneca. She won't even let me wear my crown! And she maked me put on all this agger-pervokin' unnerwear, too! I cain't breathe. 'Sides that, I was a-doin' jest fine afore yore aunt come. I have that list o' all them ladylike things, and I was a-doin' 'em all one by one. Please tell yore aunt to go home."

Her sweet plea tore at him. He wrapped his arms around her waist and tried to embrace her. But her full skirts hindered his efforts, and her corset prevented her from being able to lean into his body the way she always did. He felt as though he were hugging a bolt of fabric instead of his bride. And what was worse was that he couldn't feel if she was scrunching her thighs together. He stepped away, noticed her unhappy expression, and felt an intense urge to make everything better for her.

But he reminded himself that he had less than a month left to the wager. The *secret* wager. If Peachy did not be-

come a true lady before that time was over, he would be
forced to wait more long years before claiming the Crown.

And Peachy would be forced to return to America.

The thought pumped dread and anger through his veins.

If only he could tell Peachy about the bet she might understand why she had to become a lady. No, more likely
she'd be deeply hurt to learn she was the object of a wager
between him and his father. And if the king learned that
Seneca hadn't kept their wager secret, he would declare
their bet invalid.

"Viridis stays, Peachy," Seneca declared, steeling himself against the disbelief that filled her eyes.

"Seneckers, please don't do this to me."

Her nickname for him made him want to take her into
his arms again. But he didn't. He had to be firm right now,
very firm, and not allow her to change his mind. It was for
her own good as well as his. "Aunt Viridis stays, and you
will learn every bit of etiquette she tries to teach you."

"But—"

"I am your husband, and you will do as I say."

She stared into his ice-blue eyes. "Roses is red, hay's
put in bales. Do me a favor, and sit on some nails." In a
flurry of gray silk, she swept from the room.

Her fragrance of jasmine lingered, hovering around Seneca like a thick fog. Half the women he knew wore the
scent.

He missed the magnolias.

Tiblock could barely contain his excitement when he
caught sight of the heathen princess running up the Grand
Staircase. He'd thought he'd be forced to wait until her
morning session with Viridis Elsdon was over before stirring up trouble, but it was obvious to him now that the girl
had succeeded in escaping her tutor's lessons. "Your Highness."

Peachy pitched him a furious glare. "What the hell do
y'want, Snort-Face?"

He was delighted to hear her unladylike curse. "It is not
what I want, Your Highness, but what the peasants want.
There is a group of them at the palace gate. Some say they
are suffering illnesses they claim madam can cure. Others

have come with sick animals. I believe I saw a lamb . . . Oh, and one old woman brought a bird with a broken wing."

Peachy flew back down the stairs. "Git Ketty and Nydia to fetch me my yarbs and all the other mess I usually use when I'm a-tendin' the ailish. Tell 'em to hurry and meet me in the tower. They'll know which one. And iffen y'don't do what I say, Tiblock, I'll hang yore sorry hide on the highest steeple this here castle's got!"

"Oh, I will, madam! I certainly will! Straightaway!"

Peachy gave him one last look of warning before lifting her skirts clear up to her thighs and racing toward the palace entrance. She shut the huge doors so forcefully the chandeliers shook.

At her terribly unladylike exit, Tiblock beamed with a pleasure that grew steadily as he dwelled on the fact that she intended to bring the revolting peons and smelly animals directly into the castle.

Oh, how the king would relish this!

Hurt bird in hand, Orabelle patiently waited her turn, Bubba fidgeting at her side. She hadn't wanted to bring the bumbling dolt, but he refused to be parted from his bird and had begun throwing a fit at the palace gates. She'd had no choice but to allow him to come.

She looked around the stifling hot tower room. Earlier, it had been full to capacity with sick peasants. One by one, Peachy had examined them all and given them cures for their complaints. She'd saved the animals for last and was now tending an old man's lamb.

Orabelle grudgingly admitted that the girl possessed an amazing understanding of the use of herbs. Unfortunately, she would be unable to benefit from her own knowledge, Orabelle mused. She wouldn't have time. The poison would render her unconscious within minutes after she began to feel ill.

Smiling, Orabelle patted the flask of cider in her skirt pocket. Her smile grew broader as thoughts of yellow gold filled her mind.

"Whatcha got there, ma'am?"

Orabelle started, realizing the old man and the lamb

were gone and that she and Bubba were alone in the tower with Peachy. She held out the tiny bird.

"Oh, the poor little thing," Peachy cooed, taking the wounded bird from the woman's hands. "He needs a splint on his wing. I ain't got no smooth sticks o' wood up here, but I got somethin' that'll work jest as good."

Without a second's worth of thought, she pulled four long pins from the wreath Viridis had made of her hair. Instantly, her thick mass of red curls tumbled to her shoulders. "We'll jest cover these here pins with a little bit o' cloth so's they'll be real soft."

Orabelle noticed that the gold pins glittered with an assortment of tiny diamonds. Although she couldn't believe the girl planned to bestow such wealth on a stupid bird, she was glad for it. The pins would pay for passage back to North Carolina.

It took Peachy only a short while to fix the expensive splint around the bird's broken wing. When she was done, she planted a kiss on its feathery head and held him up for the woman to take.

But it was Bubba who retrieved the sparrow. Happiness spilling from his eyes, he, too, kissed the bird.

Peachy gasped when she saw his bruised and swollen face. "Sweet Lord o' mercy, yore worse offen than yore little bird! What—"

"The boy is a mute," Orabelle hastened to say, careful to accent her speech. She threw Bubba a look meant to remind him that he was not to say a word. "He fell from the hayloft a few days ago, but he's fine."

"Well, he ain't neither fine!" Peachy raised her hand to the young man's black-and-blue face. But before she could touch him, he winced and stepped away. "You come on back here, honey. I cain't fix yore broken nose, but I can give you a poultice that'll bring down the swellin'." She wiped her perspiring forehead with the sleeve of her gown and prepared to make yet another remedy.

While Peachy busied herself making a poultice of poke roots, lard, and mashed onion, Orabelle withdrew the flask of cider. "Your Highness must be thirsty. I've some cool cider here. Please accept it as a token of my gratitude."

The sight of the flask of cider made Peachy lick her dry

lips. "Mighty obliged." She took the flask and set it down. "I'll drink it in jest a minute."

Orabelle shook with impotent rage.

Peachy finished mixing the poultice and smiled at the big man. "Come on now, darlin'. Let me put this on. I promise I ain't gonna hurt you."

Bubba looked down at her, thinking her the prettiest woman he'd ever seen. And when her poultice-covered fingers touched his face, her gentle caress was the most wonderful thing he'd ever known.

"There now, ain't that better?" Peachy asked him. "Smile so's I'll know yore a-feelin' all right now."

He smiled. And then he reached out and touched a lock of her bright hair. "Uh . . . you're nice," he whispered, forgetting he wasn't supposed to speak.

"Sometimes he can whisper," Orabelle blurted. "Will Your Highness drink the cool cider I brought?"

Peachy continued to study the huge man before her. He was simple-minded, she realized. Her heart went out to him.

"Your Highness, the cider," Orabelle pressed.

"The cider." Peachy turned and picked the flask up from the floor. Wiping damp, sticky hair away from her face, she lifted the bottle to her lips.

Watching her, Bubba squeezed his fingers around his bird. The creature squawked, flapped its good wing, and leapt out of Bubba's hand. Reacting instinctively, Bubba lunged to catch it, failing to heed the scattered sacks of herbs lying on the floor. He stumbled over them, then began to fall, his huge shoulder ramming into Peachy's chest.

Orabelle cringed as Bubba crashed to the floor. Peachy landed directly on top of him, the flask of cider flying from her hands.

It hit the far wall and shattered. Its contents dripped harmlessly through the wooden slats of the floor.

Orabelle went numb with icy fury. All words froze in her throat. She simply stood there, staring coldly at Bubba and Peachy, disbelief spinning crazily through her.

"You all right?" Peachy asked the man. She struggled to rise, a difficult task what with all the stiff underwear hindering her efforts.

Bubba rose first. Extending his hand to her, he helped her to her feet, then showed her his bird.

Peachy grinned, "Y'didn't hurt yore little bird when y'falled down, huh? Yore a real sweet man, y'know that? Real gentle and carin'."

He beamed. And nodded. And reached out to touch her cheek.

Orabelle cleared her throat. "Come now," she said to Bubba.

He heard the chill in her words. His hand fell; his smile faded. Orabelle was going to hit him when they left the palace. He knew it. Head hung so low that his chin touched his chest, he trudged out of the room, his feet falling heavily on each step of the staircase.

Orabelle stared at Peachy. "Thank you."

When the woman was gone, Peachy thought about her strange way of speaking. She'd never heard the accent before and decided the woman was from some foreign land. Shrugging, she grabbed a broom, dodged the long rope that hung from the ceiling, and approached the far corner of the room where the bottle had broken. For lack of a dustpan, she swept the shards of glass into a pile near the wall and made a mental note to remove them later.

Done with the chore, she leaned the broom against the wall and noticed a trunk in the darkened corner. She remembered seeing it before, but she'd not had time to look inside it. Curiosity prompted her to do so now.

It wasn't heavy; she was able to drag it toward the sunny window. Hoping it wasn't locked, she pulled at the latch and was glad when it opened easily.

A flurry of dust blew into her face when she lifted the lid. Waving it away, she peered into the trunk and saw a collection of silver spoons. She picked one up, confused when she found that a second one was attached to it.

Kept together by means of a thin strip of leather, the stems of the spoons were crossed at the bottom, forming an X. A longer and wider strip of leather was tied at the base of the spoons' bowls.

Upon further inspection, Peachy discovered that all the spoons in the trunk were tied together in the same odd fashion. Try as she might, she couldn't understand what they were meant to be, meant to do.

"Peachy?"

She looked up, spying Ketty in the doorway. "The ole bat's a-lookin' fer me, huh?"

"She's beside herself. Not only is she upset because you escaped her this morning, but she's not at all pleased that you invited the peasants into the castle."

"Did Tiblock—"

"No, she spoke with several of the peasants herself as they were leaving. They told her you had cured them of their illnesses in the tower. But there are so many towers in the palace, she hasn't found this one yet."

"And Seneca?"

Ketty fingered her apron. "He's been out riding all morning. Nydia and I saw him leave. He rode as if Satan was chasing him."

"He's riled at me, Ketty. We—"

"Well, *here* you are!" Viridis's voice filled the room like a cannon blast.

Frightened, Ketty cast a look of sympathy in Peachy's direction, then fled the room.

"I have been searching *everywhere* for you!" Viridis continued. "And just *look* at you! Why, you're absolutely *filthy!* Peachy, how *could* you indulge in such behavior? Those people and their beasts have no place in the castle. You are *not* to associate with the lower classes!"

Peachy gritted her teeth. "You listen to me, Aunt—"

"No, *you* listen to *me.*" Viridis clasped her hands in front of her bosom. "Do you have any feelings at all for your husband?"

"What?"

"Do you care for him at all?"

Peachy slammed down the lid of the trunk. "What's betwixt me and Seneca ain't none o' yore—"

"It most assuredly *is* my business. I am here at Seneca's request. He wants you to become a lady."

"I've been a-doin' ever'thing he tole me to—"

"But you have misunderstood his wishes, Peachy. You have been obeying him in your *own* way, not his. That is why he asked my assistance in creating a proper lady out of you. I would think that if you were at all fond of him, you would endeavor to make him happy. I have never been married, but my guess is that a wife's obedience to her husband would endear her to him. Or doesn't winning Seneca's affection matter to you?"

"O' course it matters to me, dang it! What wife don't want her husband to love her?"

Viridis raised both of her silver eyebrows. "Well, if it is his love you covet I suggest you begin trying to earn it. I am here to help you do just that. If you will only stop fighting me, you might be pleasurably surprised by Seneca's reaction."

"You—" Abruptly, Peachy became silent. Her eyes widened, then narrowed. Her mind whirled; one word tapped into her thoughts.

Obedience.

Was that the one sure path to Seneca's heart? If she began doing everything he wanted her to do, would he love her? And would he finally accept her love in return?

God Almighty, had she been seeing obedience in the wrong way?

Peachy's thoughtful expression gave Viridis hope. "He has given you what most women can only dream of having. You live in a palace. Your clothes, your jewels . . . He has poured his wealth upon you. And he has given you the title of princess. I cannot think of anything you might ask for that he wouldn't give. And in return, he wishes only that you learn the ways of a lady."

Peachy ached with guilt. Viridis was right. Seneca had made his wishes plain the very night of her arrival. She'd agreed on the condition that he would grant all her own wishes.

He'd granted them.

But she hadn't granted his. Not the way he desired.

"Well?" Viridis pressed.

"All right," Peachy whispered. Dodging the rope hanging from the ceiling, she followed her teacher downstairs.

"Peachy, what overwhelmingly interesting thing is it that you see out that window?" Viridis demanded.

Sitting by the bowed window in the queen's chambers,

Peachy surveyed the landscape before turning away. She bent her head, staring down at her hands, which lay folded on her ecru velvet gown. She was glad to have taken off the ugly gray silk, but the velvet, combined with everything she wore beneath it, sent heat waves throughout her body. "I was a-hopin' to see Seneca. Ketty said he was out ridin'."

Viridis laid her hand on the arm of the cream settee. "You will not be seeing him for a while. I asked him to keep his distance. His presence will only hinder us."

Peachy wondered if she'd see Seneca at night. The thought made her scrunch her thighs together.

"Stop fidgeting, Peachy. And you would do well to know that I am perfectly aware of what you are thinking. Our lessons will continue until you retire at night, and then you will get a good rest in preparation for the next day of study and practice. Therefore, you will not see Seneca in the evenings, either."

Remembering that Seneca's love might possibly be the reward for her patient efforts, Peachy resigned herself to Viridis's wishes and gave the woman her full attention.

Viridis spent an hour discussing the proper way for a lady to move her head. Peachy ended up with a headache.

Footmen arrived and served tea and cakes. Only Agusta enjoyed the repast. Viridis was too busy instructing Peachy on the proper way to hold a teacup, and Peachy was too occupied wiping spilled tea off her gown.

"Look at Agusta," Viridis said after the footmen had rolled the tea trays away. "She has had her tea, and now she is enjoying a very ladylike pastime."

Agusta was working on a piece of embroidery. "Iffen y'ask me, Gussie lookes plumb sick o' that sewin'. She's been a-workin' on it fer three dang hours withouten stoppin'."

"Peachy, you will watch your language," Viridis scolded. "Agusta is a true lady, and you would be wise to imitate her gentle ways."

Agusta laid her embroidery aside. "Lady Elsdon, Peachy is the most gentle person I have ever known," she dared to argue. "Her ways may be different than ours, but—"

"Contradicting me is most unseemly, Agusta. Why, I have just told Peachy what a fine lady you are, and now you are proving otherwise. I am beginning to wonder if you have absorbed a few of her bad habits."

"Oh, Lady Elsdon, do you really think I have?"

"My comment was *not* a compliment!" Lips pursed, Viridis turned back to Peachy. "A true lady, my dear, demonstrates only surface emotions. You are much too outspoken. That is one of your many faults."

Peachy struggled to conceal her hurt. She knew she wasn't perfect, but she hadn't realized she had so many faults. She cringed, wondering what Seneca had thought about her in the past.

"We shall practice walking now," Viridis announced. "When you walk, Peachy, you must glide."

Peachy remembered that Seneca had mentioned gliding too. It was one of the things she'd written on the list of ladylike things to do, but she'd forgotten to practice it.

She rose and did as Viridis told her.

"You still have a spring to your walk," Viridis said two hours later, and sighed. "But you may sit down now. We shall glide more after the evening meal."

Rivulets of perspiration trickling between her breasts, Peachy returned to the hard upright chair by the window, remembering that a real lady always chose the most uncomfortable seat.

"Before we change to dine," Viridis began, "I want you to repeat what you have learned today."

Peachy closed her eyes, trying to remember. "I cain't do much o' nothin' with my days. I cain't cuss, yell, or use wild expressions. I cain't do no more silly stuff. Any sorter affection betwixt me and my husband has to be seed to in the privacy of our rooms. I cain't never raise my voice or git riled at Seneckers. I—"

"I have told you not to call the crown prince *Seneckers*," Viridis exclaimed. "That is most unseemly."

Peachy wanted to scream. "I can go fer rides in a carriage, but not never withouten some o' my ladies with me. And when I go, I have to have them men-at-arms go too, on account o' somebody might try to hurt me. I cain't never put mysef into a situation where I can git hurt."

Viridis joined Peachy by the window. "That is correct. And the reason you must take precautions with your person is because your most important obligation to Seneca—indeed, to all of Aventine—is to produce an heir to the throne."

Peachy glanced at the floor, unwilling to allow Viridis and Agusta to see the pain that filled her eyes. She doubted she would be alive long enough to give Seneca children. She could only hope that her death wouldn't come before she'd have time to give him her love and know the profound pleasure of receiving his in return.

"Of course, you needn't worry yourself with the children when they arrive," Viridis cooed, thinking that Peachy's dismay was connected to the unpleasant duty of bearing children. "While they are very young, the royal nanny will see to them. And when the children are a little older, the royal governess will supervise them."

She patted Peachy's shoulder. "Actually, you won't have to see much of them at all, my dear. Once a day—less if you prefer—they will be brought to you and Seneca for a short time. They will be clean, well-dressed, and hopefully well-behaved. When you tire of them, they will be taken back to the nursery, and you won't have to see them again until the next day. Even then, you mustn't feel obligated to do so."

Peachy looked up and stared at Viridis, the woman's explanation of royal childhoods still drifting through her mind. "Did Seneca spend his little-boy days like that?"

Viridis returned to the settee. "Yes, and his nanny and governess, Lady Muckross, did not have an easy time of it. Seneca has certainly become a man of impeccable manners, but when he was young ... My, he was a rebellious child. Poor Lady Muckross practically ruined herself trying to keep up with the lad. He used to disappear for hours at a time, and no one ever knew where he was hiding. When he reappeared, he would try to convince Lady Muckross that he had been with his very best friend."

"Who was his best friend?"

Viridis shrugged. "He said she was an angel. His head was bursting with all sorts of nonsense. Why, I remember one occasion when he announced that he wanted to go to

Africa and swing from trees as the apes do. Another time, he cried when Lady Muckross refused to acquire a slingshot for him. He had a nursery full of fine toys and books, yet he wanted a slingshot. Thank goodness he grew into his title. Now he wears it like a glove. But he certainly had a time learning the proper behavior of a future king."

Peachy fell silent, concentrating intently. A burst of realizations swept through her.

The tower. The day she'd brought Tivon's ram into the castle, Seneca had taken her directly to the tower. He hadn't had to think twice before leading her there. *The tower.* That's where little Seneca had been hidden when Lady Muckross couldn't find him. It had been his haven.

The spoons. The spoons she'd found in the trunk. She pictured them in her mind, recalling exactly how they'd been tied together with the pieces of leather.

Slingshots. Seneca had made them himself, using the only materials he had at hand.

And the rope. He'd hung it from the ceiling. He'd swung on it. Like an ape.

But what of the angel? Had he invented her out of loneliness? Had she dwelled in the tower room, ready to comfort him when he needed her? When no one else wanted him?

Peachy turned to the window. Sunlight glinted off her tears. She wept for Seneca. For the little boy he'd never had the chance to be, and for the man he had been forced to become. Now he was nothing more than a well-mannered title.

And she wept for herself, too. Once upon a time she might have been able to find, nourish, and bring back to life the sad little boy Seneca had been. But now she couldn't.

She had no more time for long-legged spiders, and word games, and stories, and teasing, and childish things like that.

She was too busy becoming a well-mannered title herself.

Chapter 14

Seneca handed Damascus's reins to Weeb. He'd been riding since dawn. The sun flamed high in the sky now, and the heat, combined with the thick moisture blowing in from the North Sea, dragged down the air. Seneca found it heavy to breathe. He yanked off his tight gloves and flexed his fingers. His gold wedding band shimmered in the bright light.

He felt lonesome.

"Your Highness's rides are becoming longer each day," Weeb commented as he removed Damascus's bridle and replaced it with a soft leather halter. "And Your Highness, you have been riding every day. I trust Your Highness has been enjoying the outings?"

"I suppose." Tapping his riding crop against his thigh, Seneca strode toward a giant oak tree that grew near the mews. He leaned against its ancient trunk and felt the woody knots massage the muscles in his back.

Nearby in a patch of clover and purple wildflowers lay a bucket. A rusty-red bucket. Seneca knew it had lain outside for many seasons.

He pictured rusty-red curls bouncing on slim shoulders. He could smell them, too. Lemon. And cream. He remembered how they felt sliding through his fingers. Soft. Like velvet.

Red velvet, he mused. The kind that made a good blanket. A much-loved one.

Deep in thought, he watched Weeb tend to Damascus,

who remained highly spirited despite the fact that he'd been ridden for hours.

The stallion threw his head and pawed the ground. Snorting violently, he lunged at Weeb.

Seneca tensed, realizing Weeb was about to receive a vicious bite.

But Weeb was ready. Calmly, he held out a vinegar-soaked rag-stick. Damascus backed away instantly. "The princess showed me this little trick, sir," Weeb explained. "Damascus continues to try to bite, but one whiff of the vinegar and he loses the fight in him. The princess certainly has a way with animals, sir."

And people, Seneca added silently. Leaning his head back, he watched pale green leaves flutter in the sea breeze. Their color and the way they danced reminded him of Peachy's eyes; the sound they made brought to mind her sweet whispers.

Three weeks. It had been twenty-one days and twenty-one nights since he'd spoken to her. And he'd had only two glimpses of her. From afar.

He missed her. The realization had come to him the first night Viridis had spent in the palace.

He longed to see Peachy smile again. He liked her smile. It was full of her thoughts, those outrageously wonderful thoughts. And he missed matching wits with her. He'd just begun to learn how to tease. There was no one else in the castle with whom he could do it. Only her.

Only Peachy.

He kicked at a stone, watching how it glittered as it rolled across the leaf-strewn sand. Picking it up, he noticed it was peppered with crystal. He guessed that Peachy would say it was "real diamondy." He decided to give the pebble to her.

The only problem was where to find her. Viridis was an expert at keeping her hidden away from him. It was true that he'd agreed to keep his distance, but he'd never dreamed three whole weeks would pass without Peachy's company.

He looked up at Weeb. "When did you last see the princess?" God, he thought. He'd been reduced to asking a stable hand about his own bride.

Weeb handed Damascus over to another groom and joined the prince by the oak tree. "Madam took a ride through the country yesterday afternoon, sir. Her ladies accompanied her. We brought the imperial coach around to the palace."

Seneca smiled, remembering Peachy's fascination with the gold coach. "And did she enjoy her ride?"

Weeb shook his head. "Madam had us return the imperial coach to the mews and bring the queen's landau instead. I fear our error caused the princess and her ladies a great inconvenience, as they were forced to wait while we readied the landau. But we were under the impression that madam was highly pleased with the imperial coach. Your Highness, I give you my word that it will never happen again. We understand now that madam will make use of the landau."

Seneca rubbed the back of his neck, contemplating this odd news. The queen's landau, while certainly an elegant vehicle what with its black-lacquered body and black velvet seats, didn't strike him as one his vivacious bride would favor. Only three weeks ago the gilded imperial coach and its pink satin seats had thrilled her beyond measure. Now she deigned not to use it.

He wanted to know why. And he was not willing to wait to find out.

Seneca searched for Peachy in vain. The palace, with its hundreds of rooms, had never seemed so huge to him. Finally, he happened upon Agusta in the queen's chambers. As he entered the room, he noticed that the hundreds of porcelain figurines he'd had taken out for Peachy's pleasure were gone. Many stood behind the glass doors of the curio cabinets; the others had obviously been returned to other rooms.

He joined Agusta at the elaborately draped window. "Do you know what happened to the figurines that were in this room?" he asked gently, lest he startle the timid woman.

Agusta met his gaze boldly. "The princess had them returned to their proper places, sir."

He was taken aback by her strong, clear voice and direct

regard. Studying her more closely, he noticed a subtle difference in her.

She was still thin, but her cheeks were touched with a whisper of pink, a natural pink he knew wasn't some sort of cosmetic. Her hair gleamed in the sunlight; her hands no longer shook. And her eyes ... they glowed. With a light that flickered from inside.

He was amazed to realize that she was really quite pretty. If she would only fill out a bit, she'd be beautiful. He almost smiled. Peachy would certainly take care of Agusta's meals.

Although he was impatient to find Peachy, he felt obligated to chat with Agusta for a moment. "You are enjoying your days in the palace?"

"I will not lie to you, Your Highness. I am as bored here as I was in my own estate."

Seneca folded his arms across his chest, his curiosity aroused. "I see. And is Peachy as bored as you are?"

"That I cannot say. She doesn't say much anymore. She mostly listens to Lady Elsdon."

"And why aren't you with them this afternoon?"

A long moment passed before Agusta replied. "Lady Elsdon became irritated with me, Your Highness, and dismissed me. She would like nothing more than to see me released from my service to the princess. I cannot seem to hold my tongue, and I have disrupted the lessons on frequent occasions. Lady Elsdon is fond of telling me that I have taken up the princess's bad habits. But, Your Highness, if you would care to hear my opinion, I don't believe them to be faults."

Seneca smiled. "And what is it you say that so upsets Aunt Viridis?"

"I may be frank?"

"You may."

Agusta lifted her small chin. "I told her she was being entirely too strict with the princess. The lessons begin at seven in the morning and continue into late evening. I stay as long as possible to try to make the princess's day as easy as I can, but I do fret over her when I leave."

"Peachy isn't sick, is she?" he asked quickly.

"No, but she's ... she's not herself, sir. Lady Elsdon, however, will hear not a word of argument."

Deliberating, Seneca glanced out the sparkling window and spied a few peasants standing by the palace gates.

"They've been there for three hours already," Agusta said. "The princess sent them the message that she was unable to see them, but they refuse to leave."

"Are they unwell?"

"Only mildly, thank goodness. I spoke with them earlier. One had a headache for two days, another has warts, and that big man standing beside the old woman has a broken nose. That woman has sent gifts of food and drink to the princess every day, but Lady Elsdon ..."

"What about her?"

Agusta went to a round marble table upon which lay a stack of unframed art canvases. "Lady Elsdon has disposed of all the woman's gifts. She insists that it isn't proper for the princess to consume food made by peasant hands."

Seneca continued to watch the peasants at the gates, wondering why Peachy had refused to see them. It wasn't like her to turn away people in need.

"Do you know that I had never held a pig before meeting the princess, Your Highness?"

Agusta's strange comment prompted Seneca to join her by the marble table. "I'd never held one, either. Nor had I ever handled a turkey."

Agusta picked up the canvas on top of the pile. "Peachy has been painting, at Lady Elsdon's request. This is the one she painted first."

Seneca smiled. Two childishly formed people were running through a green field filled with sheep. A man with black hair, and a woman with red hair and a crown on her head. Both were smiling and barefoot. Recalling the time she'd asked him to run through the meadows with her, he knew the painting was of him and Peachy.

Agusta held up another canvas. "This is the second one she painted."

It was almost the same as the first one, Seneca noticed. But in this one, he and Peachy wore shoes.

In the third, neither of them were smiling.

The fourth was of yet another meadow scene. But Peachy hadn't painted her crown. And she wasn't running through the grass. Neither was he. They stood proud and tall, their gazes directed straight ahead. A peasant man, cap in his hands, knelt before them, begging for their attention. It was obvious to Seneca that the man was pleading in vain.

The fifth was not a landscape. It was a painting of the castle without its surrounding meadows. Snow covered its towers, and icicles dripped from its balconies. And though Peachy had little artistic talent, Seneca could *feel* the coldness of her painting.

"And this is the one she painted this morning," Agusta murmured, holding up the last canvas.

Seneca stared at the ivory blob. Streaks of dark brown ran through it, and it hung off a thin black curve. "What is it?"

"She said it was a magnolia. A dead one."

Seneca inhaled sharply. "Where is she?"

"In the gold drawing room. Learning the formalities of holding court. She will, after all, become the Queen of Aventine one day soon. And a very proper queen she'll be too. Your Highness must be very happy."

He detected a hint of hostile accusation in her voice. It disturbed him not because it was impertinent for Agusta to speak to him in such a fashion . . .

But because it brought forth overwhelming guilt inside him.

Seneca paused in the threshold of the ostentatious gold drawing room and saw her immediately. Her gaze cast to the white marble floor, she was seated in an elaborate gold satin chair, nodding over something Viridis was saying to her. Light from the chandelier sparkled in her hair.

He missed the dazzle of her crown.

He started toward her, but halted abruptly when he saw her rise from the elegant chair. She wore green. A drab shade of green that made him think of overcooked vegetables.

The color was a far cry from the splendorous green of her eyes.

"Peachy," he called softly to her.

She kept her gaze riveted to the floor, but the sound of his voice sent excitement rushing through her. She hadn't seem him in so long. It seemed like years.

Viridis moved closer to her. "He's here," she whispered. "Heaven only knows why he has chosen to interrupt our lessons, but there is naught we can do about it. It might be that he has decided to test you. This is your chance, my dear. Your first chance to show him what you have learned. Make him proud."

Make him proud, Peachy repeated silently. Yes. *Make him proud.*

She lifted her head. A current of warm emotion drifted through her as her gaze met his. He was dressed casually. Black riding breeches and shiny black boots hugged his powerful legs, and a white shirt stretched tightly over his broad chest, its loose sleeves flowing over his long arms. His hair curled rakishly about his head, a few sable waves lying upon the pristine collar of his shirt.

He dominated the room. Filled it with his presence.

Lord, she'd forgotten how devastatingly handsome her husband was. She wanted to dash across the room and fling herself into his arms.

But Viridis took hold of her wrist. "Would you forget everything I have taught? *Glide,* my dear. Remember the royal bearing. You have worked diligently to become his lady, and you must show him what your efforts have wrought."

Trying to quell her nervousness, Peachy gave a slight nod of her head. Chin lifted high, shoulders held back, she walked across the room, her arms by her sides, her fingers lying delicately upon the rustling skirts of her silk gown. Confidence flowed through her when she heard Viridis's murmured approvals.

Seneca watched her draw near to him. She took tiny steps that made him feel impatient. It took her a full five minutes to walk across the room. When she arrived before him, he noticed that her hair was arranged in some sort of braided ball at the nape of her neck. And it was pulled back so tightly her eyes were slanted.

She curtsied, her head bent low.

The very proper show of respect irritated him. He wanted her to throw herself into his arms. At the very least, he wished she'd stop moving so slowly. Her curtsy seemed to last an eternity. "Rise." The stern command erupted from him before he could halt it.

She straightened and looked up at him, becoming wary when she saw the annoyance in his eyes. She couldn't understand what she'd done wrong. "Are y'riled—"

"Peachy," Viridis whispered.

Peachy looked down again, deeply disturbed by her mistake. "I— What I meaned to say ... Have I displeased you in some way, Seneca?" She kept her head bent low while awaiting his answer.

Her voice was so quiet, he wondered if he'd even heard it. "I wish to speak to you."

"O' course," she agreed softly, careful to keep her face void of all emotion. "What do y'want to talk about?"

He couldn't read her expression. After a moment, he realized she *had* no expression to read. Her features were blank. He turned to Viridis. "Please excuse us."

Viridis sighed. "Seneca, I had planned on formally presenting Peachy to you and the king tomorrow afternoon. She has made splendid progress, but there are still a few things I wanted to go over with her."

"They will wait. You are dismissed."

Viridis pursed her lips and left.

Seneca waited until he heard the doors close before speaking. "Walk."

Peachy struggled to keep from frowning in confusion. "Walk, Seneca?"

"Walk."

She realized his odd command must be another test. Determined to pass it, she turned and glided across the room, then returned to him.

Seneca glowered. He'd seen turtles move faster. "Why are you walking that way?" he demanded.

She did her best to ignore the irritation in his voice. It wasn't her place to question his mood. "I'm a-glidin', Seneca."

"You walk as though the floor were made of eggshells and if you crack one you'll fall."

She forced herself to accept his comment as a compliment. With graceful movements, she picked up her skirts, careful not to lift them indecently high.

Seneca looked at her ankles. Profound anger made him clench his teeth.

Her ankles were tied together with a velvet ribbon that allowed her no more than eight inches per step. There were also strange, satin-covered tubes encircling each ankle.

"What are those things?"

Peachy still didn't understand what she'd done to earn his wrath. She wanted to ask, but remembered that she was never to question her husband's behavior. "They're sandbags."

"Sandbags?"

"Satin tubes filled with sand, Seneca, and they're real heavy. The weight heps me mem'ry— I mean ... The weight heps me to *remember* that I ain't— That I'm not s'posed to let my feet rise too fur offen the floor when I walk. Yore aunt says I glide real good now. Don't ... Don't you think so, too?"

He heard the hope in her voice. But he hated the way she was walking. She moved like a machine instead of a vibrant young girl.

"Seneca?"

He picked up her hand. Her fingers felt like sticks of ice, but her nails were well-manicured. Each one was long and gently rounded.

To Seneca they looked like claws. "You don't look well. You don't act well, either."

Was his comment an insult? she wondered, bewildered. She looked at the floor again. "I'm fine."

"Look at me when I speak to you."

She had to shut her eyes for a moment to keep back the tears. She was failing his test. She knew by the sharp tone of his voice. "Seneca ..."

Seneca rammed his fingers through his hair. "For God's sake, what's the matter with you? You look as though you're about to cry."

She forced herself to swallow every dismal emotion she felt. "I'm fine."

He let go of her cold hand and took a step away from her. "You're fine."

"Very fine."

As gently as his irritation would allow, he lifted her chin. "We haven't seen each other in three weeks, and all you can say is that you're fine?"

She struggled to think of a proper response. "How have you been?"

He didn't answer. Truth was, he'd been miserable without her. Peachy, however, was fine. Very fine.

"The weather's fine, too," she added.

His gaze drilled into her. He wanted desperately to know what thoughts dwelt behind her senseless small talk. But if she was thinking at all, she certainly didn't show it. She'd become a master at concealing her emotions. Indeed, her expertise rivaled his own. "Yes, the weather has been nice enough for a carriage ride through the country, isn't that right?"

She inclined her head.

"You took the queen's landau yesterday. The imperial coach no longer suits you."

Relief filled her. Finally, he'd touched on a subject she could handle. "The imperial coach is fer grand occasions sech as weddin's, coronations, royal birthdays, and special days like that. It ain't— I mean, it *isn't* correct to take it fer a simple ride. The landau is—"

"But you liked the imperial coach. You asked me for a gold carriage, and I gave you one. I went so far as to have the interior done in pink satin for you."

She didn't reply. It wasn't proper to argue with her husband.

Her silence aggravated him further. "The figurines you professed to love are all back in the cabinets. You spent almost an entire afternoon telling me that you wanted to much-love them, yet you have had them put away."

"They ain't— I mean, they are not playthings, but very expensive objects o' beauty that are to be admired only with the eyes."

He realized she was quoting Viridis. He could almost hear his aunt saying what Peachy had just told him. He glared at her. God, she appeared so plain to him now. As if she'd just stepped out of the mold that had fashioned every other woman he knew. "You aren't wearing a single piece of the jewelry I gave to you."

"I am." She touched her earlobes.

The pearls were so tiny they were hardly noticeable. Not so very long ago, she'd glittered from head to toe with a veritable fortune in jewels. Now she didn't glitter at all.

The thought made him remember the glittering stone. Hoping the gift would prompt her to smile at him, or maybe tell him something nice, he withdrew it from his pocket and held it out to her.

She looked at it, thinking it very diamondy. "It's a rock," she said flatly.

"It glitters. Like a diamond."

"But it ain't— It isn't a diamond, Seneca. It's a rock."

He closed his fingers around the stone and let his arm drop to his side. "I thought you would pretend it was a diamond."

"Pretend?" She smoothed a pale hand down her skirt. "Seneca, I am too busy to play games."

"I see." The words swished between his clenched teeth. "And what is it that fills your time?"

His anger was growing, she realized. He wasn't pleased with her in the least. "I . . . The lessons. They keep me busy. And I embroider. And—"

"Paint?" he supplied.

"I have painted six pictures."

"I saw them."

She waited for him to compliment her on the paintings. He didn't. He simply stood there, scowling down at her. Her heart ached with misery, but she successfully kept her emotions hidden. "Was there somethin' else you wanted to talk to me about, Seneca?"

He hated the tone of her voice. It was soft, yes, but like frigid air that made him shiver. "The peasants are still at the gates. Agusta says they've been there for several hours."

Her heart rolled over within her chest. Sweet Lord o' mercy, she hoped the people weren't very ill. "I know," she whispered. "But it ain't— It is most unseemly fer to me fill the palace with sick people. The castle is not a hospital."

"You could see to them at the gates."

She shook her head. "I would dirty my gown, Seneca. You've been good enough to provide me with beautiful clothes, and I'm s'posed to make shore I don't mess 'em up."

She could set *that* gown on fire and he wouldn't care, he thought. "You will no longer call me Seneckers. Correct?"

He was continuing to test her, she realized. She chose her words carefully. "Yore the crown prince. It weren't very respectful fer me to give you a nickname. I hope you'll soon fergit that I did."

He wanted to shake her. Instead, he taunted her, hoping to get a reaction out of her. "I gather the Mistresses Molly and Polly have lost their names as well? And what of Guinevere? And let us not forget Lancelot."

"Seneca, please." She bent her head again, praying she was passing his tests.

"Please what?" he snarled. "Please hold me, Seneca? Please kiss me, Seneca? Is that what you were going to say, Peachy?" He reached for her, hauling her up against him.

"Sen—"

His searing kiss swallowed her words. His hands cupped her breast; his fingers kneaded her firmly. He thought he heard her moan, but the sound died quickly, as though she'd killed it herself.

Determined to force her sensual response to him, he deepened his kiss, granting her no quarter when she tried to squirm out of his arms. His tongue plunged into her mouth. He wanted to taste her. Wanted to find some shred of sweetness that might yet dwell inside her.

God help him, he wanted to find her again. The real Peachy. The one who cursed and bounced when she walked. The one who caught spiders and told him stories and taught him how to play games. The one who scrunched her thighs together when he touched her and stood up to him when he was angry at her. The one whose imagination sparkled as brightly as the midnight stars.

He wanted the real Peachy back again.

But if she existed, he couldn't reach her. The woman he held in his arms had gone completely limp. Her soft lips were parted, but not in passion. In submission.

Gone was the passionate girl she'd once been. The fiery hellion who had so intrigued him was now a cold and impeccable woman.

A well-mannered title.

Seneca released her so suddenly she almost fell. Fingers trembling, she reached up and touched her bruised lips. Had his brutal kiss been another test? And if so, had she passed it by showing no response? Or had he sensed her deep desire? Perhaps he'd felt it heat her body and make her quiver with longing for him.

Her mental questions alarmed her. She had to say something proper. Something that would further prove what a lady she'd become for him. "What iffen someone had come in?" she whispered. "I would've been very embarrassed. We are s'posed to see to the intimate side of our relationship in the privacy of our chambers."

"The intimate side?" he bit out. *"What* intimate side? I've yet to bed you. And did you know, Princess Peachy, that by law you are are not truly my wife? Nor will you be until we have consummated our marriage. Did Aunt Viridis explain *that* bit of information to you?"

"No," she whispered. A tight knot formed in her belly. "Why didn't you ever tell me? I didn't know—"

"I thought to give you time." His words crackled with anger. "I bent to your wishes. You spoke of love and your dreams of the specialness it would lend to our lovemaking. I couldn't make myself take you. And it was hell, Peachy. Sheer hell. I burned for you. Dammit, I've *never* wanted a woman the way I wanted you!"

Filled to the very brim with fear and bewilderment, she searched her memory for a proper response. She recalled nothing. Nothing except the fact that a wife was supposed to give her husband whatever he desired. "We— We could retire to yore chambers now, Seneca."

He stiffened. "Just like that? One, two, three, you'll spread your legs, accept me between them, and that's that?"

Her bottom lip quivered. "It's what you want, ain't—Isn't it? It's what I'm s'posed to do, isn't it?"

He stared at her, her questions crashing through his mind like giant waves that dragged him down, drowning him with remorse and frustration and deeper rage. Yes, he thought. Once, not so very long ago, her docile submission had been *exactly* what he'd wanted.

But not anymore. She was a stranger to him now. And he had no desire to make love to a woman he didn't even know. What a turnaround, he mused darkly. She'd once felt the same way about him.

"Seneca?" She was at a complete loss at how to act, and felt her ignorance keenly. God Almighty, what did he want her to do? "I . . . Do you want me to go to yore chambers with you?"

His jaw clenched. "No." He spun toward the door, stopping when he reached the threshold. Opening his hand, he looked down at the glittering rock, then tossed it at her satin-slippered feet.

She watched him stalk out of the room. When he was gone, she bent to pick up the stone.

And the diamonds of her tears splashed to its diamondy surface.

The tower door creaked as Seneca pushed it open.

The noise lifted memories from his soul. He didn't resist them. He didn't want to.

God, he wanted them to take him away. Back over the years. Back to little-boy times. The times he'd spent hidden here in the tower.

He stepped inside and breathed deeply of the musty, familiar, and deeply satisfying scent. He sucked in great gulps of it, wanting it to fill not only his empty lungs but each and every void inside him.

Just for a while . . . only a little while, he longed to immerse himself in youthful pleasures. It was an escape, but he needed an escape tonight. Just as he'd needed to escape as a child, when he didn't want to be the crown prince anymore.

When he wanted to forget what was happening downstairs in the palace.

Dusk had settled over Aventine. The weak light wasn't enough for Seneca. He yearned to see everything. Every splinter of his childhood haven.

He lit all the lamps he could find and three tall tapers as well. As the light washed the darkness away, the first thing he saw was Thurlow Wadsworth McGee sitting among Peachy's scattered bags of herbs. The squirrel must have followed him, he thought. Odd. The creature had never paid an ounce of attention to him before tonight. Perhaps Thurlow Wadsworth McGee was as lonesome as he was.

Seneca clapped, and the squirrel flew into his arms. "You're not wearing your crown," Seneca murmured, gliding his finger over the creature's soft head. "She probably decided it was unseemly for squirrels to wear satin and chandelier crystals. Maybe she's even decided you aren't fit to be a member of the royal family."

Thurlow Wadsworth McGee rubbed his tiny head on Seneca's chest and emitted a small squeak, which to Seneca's ears sounded sad.

He held the squirrel close to his chest, feeling the beast's body heat warm his skin.

He went to the window and set the squirrel on the sill. Looking out at the dusky landscape, he recalled all the times he'd stood here and looked out as a child. The peasant children used to play in the same wide meadow he was seeing now. "Sometimes the wind would carry their laughter up to the tower room," he told Thurlow Wadsworth McGee. "And I would laugh with them. I had no idea what they were laughing about, but I laughed anyway just because I wanted to laugh."

He sighed, and the memories continued to sweep over him. "Sometimes the children saw me wave to them. The shy ones ran away. The bolder ones tossed paschal flowers up to me. Then they'd return to their games. They played hide-and-go-seek, and from my spot here in the tower, I saw each child's hiding place. But I didn't want to *watch* them hide. I wanted to hide *with* them."

Thurlow Wadsworth McGee stood up on his hind legs and pressed his tiny front paws against the windowpane. It seemed to Seneca that the squirrel was looking for the children down below.

He hunkered down so that he was eye level with the squirrel, and rested his chin on the sill. "This is about how tall I was when I first discovered this tower. I grew, though. Even when I was tall, I kept coming here."

He swiveled on the balls of his feet and sat down, the wall at his back. Thurlow Wadsworth McGee sprang from the windowsill to a trunk beside the window. The dust that rose from the top made him sneeze twice. Chattering with displeasure, he leaped to Seneca's shoulder.

Seneca stared at the trunk. There was no need for him to open it. He knew what was inside.

He opened it anyway, and the lamplight and candle shine touched silver. Spoons of silver, tarnished now but still gleaming.

Seneca reached for one. Two came away in his hands, just as he'd expected since he was the one who'd tied them together with bits of leather. "Do you know what this is, boy?" he whispered, intense emotions rushing through him. "This is a slingshot. A very expensive one, I might add. Lady Muckross wouldn't allow me to bring sticks into the palace, so I had to use what I had at hand. I filched these spoons when I was eight and when Tiblock wasn't looking. The man searched the castle for a solid month. A pity he never thought to look in this tower."

Seneca held the homemade slingshot higher and looked through the V shape that the crossed spoons formed. In that space, he saw a rope. He followed its dangling end upwards to the rafter.

What fun he'd had swinging on that rope.

Rubbing the stubble on his cheek, he remembered how difficult it had been to attach the rope to the rafter. "I used a stack of crates," he murmured to himself. "Just when I had the rope tied to the beam, the crates fell, and I was left hanging there. It was the most exciting thing that had ever happened to me. There I hung, the Crown Prince of Aventine, whose very important person was never to be placed in danger. The future king . . . And then I became an ape. So I didn't fall, because apes don't fall from their vines. I swung, flying past imaginary trees."

He was too heavy to swing on the rope, but he didn't have to be a child to use a slingshot. Was he still as good a shot as he used to be?

There was no reason why he couldn't find out. He felt sure his bag of rocks was still here somewhere.

He began to look for it, Thurlow Wadsworth McGee hopping beside him. As he approached a darkened corner, he saw it—his pouch of stones. He picked it up, smiling as he ran his thumb over the filthy yellow satin sack. "I stole this too," he told the squirrel. "It was the bag in which my mother used to keep her threads. I was quite a thief when I was young. I thought about becoming an infamous highwayman when I grew up. But I couldn't, of course, because I had to be king."

He set the lamp on the floor and opened the bag. Only two rocks lay inside. He'd have to make them count. Turning, he faced the trunk, loaded his spoon slingshot, and took careful aim at the trunk's latch.

He broke the window.

"I'm out of practice," he murmured sheepishly.

He withdrew his last rock and loaded it into the slingshot. This time he would shoot merely for the pleasure of shooting. He wouldn't aim for anything.

He shot it toward some dark shadows on the opposite side of the room. He heard a thud, but not like what he would have heard had he hit the wall. Unable to guess what he'd struck, he picked up the lamp.

The shadows fled at his approach. The rock lay at the base of a large, square-shaped object that leaned against the wall. The square was draped with a long piece of blue velvet.

Seneca swallowed hard. He'd forgotten about the portrait. The one of *her.* He hadn't thought of her in years.

He remembered her now. She called to him, just as she always used to. Her voice sang a sweet melody that caressed him as if with hands and hugs and kisses, and all the wonderful things he never had when he was downstairs in the palace.

He wanted to see her again. The only being in his life who had truly loved him. Who had listened to him. God, how many hours had he spent talking to her? Pouring his heart out to her?

His angel. His best friend in the whole wide world.

He approached the covered portrait, his heart battering his ribs. The velvet slithered to the floor with a swish, landing atop his boots.

And the golden light of the lamp met the golden light of his angel.

Seneca felt intoxicated. With deep-seated astonishment. He didn't breathe. Didn't speak.

He only stared. The angel ... Her hair fell past her shoulders in rich, red waves that shimmered with gold highlights. Her skin ... magnolia skin ... was smooth, creamy, and soft. A smile touched her pink lips, full of secret thoughts, thoughts that weren't really secrets because they were all there in her smile. And her eyes. Pale green and brimming with love for him.

She wore white. The heavenly light that surrounded her cast streams of gold over her alabaster gown, her brilliant halo, and her large, graceful wings. The celestial shine glistened through her hair, too, and flickered across her beautiful face.

Seneca's eyes burned with the need to blink, but he refused to close them. This portrait ... his angel ...

She was Peachy. From the glowing crown of her red-gold hair to the tips of her bare, pink toes. The resemblance was extraordinary.

Finally he understood what he'd been at a loss to explain earlier. Whenever Peachy had neared the golden flames in the hearth, he'd been overcome by the feeling that he knew her. That he'd met her somewhere, sometime, long, long ago.

He'd seen his angel in her. Bathed in the golden fireshine, her image had sparked memories of his angel. The angel who knew all his secrets. Who let him be the little boy he needed so desperately to be. Who'd loved him. *Him.* Not the prince. *Him.*

He'd abandoned her in the tower.

But she'd come back to him.

In Peachy.

Peachy. She'd told him once that she'd be his friend.

He'd refused her. She'd tried to get him to talk to her. He'd told her nothing. She'd yearned to know the man behind the title. He'd not allowed it.

She'd attempted to give him her love. He'd rejected that as well.

She'd offered the very things he'd cherished as a child. All the things his angel had bestowed upon him.

And what had he told her? *It's not your love I want, Peachy. It's your obedience.*

Regret twisted his insides. She'd obeyed him. Yes, she'd followed his every instruction. She was a lady now. A replica of his mother. Of Callista.

"And all the other impeccable women I've ever known," he whispered brokenly. "Every damned one of them."

Anguish tore through him at the grim realization.

He'd lost his best friend a second time.

Chapter 15

Viridis clasped her hand over her chest. "Peachy, Seneca will be unable to find a single fault in your appearance. You are truly exquisite, child."

Peachy faced the full-length mirror in the corner of her room and scrutinized her reflection.

Her elaborate gown was of pale gold tissue. Floral sprays done in silk thread of darker gold embroidered the luscious fabric. Long and intricate blond lace edged the bodice and flowed from the sleeves past her elbows. But though the lace covered her arms, it did nothing to hide her lush breasts. Indeed, she dared not take a deep breath for fear they would spill out completely.

She wore gold and diamond jewelry. Queen Diandra's crown encircled the wreath of curls on the top of her head.

"I'm dressed fer a ball," she murmured. "My bosom— It ain't— I mean, it *isn't* dark outside yet and it won't be fer a few more hours. And what about this crown?" She touched a finger to the diamond crown she'd once worn every day. "I thought it was only fer special things."

At Peachy's concern, Viridis beamed with approval. "But this is a special occasion. I chose the most beautiful gown you possess so that your charms will be apparent to all. Our goal is to enchant Seneca, is it not? Besides, by the time your exhibition is over, it will soon be dark and we will sit down to the evening meal. After supper, we will enjoy a quartet in the music room, and I thought perhaps you and Seneca could dance a waltz. He should know that you've learned the steps.

"Oh, and the king will be joining us," she added. "Now, Peachy, listen carefully. His Majesty will more than likely put you through a series of tests. I mean no disrespect, of course, but— Well, I have known him for many years, and he has always enjoyed such sport. You must be alert for any traps he might set, for Seneca will be listening to your every word. Today is the day you have worked so hard for, Peachy."

Agusta rose from her chair and held out a nosegay of peach-colored roses. "You are very elegant, Peachy," she managed, her words clipped.

Peachy accepted the bouquet. "Is somethin' wrong, Agusta?"

Agusta dropped her gaze to the floor and spied the satin slippers peeking out from beneath Peachy's shimmering gown. The gold slippers were immaculate. Just like their owner. "No, there is nothing wrong . . . Peachers."

Viridis gasped. *"Peachers?* What sort of name is *that* to call your princess, Agusta?"

Agusta looked into Peachy's eyes. "Peachers is a name Her Royal Highness once asked me to call her. And on that day, she called me Gussie."

"Yes, well, that day is long past," Viridis said. "Come now, Peachy. It is time to exhibit your impeccable manners and exquisite beauty to your husband and father-in-law. I have no doubt that your display will captivate them both!"

Peachy looked away from the sadness in Agusta's eyes. Gracefully she lifted her wide skirts and followed Viridis.

She was to be presented tonight, she reminded herself as she glided down the corridor. For some reason she had yet to understand, her audition for Seneca yesterday afternoon had gone awry.

Tonight she wouldn't fail. Her performance would be perfect.

So perfect it would surely win her Seneca's love.

Seneca could see no reason why tonight's presentation had to take place here, in the green drawing room. Decorated in pale green silk, white marble, emerald brocade, shining mirrors, gleaming gold, and twinkling chandeliers, it was the largest and most ostentatious of the palace's twenty-three parlors.

The gilt plasterwork on the vast ceiling boasted elaborate scenes taken from Greek mythology. All one had to do to learn the ancient myths was lie on one's back and memorize the ceiling. There had to be at least fifty chairs lining the silken walls; their legs sank deeply into the plush raspberry-colored carpet. And there was nothing in the middle of the huge room except a monstrous satin-wood table upon which sat a green malachite vase filled with bright pink paschal blossoms.

Peachy would have a lot of room in which to glide, he mused bitterly.

A footman offered him a glass of champagne. He shook his head. "Brandy. And one of those nuts for my friend." He gestured toward Thurlow Wadsworth McGee, who sat at his heels.

The attendant handed a snifter of brandy to the prince before placing a fat walnut on the floor for the squirrel.

Seneca finished his brandy in one swallow and held the glass out for more.

"Good evening, Your Highness."

Seneca gulped down his second glass of brandy before turning to see Tiblock standing in the arched doorway. "You've come for the presentation as well, Tiblock?"

Tiblock bowed his head. "I have, Your Highness. At the invitation of His Majesty."

Seneca accepted his third glass of brandy from the footman and made his way to a chair. "Are you taking Father's place, then? You'll take notes on the princess's decorum so that you may rush upstairs and describe her behavior to him?"

Tiblock's smile was thin as he moved into the room. "His Majesty will join Your Highness."

"Ah, so he has decided to leave his bed for such a memorable evening as this."

The king limped into the room. "Indeed I have, Seneca. No amount of pain could keep me from missing tonight's performance. The month is over, and I would see the outcome of our wager with my own eyes." He allowed

Tiblock to assist him into a chair, then rubbed his throbbing knees.

"I see you haven't taken advantage of the medicines. Peachy prepared for you," Seneca commented.

"No, nor will I. I employ my own physicians and have no need of some ludicrous mountain herb doctor."

Seneca sneered. "And the royal physicians have done so well by you all these years?"

The king shrugged off Seneca's derision. "Well? Where is the little yokel? It is ill-mannered of her to keep me waiting, don't you think?"

Seneca glanced at the clock on the mantel. "The hour of the presentation is at precisely five o'clock. It is now five minutes till. She is not late; you are merely impatient. Impatient to find fault with her. I fear, however, that your high hopes are about to be dashed. I was in her company yesterday, and I assure you that I've never known a more proper woman." His mouth twisted as he spoke.

"Then you must be very pleased."

Seneca twirled the stem of his brandy snifter. "Deliriously so."

"So it is your belief that you have won the wager."

Seneca closed his eyes for a moment. He hadn't won anything. He'd lost everything that mattered.

He'd lost Peachy.

"I have won, Father," he muttered. "I've won it all. The wager, the throne, and the right to keep my very well-mannered wife."

The king glanced up at Tiblock and smiled. His smile broadened when the servant nodded.

Seneca watched the silent exchange. Both men were extraordinarily pleased with themselves, and Seneca realized that they were involved in some sort of scheme. "Father—"

"Ah, here are the ladies now!" the king exclaimed, his eyes gleaming with excitement as Viridis and Agusta entered, followed by their princess.

Seneca's gaze fell upon Peachy. Her gown looked like a golden cloud; her diamonds shone like raindrops. As if transported on a gentle summer breeze, she floated toward the king. Her deep curtsy sent her shimmering skirts billowing out around her.

Seneca felt choked by the sickeningly sweet scent of jasmine.

"Yore Majesty," Peachy said. "I am deeply honored that you have joined us."

Seneca noted that her voice rang with a profound veneration he wondered if she really felt. He doubted it, but couldn't be sure because there existed not a shred of emotion on her face.

She was good. Very good.

And he detested her excellence.

The king held out his hand.

Peachy pressed her pink lips to his huge ruby ring.

Seneca knew that not long ago she'd have bitten his father's hand rather than kiss it. Not to mention the fact that she'd once told him rubies meant anger and cruelty. If she still believed the omen, how could she kiss the red stone?

It made him feel very sad that she'd apparently given up her refreshing mountain ways.

"Rise," King Zane commanded.

Peachy straightened, then inclined her head at her husband. "Seneca."

"Peachy." He drained the glass of brandy and watched Thurlow Wadsworth McGee scamper to the window.

At his icy demeanor, Peachy stiffened. But she would not allow his coldness toward her to spoil her presentation. He would soon see that she could meet his every expectation. She returned her gaze to the king. "Yore Majesty is well?"

King Zane studied her carefully controlled features and elegant carriage. The girl had certainly improved.

But just how deeply had those spotless manners been ingrained within her? Was she a lady through and through, or behind that polished exterior was she the same hellion she'd been a month ago?

The time had come to find out. "I did not make use of the potions you made for me," he said. "I believe them to be repugnant in nature and quite useless in value. Moreover, I am unaccustomed to being treated by backwoods wenches who don't know the first thing about medicine."

Seneca realized his father was baiting Peachy and that he'd planned to do so all along. Ladylike though she'd become, surely she wouldn't ignore such cruel offense. He wondered anxiously if the real Peachy, the proud and spirited mountain girl, would rise to her own defense.

Peachy kept her gaze nailed to the King's, but she felt Seneca's censorious eyes upon her. He was waiting for her to make a fatal error. The king's blatant scorn had sent a stream of choice curses to her lips, but not one escaped. It was as Viridis had suspected; King Zane was setting traps for her.

She forced a tilt to her mouth. "Please accept my apology fer a-givin' the cures to Yore Majesty. I promise never to insult you in sech a way again."

Seneca's temper rose. "Yes, try never to help the man again, Peachy," he bit out.

She fought to keep from frowning. She was being as polite and well-mannered as she knew how to be. God Almighty, what more did Seneca want from her?

The king savored the animosity he sensed between them. Settling back in his chair, he continued to think up ways to further his plans. "It has come to my attention that you are well-versed in the art of feeding swine."

Viridis hurried forward before Peachy could respond. "Your Majesty, the princess has learned that her preoccupation with barnyard animals is most unseemly."

"That is enough, Viridis," the king snapped. "I am not speaking to you, but to the girl. Or are you interfering because you are afraid she will forget the manners you have endeavored to teach her?"

Viridis shook her head and backed away.

Peachy kept her chin high. "I know a lot about pigs, Yore Majesty. My father used to raise 'em."

The king lifted a brow. "That would suggest that you were raised with swine."

Seneca gave Peachy a withering glance. "What have you to say to that, Princess? Father declares you were raised with pigs. Will you allow him to insult you in such a way?"

Peachy bristled with indignation. Afraid she would give her real feelings away, she refused to look at Seneca. Concentrating hard, she replied, "I weren't raised with the pigs, Yore Majesty. I only watched my father with 'em."

Upon hearing her humble and very proper answer, Seneca stormed to the window and presented his back to her.

"Seneca?" Peachy called softly. "What—"

"Tell me, do you like pigs?" King Zane interrupted.

Peachy struggled to understand why he was harping on the subject of pigs. "I like 'em all right."

"I don't care for them. Especially when they are running around my kingdom. They are to be kept in pens, and yet there are herds of them meandering through my forests. Would you happen to know anything about that?"

Peachy's fingers curled into her palm. "I . . . Yes, Yore Majesty. I'm the one who tole the people to let their pigs into the woods."

Seneca realized that his father was about to chastize Peachy for what she'd done. Granted, he abhorred the way she was conducting herself, but even so, he felt an intense desire to defend her. "Father, Peachy instructed the peasants to release the swine into the forests because—"

"Champagne," the king ordered, effectively cutting Seneca off.

The footman poured a glass of champagne and handed it to a young maid, who promptly carried it to the king.

King Zane took the glass and bent to massage his knees. His movement upset his glass; champagne sloshed all down the front of his coat.

Instantly, Tiblock realized the accident had provided another opportunity to further the king's plans. He reached out and slapped the young maid across the face. "You clumsy little idiot! You have soiled His Majesty! You are dismissed from service in the palace! Pack your things and leave immediately."

Seneca and Agusta moved swiftly to steady the sobbing maid, but she fled the room before they reached her. Agusta, her thin faced pinched with fury, followed suit and left quickly.

Peachy felt her cheeks flame with rage. To keep anyone from noticing her anger, she bent her head and pretended to smooth her skirts.

Seneca felt sickened by her uncaring attitude. Tiblock

had struck the maid for no reason, and Peachy hadn't said a damn word! Dear God, what kind of person had she become? He stalked back to the window and had to curb the urge to slam his fist through the sparkling pane.

The king smiled, silently congratulating Tiblock for his quick thinking. But the servant had more to do. "I believe you have duties to tend to, do you not, Tiblock?"

At the cue, Tiblock bit back a smile. "I do indeed, Your Majesty. I will see to them this very instant." Hands clasped together at his waist, he scurried from the room.

"Domestics," the king said with a deep sigh. "With the exception of Tiblock, the servants are coarse and cloddish, all of them. Ignorant beyond measure and totally repulsive." He looked up at Peachy. "You must feel right at home among them. Am I correct?"

Peachy bent her head again, blinking back tears. She didn't know how to be more mannerly, and yet she was failing dismally.

She sensed that every eye in the room was trained upon her, every ear cocked to hear her answer to the king.

A sixth sense told her that her response would be the deciding factor in her husband's ultimate opinion of her.

Taking a deep breath, she lifted her head and met the king's stare. "Iffen my behavior still ain't—*isn't* what it's s'posed to be, I apologize again, Yore Majesty."

Seneca felt as though he'd been struck by lightning. The fire of white-hot rage sizzled through him. What would Peachy do next? Kneel and kiss his father's feet?

He hated her spinelessness, her subservience, and her absolute obedience.

He hated his father for taking such pleasure in taunting her.

He hated Viridis for having succeeded in changing her into a marionette.

But most of all, he hated himself for what he'd forced her to become.

He could stomach no more. If he didn't leave, he would explode into a million bits.

As he stormed toward the door, Peachy saw blue fire in his narrowed eyes. "Seneca?" She moved to follow him, but stopped abruptly when the king spoke.

"You had no right to issue orders for the peasants to release their animals into my woods. I have, of course, countermanded your instructions. The swine will no longer sully Aventine's forests."

Peachy felt deep dread mingle with her heightening anger and profound confusion. "What have y'done?" she asked, her voice soft but tight with wrath.

The king took a moment to admire his ring.

Peachy almost choked with bitter foreboding. "Did you tell the people to call the hogs in?" she pressed shakily.

"The peasants would not be able to perform such a feat quickly enough to suit me."

Peachy grasped handfuls of her gown. "Then what—"

"Your Majesty!" Tiblock shouted as he rushed back into the room. As if in a true panic, he wildly shook his head, hoping his performance was a convincing one. "I couldn't stop them! They have broken into the palace! I tried, Your Majesty, truly I did, but—"

"Princess! Please help us!"

Peachy's face drained of color as Mintor entered. The man's expression was one of horror and helplessness. Following him were several other peasants, each as frightened and desperate as Mintor. "What is it?" she exclaimed. "What—"

"They're going to shoot our swine! We came to the palace as soon as we realized . . . At this very moment they're gathering near the woods—"

"Who?" Peachy demanded. "Who's—"

"A few of my subjects," the king answered, still admiring his ring. "I believe there were twelve or so noblemen who volunteered to rid the woods of the swine. They're hunters and enjoy the sport. I imagine it will take but an hour to complete the task. Why, we shall have enough fresh meat to feed the entire kingdom, shan't we? What a good king I am to provide so much food for my people."

Peachy gasped. "You *arranged* fer the hogs to be slaughtered?"

Viridis grasped her elbow. "Peachy, my dear, the swine are of no concern to you. You must leave the matter to His Majesty. Come now. We shall retire to the music room and listen to the quartet perform until it is time to dine."

Absolute silence settled over the room. Time hung suspended as Peachy's gaze went from one person to another.

Viridis's eyes begged. Mintor's and the other peasants' held panic. Tiblock's glittered with excitement, and the king's gaze gleamed with smugness.

The king. Peachy stared at him so hard she felt his image being branded into her brain. Disputing the sovereign was an extreme breach of etiquette, yet she'd dared to question his order that the hogs be hunted.

She dared to do much more than that. To hell with the rules! If being a lady meant turning her back on people in dire need, then she'd rather be the most ill-mannered woman in the universe.

She took a step toward the king, her fists whitening with tension.

Viridis tightened her hold on Peachy's arm. "Are you all right, my dear?"

Slowly, Peachy turned to the woman whose bossiness she'd endured for three whole weeks. "Git yore gawdang hand offen me."

Viridis paled. "What? Peachy—"

"Lady, iffen you don't git yore hand offen me, I'm gonna knock you upside the head so hard that you'll be dead fer four days afore it quits a-hurtin'!"

Mortified to the very marrow of her bones, Viridis struggled for composure. "Peachy, I must insist that you apologize to His Majesty and then come with me."

"Yeah? Well, a snake would have better luck a-tryin' to make love to a buggy whip than you'll have a-gittin' me to foller one more o' yore agger-pervokin' orders!"

"Oh my!" Viridis clutched her bosom. "I feel faint! Something is terribly wrong— My heart— My nerves— My— Good heavens, I believe I'm quite ill!"

Peachy rolled her eyes. "Lady, you ain't got nothin' a good case o' lockjaw wouldn't cure." She yanked her arm out of Viridis's grasp and whirled on the king. "And as fer you, I got it figgered now that you was baptized in vinegar. I ain't never in my whole life meeted up with somebody as bitter as you. It's that gawdang ruby y'wear, y'know. It makes you so coldblooded that I reckon iffen a mosquiter was to bite you it'd git pneumonia!"

The king grinned, thoroughly enjoying her display of unladylike decorum. "Do continue. But speak more slowly. I want to be sure to relate everything correctly when I speak to Seneca. He so hoped you would become a lady. I shall have to break the distressing news to him gently."

Peachy's rage knew no bounds. God help her, she was going to hit the man. King or no king, she was going to hit him so hard he'd have to look out of an ear hole to see anything.

The king watched her raise her balled fist. For the first time since he'd begun mocking her, he felt afraid. "What— Are you . . . going to *hit* me?"

"Yore Majesty, when I git through with you, yore gonna feel like you was et by a goat and vomited up over a gawdang cliff!"

She prepared to deliver the blow, but a gray blurr at her feet caught her attention. Looking down, she saw Thurlow Wadsworth McGee nibbling at her gown.

She smiled and pointed to the king. "Git him, boy."

The squirrel took a flying leap onto the king's broad chest and dug in his claws, so surprising King Zane that he toppled out of his chair backwards, his fat legs extended straight into the air.

Satisfied, Peachy spun to join Mintor and the other men—and ran directly into Tiblock. "And here we have Rupert-Dupert-Figgymoopert! Y'know what, Tiblock? The last time I seed somethin' like you, it was a-covered with flies. Now, git outen my way afore I scatter the landscape with you!"

Tiblock could not remove himself from her path quickly enough.

Mintor and the other peasants followed Peachy as she called out, "Y'all go on to them woods, and I'll meet you there."

As they hurried to obey, she headed for the exit closest to the royal mews and moments later, entered the immaculate barn. Unable to find Damascus, she realized Seneca was out riding him.

The thought of her husband turned her heart over. God, he was going to pitch a fit over her behavior.

He was never going to love her now. Not ever. Tears sprang to her eyes.

The white stallion nickered. The sound recalled her to her purpose. Doing her best to push thoughts of Seneca from her mind, she dried her tears and hurried to the stallion's stall.

He wore nothing but a leather halter. Having no idea where the bridles were kept, she attached a lead line to each side of the halter, led him from the stall, and tried to mount. But the many petticoats beneath her gown hindered her efforts. "Dang this blasted unnerwear to hell and back!" she swore, swiping at her billowing skirts.

"Your Highness!" Weeb exclaimed as he entered the barn, a bucket of oats swinging from his hand. "Please allow us to ready the landau! We—"

"I ain't got time fer you to git that ugly thing ready." Quickly, she turned her back to Weeb, reached way under her gown, and untied and tugged off the multitude of ruffled underwear. Her gold tissue skirts clinging to her legs, she stepped out of the cloud of petticoats, led the stallion to a hay bale, and mounted.

"Your Highness, please!" Weeb begged. "Oh, dear God!"

"Don't pray fer me, Weeb. Pray fer the hogs. Or better yet, pray fer them noble cusses who's a-gittin' ready to shoot the swine. By the time I catch up with 'em they're gonna need all the prayers they can git."

She urged the steed out of the barn, over the bridge, through the gates, and out into the wide-open countryside. As the horse broke into a full gallop, she leaned low over his thick neck and felt her princess crown fly off her head.

She didn't care. She wasn't Her Royal Highness, the Princess of Aventine anymore.

She was Peachy McGee, the mountain girl of Possum Hollow, North Carolina.

Damascus sailed over the fence as if borne on wings, then tore across the meadow, slowing only when his master pulled on the reins.

Seneca halted the stallion in the middle of the verdant

field. Several sheep, their fluffy legs hidden by the tall vegetation, lifted their heads and stared.

Seneca dismounted and watched his boots disappear into the lush pink-and-white wildflowers. The blossoms looked soft; the grass appeared even softer.

He'd once had a chance to run through these meadows. Peachy had invited him; he'd refused. She wouldn't invite him again.

He'd run through this field without her. He'd run so fast that he'd leave all his sorrows behind him. He kicked his boots off and peeled his stockings down as well.

In the next moment, he bolted into the meadow, Damascus following. Man and stallion raced among the sheep. Through the flowers. Around a tall and graceful oak tree.

Finally, after a very long while, they stopped before a crystal-clear pond. Together, they looked into the water and saw small silver fish darting through it. Damascus snorted and pawed the moist ground. Seneca scooped cool water into his cupped palms and splashed it on his face. He drank some, too, and discovered it to be sweet and wonderfully refreshing.

Sweet and wonderfully refreshing. The description reminded him of the way Peachy used to be. He cast a glance toward the palace, wondering if she was still performing for his father.

The full measure of his misery caught up with him.

He bent his head. The pond water sparkled. Like Peachy's smile. If only he could see her like she used to be. Just once. With her fiery curls flying all around her beautiful face. With her green eyes afire with passion and courage. And with her soft lips parted to deliver a stream of verbal outrageousness.

In all her wild and brazen glory. In all her . . .

The sudden sound of pounding hoofbeats scattered his thoughts. He snapped up his head. The sight that met his wide-eyed gaze sent disbelief zigzagging through him.

An alabaster stallion thundered down the dirt road that skirted the meadow. As quickly as he'd appeared, he vanished around a bend in the path, his rider's copper-flame hair whipping in the wind.

Peachy. In all her wild and brazen glory.

Seneca was back in the saddle before he thought to mount.

As the white stallion rounded yet another bend in the road, Peachy saw a dense forest ahead. A large crowd of peasants was gathered at the edge of the woods, blocking the way of the small assembly of armed men who stood before them.

A hedgerow was the only obstacle separating her from the opposing groups. She would have to jump the stallion over it. It was too tall for her to get over by herself, and searching for the end of it would require precious time.

She kept the steed cantering toward the tall bushes. When the horse was almost upon them, she prepared herself for his flight over them, gripping handfuls of his long mane and squeezing his sides with her knees.

But when he was several feet away from the jump, the stallion stopped short. His abrupt halt yanked Peachy from her seat. She felt her legs fly up behind her, and in the next second the world turned upside down as she catapulted over the stallion's head, turning a perfect somersault through the air.

Neatly, she landed square in the middle of the prickly thick hedgerow. Blinking, she stared up at two black holes. A moment passed before she realized she was looking up into the stallion's nostrils.

He sneezed, spraying her face.

She grimaced and sputtered with outrage. "You great big, evil-minded, contrary, bedevilin'est, slobberin', *varmint!* What the hell's the matter with you, a-flingin' me offen the way you done! And then y'go an snort all over me! Gawdang it, iffen you ever walk through the valley o' the shadder o' death, you ain't gonna fear nary a bit o' evil on account o' you'll be the meanest critter there!"

"Princess!" Mintor shouted as he and his companions arrived from the palace. "Is Your Highness hurt?"

She struggled to remove herself from the tall bushes, but her efforts were hampered by her skirts, which were caught fast within the maze of branches.

His cheeks aflame with embarrassment, Mintor stuck his slingshot into the waistband of his pants and began picking the delicate gold tissue of her gown off the branches. The fragile fabric shredded as he tugged on it.

Impatient, Peachy ripped it herself. When Mintor was finally able to lift her from the shrubbery, she was wearing nothing but her satin slippers, her lacy drawers, and the shimmering bodice of her dress.

Heedless of her shocking appearance, she marched straight toward the cluster of aristocrats, noting that each of them clutched a rifle in his hands. As she neared them, one nobleman stepped forward.

Veston Sherringham sneered as his eyes traveled down her scantily clad body. *This* was the well-mannered princess that Agusta had spoken of for the past three weeks?

Turning to his companions, Veston threw back his head and laughed out loud. The other nobleman began to chuckle as well.

Peachy stopped abruptly, Mintor close by her side. The taunting laughter made her cringe. Recalling the king's show of contempt earlier, she decided she'd put up with quite enough mockery for one day.

Spying a smooth pebble on the ground, she picked it up, snatched Mintor's slingshot from the waistband of his pants, loaded it, and took careful aim.

Veston yelped, his lingering laughter turning to a shout of pain. Pressing his hand to the stinging spot on his backside, he swept his furious gaze over the crowd of peasants. It stopped on Peachy and the slingshot in her hands. "You hit—"

"Yeah, dead square in that lard ass o' yores. Now, you and the rest o' them would-be hog killers git on outen here. There ain't gonna be no hunt."

Mute with anger, Veston watched her sashay to the edge of the woods. The peasants parted for her, flanking her on either side. He tightened his hold on his rifle. His Majesty would support his every action. And as for Prince Seneca's displeasure ... Veston's fury was so great, he no longer cared what the prince thought. He raised his voice to be heard. "We've the king's command to hunt down the swine, so it would seem that *you* are the one who should leave the area. And take your rabble with you."

"No," came Peachy's simple but firm reply.

Veston motioned for his companions to join him. "We are thirteen and well armed."

Peachy took a good look at the crowd of people standing with her. "And we're about thirty and gawdang riled."

Veston swiped at a fly that buzzed around his face.

" 'Pears yore a-fixin' to meet up with a stranger, Veston," Peachy told him. "That there fly that's a-pesterin' you is a omen."

He ignored her. "Disperse so that we may proceed with the king's demands." To reinforce the seriousness of his order, he pointed his rifle toward the sky and pulled the trigger twice.

Peachy's smile calmed the nervous peasants. "Good shootin', Veston. Y'reckon y'can larn me how to shoot holes in the sky like that?"

His eyes gleaming with smug maliciousness, he lifted his rifle again and shot at a skinny tree branch.

Peachy didn't move so much as an eyelash when it fell to her feet, its leaves brushing her legs.

"A thousand apologies, Your Highness," Veston jeered. "It wasn't my intention to fell the branch so close to your royal person." His beefy hands whitened around the rifle.

Still smiling, Peachy borrowed a rifle from the peasant standing beside Mintor. She, too, shot a branch off a tree. While it was still in midair, she shot at it again, cracking it into four pieces. One by one, the four twigs hit Veston on the head. "A thousand apologies, Veston. It shore weren't my intention to fell them sticks on top o' yore empty head." She handed the gun back to the peasant.

Veston made a growling sound. "Be on your way. I have organized this hunt and mean to see it through."

It was Peachy's turn to laugh. "Lord o' mercy, Veston, you couldn't organize a piss-off at a brewery. Y'don't really think I'm gonna leave here and let y'shoot them hogs, do you?"

He advanced toward her, his fellow hunters following close behind.

Peachy turned to the group of peasants. "Y'all go on into them woods and call yore hogs. Take 'em on home, and don't let 'em go again till y'git word from me, hear?"

The older peasants, women, and children trampled into

the dim woods. The younger men stayed with their princess. "Yore downright displeasurin' me now, Veston," she warned. "And iffen y'try to kill them pigs? Well, I'll bang a knot on yore head so high you'll have to git on a ladder to scratch it. Now, go on home."

He smiled. "I am here at the express orders of the *king,* and you expect me to obey *you?* Just what kind of idiot do you think I am?"

"I don't know. What other kinds are there?"

Veston heard the peasant men chortle under their breaths. He raised his rifle again.

Peachy tore the rifle from his fat hands and shoved the barrel into the blubber of his belly.

Still, he dared to take another step toward her.

She slid the rifle down to his groin. "Y'got balls, I'll say that fer you, you thin-lipped varmint, but iffen y'make one more move, I'll shoot 'em plumb offen. I mean it, Veston. Mess with me, and you'll wake up in a coffin."

Enraged and sure she was bluffing, Veston reached for her.

An explosion of gunfire interrupted his hostile intent.

Veston gasped, expecting to feel horrible pain sear into his loins. When none came, he looked down at himself, but saw no blood either.

"Veston, you will take your hands off my bride!"

Whirling, Peachy caught sight of Seneca mounted astride Damascus and holding a gleaming pistol in his hand. And, Lord o' mercy, but blazes of fury burned from his narrowed gaze.

"The Princess was going to shoot me, Your Highness," Veston argued. "By royal command, my companions and I are to rid the forest of swine, and the princess barred our way."

"She would not have shot you, and if you ever dare to touch her again, I will personally see to it that you are stripped of your land, your title, and your wealth. Hear me well, Veston, for I do not speak lightly."

Veston stepped away from Peachy, his fat hands balling into fists.

Seneca urged Damascus forward and dismounted. His gaze slid to Peachy, his eyes widening when he saw how she was dressed. To shield her from Veston's view, he stepped in front of her, but realized the peasant men behind them could still see her.

There was nothing he could do about her indecent state. He glowered at Veston. "You will not hunt the swine."

As if on cue, the herd of hogs began to emerge from the forest, grunting loudly as the peasants prodded them with long sticks.

Realizing he was on the verge of losing his quarry, Veston threw back his shoulders. "Your Highness, with all due respect, we are here at His Majesty's orders, and—"

A loud clattering interrupted him. Looking up, Veston saw Agusta's carriage. It came to a halt and she jumped out. "Veston!" she screamed over the hedgerow. "You come here right this minute!"

He stared. He couldn't believe his eyes or ears. Agusta was *shouting* at him.

Peachy sauntered over to his side. " 'Pears you've done meeted up with the stranger that buzzin' fly warned you about, huh, Veston? That ain't the Agusta y'know, is it?"

He shook his head, still staring at his angry wife.

"Veston!" Agusta yelled again. "If you've shot even *one* of those helpless pigs, I will never speak to you again! I *like* pigs! Do you hear me?"

Her threat dispelled his astonishment. How *dare* the woman threaten him in front of all these people! He stalked over to the hedgerow. "Agusta, you will never raise your voice—"

"Shut up, Veston. I have endured your domineering behavior for long enough. You will cease to dictate to me, is that clear?"

He gasped. "It's that ... that heathen princess! She's turned *you* into a heathen as well! My God, you're as mouthy as she is! And you're getting fat, too! You're—"

"I'll be getting a lot fatter, Veston, and you better get used to it."

"Agusta—"

"That is, unless you know of a way I may remain thin and still give birth to your child."

His mouth fell open. "Child?"

"Yes, and I must tell you, Veston, it certainly isn't a

very wise thing to upset me. Now, unless you wish to harm your unborn child, I suggest you get on your horse and follow me home. I will not have you shooting the hogs, and that is my final word on the subject." She waved to Peachy. "Can I call you *Peachers* again, Your Highness?" she called, a huge smile on her face.

Peachy smiled and waved back. "Y'shore can, Gussie!"

"Well, Veston?" Agusta pressed. "Let's go home."

In an absolute daze, Veston turned and started for his horse. Mounted, he looked down at all the people staring up at him. "I cannot shoot the baby," he mumbled. "I mean— A son. I'm sure of it. I'm going to be a father. The hogs— Agusta would be terribly upset, you see. She'll be getting very fat, but I— Well, she cannot help it. The baby— The hunt ... How could I participate? The king— Oh, dear—"

"I will explain the way of things to my father," Seneca assured him. "But first, you will apologize to the princess."

His head still hopelessly muddled, Veston nodded, trying to remember what evil thing he'd done to her. Only bits and pieces of the afternoon's activities came to him.

"I'm grievously sorry that I hit Your Highness with a slingshot. I hope very much that madam does not have to climb a ladder to scratch the knot. Now, if Your Highnesses will excuse me, I must follow Lady Sherringham to the brewery. I believe she said something about organizing a piss-off. I am at a loss to understand what such a thing has to do with the baby, but I mustn't upset her. No, I mustn't do that. I'm to be a father soon, you know."

Still in a stupor, Veston rode his mount over the hedgerow and followed Agusta's carriage down the winding road. Their leader gone, the other noblemen followed suit.

Seneca saw that the peasants were a good distance away, herding the hogs back to their respective villages. He turned to Peachy. "You had no business coming out here to confront the hunters."

Pain squeezed her heart. She knew he was dismally disappointed by her behavior, but she'd prayed he would understand her actions. "I done what I had to do, Seneca. And iffen I had to, I'd do it again."

"You should have come to me."

She couldn't read his expression, nor could she decipher the tone in his voice. Confused, she lowered her head and kicked a stone. As she did, she noticed Seneca's bare feet. "Where the hell are yore shoes?"

"Where the hell is your gown?"

At his rare cursing, something gave way inside her. His anger sparked her own. Raising her head, she poked a finger into his shoulder. "You listen to me, Prince Seneca. I—"

"I will listen to everything you have to say, Princess Peachy, but not here." Without warning, he reached for her waist, lifted her high off the ground, and tossed her over his shoulder.

She fought to escape, but to no avail. "Seneca! What the hell do y'think yore a-doin'! You crazier'n a outhouse rat, lower'n a mole's belly on diggin' day, gawdang sorry cuss, put me down!"

Paying not a bit of mind to her flailing legs and choice curses, he carried her to Damascus and lifted her into the saddle. Before she could squirm off, he mounted behind her and sent his stallion into a gallop.

The powerful steed was soon racing full out over the countryside, the white stallion trailing behind. Seneca leaned down low, capturing Peachy within the hard prison of his arms and torso. But though he effectively kept her where he wanted her, he could not stop her from cursing at him. He'd never heard such language in all his life.

And he loved every obscene word of it.

Upon reaching the palace, he didn't bother to direct Damascus to the mews, but rode to the Grand Entrance of the castle instead. He dismounted, pulled Peachy back over his shoulder, and hauled her inside.

Viridis had just stepped off the last step of the staircase when Seneca entered the foyer. At the shocking sight of an almost-naked Peachy draped over the prince's shoulder, she was forced to grab the banister for support. "Oh! She— Her gown— Seneca, I am terribly sorry— I don't know what to say!"

He brushed past her and headed up the stairs. "Say good-bye, Aunt Viridis. You are dismissed from service."

He continued up the stairs and headed straight for his apartments. Once inside, he bolted the door, strode into the bedchamber, and finally set Peachy on her feet.

Her lush bosom heaved with fury.

He relished the delectable display. "I believe you had something to tell me while we were in the forest. You may speak now."

Her rising temper painted her cheeks with twin spots of crimson. "I'll speak whenever the hell I want! You *ain't* my master!" She stepped away from him, walking backwards until the heels of her feet met the bottom step of the dais that supported his massive bed.

Casually, Seneca took off his soiled shirt and dropped it to the floor.

She had a hard time keeping her gaze from slipping to his bare chest. "And I *ain't* gotta be obedient no more! I'm plumb sick to death o' all them agger-pervokin' ladylike rules, hear? Iffen I *ain't* ladylike enough fer you, then that's too dang bad! I *ain't* gonna spend what little life I got left a-stitchin' flowers! I hate embroiderin', I hate paintin', I hate unnerwear, and most o' all, I hate *glidin'!"*

"Then don't sew, don't paint, don't wear underwear, and don't glide."

"And I got more news fer you, mister. *Ain't* is a good word! I'll use it whenever I got the mind to use it. And iffen you don't like it, you can jest go around the block three times and come back only twice, hear?"

"I hear. I *ain't* deaf, you know."

"And I *ain't* gonna be some well-mannerable title! I *ain't* no title! I'm a person, and I got feelin's that I *ain't* gonna hide no more. Iffen I'm happy, you'll know it. Iffen I'm riled, sad, worried, sick, surprised ... *Whatever!* I love you, Seneca, but I *ain't* gonna give you that gawdang obedience yore so frenzyfied to git!"

"I don't want your obedience."

"Yeah? Well, you can jest— Jest . . ." She frowned, unsure she'd heard him correctly. "What did y'say?"

"I said I don't want your obedience." One purposeful step at a time, he walked toward her. When he stood before her, he placed his fingers beneath her chin. "I want your forgiveness for having forced you to endure those insufferable weeks of etiquette lessons. And if you can find it in your heart to pardon me, then I would ask one more thing from you."

"What?"

"Love me, Peachy. Love me, my wild and beautiful mountain princess."

His plea thrilled her to the bottom of her heart. She swayed with astonishment.

Seneca pulled her close. One arm was around her waist; he raised the other so he could slip his fingers through the tangled mass of her unruly hair. God, how he'd missed the feel of her silken mane. "I was wrong, sweetheart. I thought love would dazzle me. Like diamonds."

He pressed a tender kiss to her brow. "But love isn't some sort of glittering thing that blinds you. Love is . . ." He paused, trying to find the right words. "It's quiet. Like a whisper that comes from deep inside. It's soft. It doesn't knock you to your knees. It's patient. It waits for you to understand what it is. For you to recognize its name."

He gazed deeply into her eyes. "Peachy, I love the way you spring up and down when you walk. I love your simple yet profoundly wise way of seeing things. I love the happiness that stems from your heart, your soul, the very essence of what makes you who you are. I love your quick temper, and the way your eyes flash with the passion of your anger. I love the outrageous way you express yourself. I love your stories, those innocent tales of your childhood that touch me and make me wish I could have lived those times along with you."

He cupped her flushed cheeks in the warm palms of his hands. "Peachy, I love you. I much-love you with all my heart."

Tears of tremendous joy filled her eyes. "Seneckers," she whispered. "Oh, Seneckers . . . I— I don't know what to say."

He smiled. She'd never been at a loss for words before, and now, when he wanted desperately for her to talk to him, she couldn't speak.

"Say you love me," he commanded softly.

"I love you."

He raised a sable brow. "Say you want to be my wife."

"I want to be—" Her breath quivered between her parted lips. She knew exactly what he meant. The realization caused her to scrunch her thighs together.

Desire melted through him. "Say you want to be my wife, Peachy."

"Yes, I want to be your wife."

He swept her into his arms and carried her to the bed. There, he laid her down and smiled at her. "I hope you're not tired. It's going to be a long night, Princess."

"Long and special, Seneckers. Very special." She held out her arms.

And Seneca filled them . . .

Chapter 16

H e wore only his trousers.
Peachy took them off . . .

And slid her trembling fingers down his naked body. "I cain't believe I was ever afeared o' you," she told him softly, loving the glimmer of light that came into his eyes.

He tugged at the drawstring of her lacy drawers. "And I can't believe that I didn't know I loved you." Slowly, he removed her pantalettes and shredded stockings. "In truth, I've loved you since I was seven years old."

"Seven years old?"

"There was an angel in the tower."

His angel, Peachy mused. "Seneca, what—"

"It doesn't matter. She's not there anymore. She's here. With me. It's a long story. But one day I'll tell you about how I lost her twice and how she came back both times."

Before she could continue questioning him, he turned her over and unbuttoned the bodice of her gown, then unlaced her corset. When it fell away from her, he took off the half-length chemise.

And when she was naked, he frowned and felt anger and an all-consuming guilt.

Bright red marks and dark bruises marred her magnolia skin. He knew in his aching heart that the corset had hurt her. And yet she'd worn it. Because he'd wanted her to be a lady.

"Peachy," he whispered raggedly. "God, I'm so sorry." Leaning down, he smoothed kisses upon each red streak and dark bruise.

His tender ministrations aroused her thoroughly. She turned onto her back. Hands beneath his arms, she pulled him until he moved to her side. And she kissed him. As she'd learned from him, she parted his lips with her tongue, not waiting but demanding that he kiss her back.

Her initiative, her innocent command, took Seneca by delightful surprise. He raised her atop him, so that her soft body rested along the hard length of his. And while her sweet kisses continued, he felt her move her hips. Cradled in his, they rocked slowly. Insistently.

The rhythm . . . The ancient beat of lovemaking. He realized she understood it. She knew it as if she'd experienced it a thousand times.

The mating ritual began. Man came to woman, woman came to man.

He moved with her, meeting her each time she lowered herself to him. His rigid manhood ground into the cushioned mound of her femininity, and when he heard her mew with escalating desire, he understood that she was floating on the same wave of shimmering passion that he was.

Gently, he placed her back on the mattress and leaned over her. Taking the stiff crest of her breast into his mouth, he glided his hand down her body. Lower still he went . . . "God, you're sweet," he murmured when his fingers found the essence of her. She opened her legs.

He slid a finger inside her. And felt her readiness for him. Her desire made him burn with a fire he knew he no longer had to fight.

Slowly, he began to move his hand, yearning to bring her pleasure. He knew he'd begun to succeed when he heard her soft moan and saw her raise her hips in cadence with his sensual caresses. It was his intention to give her ecstasy.

Before he had to give her pain.

The first timid currents of bliss rippled through her. She longed for the waves . . . But not without Seneca. Sighing, she reached down and folded her hands around his. "Not like this. I don't want it like this tonight, Seneca. Tonight . . . I want it to happen with you."

Her sentiment touched him, but not deeply enough to

destroy his apprehension over hurting her. "I only thought to prepare you."

"I ain't afeared, Seneca. It cain't be no worser'n the ache o' wantin' you."

She ran her fingers through his midnight curls. "I know it'll hurt, but y'know? It's gonna make me feel so happy, Seneca. I'll be able to take ever' bit of it on account o' it'll mean that I'm finally yore wife, and yore finally my husband. And y'want to know what else?"

He wanted to know everything she could possibly tell him. "Tell me."

She closed her eyes, savoring her thoughts for a moment before revealing them. "I don't know nothin' a'tall about what we're a-fixin' to do. But you do. It makes me go all squishy inside to know that a man like you's gonna make love to me for the very first time. My virginity . . . Seneca I want you to have it. And it'll make me so happy to give it you. I wish I had a trillion virginities. I'd give ever' one of 'em to you. I would, Seneca."

He bent his head and chuckled softly. "But perhaps we should concentrate on the only one you'll ever have."

"Yeah, and I— I'm shore it'll fit. Sorter almost shore. The shortest kind o' almost shore. But jest in case it don't—"

"It will, Peachy."

She smiled and opened her arms. "Make me your wife, then."

His amused smile faded. Raw desire took over his senses. He moved atop her. Hands beside her shoulders, he straightened his arms and lifted his upper torso. His action pushed his hips more firmly into hers.

"Seneca?"

"Peachy."

"Don't stop this time. No matter what, don't stop."

"No."

"Swear on Aventine?"

"And the Blue Ridge, too."

Peachy needed no urging to open her legs for him. Everything he wanted her to do was written in his smoldering eyes.

He pushed his hips forward, entering her slightly and stopping when he met her maidenhead.

She continued to read the sensual commands in his hot gaze. Obediently, she wrapped her legs around his waist.

His steady, penetrating gaze held hers, and he willed her to understand how very much he loved her. Every lean muscle in his body coiled with power, he drove into her soft depths, accepting at last the precious gift she'd offered him.

She gasped, her body stiffening. "Seneca!"

"Wife," he answered, his eyes still riveted to hers.

A tear trickled down her cheek.

Seneca dried the drop away with his thumb. No words could express the profound remorse he felt over having to hurt her, and so he said nothing.

But he moved. Inside her. He loved her intimately, gently, and tentatively, hoping slow-mounting pleasure would come to her and soothe away all traces of the pain.

Peachy felt her body stretch and accept him. The pain receded, replaced by a feeling of fullness "Yore in me," she whispered tremorously. "Really and truly in me."

The wonder in her voice hummed through him. "I am."

"It *did* fit. You was right. Seneca . . . I cain't hardly believe the way it felt. All hard and big. It was—"

"Wife?"

She loved his new name for her. "What, husband?"

"It's not over yet."

She grinned up at him. "Oh, yeah. Y'ain't done all that wigglin' yet, huh?"

He couldn't quell another chuckle. "Peachy," he mumbled, lowering himself upon her. "You and your outlandish way of describing things. It's not a wiggle, love."

She kissed his chin. "Then what is it?"

"This." He began to withdraw from her.

"Wait!" She clutched the hard cheeks of his bottom, trying to push him back into her. "Seneca, you said it weren't over. You said—"

"I know what I said, Peachy." He laughed again. He'd never had this much fun making love, and the physical pleasure had barely begun! He smoothed his thumbs over her lips. "How can I teach you the things you say you want me to teach you if you keep stopping me?"

She nibbled at his thumbs. "Sorry. I won't stop you again."

"If you decide to try, I assure you that you will fail miserably." He slipped his hands beneath her bottom. Lifting her from the mattress, he plunged back inside her and withdrew again, stopping right before his body left hers. Then he filled her once more. Buried himself inside her. He made love to her with strong, steady strokes, never allowing his sensual rhythm to break.

After a moment, Peachy caught the pace he'd set and moved with him. Wrapping her arms around his neck, she breathed deeply of his musky and intoxicating scent, and concentrated on the incredible pleasure coming to life inside her. The pulses of bliss began, soft and shy ones at first, and then they mounted, boldly taking over her body.

But her fulfillment was in Seneca's keeping until he chose to give it to her. He yielded it to her slowly, determined that she savor each tiny tremor.

She'd never wanted anything so badly in her life. And nothing had ever seemed so far from her grasp. "Varmint," she whispered, unable to say more.

He grinned and decided to show her mercy. He quickened and deepened his thrusts. His own pleasure skimmed through his loins, intensifying with each breathy sound Peachy made.

And still he took her higher. As high as he could take her before she reached the brink.

And when she came to it, he was with her. Driving into her, he pushed her over the peak of pleasure and held her tightly to him so she would know she hadn't found her paradise alone. "Peachy." The word exploded from his lips as he shuddered and spilled his seed inside her.

As he called out her name, she felt him grow harder. He throbbed inside her, and his body tensed and shook. The sensation made her feel wonderful beyond comprehension before an ageless instinct told her what had happened. The deep pulse of his climax increased the intensity of hers.

She'd never known such joy was possible. And to have

discovered it with her husband who loved her made it total and absolute.

Seneca sensed her happiness. Indeed, it rose around him, surrounding him in an unseen mist that sparkled and enchanted him and whispered the most wonderful things to him. "Peachy," he said again, this time without the urgency, this time with all the soul-drenching emotion he felt for her. "I love you, Princess."

"And I love you, Seneckers. With all my heart. And my soul. And my mind and my body and my ever'thing and even my eyes and mouth and toenails. But y'know what?"

"What?"

She tempered what she was about to say with a beautiful smile. "Yore heavier'n a frozen bear."

He laughed out loud and slipped to the mattress.

It sagged under his weight; she rolled onto his chest and placed her palm over his left nipple. His heartbeat meshed with the pulse in her hand.

"What are you thinking, Princess?"

She lifted her face to him, resting her chin on the firm pillow of his arm. "I was a-thinkin' on how wrong Paw was. It *is* possible to fit two pounds o' rocks in a one-pound bag."

He laughed again, long and loud. And after his merriment calmed, he smiled into her eyes. "Would you care to swap spit now, wife?"

His question surprised her into delighted laughter. "Husband, I'll swap spit with you any ole time y'want."

His lips brushed hers in a whisper-light kiss that gradually became more demanding. He wanted her again, his wife, and he knew he would never cease wanting her. "Peachy."

She felt his lips spread into another smile and wondered what he found so amusing. Pulling away from him, she saw that his eyes danced with mirth. "Well, Seneca, what in the world's so funny?"

Sliding his fingers through her hair, he thought about all the romantic and sensual ways he once would have told her that he longed to make love to her again. *You make me wild with desire. Tender your surrender to me, and I'll take you back to heaven.*

His grin broadened; a low chuckle rose from his throat. "Peachy, I'm going to give you more gravel for your goose now. And I want more for mine, too."

Her bright giggle filled the room.

The night stretched endlessly and gloriously on. The crown prince and his Appalachian mountain girl filled each second of it with love and laughter.

And when the mellow light of dawn shimmered through the room, Seneca gathered a sleepy and completely sated Peachy into his arms.

Holding her close to him, he whispered the words in his heart. "I love you. More than you'll ever understand. You're my angel. My friend. The very best one I've ever had."

On shaky legs, Peachy made her way to the pool of buttery sunshine that spilled through the windows in her rooms. Behind her, a clock struck three. She'd been awake for only a little over an hour. And she'd probably still be asleep had Seneca not been urgently summoned to his father's chambers.

She stopped by the window and sat down in a bright pink satin chair. Thurlow Wadsworth McGee sprang into her lap.

She wouldn't cry. She wouldn't. There were too many things to be happy about. She was *not* going to cry.

Her legs continued to tremble, as did her stomach muscles and those of her bottom. Even her arms quivered.

She cried. One hot tear splashed to her hand.

Trembling muscles. That was yet another symptom of tipinosis. And no herb on God's green earth could rid her of the disease. She'd helped so many people and animals with her skills, but was powerless to help herself.

Choking back a moan, she turned to the window, wishing with all her heart that the sunbeams that warmed her face could also warm the cold anguish growing steadily inside her.

Memories of last night settled over her. Her night with Seneca, so full of passion and love. Laughter and joy.

"I ain't got many o' them nights left, boy," she whispered to her squirrel. "Not many more to hear him tell me he loves me. That I'm his best friend. God Almighty, jest when ever'thing's so wonnerful ..."

God Almighty. She'd be meeting Him soon. Of course there was her roasting in the Purgatorial flames to deal with first, she reminded herself. She'd had terrible thoughts about Viridis. Thoughts so awful that they'd surely get her a few million years in Purgatory. And she'd almost struck the king. That had to be worth at least a zillion years. Unless God thought the king deserved to be smacked.

And the peasants ... She'd ignored their pleas completely during those three weeks of manner lessons. There existed no sin worse than shunning people in need.

She wasn't going to roast in Purgatory. She was going to burn in hell. She knew it. She'd be there, soon, too. Just when her life had become pure heaven, it would end in hell.

Another sob swelled inside her. But before she could release it, her door opened. Seneca stood in the threshold.

His chest rose and fell as he tried to catch his breath. From his eyes poured fear and a terrible expression of torment.

His obvious anguish tore from her mind all thoughts of her own misery. She ran to him. "Seneca, what's the mat—"

"Father."

His voice cracked, like a piece of glass shattering into innumerable bits. "Yore paw? What—"

"The physicians— They said— They don't know what to do." He rammed his fingers through his tousled hair and sought to control his turbulent emotions. "They've given up on him."

"Given up? But what's wrong with him? Seneca, tell me!"

He took her shoulders, his gaze piercing hers. "I know you hate him. I know he's mistreated you ever since—"

"Dang it, Seneca, what the hell's the *matter* with him!"

He took a deep, shuddering breath. "It's his heart. It's beating, but barely. Peachy ... God, Peachy, please help him."

* * *

His hands shaking with apprehension, Tiblock pressed warm compresses to the king's clammy forehead. He watched the princess's every action. Without realizing it, he began to voice his thoughts. "His Majesty is quite fond of me. What would he do without me? His Majesty would never be able to plump his pillow the way I do it for him." With trembling fingers, he poked at the king's pillow.

Peachy couldn't miss the man's deep anxiety. Tiblock's face was almost as pale as the king's. "You all right, Tiblock?"

"I have taken care of him for twenty-one years," Tiblock added. "His Majesty is my family."

"Y'done real good, too."

"Yes. I truly have."

Peachy returned to her task with the king. Drop by tiny drop, she fed him an elixir of foxglove leaves, heartleaf, and rat's-vein plant leaves. He drifted in and out of consciousness, too weak to speak, move, or open his eyes. After each minute dose of the medicine, Peachy was forced to rub his throat in order to get him to swallow.

Seneca stood by her side, searching desperately for signs of his father's improvement. He found none. His sire's face was as white as the pristine sheets, his breathing alarmingly shallow, and the beat of his heart faint.

But Seneca clung to hope. It was Peachy who worked to help his father survive. And if it took a miracle to save the king's life, an angel would surely be the one to bring it about.

The king groaned suddenly, his massive frame shuddering, his fleshy face contorting.

Tiblock grabbed the bedpost for support. "Oh, God, he's dead!"

Peachy raised her head and looked at the servant, understanding then that whatever affection the man was capable of feeling, he felt it for the king.

The realization did much to soften her opinion of him. "He ain't dead. He's too ornery to die. He's a-carryin' on right now on account o' ever' time he comes awake fer a few minutes, he feels the pain in his joints. He ain't been a-usin' them cures I give him, huh?"

Tiblock shook his head. "He— He said they wouldn't work."

She noted that Tiblock had begun to shake, and decided he needed something to do. "Tell y'what. Go fetch them cures, hear? Now's a good time to rub the poultice into him, y'see, on account o' he's too weak to fight you offen."

Seneca was just about to echo Peachy's request when Tiblock moved to obey it. The servant soon returned with the poultice.

As carefully as he knew how, Tiblock began to massage the medicine into His Majesty's red and swollen legs. The king jerked spasmodically, causing Tiblock to shriek with hysteria.

"Tiblock," Peachy said, "iffen y'don't calm yoresef down, we'll be a-givin' *you* this here heart medicine."

"I cannot help it. When I touch him, I hurt him. I simply cannot bear to hurt him." He turned away.

Peachy saw tears shining in his beady eyes. She handed the heart medicine to Seneca. "You give yore paw this, and I'll hep Tiblock with the poultice."

The afternoon stretched on, finally turning to early evening. Seneca continued to feed his father the drops of heart elixir. Side by side, Peachy and Tiblock worked at massaging His Majesty's painful limbs.

Footmen brought trays of food. "Eat, Peachy," Seneca said, noticing her exhaustion.

"No."

"Tiblock?" Seneca offered.

"I am not hungry, Your Highness."

The food remained untouched.

Moonlight frosted the windows. Tiblock fell asleep in a chair beside the king's bed. At midnight, Seneca forced Peachy to lie down on the sofa in the sitting room. She slept only a few hours before waking and tending the king again. To pass the time, she whittled and prayed.

Seneca would not rest at all. His only parent lay dying. That the king had never showed a bit of affection toward his son ceased to matter.

The man was his father. And as Seneca gazed down at him, the lonely little boy inside him crept out from the place where he'd been hidden so many years ago. The child who still needed and wanted to love his sire. Who still yearned to be loved in return.

Fairly choking with his inner torment, Seneca bent close to the king's face and whispered too softly for anyone but his father to hear. "Always . . . I always wanted to call you 'Papa.' But if you— If you die, my chance will die with you."

Three days passed before the king finally responded to Peachy's medicines. Blinking, he tried to bring into focus the three people standing beside his bed.

Seneca was the first to notice his father's improvement. "Father?" He broke into a huge smile when the king glowered at him. There was recognition in his father's frown, and Seneca welcomed the terrible scowl as the most wonderful one he'd ever seen.

Tiblock lost control of himself and toppled off the dais, landing on the marble floor with a thud. "Your Majesty!"

"For God's sake, Tiblock, stop yelling," the king whispered. He stared at his attendant on the floor. "Whatever are you doing down there?"

Tiblock jumped to his feet. "She did it! She did it, Your Majesty! I was highly doubtful that she would, but she did! Oh my, yes, she truly did!"

Peachy took a careful look at the king's face and was satisfied when she saw that color was returning to his cheeks. "You a-feelin' all right now? Are y'hungry?"

The king glared at her. "What are you doing—"

"Three days ago, your heart all but stopped beating," Seneca explained. "Your physicians had given up trying to help you. Peachy made you a medicine. She saved your life, Father." Taking Peachy's hand, he waited for his sire's reaction to the news.

"What?" the king exclaimed as loudly as his weakened condition would allow. "You let her feed me those disgusting mountain cures of hers?"

Seneca went rigid. "The medicine worked. Father, she— You're alive because of her. Have you no gratitude?"

The king sneered at Peachy. "Get out. Leave immediately."

She moved to step down the dais, but Seneca caught her hand. "Peachy—"

"Iffen I stay, he'll work hissef into a frenzy, and then his heart'll act up again." After one last look at the king's pinkening cheeks, she stepped off the dais and stopped in front of Tiblock. "He's gotta have more o' that heart medicine," she whispered. "A spoonful ever' two hours. Git him somethin' to eat. Some soup, maybe. And see iffen y'can git him to take them other cures I maked fer him, too. The ones fer his swolt-up joints, his pain, and his orneriness. I give him a blood-richenin' tonic, too. I swear them yarbs'll work iffen y'can jest git him to swaller 'em."

Tiblock nodded. Hesitantly, he patted her hand, snatching his own hand back soon after touching hers.

Peachy realized the gesture was the closest he would come to showing his thanks. She smiled at him before leaving the room.

When she was gone, Seneca returned his attention to his sire. "Father—"

"Do you think I am without sense?" the king whispered, his earlier efforts at speaking having tired him considerably. "I understand precisely what you are trying to do, Seneca. The wager . . . You lost. So you have now hatched up a plan to force me to waive the terms. You—"

"I've done no such thing. Peachy—"

"You seek to make me feel indebted to the heathen. I have not been ill, have I? She— She gave me some sort of drug that rendered me unconscious, and now you would have me believe that if not for her, I wouldn't be alive."

Seneca's anger became a boiling rage. "Your illness wasn't part of some scheme. Peachy *did* save your life."

The king waved his hand, pushing away his son's words. "She did nothing of the sort."

"You were *dying!* Tiblock, what was Father's condition before the princess administered her medicine?"

Tiblock scurried to the king's bed. "Your Majesty," he said gently, "Your Majesty was very ill. The princess—"

"Out, Tiblock. Get out."

Tiblock began to wring his thin hands. Throwing a look of frustration to the prince, he quit the room, shaking his bald head as he left.

Seneca searched for a way to force his father to believe the truth about Peachy. "Try moving your legs, Father. Move them."

"Are you aware of the fact that the hellion you married tried to strike me?"

"Instead, she saved your life. Move your knees."

"Her squirrel attacked me. The animal nearly ripped my chest to shreds."

"Father, I have been staring at your chest for three days, and there is not as much as a scratch on it. Now, move your knees. Move your body."

Huffing with indignation, the king flexed his knees.

Seneca folded his arms across his chest. "Why doesn't your face betray your pain?"

King Zane didn't reply.

"For three whole days and nights," Seneca continued, "Peachy and Tiblock have been massaging the poultice into your limbs. Not the one your physicians concocted for you, but the one Peachy made. Her remedies worked, and you know it. Say it's true. Say it, Father."

"I will say no such thing. And I will *not* believe that I have been dying. Lies. All lies."

Seneca's features twisted. "It's your pride, isn't it? You can't bear the knowledge that the girl you so want to hate has helped you. You cannot stand it that she has—"

"Hear me well, Seneca. Send her away. You are to be married to Callista. You lost the wager, which means, of course, that you have lost the Crown as well."

Seneca lowered his head, battling a wealth of emotions. He tried to find his mask, the one that would hide everything he was feeling, the one he'd worn for most of his life.

But he had no idea where it was, and he was powerless to keep his real emotions from surfacing. "The entire time you were ill . . . I hoped that if you survived we could . . . I wanted— While you lay dying, I saw your recovery as one more . . . chance. I knew it would be slim, but I hoped—"

Swallowing hard, he lifted his head. "I understand now that I've never had that chance. Not since the day I was born. I was foolish to hope for it now."

The king couldn't remember ever being able to read Seneca's thoughts so clearly. Bare, they were, lying naked in his son's blue eyes.

"I will send Tiblock back to you," Seneca murmured. He stepped down from the dais and spotted the cane Peachy had made. She'd finished it while holding the vigil by the king's bedside.

Seneca retrieved the beautifully carved walking stick and held it up for his father to see. "She says that if you would only make use of this cane and the medicines she made for you, you would make a complete recovery. She also said that you should take up whittling." He ran his fingers down the cane's length, made smooth by Peachy's talented hands. With a sigh, he leaned it against the wall.

The king watched as he went to the door. "That chance you spoke of," he called. "What chance was it you wanted?"

Seneca stopped before the door. "Do you really want to know?"

"I am not in the habit of asking questions on subjects that don't interest me."

Once again, Seneca could not conceal his real feelings. Indeed, he didn't want to. "I wanted to call you 'Papa'."

A long moment passed. "Papa?"

"You don't even remember, do you, Father? I've wanted to call you 'Papa' ever since I was a small boy. You wouldn't allow me to do it then, and you have destroyed my chance to do it now."

He took a few steps back into the room, suddenly realizing he had much more to tell his father. He wouldn't leave until he'd emptied his mind of every thought it held. "You hate Peachy, and I know why. She is the only person who ever stood up to you and dared to tell you exactly what she thought of you. You demand that everyone see and treat you as the sovereign, but Peachy . . . She looked past the king and saw you as the man you are. A selfish, stubborn, and uncaring tyrant. But as cruel as you have

been to her, she *still* found it in her to help you. If not for
Peachy, we would have buried you three days ago."

"She—"

"As for the wager . . . I will not marry Callista. I am already married. To a lady. A *real* lady."

"That girl is not a—"

"Yes, Father, she is. A true lady is . . . is *mannerable.* A
true lady sees and acts with her heart. A true lady much-
loves everyone around her. A true lady would rather concern herself with a sick pig than a damned piece of silly
sewing. Peachy has more manners in her thumbnail than
you, Callista, Aunt Viridis, and I could ever hope to have
in our entire bodies."

He lifted his chin and gave his father a cool and steady
stare. "Nothing you say or do will force me to send
Peachy away. I will, however, *take* her away. I'm leaving
Aventine. There is a ship departing for England this very
afternoon. As your fortune in paschal flowers leaves the
island, so will Peachy and I. So wear your glittering
crown, Father. Sit on your precious throne. I want neither,
for in truth, I possess something far more valuable. And
that is my wife. And I do assure you that she is my wife
in the truest sense of the word."

"You would give up the Throne of Aventine for her?"
the king asked in disbelief.

"I would give up my very life for her."

The king had no chance to reply. His son stormed out of
the room.

And while His Majesty laid in his bed, one word echoed
endlessly through him.

Papa.

Sitting in the middle of Seneca's huge bed, Peachy
gasped with delight. "A weddin' trip?"

He sat down beside her. "We leave this afternoon on the
merchant ship that sets sail for England. After a brief stop
at the Yorkshire port of Scarborough, we'll sail for London. I could arrange for you to be presented to Queen Victoria if you like. And in London I'll procure our own
private ship. I'll take you to France, Peachy. To Italy—
Anywhere in the world you want to go."

Her smile faded gradually. "But— I . . . Seneca, do we *have* to go see Queen Victoria?"

He noted a dim light of sadness in her eyes. "A moment ago you were happy as could be, Princess, and now you're upset. What—"

"God Almighty, sudden mood changes," she murmured. Head hung low, she got off the bed and began to pace around the room. "It's another tipinosis symptom. Lord o' mercy, they're a-comin' fast now. I weren't gonna tell you about this, Seneca, but the day yore paw tuk sick? Well, my muscles was a-tremblin' somethin' fierce. I couldn't hardly walk. That's another symptom. I ain't got long now."

He took a moment to deliberate. "Peachy, think about the night before Father became ill. We made love all night long. Not to mention the fact that that was the day you rode bareback through Aventine."

"So? What's that got to do with—"

"Your muscles were shaking from so much exercise! From doing things you aren't used to doing!"

She stopped before him and laid her hand on his shoulder. "Seneca, y'jest ain't never gonna accept the fact that I'm a-headin' fer them pearly gates, huh? I reckon I'll have to be a-layin' in my buryin'-box afore you believe it."

He started to reply, but what good would it do? He'd disputed her morbid beliefs many times, to no avail.

From now on, he'd go along with whatever she said. And when she was eighty years old and holding her great-grandchildren in her arms, he'd ask her why she wasn't dead yet. "You're right," he whispered, hoping he looked very sad. "I cannot face losing you. I will, however, try to be brave. And I will also give you the most exciting wedding trip any woman has ever had. After all, it might be the last trip you ever take before— Well, before taking that spiritual trip into the sky. By the way, how many flame-filled years in Purgatory have you amassed now?"

"Oh, Seneca, trillions. I might not even git to Purgatory, though. I might go straight to the devil."

"I'll pray that you don't." He stifled his laughter.

"Thanky, Seneca," she whispered.

"You're welcome. Now, if you don't care to meet Queen Victoria, what would you like to do during your final days on earth? Before spending those trillions of years roasting in flames?"

She sat back down on the bed and ran her fingers over the satin coverlet. "I cain't believe I'm really gonna say this, but I'm a-gittin' sorter tired o' all this royal stuff. Whilst I was a-takin' them mannerable lessons? Well, I'd sit there with yore aunt, a-missin' the things I used to do back home. I missed my cabin and a-cookin' my own vittles. I missed my yard and my dried-up crick. I missed a-rollin' down the hills, a-pitchin' pebbles, and a-singin' songs on the porch in the evenin's."

"Do you want to return to your mountains, then?"

She shook her head. "I ain't got time. I'd die afore we got there."

"I see." He rubbed his chin and mouth so she wouldn't see his smile.

"What I'd really like to do, Seneca, is go somewhere's where nobody knows who we are. Somewhere's close so's we wouldn't have to spend ferever on the ship-boat. A place where we could be plain Seneca and plain Peachy. We could git us a little cabin somewhere and spend our days a-bein' common folk. Iffen we was to do that, I could git back to the simple life I miss, and you'd git to taste it fer the first time."

She heaved a great sigh of longing. "But I reckon y'cain't take me nowhere's like that, huh? It ain't possible."

He trailed a finger along the curve of her cheekbone. "Who said it wasn't possible? I told you I'd take you anywhere you wanted to go. The ship we'll be sailing on stops in Scarborough. We'll spend our honeymoon in the countryside of Yorkshire. I doubt there are any cabins there, but we can rent a cottage. And no one will know us there, Peachy, so we can be as plain as you want us to be."

"Do you know how?"

"No, but you could teach me."

She buried herself in his arms. "We'll spend our days a-playin', Seneca."

Bending, he kissed her tenderly. "And we'll spend our nights a-loving."

"I'll drive." Seneca reached for the reins of the rickety wagon. The people in the port of Scarborough had been glad to sell him the ancient donkey-driven vehicle. And no wonder, Seneca mused. He'd paid for it with solid gold, enough to buy a hundred donkey-driven wagons just like it.

He smiled, thinking of the townspeople's expressions when he'd shown them the gold. Garbed in simple buff trousers, a common white shirt, a plain black coat, and a very ordinary pair of black boots, he certainly wasn't dressed like a man who would possess gold. Peachy's appearance had done nothing to temper the people's surprise, either. She was back in her homespun clothing.

And he thought her even more beautiful in linsey-woolsey than she'd been in satin.

But he liked her best of all when she was wearing nothing, which was exactly what she'd worn for most of the voyage from Aventine. They'd rarely left their small cabin aboard the merchant ship, spending almost the entire trip in the lumpy bed, loving and laughing in each other's arms.

"Seneckers?"

Her soft voice broke through his lusty thoughts. He looked at her blankly. "What?"

She took a moment to settle down a very excited Thurlow Wadsworth McGee. "I asked iffen you've ever drived a wagon with a donkey a-pullin' it."

"No, and that is precisely why I want to drive. I'm a commoner now and must accustom myself to such things. Now, give me the reins."

Smiling indulgently, she handed him the reins and watched him slap them over the donkey's back.

The beast didn't budge. "He won't go," Seneca said. "I'm going to buy a horse." He moved to alight from the wagon.

Peachy grabbed his arm. "Quit a-flashin' yore princely wealth around," she whispered, lest one of the nearby townspeople overhear her. "We're s'posed to be common folk. S'why y'brung me here to England, ain't it? To git away from all that royal stuff fer a while? Now git yore spoiled sef back in this here wagon."

"Peachy," he murmured, "even a commoner would prefer a spirited horse to that long eared jackass. And I'll have you know that I take exception to being called spoiled. I am not spoiled but merely—"

"Yore a brat, Seneca."

"Peachy—"

"Nobody's s'posed to know who we are!"

"I am acting as common as I know how to act," he argued. "All I want is a horse with a bit of energy."

"Yeah, but commoners don't got the gold it takes to git 'em one o' them kind o' horses. 'Sides that, y'don't need no horse nohow. This here donkey'll go jest fine."

She showed him a long, flexible pole. A string was tied to its tip, and from the string hung half of an apple. She held the pole out so the fragrant fruit dangled before the donkey's eyes.

In an effort to reach the apple, the animal broke into a trot, his sudden movement nearly causing Seneca to fall from the cart. "Peachy!"

Laughing, she sent the donkey into a brisk canter. In only a few moments they'd left the town of Scarborough behind and were heading out into the rolling hills of the Yorkshire countryside.

Seneca allowed Peachy to drive until she turned the wagon onto a winding dirt road lined by an endless stretch of stone wall. "It's my turn now." He took the reins.

As soon as he had them, Peachy lifted the apple-baited pole away from the donkey's view. The animal stopped abruptly and pawed the dusty ground.

Seneca met Peachy's mischievous gaze. "Give him back his apple."

She ate it, then spit out the string onto which it had been tied.

He waited patiently for her to swallow the last bite. When she commenced to lick the apple juice from her lower lip, he caught her waist and lifted her high off the cracked wooden seat, holding her up over his head.

Her high-pitched squeal shattered the peaceful stillness. "Seneca! What the hell—"

"I am not the brat, Peachy," he informed her, looking up into her wide eyes, "you are. And as such, you deserve a spanking."

She tried to squirm out of his hold, but to no avail. He was too strong for her to fight. "You might be a prince, Seneca, but yore built like a hardworkin' commoner. Lord o' mercy, I bet you've even got muscles in yore hair, huh?"

"Don't try to flatter me, Peachy. I daresay it will get you nowhere."

She screamed again when he began to lower her to his lap. Renewing her struggles, she tried to keep him from turning her over.

Her wild battle dumped them both on the ground. They groaned as they hit the hard dirt and rolled over and over as each fought to gain the upper hand.

"What is this?" a stern voice demanded. "Miss, are you in need of assistance?"

Recovering from his laughter, Seneca looked up and saw a heavyset man of about fifty years old. He held a fine ebony walking stick, and a big well-groomed white dog sat panting by his heels. "We are in no need of aid, sir."

"I wasn't talking to you, young fellow," the man snapped. "I was speaking to the lady."

Unaccustomed to being addressed in such a way by a mere member of the gentry, Seneca bristled. "I am not a *fellow*. I am the—"

"No, I don't need no hep," Peachy interrupted quickly. Sprawled flat in the dirt, she sent Seneca a look of warning. "But thanky anyway."

The man laid down his walking stick and assisted her to her feet. "It appeared to me that this fellow was accosting you, miss. I hope he didn't harm you."

Seneca rose from the ground. Oblivious to the fact that he was covered with dust from head to toe, he held himself stiffly. Formally. *Royally.* "Sir, this woman is my wife, and I am not in the habit of accosting—"

"Why did you pitch your wife out of the wagon?"

"Yeah, why'd y'fling me outen the cart, Seneca?" Peachy repeated.

He took careful note of her naughty smile. So she wanted to play games, did she? Fine. He would play, too. She had, after all, taught him how. And perhaps this was the sort of thing commoners were supposed to do.

He faced the man. "I threw her out of the cart because she was talking back to me. You look to be the sort who is the man of his house, sir. As such, what would you have done had your own wife informed you that she was moving her mother in to live with you?"

The man frowned. "I would forbid her to do it!"

Seneca nodded in all seriousness. "And what would you do if your wife informed you that she had decided to deprive you of your husbandly rights and that she was moving your sleeping place into the kitchen so that her mother could make use of the bedroom?"

The man inhaled sharply. "I would throw her out of the house, that's what!"

"Precisely," Seneca agreed. "And that is why I threw my wife out of the cart. She pulled me out with her. Really, sir, I was not accosting her, but only showing her who is boss."

The man nodded vigorously. "Women need a firm hand, son. You did right. Yes, you did exactly what I would have done. And as for you, young lady ... Move your husband's bed into the kitchen, would you! Why, I have never heard such codswallop! You would do well to learn that your husband is master. He is king of the household, that he is, and his cottage is his palace. Indeed, a wife's duty is to treat her husband as if he were royalty!"

His eyes sparkling, Seneca looked at Peachy. "What have you to say to that, wife?"

Peachy burst into laughter and began to stagger around while trying to get hold of herself.

The man watched her for a moment. "You've got your hands full with that one, don't you?"

"If only you knew," Seneca replied. "Tell me, sir. Do you know of any cottages for rent? We are new to the area. As you said, a man's home is his castle, and I would like to find my palace as soon as possible. Nothing large, of course, as I don't wish to have any excess space for my mother-in-law."

The man broke into a huge smile. "As a matter of fact, son, I have in my possession a place that I think you'll enjoy. It's small, but cozy. Two rooms. When you come to a grove of oak trees, turn in to them. The cottage sits right in the middle of them. And you won't have to make the trip to Scarborough for supplies. The village of Gladensham is but a ten-minute walk from the cottage. Will that do?"

"I imagine it will more than do." Seneca withdrew a handful of solid gold coins from his pocket. "Will this suffice for a month?"

The man's eyes grew wide. "I'm an honest man, sir, and therefore I will tell you truly that that is enough for almost an entire year. How did you come by so much—"

"Seneca!" Peachy exclaimed, recovering from her laughter when she saw the stack of gold gleaming from his open palm. "So *yore* the one who filched my life's savin's! That's my gold," she told the man. "I been a-savin' fer years so's I can— Um . . . Well, y'see, I always wanted me one o' them diamondy crowns like princesses wear. They cost a lavish o' money, y'know. I hope to have enough gold to buy one in about sixty-eight years."

Seneca swallowed his laughter. "My wife speaks falsely, sir. The sad truth is that she drinks. I took her gold so she wouldn't waste it on wine and ale. Aside from the fact that a woman has no business indulging, she . . . Well, it mortifies me to admit this, but when she is in her cups, she likes to pretend she is Lady Godiva. I'm sure I do not have to explain what she does to act out the role."

The man gasped again. "You must see to it that she does not avail herself of strong drink, son. I cannot begin to guess what the people here would do . . . well, should she become Lady Godiva."

"I'll do what I can," Seneca promised. "If I may ask, how are you called?"

"I am Tanner Wainwright, and this is my dog, Morton. And you?"

"Seneca Brindisi. My wife is Peachy, and that is her squirrel, Thurlow Wadsworth McGee. Thank you ever so much, Mr. Wainwright." Seneca handed a few of the gold coins to the man, then climbed into the wagon. "Wife, get in."

Giggling, Peachy climbed in beside Seneca and attached another apple to the pole.

"Mr. Brindisi," Mr. Wainwright said. "Ordinarily, we've not a spot of trouble around here, but a band of gypsies has been in the area for a few days. I'm sure they will be moving on soon, but do watch for them. A dishonest lot they are, too. They're inclined to steal, you know, and you've quite a bit of gold."

At that news, Peachy took hold of Seneca's arm and squeezed tightly. "Seneca! Can I dance with the gypsies? Do y'mem'ry when I tole you I wanted to dance with 'em?"

He took the apple pole and turned to Mr. Wainwright. "I must get her out of the sun. I believe she's quite addled. Good day."

As the wagon rumbled down the road, Mr. Wainwright looked down at his dog. "I don't believe I have ever encountered such an outrageous wench. We'll keep a sharp eye on her, boy, that we will. No naked woman is going to ride around dancing with gypsies in *our* peaceful area! Poor Mr. Brindisi. Aye, he's certainly got his hands full with that one."

Chapter 17

"Uh . . . There it is, Aunt Orabelle!" Bubba shouted, pointing wildly toward a thick cluster of oak trees. "The donkey! And the wagon! The same one we seed Cousin Princess Peachy and her prince-husband git into in that town! 'Member we seed 'em gittin' in the wagon after we snuck off the ship? 'Member, Aunt Orabelle? 'Member—"

"Bubba, shut up!" Whirling on him, she landed a sharp slap to the side of his face. Grabbing his sleeve, she pulled him down the road. It certainly wouldn't do for Peachy to see them now. She'd recognize them immediately. Orabelle sighed, realizing she would have to invent some disguise before coming face-to-face with Peachy again.

God, the girl was almost becoming more trouble than the gold-filled creek was worth.

Almost.

A way down the road, Bubba turned back to the oak forest. He wiped a tear off his crooked nose. "Can we go see Cousin Peachy now, Aunt Orabelle? I want to tell her that I let my bird go. My bird got all better. Uh . . . He flyed away real good. Can I have another bird? And can I have a big white dog, too? Can we go see Cousin—"

"No." Hand at the small of her back, Orabelle approached the stone wall that lined the dirt road and sat in a clump of clover. Her entire body ached. And with good reason. The voyage from Aventine had been miserable. For almost a week she'd been forced to remain in the ship's belly, unable to stop Bubba's never-ending tears and verbal ramblings, unable to escape the overwhelmingly sweet scent of the paschal flowers, unable to move ... unable to do anything but become more and more furious.

And all because their Royal Highnesses, the Prince and Princess of Aventine, made the sudden decision to visit England. If not for the incredibly swift spread of palace gossip, Orabelle never would have known Peachy was leaving the island. Even as it was, she and Bubba had had to scramble to gather enough food to see them through the journey and sneak on to the ship before it set sail.

Peachy. The bitch certainly led a charmed life. She'd escaped death by the bullet. She hadn't tasted a drop of the poisoned cider. And although Orabelle had sent numerous items of venom-filled food to the castle for Peachy's consumption, the girl obviously hadn't tasted a crumb.

Well, she wouldn't last long now, Orabelle mused, rubbing her sore shoulder. Peachy was no longer protected by the thick stone walls and impassable gates of the palace. She had no access to fine, swift horses and none of the royal men-at-arms to guard her precious person. There was only the prince, and Orabelle was sure he wouldn't be much of a hindrance. He was but one man, and what could a prince do, anyway? The man was used to soft living.

"Can Cousin Princess Peachy have two husbands, Aunt Orabelle?" Bubba knelt in the sand and played with a furry green caterpillar. "I'm gonna marry Cousin Princess Peachy when I grow up. I bet she'd git me a white dog if I asked her, Aunt Orabelle, 'cause she's my sweetheart. She called me her darlin'."

Gently, he placed the caterpillar on the side of the road. "I taked the caterpillar outta the road so he won't git runned over by a cart. See, Aunt Orabelle? The caterpillar's safe now. Sweet little caterpillar. Good-bye. Uh ... Don't tell nobody my secret." He touched its hairy back.

Orabelle wondered if her nephew would forget his affection for Peachy. Lovestruck as he was now, it was doubtful he would stand idly by and allow Orabelle to proceed with his sweetheart's murder.

She would have to think of some way to occupy Bubba while she proceeded to kill Peachy. But it wouldn't be easy. Afraid to be alone, he followed her around like a frightened puppy.

Orabelle gritted her teeth. The time it would take her to come up with a way to get rid of Bubba would be yet another stay of execution for Peachy.

Yes, the bitch certainly did lead a charmed life.

But not for long, Orabelle vowed. Not for long.

Peachy placed a mug full of wild red roses on the wobbly table beside the small bed. Just as Mr. Wainwright had said, the cottage was tiny. But he'd also promised it was cozy, and he hadn't lied about that.

A blue, red, and yellow patchwork quilt covered the bed. Lemon-yellow curtains tied back with vivid blue sashes ruffled in the sweet breeze that swept in from the window. At the foot of the bed lay a red throw rug, its long fringe splayed out upon the wooden floor.

Humming, Peachy waltzed into the sunny kitchen. There, she caught Seneca sweeping dirt under the vivid green rug before the fireplace. "Seneca!"

He stared straight back at her. "It was only a bit of dust. Barely enough to bother myself with."

"I don't keer iffen it was only a speck. Y'ain't s'posed to sweep it unner the rug."

His hand tightened on the broom handle. "You have become a shrew, wife. Moreover, I am not at all certain that common men sweep their homes any more than princes sweep their castles. I thought you wanted to come here to play, and yet all we've done since we arrived is work."

"We had to clean, Seneca. And now the work's all done. Look around you. Ain't ever-thing purty?"

He glanced around the cottage. It smelled of soap and lemon oil and wild roses. The hearth gleamed. The tin cups and plates sparkled, as did the brass lamps and candlesticks. But by far the cleanest thing was the floor. "I swept well, didn't I, Mrs. Brindisi?" he asked proudly. "I don't imagine any other common man could have done better."

"Where'd y'hear that last name, Brindisi, Seneca? When Mr. Wainwright asked you yore name, y'come up with it real fast. Like y'didn't even have to think on it none."

He leaned the broom against the wall. "It's my last name, Peachy. I had little trouble thinking of it."

It was a moment before she replied. "Well, don't that jest beat all? I didn't never know royal folks had last names. I thought they was just King This and Queen That. Here I've had a new last name ever since we got wedded up, and I didn't even know it. Peachy McGee Brindisi."

Still dwelling on her new last name, she untied her apron and laid it over one of the chairs at the small table. "Y'ready to go a-shoppin' now, Mr. Brindisi?"

"I'd something else in mind."

She recognized the fire of desire in his eyes. "One thing commoners cain't do is fall into bed whenever they git the hankerin' to do it. There's jest too many chores."

He joined her by the table and took her lush breasts into his hands, kneading them gently. "The shopping can wait. Lancelot cannot."

Laughing, she caught hold of his hands. "Lancelot'll have to wait on account o' later on yore belly ain't gonna want to. We ain't got no food in the house, Seneca, and iffen we don't go on to the village, the shops'll close."

He sighed and went for his coat, which hung on a nail beside the door. "Very well, but I must tell you that I'm not at all certain that I like being a commoner. As a prince, I had more time for the finer things of life."

Peachy smiled. He had no idea what the finer things of life really were.

But she was going to show him.

As if it weighed no more than one of the sunbeams flickering through his sable hair, Seneca heaved the heavy sack of flour over his broad shoulder and carried it to the wagon. Watching him, Peachy began to wish she'd given in to his desire to stay in the cottage and indulge in the lusty activity he'd had in mind. Lord, the man looked good. His white shirt, damp with sweat, molded to every muscle in his torso. And his tight breeches and snug, knee-high boots clung to him, outlining each sinewy stretch of brawn in his powerful legs.

She scrunched her thighs together.

He saw her do it. Because several villagers were within hearing distance, he chose his words carefully. "None of that now, wife. You know as well as I that this is neither the time nor the place to think about such things as gravel and geese."

The silvery sound of her laughter danced through the cool, fresh air of the village. "Seneca— I . . ." She blinked, then shook her head a few times. "My eyes . . . They're a-twitchin'."

"You're tired. We've had a long day. We're finished shopping, so let's go home." He stepped away from the heavily laden wagon and reached for her hand.

She snatched it away. "Seneca, y'don't unnerstand."

He noted the panic in her voice. It took only seconds for him to comprehend. "Another symptom of the dreaded tipinosis?"

She nodded. "Now, Seneca, don't git sorrerful. But the symptoms . . . They're a-comin' more'n more now, so there's somethin' we're gonna have to do. It won't be no fun a'tall, but we cain't put it offen no longer."

He struggled not to laugh. "Very well, tell me what it is. I'll try not to be sad."

She patted his arm. "Seneca, we gotta git my coffin maked. Once I'm gone, you'll be a-grievin', y'see, and y'jest won't have the strength to face the chore. This way, the coffin'll be maked and ready. And I'll git to design it mysef. It'll be jest the way I want it."

He could barely control his amusement. "And when I lower you into the ground, I'll feel good knowing that you are in the box of your dreams."

His calm acceptance relieved her enormously. "That's right. Now, let's go visit the carpenter."

Seneca scanned the small village, finally spotting the carpenter's shop. Taking Peachy's elbow, he led her across the street, sidestepping running children and squawking chickens.

"Well, Mr. and Mrs. Brindisi, we meet again!" a deep voice exclaimed.

Seneca turned and saw Mr. Wainwright. The man's big

white dog, Morton, sat panting by his heels. "Good afternoon, sir."

"What brings you to Jonah's?"

"Jonah's?" Seneca asked.

"Jonah Mead," Mr. Wainwright said. "He's the carpenter."

Seneca patted Peachy's hand. "We've come to order a coffin."

"A coffin? Good heavens, who died?"

Seneca enfolded Peachy in his embrace. "My wife."

Mr. Wainwright's brows shot up. "Your wife?"

"Well," Seneca answered, "as you can see, she's not dead yet, but her eyes were twitching. That, of course, makes it imperative that we order her coffin without delay."

Mr. Wainwright stepped away. "Twitch— Twitching eyes? I— Yes. Yes, I see. Eh ... Good day." He left quickly, deliberating on the fact that Mr. Brindisi was just as odd as Mrs. Brindisi. He would certainly keep an eye on the couple. Yes, indeed, he would at that.

Seneca had never tasted fried squash blossoms. Or chicken and dumplings. Or corn sticks, or cowpeas and hog jowl. Or green tomato pie, either.

As he devoured the food now, he decided the dishes were among the finer things of life.

Peachy, who had finished her supper long ago, sat by the fire, knife and wood in hand, Thurlow Wadsworth McGee digging through the pile of wood shavings by her feet. She glanced up and saw Seneca helping himself to his third piece of pie. "Keep on a-eatin' like that, Seneca, and yore gonna fill up this room like you was a-wearin' it."

He paid her no mind. When he finished the pie, he patted his belly and joined her by the fire. "What are you making?"

She whittled for a few more moments, then held her project up for him to see. "It's fer you. I maked it this afternoon whilst you was a-sweepin'. Tonight I was jest a-smoothin' the handle."

A soft breath escaped his parted lips when he realized what it was. "A slingshot," he whispered.

She smiled. " 'Pears so. Y'ever had one?"

He took the weapon and ran his fingers down its sleek handle. "Yes. Well, not a real one. Not one like this."

"Y'want to go try it outen?" She placed a small bag of pebbles in his lap. "It's too dark to aim real good, but y'can shoot jest fer fun."

He needed no further urging. Once outside, he shot every rock he had into the thick grove of oak trees. Some part deep inside him leaped with excitement every time he heard a pebble swish through the air and smack into something.

"There's more rocks by the stream," Peachy hinted. "It's where I finded the ones y'done shooted already."

He followed her to the stream, which ran through a clearing in the oak forest. Moonlight poured into the water, making it sparkle as though its bottom were covered with diamonds. With the aid of the bright light, Seneca had no problem finding more rocks. Bent at the waist, he walked along picking them up, but when he felt something rough brush across his cheek he stopped.

He straightened. A rope swayed in front of his face. Looking up, he saw it was attached to the high branch of an oak tree.

He dropped every one of his rocks and turned to Peachy.

She stood in a pool of moonlight beside the stream, dipping her bare toes into the cool water. "Y'ever swinged from a tree branch afore, Seneckers?"

Deeply moved, he could not at first reply. "The slingshot. The rope in the tree. How did you know?"

She lifted her skirt and waded into the stream. "Don't differ none how I finded outen. Y'wanted a slingshot. Y'wanted to swing through trees. Well, now y'got yore slingshot and yore rope. Have at it."

He felt overcome by a need that no slingshot or hanging rope could satisfy. With a ragged groan of desire, he strode toward her, brittle twigs snapping beneath his boots. He splashed straight into the stream and when he reached Peachy, he crushed her to him. "I love you, Peachy," he ground out. "I love you more than I ever thought it possible to love a woman. You touch something so deep inside me I cannot begin to guess what or where it is."

She folded her arms around his neck. "Show me. In these here woods. Right now. Show me how much y'love me."

He lifted her out of the water and carried her to a soft, leaf-strewn area beneath the rustling oaks. In only moments, neither of them wore anything but moonlight.

Peachy slid her hands down his naked body, loving the swells of muscle she encountered. "I reckon y'ain't never been outside buck-nekkid afore, have you, Seneckers? Don't it feel good? The night breeze a-touchin' you all over, 'specially in places where it ain't never touched you afore? A-wanderin' around outside nekkid's a real fine thing life lets y'do."

He drew her closer, wanting the feel of her bare hips next to his own. "Since meeting you, Peachy, I've done a lot of things I'd never done before. Why, what would my life have been had I never gotten to see a daddy long-legs?"

"Yeah, spiders is another one o' life's fine things. What happened to yore spider, anyway? Y'didn't kill him or nothin' like that, did you?"

"What? And have all the cows go dry? I should say not." He kissed the tip of her nose. "He was too beautiful to keep in a jar. I put him back in the garden a few days after you gave him to me."

She felt his rigid manhood move. It slid across her belly. "Seneca?"

"Tell me."

"I don't want to talk about spiders no more."

"Indeed. What, then, do you want to do?" He gave her a rakish smile.

She pushed at his shoulders until he lay on the ground. Standing above him, she grinned down at him. "I want to be on top. We ain't never done it like that afore, and I'm a-thinkin' that I might like it."

He couldn't resist teasing her. "Peachy, I'm very sorry, but what you suggest is impossible."

"Why?"

It was an effort, but he succeeded in keeping a straight face. "Because it won't fit like that."

At his admission of the one fear she'd ever had concerning lovemaking, she gasped. "Really?"

Her surprise tickled him so thoroughly he rolled to his side and laughed into the oak leaves.

Only then did she realize he'd been teasing her. He'd become quite good at it. But she was better. "Oh, my God, Seneca, a *snake!*"

He bolted instantly to his feet.

Peachy peered down at where he'd been. "Oh, how dumb o' me. It was only a stick I seed. Shore looked like a snake, though. Hope I didn't skeer y'none."

As casually as possible, he flicked a bit of leaf off his arm. "Don't be ridiculous. I merely jumped up to save you. I was going to kill the snake as soon as you were out of harm's way."

"You was gonna kill a stick?"

They looked into each other's eyes, recalled each other's lies, and burst into loud laughter.

Seneca was the first to recover. "It's time to get serious now. Our silliness has gone on long enough." He laid back down in the leaves and patted the ground beside him.

She stretched out next to him. "Yore right. Lovemakin's serious business. I jest got one comment."

"What is that?"

"Well, when I yelled 'Snake,' *you* might not've been afeared, but ole Lancelot got the life skeert plumb outen him." She dropped her gaze.

Seneca felt more laughter rumble through him. "It's your fault. If you hadn't yelled 'Snake'—"

"Yeah, I'll take the blame. I'll fix the problem, too."

He was just about to ask how she planned to fix it, when she showed him.

She caressed him in the most intimate way possible, sprinkling warm, light kisses up and down the hardening length of his masculinity. Bliss almost too great to bear shot through him when she took him into her mouth and loved him thus for many long moments.

"Peachy." He moaned her name over and over again, like a beautiful chant he couldn't stop singing. Strong tremors ran through his body, and still the pleasure mounted.

Inexperienced though she was, Peachy realized he'd just about reached the point of no return. She ceased her sensuous ministrations. "Seneca, you'd have better luck a-hearin' a worm sneeze than you'll have a-gittin' yore jollies withouten me a-gittin' mine right along with you."

"Peachy—"

"I know, I'm a-hurryin'." Adjusting her position, she straddled him. "Giddyup," she told him, unable to resist aggravating him one last time.

Wild with unappeased desire, he caught hold of her hips, lifted her, and impaled her swiftly.

She gasped with deep surprise and pleasure, and began to circle her hips. It was wonderful this way, she thought. Being on top. In control. Mastering the feelings.

Mastering Seneca . . .

"Who's got the key to the gate now, Your Royal Highness?" She lifted her hips so high that he almost slipped out of her, and then she lowered herself onto him again, savoring his low moan of desire and impatience.

She slowed her pace and laid down on him, smiling into the muscle of his shoulder when he growled his displeasure with her. "Slow, slow," she whispered. "Slow like a herd o' turtles, yeah, slow, slow, this is real slow."

"Dammit," he whispered. Hands at her hips, he tried to make her move the way he wanted.

"Deep, too," she continued. Placing her hands on his shoulders, she pushed herself up. In a sitting position now, she felt him penetrate her farther; she felt all of him, every hard and throbbing smidgeon of him. He'd never filled her so completely before. "Deep, huh, Seneca? So deep, I reckon you feel like you've done hit bedrock."

"Cease this torture, woman," he demanded. "Move. Move!"

She did, but only slightly, just enough to make him wild with elusive pleasure. Smiling, she walked her fingers up his chest, then slid her thumb over the grimace on his mouth. " 'Course, there's fast too. Like a whipstitch. Fast like a bullet with legs. But I've got a mind to keep things real leisure-like."

His breath came in ragged pants. He ached with the pleasure she doled out so slowly. "And I've got a mind to—"

The sudden rotation of her hips cut short his threat. She lowered herself down to him again, curtaining the sides of his face with her soft, fragrant hair. "Wait fer me," she instructed him. "Wait till I tell you that y'ain't gotta wait no more."

He closed his eyes, every fiber in his body warding off the sensual explosion she'd denied him for too long already. Determined to find release, he cupped her bottom and pushed her into him, meeting her, matching her thrust for thrust.

The thick mat of hair at his groin tickled and increased her own pleasure. The sensuous feeling of his large, hot hands on her bottom and the raw strength that surged through his hard body made her whimper with delight. "I'm within a lash now, Seneca," she panted into his ear. "Lord o' mercy, I got the wigglies. Don't wait no more!"

As if he could. The thought burst into his mind as ecstasy shot through his body. The bliss spun through him, touching parts of him that had never been touched. His entire frame, every nerve he possessed, quaked with the rolling pleasure, and he realized then that it had never been like this before. "Peachy." He spoke her name with all the passion she made him feel, with every shred of love he had for her.

"Sen— Oh! Oh, Lord, Seneca, them jollies is a-comin' back!"

Her second bout with pleasure was the crowning glory of his own. He felt her quiver around him again, her body surrendering once more to the rapture. She called out his name, and he knew in his heart that there was no sweeter song than the sound of his name on Peachy's soft lips.

"Peachy," he whispered, losing his hands within the untamed splendor of her silky hair.

Her body continued to tremble with the last tremors of pleasure. "Y'didn't never tell me it could happen two times in a row," she murmured, her face still buried in his shoulder. "It come up on me real quiet-like. Like a snowflake on a feather. And then, all of a sudden, it tuk holt o' me, and I couldn't do nothin' but hang on like a starvin' tick on a fat dog's ear."

He smiled into her hair, relishing the way her soft curls felt on his lips.

Slowly, she rose, slipped to the ground beside him, and placed her leg over his stomach. "Did it happen two times fer you, too, Seneckers?"

He remembered the intensity of his climax, the bone-melting strength of it. "Once was enough."

She snuggled closer to him, gazing up at the stars twinkling through the swaying branches overhead. "I liked a-bein' on top. Whatcha got to say about that, darlin'?"

He turned and took her lips in a tender kiss. "I would say that it was definitely one of the finer things of life."

The days passed. Seneca didn't trouble himself keeping count of how many slipped by. He spent each of them as if no tomorrow existed, and when tomorrow did come, he lived it laughing. And playing. And loving the girl who had stolen his heart, his soul, his very self.

But Peachy knew exactly how many days came and went. Each night, while wrapped in Seneca's arms, she prayed for just one more day with him. And although she continued to mourn the fact that she was going to die, she knew in her heart that in her short life she'd experienced more happiness than some people whose lives took them into old age.

"I'm going hunting," Seneca announced one morning, after having eaten his fill of Peachy's hot and fluffy biscuits, fried pork chops, potato cakes, and fresh apple chutney. "I'll bring back supper."

He smiled to himself. Hunting was illegal here. The land belonged to some aristocrat who'd left his country estate to enjoy the London Season. But Seneca hunted at least three times a week. He hadn't been caught yet, and he didn't intend to allow it to happen.

Still, the thought struck his sense of humor. His Royal Highness, the Crown Prince of Aventine—a common poacher.

"See iffen y'can git a possom," Peachy said, up to her elbows in a pan of soapy dishwater. "I make a sloppin'-

good possum stew, Seneca. So good yore tongue'll slap your brains outen whilst yore a-eatin' it."

He bent his head and chuckled. "Peachy, I don't even know what a possum looks like. How about rabbit?" He retrieved the rifle he'd purchased in the village.

"Well, dang it to hell, Seneca, all's y'ever bring home is rabbit. We've et rabbit four times this week. Cain't y'git nothin' else?"

He gave her a good frown. "Do you think you could do better, wife?"

At the prospect of hunting, excitement whirled through her. She yanked her hands out of the dishwater and quickly dried them on her apron. "Yeah, give me that there shootin'-raffle, and I'll go—"

"No." He held the rifle over his head. "Hunting is man's work. You go chop the firewood." As soon as the words were out of his mouth, he smiled. Peachy's sudden giggle soon prompting his laughter.

He took her into his arms and kissed the top of her head. "Behave yourself while I'm gone," he warned, his breath ruffling her hair. "Don't wander away. Stay—"

"I will," she promised. "I'll stay right here a-choppin' firewood jest like a good little wife should."

He was still chuckling as he left the cottage. When he was gone, Peachy finished the breakfast dishes and stored the leftover food in a cabinet that the numerous field mice couldn't reach.

Outside, she found her ax leaning against the cottage wall, and approached the thick logs stacked beneath the shade of an oak tree. It was true that she'd been chopping all the wood. Not that Seneca didn't know how; on the contrary, he'd mastered the technique with little trouble. And because of the sheer power he was able to put behind each stroke of the ax, he was capable of finishing the chore much more quickly than she could.

But she *liked* to chop wood. There was something about the scent of the freshly split logs that soothed her senses. She savored the sight of flying wood chips and took delight in the way they peppered her skirts. She enjoyed the feel of the ax handle in her hands and even relished the way her body was jarred as the blade sank into the log. It was a good sensation. It made her feel alive.

And she so loved being alive. God, she was so happy. She couldn't imagine that any kind of happiness surpassed what she had with Seneca. He was her heaven on earth, and she loved him beyond comprehension.

Before long, she'd chopped enough wood to last for several days and nights. Wiping her moist brow with the sleeve of her blouse, she heard a jingling sound, then caught sight of a wagon. The horse that pulled it wore a necklace of bells around his neck.

Curious, she walked to the edge of the road. Her eyes widened with surprise when she saw the bright yellow wagon wheels. Vivid paintings of suns, moons, and stars covered the sides of the vehicle. A crate of noisy chickens rode on top, and two goats were tied to the back.

She couldn't suppress a squeal of delight. "The *gypsies!*" Sweet Lord, she was finally going to meet and dance with real live gypsies! "Stop!" she shouted, waving frantically. "Stop and let me see y'all!"

The olive-complected, white-haired man driving the wagon turned his caravan onto the small path that led to the cottage. As soon as he'd stopped the jingling horse, three other people emerged from inside the wagon.

Peachy realized this was a gypsy family. The man driving the wagon was the elderly father. His wife, her black hair streaked with silver, held the hand of a young girl. Both women wore gold jewelry and brilliantly colored clothing. Lost in swirls of orange, purple, red, green, and yellow, they resembled bold rainbows.

Another man stood beside the women—a young man, his skin as dark as Seneca's, his body full of muscle. His coal-black hair fell past his shoulders; a gold earring sparkled from his right earlobe. A crimson silk scarf shimmered around his neck above two heavy gold necklaces, which glittered against his flowing white shirt. Tight black pants encased his thick legs, black suede boots rose to his knees, and a long sword flashed at his side.

He turned to his mother. Peachy saw the woman smile at him and realized they'd communicated silently. She was thrilled to have seen real gypsy mind reading with her own eyes and suddenly wondered if one of them could read hers.

"Can y'read my mind?" she gushed. "My palm?" She held out her hand. "Can y'tell me how long I got to live? Do y'all dance? Is there any o' them tambourines in yore wagon? Oh, Lord o' mercy, y'jest cain't know how tickled to death I am to meet real live gypsies! We ain't got nary a one in the Blue Ridge, y'see, and I only seen pictures o' y'all in a gypsy book."

The young man approached her, covering her out-stretched hand with both of his. "I am Tas. And you are?" While waiting for her answer, he studied the gleaming di-amond ring on her left hand.

"I'm Peachy. God-proud to meetcha, Tas. Can we dance?"

His gaze settled on the enticing glimpse of creamy breast that peeked out from the vee of her blouse. His black eyes gleamed with a desire that had little to do with her diamonds. "We can dance. We will make gypsy music for you." He glanced warily at the cottage. "There is a man who lives here with you?"

"I live here with my husband, Seneca. But he ain't here. He went to git a rabbit. Or a possum iffen he can figger outen what one looks like."

"Seneca?" Tas deliberated for a moment. "I have heard this name before, but I cannot think where." He smiled, his white teeth a striking contrast against his dark skin. "It is a shame that your Seneca cannot dance with us. But first you will give us cool water? We have been traveling since dawn, and our water has grown warm. This is my father, Camlo, my mother, Padma, and my sister, Miri."

Peachy gave each member of his family a big smile. "I'll fetch the water." She scurried to the cottage.

They followed her inside. Sipping their water, Camlo, Padma, and Miri began examining the cottage with black eyes that missed nothing. It was Camlo who spotted the bulging sack that hung near the hearth. From where he stood, he scrutinized the bag carefully, soon discerning round shapes pressing against its sides. Round as coins, they were, and the pouch was fairly bursting with them. He slid his gaze to Tas, who read the signal clearly.

Peachy was refilling Tas's cup when he took her other hand. "Come, Peachy. While my family soothes their thirst, we will walk, and I will tell you about the life of the gypsy. Later, my mother will tell your fortune, and then we will dance while Miri plays her tambourine."

His offer stirred her anticipation once again. After setting a plate of leftover biscuits and a bowl of apple chutney on the table for his family, she followed him outside and into the oak grove. "Can y'read my mind, Tas?"

He stopped and lifted his dark hands to the sides of her face, his fingers caressing her temples. "You are pleased to meet the gypsies. It is a wish come true for you."

She inhaled a slow breath, amazed by his ability.

"And now I will tell you what thoughts are in my own mind," he murmured, his voice as heavy with desire as the summer air was with sultry heat. "You are very beautiful. With hair bright as copper, skin pale as moonlight, and eyes that frolic like happy dancers dressed in green."

His raven gaze pierced hers. Something in it, some glowing intent, made her uneasy. She backed away. "We—dance. We're s'posed to—to dance."

It took him only two long steps to reach her. He curled his dark hands around her tiny waist. "I do not lie to women as beautiful as you. We will dance."

Her body went rigid when he tugged her against his powerful frame and ground the solid proof of his desire into the coiled muscles of her belly.

Before she could react, he moved his hips, rotating them slowly. "We dance in this way," he murmured, holding her to his loins. "You can dance to the rhythm I set?"

Sickening fear lent strength and momentum to her body. She struggled violently, twisting and turning in brawny arms that gave her no quarter. Lifting her hand, she ripped her nails down his cheek and was horrified when the pain she'd inflicted kindled flames of excitement in his eyes.

The sound of furious chattering broke the tension of the moment. From the corner of her eye, Peachy saw a gray ball fall from the tree above and land directly on Tas's back.

Thurlow Wadsworth McGee dug his claws into the man, his sharp teeth sinking into a thick slab of muscle. With a roar of pain, Tas reached over his shoulder, grabbed the tiny animal, and threw it into the forest. His chest heaving, he peered into the woods, trying to see what kind of vicious creature had attacked him.

Peachy took full advantage of his loosened hold and turned to flee.

Tas caught her easily. "Do you think a small wound to my shoulder takes away my desire for you? It is time for you to read this gypsy's mind. Read my intent, and you will understand that I will not be denied."

He dragged her back into the oak glen and smiled down at her. "You are a woman of fire, of spirit, one who will scream. You will battle me while I take you, and I will savor your cries for help. There is no one about," he reminded her. "We are alone." With one fluid motion, he lifted her off her feet and laid her on the ground, covering her body with his own. "Scream," he commanded her.

She did.

And the name she screamed was Seneca's.

Seneca stopped. Something moved ahead. Something small, gray, and running so swiftly that a small cloud of dust shadowed its flight.

It chattered. Furiously.

In the next moment, Thurlow Wadsworth McGee sprang to Seneca's chest, then leaped back to the ground. He repeated the action several times.

Seneca stared at the agitated squirrel. A sense of disquiet ribboned through him. He lifted his head, pinning his sharp gaze to the tiny cottage in the distance.

The rabbit-filled bag fell from his hands, landing in the dust. The thud it made as it hit the ground mingled with a scream, a faraway scream, more like a whisper, but it roared through Seneca's mind like thunder, deafening him to everything except the sound of Peachy in danger.

He bolted forward, his thick legs pumping with all the raw power of his fear for her safety. Clods of dirt flew all around him, stones battered his torso, and the wind whipped through his hair.

And still he ran faster. So fast the stone fence that guided his way became nothing but a gray-and-white blur.

The endless distance shortened; the cottage came closer. Through narrowed eyes, he saw a wagon, a caravan, and dread shot through him when he realized that Peachy had fallen prey to the gypsies.

"Seneca!"

Her cry for his aid was so filled with terror that Seneca felt bile rise into his throat. His rifle clutched tightly to his chest, he spun onto the path that led off the road and tore into the cluster of oak trees.

And then he saw her. She was struggling desperately to escape the grinning man who held her pinned to the ground. Her wild gaze caught Seneca's and the chilling horror he saw within it brought him a fury so intense, its burning blaze destroyed any shred of mercy he might have shown.

He was going to kill the bastard who'd dared to touch his angel.

"Seneca! Seneca!"

Tas raised his head, his eyes widening when he saw the huge man bearing down upon him.

He had no time to rise on his own. Seneca grabbed the skin of his back and lifted him high into the air. With a giant burst of strength, Seneca sent the man flying.

Tas crashed against the trunk of an oak tree. But though the impact dazed him, he roused himself and staggered to his feet, his eyes never leaving the man who'd tossed him through the air.

Anger and humiliation collided within him. He wiped a trickle of blood from his mouth and ignored his mother's cry of concern as she and his father and sister appeared in the clearing. "You must be Seneca," he bit out, eyeing the rifle in the man's hands. "You have hunted this morning, and now you will shoot me. That is what you will do?"

His slitted gaze still riveted on the gypsy's face, his instincts trained on the three other gypsies who stood huddled together a short distance away, Seneca reached down, his fingers curling around Peachy's wrist. Gently, he pulled her to her feet. "Did he—"

"No. Y'come jest in time."

It didn't matter that the gypsy hadn't violated Peachy.

Seneca was going to kill him anyway. He motioned Peachy behind him. His hands whitened around his rifle.

The gun was useless to him. He'd fired his last bullet to bring down the rabbit. But the gypsy wouldn't discover that fact. Seneca had never been in more need of the mask that hid his every emotion.

Wearing it now, he dared the gypsy to read his mind.

Tas stared at the gleaming gun. He knew that these English farmers were well-practiced in the art of shooting.

Tas was not willing to test the skill of this Seneca. He took a few steps away from the tree, stopping short when Seneca lifted the rifle. "I have no gun, Seneca. You would slay me in cold blood? Have you no honor as the gypsies have honor?"

Seneca remained silent, his face void of all emotion, all thought.

"I am not afraid to die," Tas continued, his hand inching toward the hilt of his sword. "But I would not care to die without the chance to fight for my life, and yet as you can see, I have no gun. I have only this."

With a flourish, he drew his sword.

Seneca almost smiled.

"You will lay down your gun?" Tas asked. "I cannot fend off your bullet with my sword."

Seneca feigned a thoughtful look. "You have no gun, and I have no sword."

Tas felt relief flood his body. The ignorant farmers could shoot, but they could not fight with swords. Sword-play took sharp skills and honed instinct. After many years of endless practice, Tas possessed both. He would kill this Seneca, and then he would take the girl for his own. "Your problem is easily solved, Seneca. Father, you must lend this honorable man your sword. He has deigned to give your son a chance to defend himself."

Camlo smiled, drew his own sword from its sheath, and tossed it to Seneca's feet. Its blade clattered against a few pebbles.

"Seneca," Peachy whispered.

His eyes told her not to fear.

She nodded slightly and backed away.

Seneca lowered his gaze to the ground. There, at his

feet, lay a weapon as familiar to him as his own hand. He bent and curled his fingers around its hilt. It fit his grasp as if his palm had been its mold. He lifted the weapon; it swished, cutting air. Seneca stared at his adversary.

Tas frowned. There was something about the way Seneca held the sword that send a current of anxiety through him. And Seneca's eyes ... They glowed.

With a confidence as lethal as the sword itself.

Tas's hand shook. "You have knowledge of swordplay, Seneca?"

Seneca only smiled. And then, one slow step at a time, he approached the man whose blood he would soon spill. Stopping a few feet before the gypsy, he raised the sword again. "En garde."

Swallowing his apprehension, Tas made a wild lunge, his sword crossing Seneca's at the hilt.

With a slight movement of his wrist, Seneca freed his sword and flicked its point across his enemy's cheek, drawing a thin line of blood. "Your gypsy blood flows," he said. "Do you surrender?"

Tas took one retreating step before rushing blindly forward.

Sunlight glinted off the blades. The clash of steel shattered the silence. Seneca kept his legs apart and his body in profile to his opponent. His guarded position, a well-balanced crouch, enabled him to counter each parry the gypsy made. He kept his own sword slightly above his waist, his arm gently bent, his right hand palm up as he deflected his adversary's attacks.

The gypsy was good, he mused. His skill was evident. But his fear made him reckless.

Seneca toyed with him, allowing him to tire and worry and become more afraid. For a long while, he didn't recoil a single step, but stood firm. And then he began to circle the gypsy, anticipating each of his opponent's thrusts with a rapid crossing of blades. His sword shone as he wielded it with quick, skillful strokes that drew blood from the gypsy's other cheek, his forehead, and his neck.

And then, without warning, he opened his right hand and tossed his sword toward his left hand. As the sword hung in midair, its blade met that of the gypsy's, but before the impact could send it to the ground, Seneca seized it with his left hand and took full advantage of his enemy's unprotected chest. With one powerful thrust, he buried the sword in his opponent's shoulder, then slid it slowly out.

Tas clutched his hand over the wound; his mouth open to emit a silent scream. Blood covered his face from the cuts Seneca had made there, blood dripping to mingle with that seeping from his shoulder.

Seneca raised his sword one more time, the muscles in his arm bulging with the strength he would use to kill. "You have dared to lay your foul hands on the Princess of Aventine, gypsy. The punishment for that is death."

Tas paled with recognition. "Seneca," he whispered. "You . . . Prince of Aventine, master swordsman."

"I'm flattered that you know me." Seneca drew back the sword, aiming its tip directly at the gypsy's heart. "Unfortunately for you, however, I am not sufficiently moved to show you mercy."

"Seneca, *no!*" Peachy screamed, running toward him. "Y'cain't *kill* him! Y'cain't! For God's sake, let him go! Seneca, please let him go!"

Seneca continued to stare into the black eyes of the gypsy. "The princess is right. A sword is too fine a weapon to sully with the death of a miserable bastard like you. I am giving you and your family one minute to leave. If you are not gone in that time, I will skewer you to one of these trees. And if I ever hear of your presence in this area again, you will sorely regret not having taken heed of my warning, for I swear it will take you agonizing hours to die."

Dragging his sword behind him, Tas stumbled toward his father, mother, and sister, who were already racing toward the caravan. When he reached the wagon, his mother and sister pulled him inside. His father urged the jingling horse onto the road.

As the steed picked up speed, Seneca spied a familiar pouch hanging from the gypsy father's belt. He gritted his teeth and squelched his anger.

No amount of gold in the world was as valuable as Peachy.

Turning, he gathered her into his arms. "Are you sure you're all right?"

"I ain't hurt nary a'tall." Laying her cheek to his chest, she heard his heartbeat. The soft, gentle sound soothed the last shreds of her fear. A deep sense of security and tranquility stole over her. "Y'saved me. Jest like them gypsies was fire-breathin' dragons, y'come and keeped 'em from a-gittin' me."

He lifted her face and peered into her beautiful eyes. "I'll never leave you alone again. I don't care if I never taste fresh meat again, I'll never leave you alone."

She wrapped her arms around his waist. "We can buy meat in the village. Y'ain't got to hunt fer it."

He closed his eyes for a moment. "I never thought I'd hear myself say this, but I've no money. None to speak of. They stole the bag of gold, Peachy."

She frowned, then smiled. "The pouch that was a-hangin' by the fireplace?"

"I saw it on the old gypsy man's belt."

Her smile grew. Her bright giggle filled the air. "Seneca, I tuk all yore gold outen that bag and poured it in the flower vase that's in the bedroom. That sack them gypsies tuk didn't have nothin' in it but Thurlow Wadsworth McGee's walnuts."

"All they got away with was a sack of nuts?" He threw back his head and laughed. Still chuckling, he threw down the sword, swept Peachy into his arms, and started for the cottage. "Tell me once more that you're all right."

"Nothin' real bad happened," she told him, "but I still feel sorter bad."

"Why?"

"Well, I got to see real live gypsies with my own eyes. I got to see one of 'em fight you with a real live sword. But y'know? I never *did* git to dance with 'em."

He stopped. "Would you settle for swinging through the trees with a real live prince instead?"

Mischief deepened the sapphire of his eyes to a midnight blue. Grinning, she combed his hair with her fingers and nodded.

Seneca pivoted toward the several ropes that now dangled near the stream, halting when he heard a familiar voice call out.

"I say!" Mr. Wainwright shouted as he sauntered into the yard. "I saw the gypsy caravan tearing down the road. There's nothing wrong, is there?"

Seneca turned to face the man and saw an old, huddled woman standing beside him, the hood of her ragged pea-green cloak drawn low over her face. She held a large covered basket in her gnarled hands. "Everything is fine, Mr. Wainwright." He set Peachy down and slipped his arm around her waist.

"Good, good. Oh, this is Mrs. Belle. Like you, she's new to the area. I met her and her nephew yesterday in the village. The young man didn't say much, but he is quite fond of my dog. I'm sure he would have come to meet the two of you, but he preferred to run in the fields with Morton."

Beneath her hood, Orabelle smiled, silently thanking the big white dog for stealing Bubba's heart. Bubba's fascination with the animal had finally given her an opportunity to meet Peachy alone.

"Mrs. Belle has brought you a basket of food," Mr. Wainwright announced.

Orabelle held out the basket, careful to keep her head covered with her hood. "I look forward to becoming acquainted with you," she muttered quietly.

Peachy accepted the basket. "Thanky, ma'am. Right nice o' you. Purty cape y'got. Reminds me of the pea soup my maw used to make. I come up on that soup, y'know."

Orabelle nodded.

Mr. Wainwright smiled. "Could we visit for a while, Mr. and Mrs. Brindisi? I'd be delighted to hear about how you are enjoying your time here."

"Perhaps another time," Seneca replied. "We're very busy at the moment."

"Oh, I see. What has you so occupied?"

Seneca grinned into Peachy's excited eyes. "We must swing from the trees, Mr. Wainwright."

"Swing . . . Eh, yes. Quite right. Swing from trees." Frowning, Mr. Wainwright turned and walked back to the road. "They are a very strange couple, Mrs. Belle," he whispered. "The oddest people I have ever known. Why, do you know that Mr. Brindisi ordered a coffin for his wife? The girl isn't even dead yet."

Orabelle merely smiled.

Chapter 18

"**W**atch this," Seneca called down to Peachy, who sat at the base of the tree he'd climbed.

"Yeah, I'm a-watchin'." Removing the checkered cloth that covered the basket of fruit, bread, and cheese Mrs. Belle had brought, Peachy examined the food. Her stomach growled; her mouth watered.

"You are not watching, Peachy."

She smiled. He sounded exactly like a little boy who wanted someone to witness the amazing feats he could perform. Recalling the fact that as a child no one had cared about the things he'd wanted to show and tell them, she felt a warm rush of tender understanding. It was becoming more and more obvious to her that the neglected but playful and mischievous little boy inside him had left his hiding place to join hearts with the very proper prince. The combination of child and adult had transformed Seneca into a whole man. A man who knew how to mix work with play, and do both things well.

A man who comprehended now that the very finest thing in life was simply the ability to find and enjoy every opportunity for happiness that came his way, no matter how small or how grand.

"Peachy!"

"I love you, Seneca."

"If you really loved me, you'd watch me."

Smiling indulgently, she glanced up. "I'm a-watchin', darlin'."

Satisfied now that he had her full attention, Seneca nodded. "I'm going to swing from this branch on this rope, and then I'm going to catch hold of the other rope and swing to that branch that's hanging over the stream."

A sprinkling of the tree dust he'd stirred up floated down, wafting through a sunbeam and glittering like diamond powder. She waved it away from her face. "Yore gonna kill yoresef, Seneca."

He stood on the sturdy branch, swiped leaves away from his head, and grabbed the rope. "Peachy, I've done this a thousand times."

"Yore the biggest liar in the whole wide world. Y'know dang well that y'aint done no sech thing."

"I have. In my mind, I have."

"That ain't the same thing. Git down afore you—"

She had no time to finish her command before Seneca was already swinging through the air. As he said he would do, he let go of the rope he held and grabbed a second one, his swing continuing smoothly to the other branch.

As soon as he landed on it, Peachy heard a sharp snap. "Oh, Lord, Seneca, the branch is gonna—"

A loud cracking sound drowned out her warning. The branch splintered off the tree, sending Seneca straight into the deep stream.

He came up sputtering, but unharmed. After wiping water from his eyes, he grinned sheepishly. "God, that was fun."

Peachy rolled with laughter, unable to stem her vast amusement until she felt Seneca lift her from the ground. "It's a gawdang wonder y'didn't break yore fool neck."

"Do you know what I'd like to do now?"

"Jump offen the roof o' the cottage and pretend y'can fly?"

He pressed his smile to her lips, then whispered into them. "I'd like to see you naked, Princess. I'd like to adore you with my body and make slow, thorough love to each silken inch of you. I'd like to bury myself in your warm, tight softness and know again the sheer bliss of being inside you, becoming one with you. I'd like to pleasure you, Peachy, as you've never been pleasured before."

She nibbled at his lower lip. The little boy in him had

moved over for the man, the incredibly sexy man, she mused.

"Well, wife?" he prompted her.

She had only to scrunch her thighs together for him to understand that his desires were her own.

"The basket," she told him. "Git the basket that sweet Miz Belle brung us."

Bending, he scooped its handle into the crook of his elbow and carried basket and woman into the cottage. He didn't even wait until they'd reached the bedroom, but started peeling off Peachy's clothes while still in the kitchen. When hers were off, he began removing his own.

Seeing his wet trousers pooled around his ankles, Peachy hurried into the bedroom. The loud crash she heard in the next moment told her he'd tried to follow.

He'd knocked a chair over while grappling at it to keep from falling. "Dammit!"

His curse brought forth her silent giggle. Quickly, she looked for a place to hide. The man had never played hide-and-go-seek, and if he truly wanted her the way he'd sworn he did, he would have to find her first.

She saw his bare feet enter the room only seconds after she'd crawled under the bed. He was so close, his toes almost touched her chin.

"Peachy?"

She struggled with the urge to bite his toes.

"Peachy, where are you?"

She watched his feet move to the end of the bed, where the quilt that hung to the floor hindered her view of his whereabouts. She listened carefully, straining to hear sounds that would tell her where he was.

She heard nothing. Seconds stretched into minutes, and still she heard not a single noise. Before much longer, her curiosity overrode her will to stay hidden.

She slipped out from beneath the bed and got to her feet. Looking all around the small room, she found no sign of Seneca. "Seneca? Seneca?"

When he didn't answer, she looked in the tiny closet, but found only clothes and shoes. She frowned. He couldn't have left the room; from her spot beneath the bed she'd had a perfect view of the doorway. And he couldn't have escaped by way of the little window, either. He was much too big to fit through it.

She looked up, expecting to see him hanging off one of the ceiling beams, but spied nothing but a few floating spiderwebs. Truly bewildered, she walked around the bed and peered around the side of the old dresser. Nothing existed there but empty space.

"Well, this is jest the beatin'est thing I ever seed," she muttered. "Seneca, where the hell'd you go, dang it! It's like y'falled into a varmint hole and pulled the openin' in after you!" Turning to the bed, the tips of her toes disappearing beneath the hanging quilt, she gave a tremendous sigh of frustration.

Her breath exploded into a scream when she felt something bite her toes. "God Almighty!" she hollered, snatching her feet away from the bottom of the bed. "Seneca! Rats! Oh, sweet Lord o' mercy, there's rats unner—"

Deep, rich laughter silenced her immediately. It poured out from beneath the bed.

Her eyes grew so wide that her eyelids ached. "Why, you plumb no-account, worthlesser'n a bucket o' spit, crookeder'n a barrel o' fishhooks, triflin'er'n hog swill, low-down varmint, you!" Bending, she snatched up the quilt and glared into Seneca's twinkling blue eyes. "I gotta good mind to meller you s'hard that yore young'uns'll be born a-shakin'! You skeert me so bad I got a mouthful o' my own heart and near 'bout strangled on it! How the hell'd you git unner here withouten me a-knowin' it?"

He reached out and smoothed his finger over the wrinkle of fury on her forehead. "You didn't hear me because the noise you made while getting out from under the bed covered up the noise I made while taking your place. When I couldn't find you, I deduced that the only place you could be was under the bed. And may I remind you, wife, that this game of hide-and-seek was your idea?"

"It's fun, ain't it?"

"I know something that's even more fun."

She stepped away while he got out from beneath the bed. When he was standing, she leaped onto him, hanging on to his neck and wrapping her legs around his waist.

Desire slammed into him.

She felt his masculinity touch the left cheek of her bottom as it grew to full arousal. "Let's git in the bed now," she whispered.

"No."

Confusion misted her thoughts, but before she could voice it, he carried her to the armless rocking chair in the corner. When she realized his intentions, she tried to scrunch her thighs together, but had to squeeze her legs around his waist instead. "Lord o' mercy," she said as he sat in the chair, "I believe I'm a-fixin' to git the best gawdang rockin' I ever had."

"Up now, wife." Hands at her waist, he lifted her onto the crown of his thick shaft, then sent the rocker into motion. Slowly, so slowly, he lowered her, filling her with himself. Bit ... by ... bit.

Peering down, Peachy watched his leisurely entry into her body. The beautiful sight and the way his languid penetration felt stirred her every emotion and brought to tingling life her every nerve. "Oh, Seneca, look at that."

He did. "You like the way we look coming together, do you?"

"I cain't mem'ry ever a-seein' somethin' so powerfully wonnerful. I feel filled to the brim with love."

When he was buried inside her, he continued to keep the chair moving back and forth. The gentle rock of the chair, the even gentler sway of Seneca's hips, brought Peachy a gentle pleasure. Sighing with contentment, she leaned down and kissed him.

"Peachy," he whispered, "I chose to make love to you in this rocking chair for a reason."

"Because y'knowed it'd feel good?"

His large, dark hands closed over her milky breasts. "I would see you rocking my son someday soon," he murmured, his eyes locked with hers. "It seems fitting to me that he be conceived in a rocking chair."

Tears floated into her eyes. "But, Seneca, I—"

"Ah, yes. The tipinosis. You don't think you'll last another nine or ten months?"

"Well, I—"

"You know not the hour of your death, Peachy," he told her softly, smiling. "It could arrive today, tomorrow, next week, in a month, or not even for years. At any rate, I would think you would do your best to give me my son before passing into the hereafter. It would be the last noble act you performed on earth. A deed so noble, I feel certain it would deduct at least a billion of your trillions of years from your stay in Purgatory."

His suggestion was definitely something to consider, she mused. "But ... Do y'really think I'll git the makin's of a baby today? Now? In this here chair?"

He rocked a bit faster, sinking into her so deeply he felt the softness of her womb caress him. "If not, we'll rock every day until we learn of our son's beginnings."

"Could be a girl."

"He will be a boy."

"But—"

"My firstborn will be a son, and I will hear no more on the subject, wife."

"Yore firstborn," she whispered. "Yore heir."

He stopped rocking.

"Y'gotta go back, Seneckers," she cooed. "Y'cain't give up the Crown on account o' yore people need you. Yore paw ain't gonna be king ferever, y'know. One day you'll be a-settin' on the golden throne, and that's when you'll finally be able to hep the people."

He put the chair back into motion.

Soundlessly, they rocked, Peachy laying against Seneca. They loved each other lips to lips, chest to chest, heartbeat to heartbeat, joined as intimately as it was possible for man and woman to join.

And when Seneca felt her pulse around him, when he heard her cry out his name, he responded in kind, and flooded her womanly depths with his essence, hoping with all his heart and soul that her body was ripe for his seed. "And now I wait," he breathed into her moist lips. "Wait to see if you swell with the son I so want to have with you."

They remained quiet for a very long while, both of them dwelling on the wonderous thing that might be taking place inside Peachy's body.

"And I do solemnly swear," Seneca said, his voice shattering the silence, "that when you grow fat with child ...

when you can do nothing but waddle, I will come to your rooms to visit you as often as my lithe and lovely mistresses will allow."

She gasped so sharply she choked.

He patted her back. "Stop that, wife. You're frightening my son with all that noise."

"Well, good Lord, the little feller shore did grow fast, huh? He weren't even maked till five minutes ago, and now he's done got him a pair o' ears!"

"Which you are quickly deafening. His and mine both."

Content to savor their gay and relaxed mood for a while longer, they continued to rock, stopping only when a sharp rap at the front door disrupted their peace.

Seneca practically dumped Peachy onto the floor in his haste to rise and dress.

"God Almighty, Seneca. A second ago you was worried about yore son's ears, and now yore a-bangin' the little young'un all over the place."

Grinning, he grabbed a pair of trousers from the closet and proceeded into the kitchen to answer the door.

"Mr. Brindisi," Jonah Mead greeted him.

Seneca nodded at the carpenter. "What can I do for you, Mr. Mead?"

"I've come to tell you that your wife's coffin is finished. I put the final touches on it only an hour ago. I thought perhaps she would like to see it. But I'll be closing the shop in only twenty minutes," he warned.

"Oh, *yes,* Mr. Mead!" Peachy hollered from the bedroom. "We'll be there quicker'n a cat can lick his—"

"His *paw,*" Seneca interjected before she could say the word that would shock the carpenter.

As soon as Seneca shut the door, Peachy came skipping into the kitchen. She'd donned her skirt and shoes, and now her fingers flew down the line of buttons on her bodice. "Hurry, Seneca!"

He realized that no power on earth would keep her from laying eyes on her coffin. Shaking his head, he made his way to the bedroom and dressed quickly.

"Well, good Lord, we didn't git no lunch," Peachy announced while draping her shawl over her shoulders. "I'm so hungry, my stomach thinks my throat's been cut."

"Very well, you stay here and eat, and I'll go see your coffin." He started out the door.

"Wait! I'll git somethin' from the basket Miz Belle brung!" She grabbed a piece of cheese and a small loaf of bread and raced outside to join Seneca.

She'd finished the cheese before she even reached the wagon.

"Y'shore y'don't want the last bite o' this bread, Seneckers?" Peachy asked as he directed the wagon into the village square. "You didn't eat nothin' a'tall."

He shook his head and stopped the donkey beside the village well. After descending, he lifted Peachy out, then escorted her across the street to Mr. Mead's carpenter's shop, Thurlow Wadsworth McGee springing along behind.

Peachy almost lost her breath when she saw it. Her coffin. There it lay, right in front of the shop atop a sturdy wooden platform. A cry of pure joy escaped her as she hurried toward it.

"Oak," she whispered, running her hand across its sleek rim. "I always thought I wouldn't git nothin' but a plain ole pine box."

Seneca moved behind her, covering her shoulders with his hands. "Only the best for my wife," Bending his head, he closed his eyes and laughed silently into her hair. "Only the very, very best."

She examined the elaborately carved sides, satisfied beyond her wildest dreams by the excellent job Mr. Mead had done in depicting the scenes she'd wanted chiseled there. On one side, he'd fashioned her tiny Possum Hollow cabin surrounded by magnolias and the mountains of the Blue Ridge. On the other side, he'd sculpted the splendorous Palace of Aventine, wooden waves of the North Sea in the background.

The interior surpassed her expectations as well. Plump cushions covered in emerald green satin lined the entire box. "Do y'like this color green, Seneca?"

He glanced down at it. "Indeed, I do. I've always loved that shade of green on you. How fitting that you will wear it for all eternity."

"Ever'thing's jest right," she exclaimed, hands at her

cheeks. "Jest as right as right can be. And it looks real comfortable, too. But y'know? I think I orter be shore and sartin that it fits."

"That it fits?"

She held up her thumb and looked at her coffin the way an artist examines his paintings. "Hep me git in it. It's the onliest way I can be shore that it ain't too small. What iffen my toes is all crunched at the bottom? Seneca, I cain't think o' nothin' worser'n a-waitin' fer Jedgment Day with my toes all cramped up. God Almighty, I'd be too crippled to rise and git jedged when it's my turn."

He noticed she was beginning to draw a small crowd. "Peachy, for God's sake, you don't have to lie down in—"

"Yeah, Seneca, I do, and iffen y'don't hep me git in, I'll git in mysef." When he made no move to assist her, she climbed into the coffin and laid down, sinking deeply into the thick satin cushions. Thurlow Wadsworth McGee jumped in as well and burrowed beside her.

Seneca groaned inwardly. The woman was crazy. Absolutely, totally, and completely crazy. "Peachy," he whispered, "this has gone far enough. Get out—"

"How do I look?"

He realized that nothing he said was having an effect on her. Short of dumping her out of the coffin, or threatening to bury her alive, he could think of no way to get her out of it.

He glared at her, biting mockery flowing to his lips. "I'm inclined to think that the dead have their hands clasped together upon their chests."

She folded her hands into a praying position between her breasts. "How 'bout now?"

"Mr. Brindisi!" Mr. Wainwright boomed as he sauntered up to Seneca's side. "Why, I've seen you twice today. Where is your wife?"

"She's lying in her coffin, Mr. Wainwright." Seneca gestured toward Peachy.

She wiggled her slender fingers in a wave of greeting.

Mr. Wainwright's shock was of such magnitude that he was forced to hold on to the coffin for support. But as soon as he realized what he was holding on to, he snatched his hand away as if the box had burned it off. "My word, Mrs. Brindisi! You are not even dead!"

"She's practicing," Seneca explained. He looked down at Peachy, rolling his eyes when he saw her make the sign of the cross. "Slipping away rather quickly, aren't you?" he taunted. "Before you go, you should know that you're supposed to have a lily in your hands." Scanning the gathering crowd, he spied a woman who held a basket of freshly picked honeysuckle. He offered her a gold coin for one long stem.

She gave him the entire basket, whereupon he proceeded to scatter the fragrant flowers all over Peachy's prone form. "Why settle for just one lily when you can have an entire bushel of honeysuckle?"

She could barely hear him. He spoke as though he was a mile away. Frowning slightly, she moved her hand to pick up a spray of the creamy flowers.

Her motions seemed distant, almost unreal to her, as if she were watching someone else do them. Curling her fingers around the stem of the blossoms, she discovered she couldn't feel it. She knew she was touching it; she could *see* it in her hand. And yet she felt no sensation of touching it at all.

"Seneca?" As she spoke his name, she felt a wave of extreme lethargy roll through her. Her limbs seemed heavy, too heavy to move. Her hand dropped back to her chest.

"Seneca." She could only whisper his name now. Panic set in. Something was wrong, she realized. Truly wrong. She opened her mouth to tell Seneca.

But she couldn't move her lips. Nor could she seem to take in enough air to quench the burning in her lungs.

Her image of Seneca began to blur. Within seconds, she could hardly see him. Her eyes closed of their own volition. As if they were sewn shut, she couldn't open them.

When Seneca saw her close her eyes, he rolled his own once more. She was playing the role of a lifeless person to the hilt, he realized. Why, she'd even managed to slow down her breathing; her breasts rose and fell only slightly. "Peachy, if you are satisfied that the coffin fits, I would appreciate it very much if you would cease your play-acting and get out of the box now. I'm hungry, wife, and want to go home."

She didn't answer. She didn't move.

Mr. Wainwright leaned over the coffin, studying her face. "She's become quite pallid, Mr. Brindisi. My, she is quite an actress to be able to pale at will. I don't believe I've ever seen such fine acting in all my life."

Before Seneca's very eyes, the color in Peachy's cheeks disappeared.

Thurlow Wadsworth McGee began to chatter wildly.

Seneca tensed, a flicker of anxiety sparking inside him. "Peachy? Peachy?"

"Oh, dear, Mr. Brindisi," Mr. Wainwright mumbled, "I do believe she's unwell!"

Seneca's hand shot out to grab Peachy's. Heinous disbelief spread through him when he discovered her hand was cold, too cold.

His stomach constricted into a hard knot of fear. Instantly, he snatched her out of the coffin, horrified when her head lolled over his arm. "My God," he whispered. "Get a doctor. Get a doctor. Dammit, get a doctor!"

"Dr. Hinston just left for Scarborough!" Mr. Wainwright declared.

"Catch him! Bring him to the cottage! *Now!*"

Mr. Wainwright rushed to obey.

Clutching Peachy's limp form tightly against his chest, Seneca jostled his way through the gaping people in the crowd and ran to the wagon. As he reached it, he spied a well-dressed gentleman riding into the village upon a fine thoroughbred horse.

Making a sudden decision, he raced toward the man. "I need your horse! Give me your—"

"Get away from me, peasant! I am the Earl of Leathshire!"

"And I am the *Crown Prince* of Aventine, dammit!" Seneca returned furiously.

The earl raised his riding crop.

The blow slammed across Seneca's neck. Instantly, another followed, sending streaks of pain into his temple. Enraged at his assailant and hysterical over Peachy's condition, Seneca growled a deadly sound and reached up to grab the man's forearm. One powerful yank sent the earl sprawling to the dusty ground.

One arm holding Peachy, Seneca used the other to pull himself into the saddle. Mounted, he sent the sleek chestnut into a smooth canter that soon became a breakneck gallop. In only minutes the snorting steed came to an abrupt stop in front of the cottage.

Seneca dismounted, holding Peachy as though she were fashioned of the most fragile crystal. One brutal kick at the door sent it flying off its hinges, and Seneca rushed inside.

In the bedroom, he lay his wife upon the bed and leaned over her. Her copper hair fell in shining waves around her white face. Her pale lips were parted, as if she were about to speak.

Seneca waited for them to move. He strained to hear the slightest sound, even the whisper of a breath.

He hoped in utter vain. His own breath came in rasping heaves.

He stared at her for a long while, memorizing each delicate feature on her face. "Peachy," he murmured at last, his voice cracking with pain. "Please—"

"Mr. Brindisi! Mr. Brindisi, I've brought Dr. Hinston!"

Seneca fairly lifted the doctor off the floor when he and Mr. Wainwright entered the bedroom. "You've got to save her! She— I— Something happened. Gold. I'll pay you in gold!" He snatched up the vase upon the small bedside table and dumped its contents at Peachy's feet.

A veritable fortune in solid gold gleamed upon the patchwork quilt. "More," Seneca mumbled almost incoherently. He raked his shaking fingers through his thick hair. "I've got more. I can get more. Jewels . . . too. Silver. For God's sake, I can give you anything you ask for!"

"Please, Mr. Brindisi." Dr. Hinston tried to soothe the distraught man. He took Seneca's arm and led him to the rocking chair. "You must calm yourself, sir. Sit down."

Seneca stared at the rocking chair, remembering the beautiful moments he'd spent in it this afternoon. With her. With Peachy, his wife. "This chair . . . No. I— I don't want to sit down."

"Very well." Dr. Hinston moved to the bed.

"I'll be outside," Mr. Wainwright said. "If you need

anything . . . I'll see to the earl's horse. And the front door, as well. It's come off its hinges. I'll be outside." He left quietly.

While Dr. Hinston examined Peachy, Seneca paced from one end of the bed to the other. His arms clasped tightly across his chest, his fingers dug into the contracted muscles of his forearms. He couldn't bear the waiting, the not knowing. The doctor was taking too long. What was the matter with the doctor?

Every glance at Peachy jolted him with fresh anguish. He perspired profusely. "Hot," he whispered. "Peachy— Maybe she's hot."

He opened the window. He closed his eyes. A country breeze swept across his face, gently ruffling his hair. He took in a deep breath of it and caught the scent of clean dirt and stream water. Trees. Furry animals. Leaves and fresh firewood and melting sunshine.

Each fragrance reminded him of Peachy.

He listened. To sounds, simple and beautiful. A bird burst into song; another joined it, and they harmonized a soft, sweet melody. A ground creature crunched through brittle leaves in the forest. The stream bubbled and splashed.

Songs. Meandering. Bubbling.

Those things were Peachy.

Seneca leaned his head out of the window; his broad shoulders wouldn't fit through it. He opened his eyes.

And he saw his ropes. They swayed in the warm breeze.

Watch me, Peachy.

I'm a-watchin', darlin'.

His heart turned over. Sickening dread exploded inside him. He couldn't think coherently. His thoughts weaved into a thick tangle he couldn't loosen. "My slingshot," he muttered. "I think I lost . . . my slingshot, Dr. Hinston."

Dr. Hinston tugged his stethoscope off his neck.

"I'll find it," Seneca whispered. He pivoted away from the window and started for the door.

"Mr. Brindisi?"

Seneca stared at the doctor. He couldn't ask the question hammering through his mind, his heart, his very soul. The words to the question wouldn't string together for him.

"She's alive, Mr. Brindisi," Dr. Hinston announced quietly. "However, I cannot say how much longer she'll— She's slipping away from us, sir. She shows all the symptoms of being—"

"Yes, symptoms," Seneca said, nodding. "She had all the symptoms. It's tipinosis, Dr. Hinston. That's what's killing her. Don't you see? You've but to give her the medicine for tipinosis!"

"Tipinosis?" Dr. Hinston scowled. "Mr. Brindisi, I have been a doctor for over thirty years. I assure you there is no such thing as tipinosis."

Seneca lowered his gaze to the floor. "I told her that. She wouldn't believe me."

"Mr. Brindisi—"

"She has herbs," Seneca remembered out loud. "You can give her the herbs." He tore up the closet, seeking Peachy's bags of herbs. "Here. They're here, right here." He opened the sack and shoved his hand inside. His fingers touched soft parcels and something small and hard. Pinching the hard thing, he withdrew his hand.

The rock. The diamondy rock he'd tried to give her. She'd saved it. Here, in her bag of precious herbs.

"Mr. Brindisi?"

Seneca pocketed the rock, then thrust the sack into Dr. Hinston's hands. "With love, she said. Yes, that's what she said. Herbs work better when mixed with love. And lard. I've seen her use lard. And onions and garlic. Eggshells. Water. I'll get the water. Mr. Wainwright and I will mix everything for you."

Dr. Hinston followed him into the other room. "I've no knowledge of these herbs, Mr. Brindisi," he said, setting Peachy's bag of cures on the kitchen table. "What I'm trying to tell you is that it appears that your wife has been poisoned. And because I've no idea what substance she injested, I have no way of knowing what sort of antidote might counteract it."

A bitter cold settled over Seneca. He shook with it, his massive frame shuddering uncontrollably.

Dr. Hinston forced him to sit down in one of the chairs at the table.

Seneca stared. At the table. At the cracks in it. At the

basket. Filled with fruit and cheese and bread. The checkered cloth that had covered it rested beside it. Bits of cheese, some white, some yellow, were scattered around the table, a few of them on the checkered cloth as well.

His tortured gaze fell upon a tiny field mouse. It lay on its back, its tiny hands and feet pointed toward the ceiling. Two more mice reposed nearby.

Seneca felt his eyes sting. "She always put the food away, Dr. Hinston," he slurred. "She locked it in the cabinet so the mice wouldn't get it. But today ... She didn't have time, you understand. We left so quickly. So very quickly. And do you see what has happened because of our rush? The mice. They've gotten into her basket."

He stared so intently at the mice that soon he could see nothing else. Why didn't they move? he wondered. They just lay there, looking as though they were dead.

A hazy thought drifted along the edges of his mind. Like fog too thick to see through. The mice were dead. He understood that now.

Another thought fluttered into his brain. Its arrival cut through the murkiness of his other musings. One of the mice had a morsel of cheese in its mouth.

A deeper realization began to haunt him. A phantom bringing grim tidings, it slithered from his subconscious. The mice had eaten the cheese.

So had Peachy.

The mice were dead.

Seneca stopped breathing. His blood slid through his veins like slivers of ice.

Comprehension struck with devastating clarity.

In his frantic haste to leave, Seneca turned the table over. He rushed blindly toward the door.

Mr. Wainwright had only just finished reattaching the door to its hinges when Seneca burst through it. It crashed to the ground. "Mr. Brindisi! What—"

Seneca grabbed the man's collar. "That woman! That Mrs. Belle— She poisoned Peachy! *Where is she?*"

"*What!* I— She— We— Dr. Hinston and I passed her and her nephew while coming here! I— Oh, Mr. Brindisi, she had your wagon! I thought little of it before, but— She must have stolen it from the village! She—"

"Dammit, tell me where you saw her!"

Mr. Wainwright's eyes bulged. "She was on her way to Scarborough!"

Seneca spun in the dirt and made a mad dash for the swift horse tethered to a hitching pole. Grabbing the reins, he leapt into the saddle and sent the steed into a thundering gallop down the road to Scarborough.

He leaned low over the horse's neck.

He raced against the wind.

Against time. The measly amount Peachy had left.

With a long, slender switch, Orabelle began to beat the donkey unmercifully. Her sack of herbs, looped around her neck, swung wildly, bumping into her scrawny shoulders.

Bubba sat beside her, his huge body taking up most of the seat. Blubbering with thick sobs, he heard the poor donkey scream and watched it shudder with pain. "St-stop, Aunt Orabelle," he murmured through his tears. "Don't hit him no more. Please don't, Aunt Orabelle."

Orabelle paid no attention to him and continued to flog the slow-moving beast. "Go!" she shrieked. "Faster! Faster!"

She had to get to Scarborough. Ships arrived at and left the port continuously. She had to be on one of them soon.

Hurry! It was imperative to hurry! The chances of anyone discovering the truth of what she'd done were remote at best, but she would take no chances.

Peachy was dead. If not, she soon would be. Orabelle had seen her lose consciousness with her own eyes. And how appropriate that she'd lost it in her own coffin!

Yes, yes, the bitch had eaten the poisoned fruit. Or maybe the cheese, or the bread. Or all three.

The golden creek belonged to Orabelle now. She struck the donkey again. She wanted the gold. The donkey wouldn't run. Her lash bit into the tortured animal's back again and again and again . . . She wanted to see the gold!

"No!" Bubba hollered. "You're makin' him *bleed!* I'm takin' him to Cousin Princess Peachy! She'll make him better!" His beefy hands grappled with Orabelle's bony ones while he tried to get hold of the reins.

Furious, Orabelle turned the switch onto Bubba, thrashing at his fat, tear-stained face until he was forced to let go of her and shield himself from the stinging blows. "Idiot! She's *dead!* She ate the poison, Bubba! She—"

She closed her mouth suddenly. A drumming sound hit her ears. Like a faraway rumble of thunder.

Like the pounding of hoofbeats.

A sense of foreboding slithered through her.

She whirled, gasping when she caught sight of a cloud of dust in the distance. It moved. Came toward her with astonishing speed. A horse galloped in the middle of it. Its rider leaned low over its neck. The man was still too far away for Orabelle to see clearly, but she knew who he was.

The prince.

Screaming, she spun around again and scourged the donkey repeatedly. The beast's scream collided with hers, creating a cacophony that battered Bubba's ears, causing him to whimper and wail with great bursts of fear and confusion and utter misery.

Completely maddened, Orabelle threw the switch into the road, then thrust her heavy bag of belongings into Bubba's lap. "Get me down! We've got to *run!* We've got to *hide!* Bubba, they're going to take you to jail! You'll never get out!"

Terror clawed up Bubba's spine. He threw himself from the wagon, grunting when Orabelle jumped on top of him. He watched her scurry down the road. "Hide," he whispered. "I gotta hide." Crazed with fear, he staggered to his feet and heaved himself over the stone wall. Just as he began to fall to the other side, he saw a big brown horse race by.

Seneca cared nothing about the man who was escaping, and directed the horse toward the old woman in the pea-green cloak. *The murderous Mrs. Belle,* he seethed. Rage narrowing his eyes, he urged the horse to an even faster gait.

The loud hammering of the horse's hooves as he bore down on her pounded into Orabelle's brain. She cast a glance over her shoulder, her panic-stricken gaze clashing with one of blue fire. A fire so close now she felt its flames sear into her. "No!"

His horse still at a full gallop, Seneca swooped down and coiled his arm around her thin waist. In one smooth motion, he hauled her off the ground and flung her over his thighs. Deaf to the woman's frenetic screams, he turned his mount around and sent him thundering back toward the cottage.

The short time it took to get there seemed like an eternity. When the horse finally galloped into the yard, Seneca pulled back on the reins so quickly the horse reared in fright. Mr. Wainwright promptly grabbed hold of the nervous animal's bridle.

Seneca plunged out of the saddle and dragged his screaming captive across the threshold of the cottage. Panting with exertion, fear, and all-consuming rage, he stopped in the kitchen and took firm hold of her thin shoulders. "Make the antidote." He heard his order flow forth on a bare whisper. "Make the antidote," he repeated, this time a bit louder. "Make the antidote, dammit!" he yelled, his voice crashing through the small room.

Orabelle stared into his glittering eyes. An eerie tranquility permeated her scrawny body. She was caught. She'd never escape. She was going to jail, and she'd rot for the rest of her life behind bars.

But she'd die in her prison cell with the sweet satisfaction of knowing that she'd killed the bitch who put her there.

Seneca watched her thin lips twist into an icy smile that froze him to the very marrow of his bones. "Make the anti—"

"No."

"Make it! *Now!*"

"No."

"For God's sake, she's dying! You've got to—"

"I want her to die." Orabelle began to laugh, her laughter a cackling shriek.

God help her, Seneca raged, he was going to kill her with his bare hands. His fingers inched toward her wrinkled neck, meeting a thin cord of leather. He looked down. Between the woman's sagging breasts lay a pouch. Seneca ripped it off.

"The antidote," Orabelle announced triumphantly. "It's

in there. Herbs. At least forty or fifty different kinds. I wish you the best of luck discovering the magical combination of the correct ones. And be very careful, Your Royal Highness. You might end up giving the bitch more poison instead."

Seneca stared at the bag, his hand crushing around it. No longer able to control his violent emotions, he threw his head back and roared with fury and helplessness ... and the profound agony he felt at knowing that Peachy was going to die.

His horrible scream brought Mr. Wainwright. "What—"

"Mr. Brindisi," Dr. Hinston called from the bedroom door, "I think you had better come now."

Mr. Wainwright pulled Seneca's arm. "Mr. Brindisi, for the love of God, go to your wife! I'll see to Mrs. Belle!"

Seneca raised his head, only to lower his chin to his chest. A wretchedness he'd never known made him stagger as he entered the bedroom.

Dr. Hinston laid his hand on Seneca's shoulder. "Go to her."

"Is she ... Is she—"

"No, Mr. Brindisi, she's still alive. Go to her now. Tell her how much you love her."

"You're saying I should say good-bye to her," Seneca answered with a hoarse groan. "You're saying ... that she'll be gone— Soon. Soon."

Dr. Hinston didn't reply. Quietly, he left the room.

Seneca approached the bed. Sunlight dappled the colorful quilt and streamed across Peachy's colorless face.

In that moment, he shattered. His mind, his heart, his soul ... Everything she'd ever touched inside him broke into millions of pieces.

And his fragile hold on rationality snapped.

With a gutteral moan, Seneca threw himself down beside her, his weight causing Peachy to roll into his arms. "Just like always," he whispered. "You always did this ... roll into my arms. Whenever I got into bed beside you, there you were, rolling straight into me."

He gathered her closer. "Cold," he rasped. "You're so cold, sweetheart." Reaching over her, he pulled the quilt atop her body and snuggled into it with her. "Don't be cold anymore. Be warm, Princess. Please be warm."

He slipped his hand into the thick flames of her hair. "I'll talk to you, wife. I'll tell you things, remind you of things you wouldn't want to forget."

Pressing kisses to her chilled forehead, he began to rock her in his arms. "Remember when you suggested I sleep on a pinto bean to prove I was a prince? I wanted to laugh, but I didn't because that was before you taught me to laugh again."

He swallowed thickly. "You wanted possum stew tonight," he recalled aloud. "I didn't find a possum for you. I don't know what one looks like. Then there was the time you informed me that Tivon's punishment of painting the stall doors was not a punishment at all. You spilled the suit of armor down the staircase and thought you'd killed a man."

He frowned, realizing he was relating the memories out of order. He wanted to tell them to her in the way that they'd happened.

But he couldn't remember their sequence. He shut his eyes and hated the darkness. He opened them again and hated the sunshine, too.

And recollections continued to twist through his mind.

"Remember when you called Veston Sherringham a 'lard ass'? Did you know, Peachy, that I laughed inside when you said that? I wanted so badly to be angry with you, but you wouldn't let me."

He positioned her so that her cheek lay against his shoulder. "Thurlow Wadsworth McGee had his own little crown. You made it for him. Remember the turkey with the yellow rock in its throat and the little figurine you wanted to hold? Do you ever miss your red velvet blanket, Peachy?"

Dying. She was dying. And he couldn't do a damn thing to save her. He, the Crown Prince of Aventine, who could buy anything in the world, could not purchase Peachy's life.

His eyes misted. "I've laughed," he whispered ever so softly. "Often ... With you. But I've never— I've never cried with you. You've never seen me cry, Peachy. Not ever."

He brushed his thumb across her slender throat and stared at the contrast, his skin dark, hers light. "Dark," he murmured. "Like shadows. And midnight. White. Like cream. And magnolias. You. And me. Me. And you. Midnight and magnolias."

He stared at his hand on her throat for a long moment, then at her closed eyes. "I promised I would tell you the story of the angel. She lived in a frame in the tower. But she wasn't really made of paint. Not to me, she wasn't. She was alive, Peachy, very alive. Warm and compassionate, and she listened to everything I told her. I loved her with all my heart, and then I left her. There in the tower, all by herself. Because, you see, I had grown up then, and I didn't need her."

He sucked in a ragged breath. "I was wrong. I needed her, but I'd forgotten about her. And then ... Then she came back. When I needed her more than ever before, she came back to me. She crashed into my room one night. She slid across the marble floor. Two weeks later I married her. And she wore a chandelier and a candlestick holder to her wedding."

He buried his face into her hair. The lemon-cream scent of magnolias swirled into him. He breathed deeply of the sweet fragrance, longing for it to soothe him.

It didn't.

"That omen ... The ruby-throated hummingbird. You were supposed to be happy for the rest of ... Were you happy, Princess? Did I make you happy?"

Raw with grief, he lifted his head and gently pressed his warm lips to her cold ones, wishing beyond all reason that he could infuse life back into her.

"Peachy, don't leave me," he begged, his voice strangled. "Don't, God, please don't."

His tear-filled gaze touched every part of her beautiful face. "Angel," he whispered tenderly to her. "Wife. I love you, Peachy. You're ... You're my very best friend."

With a cry of soul-wrenching anguish, he sat up and swept her into his lap, holding her as he would a newborn child. His shoulders shook as deep sobs broke free.

Seneca wept. His low cries filled the room; his hot tears spilled to Peachy's breasts.

"Cousin Prince Seneca?"

At the sound of the unfamiliar voice, one that had interrupted his last moments with Peachy, Seneca felt fury burn into him. He snapped up his head. Through his tears, he made out the shape of a man, a very large man.

"I'm Bubba. I come back. I have a secret. Uh . . . I thinked about jail for a long time. I can't go to jail, Cousin Prince Seneca. I didn't do nothin' wrong. Aunt Orabelle— She musta lied to me. I come to tell you the secret."

Secret. Seneca mouthed the word, unable to speak, unable to understand anything the man said.

Bubba walked into the room, stopping by the bed. He held up a pouch.

Seneca recognized it as Mrs. Belle's sack of herbs.

"The secret," Bubba tried to explain. "Uh . . . It's in this bag. She didn't never know. I never told her. I watched her make it one time, y'see, and I 'membered. Aunt Orabelle never, ever knowed. I keeped the secret."

Seneca stared at the dim-witted man, wondering who he was.

"Cousin Princess Peachy ain't gonna die."

Seneca's heart began to thrash. "What did you say?"

Bubba leaned down and laid his massive hand upon Peachy's shoulder. "She ain't gonna die."

"Why do you say that?" Seneca demanded.

Bubba grinned and held up the pouch again. "Cuz I— Uh . . . Cuz I know the secret to the medicine."

Chapter 19

❧❧

"**D**ang it, Seneca, put me down! I can walk to the ship-boat landin' by mysef!" Peachy declared, swiping at her hair as the swift sea breeze blew it into her face.

Looking around, she saw that her shouting had attracted stares from the Scarborough townspeople who milled through the street. But she didn't care. She'd had more than enough of Seneca's overwhelming concern for her well-being. Lord o' mercy, he'd been hovering over her for more than a week! "Quit a-treatin' me like I was as helpless as a gawdang mute in handcuffs, and put me down."

Smiling, he hugged her tightly to him. God, it was so good to hear her cursing at him again. He looked forward to many years of her obscene language.

"Uh . . . I'll hold her now, Cousin Prince Seneca," Bubba offered. Gently, he placed Thurlow Wadsworth McGee onto his shoulder, then lifted his thick arms in preparation to receive Peachy. "I'll carry her to the ship. I'll take her, and you can bring the donkey. You said I could take the donkey, Cousin Prince Seneca. You said he could live with your horse. Uh . . . You said nobody wouldn't never hit him again. I'm takin' my donkey to Aventine."

Looking into Bubba's huge, hope-filled eyes, Seneca felt deep affection. The young man had a heart bigger than the Aventine merchant ship that swayed near the landing. And if not for him, Peachy would have died.

But she hadn't. Bubba's secret, the recipe to the antidote, had revived her only a few hours after Dr. Hinston had administered it to her. By the next day she'd eaten a bit of food, and by the second day she'd tried to get up to bathe in the stream. On the third day there had been no holding her back. She'd seen to the lashing wounds on the donkey's back, cleaned the cottage, hunted down a possum, made stew, and carved another slingshot to replace the one Seneca had lost.

And he'd not left her side for an instant.

"Can I hold her, Cousin Prince Seneca?" Bubba asked again, his arms still outstretched. "Iffen— Uh ... Iffen y'let me hold her, I promise I won't ask her to marry me no more."

His promise brought a smile to Peachy's mouth. "Bubba, I done tole you that iffen y'weren't my cousin, I'd leave Seneca and marry you quicker'n the flames o' hell can scorch a feather. Y'know yore my darlin'est darlin'."

Bubba blushed scarlet. Blinking bashfully, he gazed at Seneca. "Uh ... It ain't my fault that she likes me better'n she likes you, Cousin Prince Seneca. I'm sorry she done falled in love with me. Hope y'ain't mad at me none." He crowned his apology with a big, toothy grin. "Can I hold her now?"

Chuckling, Seneca nodded. "Of course you may hold her, Bubba. I'm sure she'd enjoy it immensely."

As she was passed from her husband's arms to her cousin's, Peachy succeeded in squirming to the ground. "Ain't nobody a-holdin' me, and that's it, hear?"

"Mr. Brindisi!"

Seneca turned and saw Mr. Wainwright running toward him, Morton loping along beside him. "Ah, I'm so glad you've come, Mr. Wainwright. We are preparing to leave, and I would have felt terrible had I not been able to say good-bye and thank you for all you've done for us."

Mr. Wainwright beamed. "You're quite welcome. For everything. You— Oh, I almost forgot why I rushed to find you. This letter arrived for you. It comes from London."

Seneca took the letter, opened it, and read it quickly. Its

contents prompted him to nod in deep satisfaction. "Your Aunt Orabelle will never hurt you again, Bubba. She's behind bars in London. The authorities possess all the evidence they need to prove her guilt, and she'll be spending the rest of her life in prison."

Bubba began to jump up and down, his actions forcing Thurlow Wadsworth McGee to hang on for dear life. "And— Uh . . . And what about Dr. Greely? What about that doctor that Aunt Orabelle paid to lie about the disease?"

Seneca folded the letter and slipped it inside his shirt. "We haven't heard from the North Carolina authorities yet, Bubba, but I'm sure we'll receive word soon. Dr. Greely will be found and brought to trial for his part in the crime. You aren't to worry about him. He's not going to hurt you, do you understand?"

Nodding, Bubba turned to Mr. Wainwright. "I git the cabin in Possum Holler," he told the confused man. "Most o' the time, I'll live in the castle, but— Uh . . . I git to go back to North Carolina anytime I want to. There ain't a speck o' gold in the crick, but I don't care nothin' about that no more. Miz Mackintosh is gonna make me socks and suppers when I'm there. But then I'll come back to the castle cuz the sheep look like big white dogs, Mr. Wainwright. They look like Morton. But I git to have real dogs. As many as I want. Well— Uh . . . Bye, Mr. Wainwright. Bye, Morton. I'm gittin' on the boat now."

"Castle?" Mr. Wainwright repeated, thoroughly bewildered.

Peachy took Mr. Wainwright's hand, pumping it firmly. "Thanky fer all y'done, Mr. Wainwright. You've been a real good friend. The kind o' friend who'll hep you outen when both yore arms is broke and yore nose needs a-pickin'."

Mr. Wainwright gasped. But in the next moment he smiled. And then he threw back his head and laughed uproariously.

"Good-bye, Mr. Wainwright," Seneca said when the man had recovered from his fit of mirth. "We are indeed very grateful for all you've done. And if there is any way

I can ever repay you, please do not hesitate to let me know."

Mr. Wainwright waved away Seneca's offer. "I wouldn't dream of asking you for a thing, Mr. Brindisi. I would, however, enjoy corresponding with you and your wife. How should I post my letters?"

"Send them to Aventine."

"Aventine," Mr. Wainwright repeated thoughtfully. "An island kingdom, is it not? Situated somewhere in the North Sea?"

"Yes."

"Ah, then your sovereign is King Zane. Yes, I've read about him in the papers. He exports paschal flowers. Makes a bloody fortune, from what I've heard. Have you ever met him, Mr. Brindisi?"

Seneca took hold of the donkey's halter. "He's my father."

Mr. Wainwright scowled and stepped backwards. "Your father."

"Yes. You see, Mr. Wainwright, I am the Crown Prince of Aventine. Farewell to you, sir. And the best of luck to you always."

"The Crown Prince ... Eh ... Yes, Mr. Brindisi. Of course. Yes, of course. Whatever you say. Farewell."

Mr. Wainwright watched as Seneca left to join Peachy and Bubba at the dock. "The Prince of Aventine, indeed," he muttered, shaking his head. "My goodness, Morton, they are truly the strangest, most bizarre people I believe I have ever known."

Peachy bent down, scooped up a handful of Aventine soil, and brought it close to her face. "We're home," she whispered, her breath blowing the glittering sand in her hands. Looking up, she saw Bubba hurrying down the path that led inland, his donkey in tow. "Bubba, don'tcha want to ride to the castle in the coach, darlin'?" she called out to him.

"No! I want to run in them— Uh ... In them meadows and play with them sheep! They look jest like Morton! Bye, Cousin Princess Peachy! Bye, Cousin Prince Seneca!

Bye, Thurlow Wadsworth McGee! Bye, soldiers! Bye, ship! Bye, sailors! Bye, ocean!"

Chuckling, Seneca waved good-bye to Bubba, the newest member of the royal family. Still smiling, he turned back to Medard, the captain of the guards. "My father knows of our return?"

Medard gave an affirmative nod. "Word was sent to the palace as soon as the ship was spotted and we learned that Your Royal Highness was aboard."

Seneca handed Medard a sealed letter. "Have one of your men take this to the palace. It is to be delivered to either Ketty or Nydia, both of whom are the princess's personal maids. The instructions detailed in this letter are to be followed exactly and are to be completed by the time the princess and I arrive."

Medard took the letter, bowed, and left to give orders to one of his men.

Turning toward the coach, Seneca saw that Peachy and Thurlow Wadsworth McGee were already seated in it. He joined them, tucked Peachy into the curve of his arm, and waved the driver onwards.

After only a few moments, the coach rumbled along the path that wound through Aventine's emerald meadows, the men-at-arms accompanying the vehicle on all sides. Peachy wished she could see the villages, but they lay behind the rolling hills to her left. Instead, she drank in the sight of the lush fields. "Well, sweet Lord o' mercy, Seneca! Look at all them shepherds! And they ain't young'uns, neither! They're grown-up men!"

Seneca studied the people guarding the sheep. Peachy was right. There was not a single child to be seen. The men were the real shepherds of Aventine.

Odd. If the men were tending the sheep, who was tending the paschal fields? Had his father sent the *children* to the flower fields? Were the little ones now stooping over plants for hours a day? What other explanation could there be?

"Seneckers?" Peachy asked, noticing his dark expression. "What's the mat—"

"It's nothing, Princess," he tried to reassure her. "I'm

only a bit worried about you. You've only just recovered from—"

"Oh, hesh up. I'm fine. As a matter o' fact, as soon as I git changed, I'm gonna go see Gussie. Then I'm gonna stop by the villages and visit the people. I want to see Marlie, and Tivon, and Mintor, and Gervase, and the hogs, too."

Seneca made no comment, but he had other plans for Peachy, plans that did not include visiting. On the contrary, his plans demanded privacy. The privacy only his bed-chambers would provide.

A short while later, the coach halted in front of the Grand Entry of the palace. Tiblock was the first person Seneca and Peachy saw as they entered the great marble foyer. The servant had just stepped off the last step of the staircase.

"Tiblock," Seneca said.

Tiblock scurried forward. "Your Highnesses," he greeted them, bowing his head. "Welcome home."

Peachy noticed something different about the man. After a moment, she realized what it was.

He was smiling. The unfamiliar sight both confused and pleased her.

"Tiblock, I wish to see my father," Seneca announced.

"Very good, sir. His Majesty is in the blue drawing rooms. I—" He broke off suddenly when he spied two young maids in the corridor, heading for the servants' stairs at the end of the hall. The maids were carrying huge sacks of pristine towels in their arms.

One of the girls dropped hers.

Tiblock turned back to the prince. "If Your Highness will excuse me, I must assist the maids with the towels. The towels are for Your Highness's bath, and as Your Highness can see, one of the girls has spilled her stack."

Astonished, Seneca could only nod his permission for Tiblock to leave.

Peachy saw Tiblock take almost all the towels from the two maids. He left them with only two each to carry, then disappeared up the servants' stairs. "That's a purty nice thing fer him to do, huh? A-hepin' them girls. And he was a-smilin', too. Jest a-grinnin' like a little dog with a big bone. Y'know, Seneckers? I'd bet all my egg money that he's been a-sippin' at that medicine I give to yore paw. That cure fer orneriness. I'm a-tellin' you, Seneca, it really does work. I ain't never knowed it to fail."

"Well, I'll be damned." Shaking his head, Seneca escorted Peachy to the blue drawing rooms.

He tensed when he caught sight of his father. The king stood before a vast collection of wooden figures that were spread out upon the table near the fireplace. Seneca had never seen the wooden objects before, but reminded himself that he was not here to discuss knickknacks.

"Father."

The king spun around. "Seneca, I will have you know that you interrupted the course of my ship. The vessel upon which you returned to Aventine was supposed to sail from Scarborough to London. My cargo of—"

"I'm glad to see you again, too, Father," Seneca quipped sarcastically. He led Peachy to the settee and remained standing beside her. "And now you will tell me where all the peasant children are."

"The peasant children?" The king rubbed his chin.

"Are they in the paschal fields?" Seneca pressed.

"The paschal fields? Why, whatever would they be doing there? To the best of my knowledge the only things you will find in the paschal fields are sheep."

"Sheep?" Peachy blurted.

"Sheep?" Seneca echoed. "The sheep are—"

"Well, not all of them," the king clarified. "The flocks must take turns. That seemed fair enough to me. One village's flock goes one day, another village's flock goes the next, and so on."

Seneca frowned in utter confusion. "Father, what are the sheep doing in the paschal fields?"

The king picked up one of the wooden figures. "I would guess that they are eating the paschal, Seneca. If you were a sheep, isn't that what you would do?"

"If I— If I were a sheep?" Seneca frowned. He'd never heard his father speak in such a manner. Mute with disbelief, he stared at his sire.

Peachy decided to handle the rest of the interrogation. "Where's all the young'uns? They're usually scattered all ever'where, but we didn't see nary a one whilst we was a-ridin' up here."

The king took a moment to caress the wooden figure he held. "The children are painting."

"They're a-paintin'." Peachy felt just as perplexed as Seneca.

The king set down the wooden figure, picked up another, and began to take a walk around the room. "Yes, they like it. Odd, really. I never thought of painting houses as something diverting, but the children are having the time of their lives. I went to see the new houses the other day, and one child splattered paint on my shoe. It was just as well. I never did like those shoes, as they pinched my toes."

Seneca raked his fingers through his hair. "What houses, Father?"

"The peasants' houses. The new ones. The old ones were torn down. At my command, all of Aventine assisted in the building of the new ones."

Peachy struggled to understand. "Even the noblemen heped?"

The king nodded. "Well, all except Veston Sherringham. He is too busy making a cradle. Agusta was of the inclination that her firstborn should sleep in a cradle made by his father's own hands. Veston is not as good with wood as I am, however, so I have consented to help him. I'm to visit him this very afternoon."

Peachy and Seneca stared at the king, then at each other, then at the king again.

"Yore good with wood?" Peachy asked.

The king pointed to all the wooden figures. "I whittled each of them. And if you would care to have a closer look, you will see how superb they are."

Obediently, Peachy examined the figures. Many were of animals. Some were of trees, and flowers, and fruits, and a wide assortment of other everyday objects. "You really whittled these?"

"I did," the king replied proudly.

Peachy picked up a carving of a pig.

"The hogs are loose again," the king informed her. "They have been for quite some time now. A little girl named Marlie came to the palace and offered me her kitten, Rainbow, in exchange for my permission to allow the villagers to free their swine. It was quite the most endearing plea I have heard, but I refused her offer. Well, I couldn't very well take the child's pet, could I? I did, however, allow the swine to be freed, but only because I always thought there were too many nuts in the forests, anyway. Those hogs— The snorting creatures are becoming rather rotund. Would you care to know why I became interested in whittling, Peachy?"

When she heard him speak her name—something he'd never done before—she was too surprised to answer out loud. She nodded instead.

The king pointed to the hearth.

Peachy saw the cane she'd made leaning against the marble fireplace.

"I was impressed with the skill you put into the making of the cane," the king informed her. "Curious to know whether I possessed the same skills, I took up the pastime of whittling. Tiblock forced me to stay in bed for weeks. The man thinks he is my mother!"

Peachy grinned.

Seneca could only stare, his mouth open.

"I had little to do during those weeks," the king elaborated. "Did you know, Peachy, that you left your knife in my bedchambers? It was only a matter of having wood brought to me, and I began. Well, you *did* advise me to take up whittling, did you not? And did you not also say that it would have a calming effect on me? God knows I certainly needed something that would calm me. What with Mother Tiblock fussing over me at all hours of the day and night, I nearly lost my sanity. I will tell you now that I am every bit as talented with wood as you are."

Peachy's grin spread from ear to ear. The king had been taking his medicines. There was no other explanation for his change in mood.

The king raised his chin at her. "You have wounded my feelings. Here I have been walking all around the room, and you have said nothing at all about the absence of my limp."

"Y'been a-usin' the remedies. I done figgered that outen."

Seneca moved to the window, where his father stood. "You made use of the cane as well?"

"I did."

"But you said it would make you look old, Father. You said—"

"Nonsense. I never said that. Why, it would be ridiculous for one not to use a cane if one needed it, wouldn't it? You aren't saying that your sire is ridiculous, are you, Seneca?"

"Well, no, but I— That is to say . . ."

"You have yet to apologize for interrupting the course of my ship, Seneca. The vessel was fairly laden with cargo, and now it will be weeks before it arrives in London."

Seneca deliberated on what his father had said. "How is it possible for you to continue with your exportation of paschal if the sheep are eating it?"

The king ambled away from the window. "I am no longer exporting paschal."

Seneca was stunned. "Father, I'm afraid I don't understand."

The king rolled his eyes. "And it is no wonder that you do not! If you had stayed in Aventine instead of running all around England, you would have been here when the all-important and most extraordinary letter arrived! As it was, you—"

"Letter, Father? What letter?"

The king sighed impatiently. "The letter from Queen Victoria! Peachy sent the queen a wool sweater, did she not?"

"Yes, but what has that to do with—"

"Really, Seneca, try to pay attention," the king blustered. "The queen expressed her astonishment over the Aventine wool, proclaiming it to be the thickest, softest, and warmest wool she had ever felt. I, of course, was already aware of its superior quality, and informed her of that fact."

Seneca gave his father a doubtful look.

The king ignored it. "Queen Victoria desired more of

our wool immediately. I have sent her eight shiploads so far, and I have sent six more to Australia. We need more ships, Seneca! We shall purchase an entire fleet!"

"Father—"

"Those Australians ... It's true they are practically overrun by sheep, but their animals are quite inferior to ours. Aventine sheep, you see, have the benefit of the paschal, which, as you well know, grows nowhere else but Aventine. The paschal is the reason why our sheep's wool is extraordinary, which is also why the sheep are in the fields consuming the flowers."

Seneca gave his father a wry smile. "And no one had to tell you about the connection between the paschal and the sheep's wool, correct? You deduced that all by yourself."

"Quite right, I did, indeed. Yes, I have known for a very long while."

Seneca saw his father's eyes twinkle. The rare sight amazed him.

"As for the shepherds," the king continued, "I have had new homes built for them because it would be unwise not to take proper care of the very people who raise the incredible sheep. The shepherds still tend to the paschal, but they do so happily because their sheep walk right along behind them eating it."

He smiled at his son. "We have a veritable gold mine in our hands, Seneca. Aventine wool is becoming more famous even as we speak, selling for five times as much as the paschal ever did. And as I was saying, if you had stayed in Aventine like a good king should, you would know all about the stupendous things that have occurred in your absence."

Seneca nodded. "I'm sorry. We were on our honeymoon. We— I ..." He frowned deeply, overcome by astonishment. "What— What did you say, Father?" he whispered.

"I said that you ought to have stayed in Aventine like a good king should."

"*King?*" Peachy exclaimed. "*King?* But Seneca's only the prince. What—"

"He will be king as soon as the preparations for the coronation are completed. I am stepping down from the throne. While I no longer suffer the pain I once did, I am tired. Too tired to continue ruling the kingdom. There is more to life than ordering people about, Seneca, and you would do well to understand that! There is whittling. Yes, whittling is definitely one of the finer things of life. I am going to spend the rest of my days whittling."

Seneca cleared his throat. "Father—"

"Seneca, you are the most ungrateful son any man could have. Why, I am giving you the throne, and you have yet to thank me. What's more, I am giving you a kingdom free of problems. The peasants are happy, the sheep are happy, even the pigs are happy. And the ships leave full every day. I cannot imagine a son more ungrateful than you."

Seneca was about to defend himself when his father suddenly tempered the admonishment by reaching out his hand for a handshake.

Seneca stared at the wrinkled hand. He didn't want to shake it. In light of all the new and profound emotions inside him, a handshake wasn't enough.

He wanted to hug his sire.

Unsure of how his father would react, he lifted his hands very slowly and gently placed them on the king's shoulders.

The king stiffened.

Dismayed, Seneca started to lower his hands.

The king covered them with his own.

And in the next moment, for the first time in all his life, Seneca understood what it was like to be in his father's embrace.

Tremorously, the king patted his son's back. "Well, Seneca, you know you want to say it. Now is the time, as I am off for the Sherringham estate."

Seneca understood immediately what his father was telling him. For a moment his eyes locked with Peachy's tear-filled gaze, then he stared into his father's robin's-egg-blue eyes. As a deep wave of love streamed through him, he whispered the one name he'd longed to say for years.

"Papa."

As soon as Seneca carried Peachy into his apartments, they saw it. It stood in front of the fireplace, gleaming in the late afternoon sunshine that streamed in from the window.

A handcarved cradle.

They both knew the king had made it.

Seneca grinned. "A rather broad hint, wouldn't you say?"

Peachy slid her hand over the sleek slats that lined the sides of the baby bed. "He must want him some grand-young'uns real bad, Seneckers."

He took her into his arms, holding her close. "And I want my son."

"Could be a daughter. I done tole you that, but yore too hardheaded to listen good."

He gave her a stern look. "I'll be king soon, wife, and I am hereby giving you the royal command to produce a son."

She smiled into his sapphire eyes. "Well, I ain't never disobeyed you since I got here. Not nary a time, so I reckon I better commence a-gittin' busy with the makin's o' that boy. Y'wouldn't mind a-hepin' me along with that, would you?"

"Mind?" He swept her off the floor and carried her into his bedchambers. There, he sat down in a chair beside the bed, keeping Peachy in his lap.

The chair moved. Peachy looked down and saw it was a rocking chair. "Where'd this come from? I don't mem'ry a-seein' it in here afore."

Slowly, he began to unfasten the buttons on her blouse, then slipped his hand inside to caress her. "I sent a message to Ketty and Nydia, instructing them to make sure there was a rocking chair in my chambers when we arrived at the palace. I told you that I would love you in a rocking chair until we learned of our son's beginnings, and I meant what I said."

She scrunched her thighs together. "Yeah, I reckon rockin' chairs is one o' the finer things o' life, huh, Seneckers? Right up there with spiders and a-bein' nekkid outside and a-swingin' from trees?"

"Those are all very fine things," he agreed. "But the very finest thing in my life is you, Peachy. I much-love you more than you'll ever know."

"And I love you, Seneckers." She smiled into his wonderful blue eyes, looking forward to many long years of smiling into them.

"You know," he began softly, "you haven't said very much about how it feels to know you aren't going to be living in that great castle in the sky any time soon."

She giggled. "There ain't no way to tell you how plumb thrilled I am." She closed her eyes, dwelling on her feelings. "There ain't nothin', not nary a thing, worth more than a-wakin' up to a brand-new day and a-knowin' y'got time to live it the way it orter be lived. To the fullest, the very, very fullest. I didn't never think on that too much till I believed life was a-bein' tuk away from me. I won't never fergit it again. And I ain't said much about a-gittin' my life back on account o' I been too busy a-makin' plans fer the next eighty wonnerful years with you. I done decided to live to be a hunnerd, y'know. That's a nice, even number."

He grinned at her. "Well, it would seem that I must endeavor to live another eighty years, too. I wouldn't want to miss a single day with you, Princess."

"That means you'll be a hunnerd and twelve years old when it comes time fer us to git our angel wings."

He nodded. "I'll need a cane and some of that tonic for old people. Promise me you'll make me those things."

"I'll make you a different cane fer ever' day o' the week and enough tonic to swim in."

He trailed a finger across the soft swell of her bottom lip. "That omen," he whispered. "It didn't lie."

"Omen?"

Seneca drew her close, kissing her tenderly. "The ruby-throated hummingbird. Sweet Lord of mercy, Peachy, we're going to be happy for the rest of our days."

Epilogue

T iblock found the queen in the blue drawing rooms. He'd known he would. She enjoyed the rooms because of the portrait of the angel that King Seneca had had mounted over the mantel.

He entered the room, but promptly turned his back when he discovered the queen rocking and nursing her infant child. "Madam, I am taking Master Bubba out for a walk. We shall be placing flowers on King Zane's grave, and then we shall be seeing to Master Bubba's dogs. One of them has recently had puppies."

Peachy wiped a dribble of milk off her baby's cheek and pondered her father-in-law. He'd passed away several months ago, but he'd died happy, having lived long enough to set eyes on his four grandchildren.

The thought prompted her to wonder where her other children were. "Where's the rest o' my young'uns?"

"The three little heathens are playing hide-and-go-seek with His Majesty and Thurlow Wadsworth McGee, madam."

Peachy giggled, knowing Tiblock meant no insult by describing her children as heathens. Only this morning, they'd locked Ketty and Nydia in a closet and thrown away the key. Seneca had had to pull the door off its hinges in order to free them.

"All right, Tiblock. But tell Bubba not to fergit that he promised one o' them pups to Gussie's young'uns."

"He has promised one to me, as well. I will be getting the pick of the litter."

When Tiblock was gone, Peachy lifted her six-month-old baby to her shoulder. The infant burped loudly just as Peachy's other children skipped into the room, dragging their red velvet blankets behind them.

"We've looked everywhere, Mama," Tilly declared.

"We can't find him anywhere," Lulu added, wrapping Thurlow Wadsworth McGee into her red velvet blanket.

Diandra nodded. "I think one of the trolls in the river got him. You said they only filched boots, but I think they steal kings, too."

Peachy grinned at her daughters. Seneca could never deny having fathered them. All three of them had inherited his dark skin, black hair, and twinkling blue eyes. "Y'cain't find him, huh?"

"No, Mama," Lulu answered. "He's lost like a goose in a snowstorm."

"A goose?" a deep voice asked.

The three little girls spun toward the door. *"Papa!"* they cried in unison.

At the loving name they'd called him, Seneca felt a deep wave of poignant emotion wash over him. He walked into the room. "What is this about a goose?" His gaze fell upon Peachy. "Do you know anything about a goose, wife?"

She grinned. "I only know that gooses like gravel."

Seneca laughed loudly.

"Papa, where were you?" Tilly wanted to know.

"We looked all over," Diandra informed him.

Seneca leaned over Peachy and took into his arms his red-headed, green-eyed son, who had arrived just a *little* later than his father had foretold. After kissing little Zane Seneca Duff Brindisi, he bent and kissed his daughters, loving each of them every bit as much as he loved his son.

"Papa," Tilly said, pulling on his coat, "where were you?"

He tweaked her nose. "In the tower."

"The tower?" Lulu repeated. "What tower?"

Seneca feigned astonishment. "Do you mean to tell me you don't know about the tower? My goodness, an *angel* used to live there! Why, she taught me about spiders, and hide-and-go-seek, and going barefoot, and laughing, and all those very fine things of life!"

"An angel?" Diandra gushed.

Tilly's eyes grew wide. "Why isn't she still there?"

Seneca pretended a sorrowful expression. "I lost her. Twice."

"Oh, Papa, how very sad," Lulu whispered.

Diandra tugged on her father's pants pocket. "We could help you search for her, Papa."

He smiled. "You know, that's a good idea. And we wouldn't have to look very far. She's in this very room."

The girls peered all around the elegant parlor.

"There's no angel in here, Papa," Tilly informed him. "Only a portrait of one."

"There is a real one here as well," he replied. "You just don't know what she looks like."

Lulu's pudgy face screwed up into a frown. "Then who is she, Papa?"

Seneca gazed at Peachy, adoring her with his eyes. "Who is she?" he murmured. "She's the queen of Aventine. Your mother. She's . . . She's my very best friend."

A tender smile tilting Peachy's lips, she slipped her pale hand into Seneca's dark one. As his fingers closed around hers, she pondered her life. She lived in a fairy-tale kingdom with four wonderful children and the most magnificent husband any woman could ever hope to have.

She possessed an abundance of love. It dwelled within her. Around her. It existed everywhere, brightening each of her days.

And Peachy knew in her heart that although life offered many fine things, love was the finest of them all.

Avon Romantic Treasures

*Unforgettable, enthralling love stories,
sparkling with passion and adventure
from Romance's bestselling authors*

FIRE ON THE WIND *by Barbara Dawson Smith*
76274-9/$4.50 US/$5.50 Can

DANCE OF DECEPTION *by Suzannah Davis*
76128-9/$4.50 US/$5.50 Can

ONLY IN YOUR ARMS *by Lisa Kleypas*
76150-5/$4.50 US/$5.50 Can

LADY LEGEND *by Deborah Camp*
76735-X/$4.50 US/$5.50 Can

RAINBOWS AND RAPTURE *by Rebecca Paisley*
76565-9/$4.50 US/$5.50 Can

AWAKEN MY FIRE *by Jennifer Horsman*
76701-5/$4.50 US/$5.50 Can

ONLY BY YOUR TOUCH *by Stella Cameron*
76606-X/$4.50 US/$5.50 Can